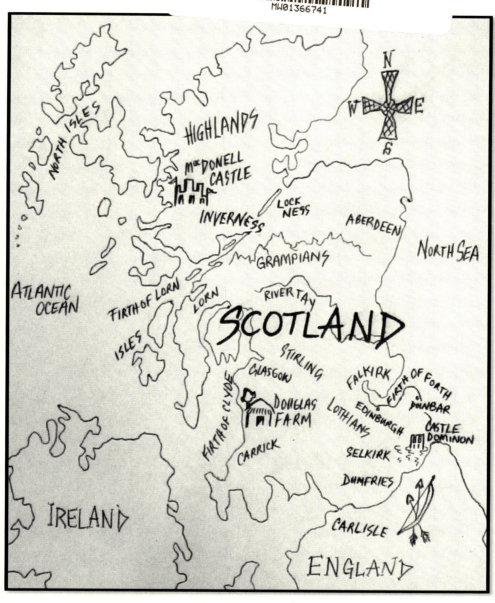

Cheryl Alleway

Of Blade and Valor

By Cheryl Alleway

Cheryl Alleway

Copyright 2013 by Cheryl Alleway
All rights reserved. No part of this book may be reproduced, stored in a retrieval system or transmitted in any form or by any means without the prior written permission of the author, except by a reviewer who may quote brief passages in a review to be printed in a newspaper, magazine or journal. Cover images and layout designed by Cheryl Alleway and Twisted Willow Press and belongs to the author and publisher. Unauthorized use is prohibited.

First printing.

All characters in this book are fictitious, and any resemblance to real persons, living or dead, is coincidental.

ISBN 978-1-304-12182-0
Published by Twisted Willow Press
Printing by Lulu
www.allewaybooks.com
www.twistedwillowpress.com
www.lulu.com

Printed in the United States of America

"It doesn't matter who you are, or where you live, or what your past was. Life isn't always perfect, but you can choose your own path. Adventure is the greatest gift we can give ourselves. Of Blade and Valor is one of mine."

To my husband: You are my best friend. Thank you for standing by me.

To Daisha: What a journey! Thank you for the wings.

Thank you to my father, my family and my friends for your support and to those who inspired me to be tougher than I thought I was. I can't forget to thank the ladies in my life that also reminded me of the softer core within by sharing stories of their challenges with me.
You know who you are. I am grateful for the lessons in life balance.

To my mother, who is hopefully looking down with my brother by her side reminding me to brush my teeth, put on a coat and be nice to people. Don't worry mom, I won't forget…ever.

"May you find 'your' adventure."

-C. Alleway

Cheryl Alleway

Prologue

"Father Can You Hear Me?"

Cheryl Alleway

Her old dress was still stained from the blood of her own wrists, but she folded it neatly and laid it by the fire. She looked down at her dirty feet and sat beside a dingy metal flask of water. Pouring it gently onto an old rag, she rubbed hard to reveal her skin again. With a sullen expression she told herself out-loud, *"You will cry no more."* It did nothing for her at this point but take her strength away. Why could she not grasp her gut wrenching fear and kick it out of her!? She knew herself better than this!

"Get hold of yourself!" she whispered, gripping the rag and wringing it with angst within her hands. The water dripped onto the floor and suddenly she found herself becoming angry. She tossed the rag into the corner and bowed her head over her knees clenching her fingers together. Her long black hair fell around her face draping over her legs. After closing her eyes and taking a deep breath, she whispered, *"Father, I need you. Please hear me."*

She took a moment to gather her senses and envisioned her home and the things in her life that made her feel safe and comforted. She pictured the beautiful fields and the sun rising over the hills. She saw the purple waves of lavender, the fireflies dancing carelessly over them and the sight of the silver moon above it all. The miles of rolling green hills gave way to the sight of tall oak trees surrounding the family croft. Its majesty made her heart ache, but its peacefulness gave her solace. She swore she could see her father standing there watching over her in the Scottish mist like a beacon of hope guiding her every step of the way. Now, as she stood in the room that had imprisoned her for so long, she looked out across the barren landscape and knew she had to be stronger than she had ever been before. The minutes were passing by so slowly. She was tired of the smells, tired of the fear, tired of his evil touch, tired of it all! She had to believe that all was not lost. Her young heart was burning for her mother's comforting embrace and her father's strong wisdom, but her old soul knew that courage must prevail. Her parents were not here to help her any longer. *"Breathe. Just breathe."*

Three months ago, they brought her here. She had been ripped from the very ground that her father swore would always be hers. Deb and her husband Liam now owned her family's land. It sat on the south west edge of Scotland near Carrick, almost bordering the ocean if not for a rolling trio of hills that were adorned with thick evergreens. The thick forest was five miles deep, dark and difficult to travel through, especially at night when one wrong step would send a person tumbling down a wet ravine layered with stone and jagged fallen trees. Bogs so deep that they would swallow a man, lined the other edge of the farm that sat quietly within its dangerous borders. Now in the dim light of evening, she envisioned it within her mind as she sat upon the cold floor of the room that had been her living hell. Blinking; breathing; holding onto it, she continued to shut the pain out of her mind.

"Remember, remember..." She pushed herself to think. The memories came flooding in like an elixir.

The wildlife that filled every crevice and hole on her family's land had sustained Deb and her family for three generations. Timber wolves ruled the food chain while hunting the bountiful deer that foraged the dark woods. A myriad of birds filled the air with songs of a thousand voices, while fox, hare and other smaller vermin flourished on in the underbrush. Biting flies were ironically the masters of them all during the start of the spring days. Salmon and trout earned their keep in the waters as the rivers were fed from runoff and connecting streams.

"Father, I can see you," she stated with her eyes closed and her hand upon her heart. Deb's father Jacob had taught her to hunt and fish while living off the harsh land. He taught her what to avoid and where the safest passages were. The humble fields had seen freezing winters, crop infestation and war. Deb was not the only Douglas born here as her parents and her grandparents' bodies were sheltered by the very soil that she loved so dearly. It was sacred to her. She continued to drift into her memories not thinking about how cold she was sitting there on the floor. She didn't care. She wanted to see it, feel it, touch it and remember it.

The fields were home to wheat, corn, and barley; along with potato and turnip. There were rows of cabbage and onion. All were easily kept over the long winter months in the deep root cellar beside the family croft. Her father's job as a child was to collect plants when they went to seed and to keep a healthy batch of seed potatoes with which to replant. Deb learned and carried on the skill. The small stone quern still sat as it did when her father was a boy. It was used to mill the barley and wheat into small batches of flour with which to make bread. The family's horse did the trick by walking around and around in circles to grind the precious grains within the two rough stones. In the summer, resilient wild raspberry and blackberry bushes adorned the forest's edge. Young Deb had also become quite adept at bringing down beehives with a smoking arrow well away from the sting of its biting soldiers. The honey inside would last for an eternity; never spoiling and always providing a sweet, healthy treat on a cool summer night, as well as an antiseptic when making a poultice for cuts or blisters. They had more than most and although not considered wealthy by any means, the Douglas' had come to be known as a small, but generous family in the area belonging to the well admired clan of the same name. Deb's grandparents and her father thereafter would provide grain and potato to those neighbors with more mouths to feed than themselves. Their kindness was known for miles in Southern Scotland.

It was working. She continued to breathe in...and out. *"Slowly. Keep going. Settle yourself."*

So much food for such a small family was uncommon. It was due to the extremely hard work the Douglas's put in each season. They had a drive within them for survival that was innate. The very fact that Deb's father and grandfather were able to live without the watchful eye and ruthless hand of a money grubbing landlord, was something they never took lightly. Deb's grandfather's reputation for protecting his land was well known and he had sought assistance on more than one occasion from the northern clans; namely Barne and MacDonell.

Deb's father also found solace in the highlands from time to time. The one saving grace for her family when talk of war would drift their way was the fact that their land was nestled far from any main villages or castle vantage points. They were secluded and the land was not desirable to passing armies as the bogs and skulking timber wolves made for a treacherous trip. The hills that would to some seem useful in attacking were saturated with sink holes, poison ivy and insects that would drive a man insane. She loved it all. She was seeing it all now in her mind. It was like paradise to her soul.

    A strange choice of land indeed for most but if one saw past the initial view, there was rich soil to be found. Being one that saw the advantage of both aspects, Deb's grandfather chose the land willingly when offered soil for his loyalty to the MacDonell clan. They were dumbfounded at the choice. They easily bargained with the lower clans to purchase it, but knew that only a hardworking, foreseeing man would select land that required so much work and diligence. It would eventually pay off for the family and was theirs for decades to come.

    Deb's father would show it all to her as the years passed. She was taught how to draw deer from the woods; to hunt them in the open grass. She was given sharp aim and steady hands to kill an attacking wolf with one shot of her bow. If she failed, the wolf would win. They were massive with some standing three feet at the shoulders. Deb's father tried to make this point unchallenged. She had to be accurate. She would stand for as long as she could, shooting arrow after arrow until the straw bale she was using was sliced to shreds. They had lost many sheep, but not before Deb and her father had taken down a few wolves in the process. As a result, a few very warm winter outfits were created. On the side of the wolves however, Deb's father had a few wounds from one attack that almost took his arm. If not for the swift reaction of their old mare and her angry hooves, he would have certainly met a different fate. Fortunately the wolf was a rogue male. If he had had a partner or two, Deb's father and their stout mare would not have survived. Life on the Scottish moors was risky to say the least at times, but the payoff for a free life was something they never forgot and prayed for every night on their knees.

Her knees; they were bruised and as she continued with her daydream, she caressed them gently as the next vision came into her thoughts.

The main stream housed a small stock of trout that they always tried to catch sparingly so as to allow the next brood to grow. They would salt and store it for the cold winter months. The water in the stream was clean and cold as it ran from the hills above and was replenished by the heavy rains that washed down on the Scottish craggy landscape.

On the north end of the farm, a small sheep herd grazed in fields surrounded by stone fencing flanked by the dark forest, but guarded by the mare. A stone wall with a small wooden gate held the sheep in at night near the croft. There were no family pets to guard them from the wolves and so, the old mare that had been bred from a Shetland stallion stood her ground in the mud. She was short legged, but wide across the shoulders. Her thick hair draped her legs and her mane was tousled, wrapping around her neck like a winter scarf. Her chocolate brown body blended into the dirt beneath her feet, but her large glossy eyes stood watch at night. She would see the eyes and smell the scent of any animal that came too close. Her hooves were deadly weapons, but even she bore the wounds of an attack by too many that she could not handle alone. Deb was alerted by the whinnies of the loyal pony and the two of them fended off the intruders once again. Her love for the old horse showed as she would often walk with her around in circles to mill the grain each season. This would prove useful in building Deb's body and the mare loved her dearly, longing for her gentle touch to the snout each day. She would neigh every time she saw her come from the croft and the two became companions; loyal to each other through it all.

"*Husband, where are you?*" Suddenly her thoughts changed.

Deb's husband, Liam, helped her work the soil and protected it as if it were his own. He promised Deb's father on his own grave. She saw his face within her vision as they tore her from him and slammed her palm upon the damp floor. "*Hear me, Liam. I'm here! Do not give up on me!*" Clenching her teeth in vain, her survival instincts were growing stronger. It was building up within her chest.

The croft came into view. It was Deb's only home and she would die for it. After her father's death, she was the last of her family to survive the years of hatred amongst the English and the Scottish.

Liam's clan, Barne, was not large and as a result, they were loyal to the MacDonells and other northern clans while still connected with the Douglas family to the south. Liam was born and raised in the frigid north. He was a stout and strong young man. His family was humble and loyal to each other to the end. Little did he know Deb would become his heart's desire after her father requested him to travel south and help them work the fields. It may very well have been Deb's father's intent to bring Liam and Deb together. His daughter was everything to him. Liam's father, Malcolm Barne, was a loyal friend to Jacob Douglas and a man who had never turned his back on Deb's father. Their history ran deep and bringing their children together would definitely be the ties that bound them together forever.

She would only be alone for so long in the room. He would come back, but for now, she was alone with her thoughts. She held onto them. She knew the night would bring another episode of physical discomfort and emotional anguish, but she would not cry any longer. She would sacrifice her body in the name of freedom, for it was close; she could taste it. His game of lust and control would continue no more.

"It shall be done. Mark my word! I shall not fail!" She promised herself with one last whisper of indelible fury.

She got up, opened her eyes, and straightened her back. She walked closer to the window and stood in silent reflection. Placing a shawl over her shoulders, she breathed in one more time deeply and then out again. Hushed by the silky, mist swept field in her view, Deb paused mid thought. These memories were all she had at that moment. Her heart ached for Liam. Was he alive? Was this really happening? Gathering her senses, she stood in silence with fists clenched, thinking about one thing only. She would not be a prisoner any longer. It was time for redemption. Deb's images of home were pushing her to be stronger.

She was ready to get it all back and no one was going to stop her; not even 'him'. As she blew out the candle that burned beside her, Deb's dark unwavering eyes watched the smoke snake out the window along with all of her fears.

Cheryl Alleway

Chapter One
Fate's Gateway

Cheryl Alleway

Jacob Douglas was just fifteen in the year 1295. The wars between the English and the Scottish were volatile and evading conscription into the English army had become a daily probability they did not want to face. His father had been hoping that soldiers would pass by the Douglas farm and leave them alone because of the difficult passage, but the two were working on the farthest edge of the fields beyond a rocky trench that day. It was here that they were most vulnerable. Jacob's mother was fearful of the danger, but the crop had to come in before it went to rot and winter was coming. Still they would not accept that he could be taken at any time. They could not bear the thought. Jacob's father had promised potato and grain to a young family just south of them. They recently bore a new baby and they needed an extended family to help them through their first winter. The food was a waste the Douglas family could not afford.

As Jacob worked alongside his father, the air seemed still and dense. A bead of sweat formed upon his forehead and as he looked up to wipe it away, the horizon gave way to five riders coming straight toward them. They were soldiers for certain.

"Jacob lad, hold fast! Do not run or they will strike you! Stand strong, my boy." His father's eyes were filled with rage. There would be nothing he could do to stop them. His body turned to stone as he realized what was about to happen.

Jacob's eyes were filled with fear. As the men rode up to them briskly and with no respect, they trampled half of the root vegetables that they had just pulled and bluntly threatened Jacob's father with sword to the head.

"It is time to join the fight. Get up and come with us, boy."

Jacob's father glared at the soldier speaking and tried to stay calm. He wanted to drag him off his horse and bury his face into the mud with his boot. Yet, he could do nothing.

The others paced back and forth upon their horses, watching and waiting. Jacob's mother stood watching from the croft doorway frozen, weeping with frustration and fear as the soldiers told them to keep their tongues about it or they would lose them to an English blade. She could see what was happening, but didn't know what to do. A burning sensation crept into her face and she felt fear like no other. Jacob looked back at his father's helpless face as they dragged him up onto the back of the horse and told him he was a soldier for the King of England. His mother gasped and lurched forward. The figures on the horses were taking her son. She saw her husband standing alone now in the mud. Her life was ending.

"Be proud, boy! You're about to join the rightful leaders of your Scottish lands! You're not the only one that will see the light!" shouted one of the men.

Another soldier glared at Jacob's father, "Your boy will be a trained archer soon! Be proud of him!"

He laughed smugly while turning his horse only to ride off with Jacob staring back at his weeping mother's shrinking figure as they rode into the far distance. She had fallen to her knees. His father was running after them, but the horses were too swift and he was getting sucked down into the thick mud. He too finally gave in and went down to his knees as if his last breath had left him.

"Father!" Jacob screamed out and was barely hanging onto the soldier who was grasping his tunic at the chest. He stretched his other arm out in desperation watching his father's frantic face disappear into the countryside as he too reached out an arm toward his son. It was no use.

His wife rose in anger and frantically tried to run to help her husband. The field was some distance away, and her lungs almost burst as she ran faster than she ever had. As the mud splashed in her face, she was grasping at anything that would pull her forward quickly. Her dress was getting bogged down in the mud as she plowed her way, staring through her tears. She cut her hands on hawthorn bushes, but didn't feel it. The pain in her chest was killing all feeling in her body.

She screamed, "Jacob! Jacob! Don't take my boy! Don't take my boy! No! Jacob! Bring him back, you devils! God, please help us!" Her eyes pleaded with the sky, but nothing came to relieve her heartbreak.

Stumbling through the trench, cutting her hands even further as she grappled over the sharp rocks, her left ankle twisted and finally shot her with pain as she was climbing up the other side.

Despite her agony, she stumbled to her husband's side and fell beside him. They grasped each other in utter defeat; tears filling their eyes as their bodies quivered together in the mud.

One soldier turned on his horse only to yell back, "You can bellow all you want woman, but this boy has a job to do now! He is a soldier!" He turned coldly and kept riding, looking annoyed at her cries to say the least.

Jacob's parents held each other and hung their heads. Their son had no choice but to do as the soldiers said.

The boy was to endure many more threats along the way to the distant English campsite on the border and made him fear for his parents if he did not do as they said. Jacob was in Hell.

Many nights he cried himself to sleep in silence, rocking back and forth quietly to comfort himself. The months went by so slowly. Jacob lived a tortured existence fighting against his own people. To further confuse his young mind, was the fact that many Scottish nobles were on the side of the English. He was becoming lost in the sea of political and warring gestures among men of power. It was all too much for him.

After a year, he knew that the only way to save his family's future was to escape the English and take arms with the people he was meant to fight with. His father had always followed the beliefs of William Wallace. This is what Jacob held onto. It would not be easy and through fear of death, he thought of many ways to escape. Jacob realized the only way was to become useless to them. It was something that he knew could free or kill him in the end. He had no choice but to chance it. Every time one of his arrows took flight, his heart burned and he knew that it might kill one of his people. Young and quick on his feet, he was often ordered to take his place alongside the knights as a low rank squire. He was also fighting with Welsh and Irish conscripts and each day was a swirl of emotions for him as he struggled with the confusion of it all. He didn't speak much to anyone as Jacob was not a young man built for battle. He was raised to farm and knew only peaceful means of dealing with conflict. This was more than he could grasp.

Although he was trained as a center field archer, his rank among the true English of his discipline was more of a slave than a soldier. If he did not perform on the field, it meant a beating that would keep him torn between loyalty and survival. His young body bore many bruises at times and a small scar on his right cheek proved to be the last thing he thought he would get after taking an extra piece of bread one night.

As the sun rose on the day that would change his life, Jacob was readying himself for battle one more time. The air was thick with fog and smelled a trifle rancid from the stagnant mud that surrounded the campsite. The English Earl of Surrey was leading his large infantry and cavalry based army to take Stirling Castle. It was long desired by leaders on both sides as its position between the two provided a formidable stronghold. High upon its perch, Stirling was a prize worth dying for during those times. The Scots were not willing to lose it easily, but it would be a huge victory for the English, if taken.

William Wallace, however, had made it clear to his men that the Scots would win that day. He had no doubt in his dark eyes as he gazed out over the landscape in the direction of the English army. Wallace was ready to fight to the death and his men would follow him to the grave. The fiery eyed Wallace had been successful in his bid to win the support of the tortured Scots and his leadership was driving the people forward with a strength that was becoming increasingly formidable against the English. He was an unequivocal enemy to the southern armies and he used their hatred for him to build confidence amongst the Scots. They were his people and he would die fighting the southern enemies that threatened their families and their Scottish way of life.

  The French were on board with Wallace's intentions while fighting their battles against the English on their own soil and the wars were now escalating to a fevered pitch. The English had their own goals and those goals were extravagant in the eyes of their enemies. Their money and power were indisputable, but overzealous confidence was beginning to show. One of their greatest advantages was the loyalty game of tug-o-war between the nobles of Scotland and men like Wallace. A seedy game of cat and mouse was being played among men of power on both sides and many of the Scottish nobles were dividing their promises and lies between their own people and the very enemy that promised devastation to their own homeland. Wallace had clearly chosen Scotland. Others had not. This was the other face of the enemy he fought.

  On that one day, the English were forced to take the path of Stirling Bridge. The muddy bogs and ditches leading to the castle would swallow their troops if they strayed from the trail. Ideally, the plan was to come within killing range of Wallace's men and bombard them with a shower of fatal longbow arrows, but because this time his troops were heavy cavalry and infantry, they decided that their sheer numbers would overcome the less skilled Scottish foot soldiers. This decision was not well received by the Earl's men. There were also people in England who wanted to see the wars come to an end for the toll they took on both sides was great. But Surrey desired the blood of Wallace on his hands and thus his pension for glory was driving his decision.

The weapon of choice for Wallace that day was the passionate hatred his men had for the English soldiers and their army. With his motley band of local warriors he intended to lure the English across the wooden Stirling Bridge and take them while they sat congested within its narrow path. There would be no other way for them to travel. Wallace made it obvious to the Earl that there were men positioned half a mile on each side of the bridge. What he didn't show were the hundreds more that were muddied and hiding in the brown sludge surrounding the bridge itself. They were like shadows sitting in the river's edge amongst the reeds dug down into the dark wet soil, motionless. Nothing but their eyes could be seen.

With his men outnumbered by thousands, Wallace waited for a large number of English to fill the bridge. The Scots knelt motionless like wolves narrowing in on their prey. They watched as the dust clouds of a thousand horses came closer; whirling up into the air like the tails of a thousand devils.

When the men were visible, William's heart began to pound and his face became crazed with adrenalin. His men were so engulfed in William's words over the last few days that they too were wide-eyed and vibrating in the mud. He cautioned them to stay still. They were silent and well hidden in their dark camouflage. One could hear the breathing of a hundred men as their cold breath mingled with the mist in the morning darkness and rose from the water. The ground above was covered in a thick rolling fog and Wallace's men poised themselves into rigid statues. The English couldn't see them even if they were right on top of them.

"Don't move until we've packed them in like grains of sand! Don't give them a damn chance to think. Take them fast! They will not be able to move once they are on the bridge! It will be their grave! Ready yourselves! Stirling will not be taken while we stand on this ground! Kill every bastard you set eyes upon! They will not hesitate to kill you!"

Wallace's other troops along the side flanks braced themselves out of sight as the English moved forward filling the bridge two abreast. They were cocky and confident and that was just what Wallace wanted. Then, he made the call. From every direction beneath them and around them, the Scots swarmed their enemy. A small pack of English made it across and headed to the right, but they were forced back toward the main group and taken down hard as the crazed Scots overwhelmed them. Wallace's brutality was horrifyingly evident and his men were fighting with the same driving force as they butchered the soldiers still trapped on the bridge. With nowhere to go for the English, the river became a sea of blood. Men were piled on top of each other as panic ensued at the front of the bridge. From yards back, the Scots had set up catapults that plunged burning bails of straw onto the men on the bridge. Inside was a large stone that made sure the strike was hard. Once a hard bale hit, the straw blew apart and spread flames onto the bodies of the soldiers and their horses. Some were lucky and were killed instantly by the stony projectiles. For others, the terrified neighing of the innocent animals could be heard for a miles. Many horse tails and manes caught fire causing the large animals to lurch in pain and throw their rider. It was a disaster for the Earl. His men were being burned to death in large groups at a time.

"Get back! Get back!" some shouted feverishly, but the huge group that was behind them surging forward could not hear them. It was chaos and the English were smothering themselves. Horses were being chopped at the legs and soldiers were diving from the bridge only to be slaughtered as they fell. The stench of blood and innards filled the scene. The water was black and the sky was filled with blood curdling screams. Surrey watched in horror as he realized what he had done. This day would see his death if he was caught by Wallace. Anger filled his eyes, as he sat poised upon his own horse. Hours went by so quickly that time was irrelevant.

There were peaks and valleys in the fighting as the English began to sort out their communication. Some of them retreated but the Scots wanted to hold their ground. Surrey made other attempts at sending men forward, but he knew he was finished. He could not and would not win this fight.

At night, the sounds changed. The moans of many men trapped in the sludge, dying, filled the air as some tried to sleep before the next surge began. They were tired, dirty, injured and in shock.

Wallace wiped his face with a cloth and looked down. It was soaked in blood. He looked around at his men and wondered if their lives would be like this forever.

Standing up, he walked over to the other key man in charge, Andrew Moray, and looked him in the eyes with conviction. "We take this when the sun comes up. It ends for them before we see another moon."

Moray was straight military. As a wealthy northern baron's son, he was trained in knighthood and had joined forces with the battle minded Wallace who was surging forward in the south. The Moray family was steadfast in their defense of the highlands and in combination, Wallace and Moray had hoped their fires would ignite an army fueled by patronage and the need to protect the north from losing their money and power. They needed both influences. Brute strength and old nobility would battle the English together at Stirling. Wallace and Moray were hoping they had made the right choice in joining arms.

Day two saw Surrey attempting to tell what men were left that they still had a chance of succeeding. If he did make it back south, he didn't want to be seen as a coward who lost a pitiful battle against such low life animals.

Suddenly, young Jacob Douglas found himself struggling for his sword and he was now in the hand-to-hand combat zone headed back to the spot where the onslaught from the morning before had taken place. It was the most deadly place to be during a battle. Jacob was not grown enough to be well suited for single man fighting. He would be overwhelmed in a matter of seconds against men twice his age and size. This was the reason for his position as an archer, where thousands of smaller, quicker bodies could become one of the most accurate and brutal killing machines ever created for battle. The longbow was a killing spectacle on the field. Today however, the English thought wrong when they attempted to stand ground with the Scots sword to sword. Thousands of English were now dropping. They were being separated and conquered by a lesser army. They were tired and beaten down.

As Jacob approached the now exhausted but steadfast wave of Scots, he found that his small stature could work to his advantage. Ducking and weaving behind the larger infantry, he made his way to the river's edge. As he held his head under the filthy water over and over to avoid the fighting, he gulped down the foul liquid as he tried to breathe and swim. He vomited over and over again while he swam. This was the worst battle he had ever experienced. He had never been at ground zero before and his mind was overwhelmed as he saw the faces of his people once again up close. They were mad and horrifyingly violent. Jacob did not blame them. Instead, he felt a deep inner pain. He shook his head to gather his senses and slapped his own face hard to gain his composure.

Finally seeing the bank, he hurled himself behind a large pile of mud and reeds. He lay completely motionless and covered in the brown stench. He was fifty feet away from the gory scene. Jacob was panicking and wondered if his plan would work. He would never get out alive unless he did something drastic. He had slipped through the wall of English and made his way here. Always within him, he carried the thought that he had been seen and would be killed for deserting. He just kept running. There was no time to second guess it. He made the choice; now he had to face it. *"God, please help me."*

On the right and moving slowly away from the main group, there was a large Scot wielding his sword like a raging bull. He was killing more men alone than was imaginable; not leaving any one man in the river alive. He plowed through, chopping off the heads of the stunned English with one swing and severing the limbs of others. His striking reach was shockingly past the sixty inches already marking the length of his Claymore sword. He terrified Jacob and his young body was beginning to freeze. He had to constantly punch himself in the stomach or shake his head violently to maintain his composure. The violence was like a sick intoxicating swirl as the adrenaline rush was coursing through every man. The black scene Jacob stood in looked like a battle from hell with flying debris, dirt, and dark blood covering the faces, making every man look as if he had no eyes. The Scots were killing machines driven by the right to hold their own land. They would defend this place to the death.

Wallace hurled himself into the fighting again and shouted profanities at his enemies. He looked insane as he pushed his men into the English like a wall.

The man that Jacob watched from behind the mound had a short auburn beard and solid stature. He was an ominous figure forcing his way through the crowd with a solid purpose to kill. His shoulders were twice the width of Jacob's and his legs appeared hard and muscular. His hands were large and covered with wounds, but it seemed to mean nothing to him. The colors he wore on a small patch of his blade sheath were that of a clan that

Jacob recognized through the mud. They were that of the Douglas clan. Jacob was in shock and although not all of one clan was of blood relation, this man could have been of his own.

The boy took a deep breath and stood up now in the sight of the large warrior. Watching, waiting, shaking; he stood there in the filthy knee high water trying not to pass out. The Scot had sliced a clean path through the other men and was looking for more to fight. The spot where Jacob had been hiding was clearing slightly as the fighting moved toward the bridge's left side with the fleeing English. At sixteen years of age, Jacob was not of size to take this man on.

In a split second, they made eye contact and as they did, young Jacob stood still with his weapon at his side. Through the blood and the muddy faces, the large warrior rushed at him. He stopped only five feet from Jacob as he strangely allowed his sword to fall into the water and closed his eyes.

Suddenly the scene froze. Jacob blinked once and his young life flashed before his eyes. He saw his mother's face, heard his father's voice and saw himself in his own cradle. Then he heard the sounds of the men around him. His mind focused on the tension, pain and anger in their voices. Their anguish filled his young heart and he felt them in his soul. He could not breathe. Feeling as if his heart would burst, Jacob spoke to the man. The Scot shook his head and looked around, thinking the boy was an ambush or insane. Jacob knew that there was a small group of English soldiers set aside to seek out deserters or traitors. Their job was to kill any conscript who tried to leave his post, but if injured, they were left behind. It was either one of them, or the Scot standing in front of him that would fit the bill. Like a stone striking his head, Jacob snapped out of his daydream.

In a rush of energy he screamed, "I am Jacob Douglas and I am a Scot! Take my leg so that I may be free of this English army! Take it now! Long live Scotland!"

His body was shaking and his eyes were filled with tears that coated his bloodshot view. His hands were vibrating; his body became painful as the fear flowed through his limbs. He could barely hold it together. The look of terror on his face was undeniable and this boy stood helpless, even terrified, as the Scot looked at him with puzzlement. *What the hell was this boy doing?*

The warrior's face was stunned and as he looked closer, he noticed that Jacob had placed a purple thistle in the strap of his English uniform. Jacob was strong looking, but small and he stared at the man upon opening his eyes. The sweat and blood dripped down his face with every shake of his bones. As he looked into the man's face, a single tear drifted down his cheek creating a clean trail through the dirt, but he remained stone-faced, standing his ground and shaking profusely as the fierce warrior moved forward slowly in the dirty water. The waves made in the water by the Scot were now lapping against Jacob's legs, he was so close. This man was going to kill him unless he could make him understand.

"Take my leg I say! I will not fight against you! Your colors are mine as well!"

The warrior spit back at Jacob in a loud deep voice, "One so young, yet so willing to feel pain? What are you doing?! Are you mad, you crazy bastard?" He looked around again to make sure he was not being ambushed and then back at Jacob.

Jacob's accent did have the same twist of the tongue to that of the Scot himself. It was not an English soldier speaking these insane words.

The man looked at Jacob's face and saw that he was quivering with the deepest fear anyone could bear.

He suddenly blurted, "You must be a Scot boy! No one else would have the balls to take my blade at will! Brace yourself, if this is what you want! I'm about to free you! I know what you're doing, but do you? If you are a Douglas, you will not die by my blade! God above bless you lad, and save me from hell for helping you!" The man did not have time to waste thinking about his deed. This was war and if this boy was asking for salvation by his blade alone, he was not going to stand there and debate the moral issues surrounding it. Jacob was wearing an English uniform and for all the man knew, this was his only option. Who was he to stop time now and make that decision? He did what the boy asked.

As if in a dream, the fear overtook Jacob's mind and body. He did as the man said and as the blade came down heavily on his right leg just below the knee, he cried out in pain. It was like a boulder had hit him and then the rush of heat came as the veins burst at the ends with bloodied force. Jacob's body lurched from his head to his toes as the extreme trauma jolted every hair on his body to stand on end. He went stiff with agony and his face contorted in wretched horror. He felt his heart begin to pump so hard that he thought he was dying. The river began to spin and his head fell back lifting his sight above the turmoil.

All became quiet in Jacob's mind and he saw the sky high above as if in a drunken state. He heard his mother's voice and felt her touch. *"Jacob, I love you son."* The pain set in only for a moment before he fell to the hard and cold stone covered embankment. The filthy water splashed up around him coating his skin in a black, muddy swirl of blood. Instinctively, he yanked a medicinal bag from his hip and tore it open. It had a honey poultice in it and he forced it over the severed end of his leg to stop the bleeding. He plunged himself into the mud and out of the water and collapsed. He tried to pull the rope on the bag tightly to keep it on, but could not. His body was going into shock. As his eyes rolled into the back of his head, his hands went limp on the ropes and he toppled into his own blood surrounding him in the mud.

The Scot could see for certain now that Jacob had planned his injury long before this moment and he stood in disbelief at what he had just helped the young man do. "God forgive me," he said with reverence.

Jacob felt the sensation of the large warrior standing over him but the darkness was pulling him in.

The Scot drug Jacob behind the mound of dirt and pulled the ropes of the bag tightly around the thigh. He tied it with one quick snap. Jacob cried out, delirious with pain. Looking around and behind him, the Scot packed clean mud on top of it as well and quickly threw some reeds over Jacob, looking around again to make sure he was not being seen. He studied Jacob's face up close and realized Jacob had to do this and he hoped he had made the right choice. He looked at the boy's hand now clutching the thistle. He was grasping it so tightly that the tiny thorns were digging into his skin and making him bleed from the punctures. This boy was no English archer. This boy was a Scot.

In a contrastingly calm voice the warrior stated, "May you live to fight again boy, but for us!" With that he turned and bolted back toward the fighting. He pushed through the water creating a wake behind him. As he met with the sea of men again, he plunged himself into the blackness.

As the chaos and killing continued so close to him, Jacob succumbed and was in the hands of God.

Hours passed until the fighting finally began to settle, the battle was nearly over and Wallace, with Moray, had claimed victory over Stirling. The Earl of Surrey retreated with his remaining troops and Wallace watched on top of the hill as they disappeared into the evening skyline. He took some men and made a rush forward to try and catch up with the Earl who was seen riding like the devil was on his heels.

The battle area was now given a sweep for survivors and anything salvageable. The stench was palatable and one felt as though they were in a butcher shop. Blood was strong on the wind and it took everything the men had to stomach the aftershock of it all. The Scots could not afford to waste anything, yet the English would leave screaming men and horses behind. These souls would quickly perish as some of the Scottish men took pleasure in finishing them off until the order came to pull back from the field. The rest were left in the bloody mud to die alone. It was ominous and chilling to watch the crows move in and the mist began to clear. They went to work feasting on the buffet that was left behind. Soon afterwards, the larger ravens and hawks made their attempt. After the sun fell, the fox and wolves would get their turn. The rest was carried downstream for fish to find sustenance. Many a Scottish mouth would eat the very fish that swallowed these men bit by bit. It was that sick circle of life no one thought about.

Jacob would soon perish at the hands of the wolves or his own demise if he stayed where he had been left. The men were almost ready to regroup when Wallace returned after turning back from the chase at Carlisle.

The man who had so aptly assisted Jacob with his plan decided to check the spot where he had last seen the valiant young man who so bravely risked his life for freedom. His own heart had slowed and now his mind could have time to think about what had happened. He wiped the mud from his face and bandaged a wound on his wrist. Exhausted, he walked to the water. The birds were heavy now and they scattered as he made his way through the scene. He passed many other men who were tending to wounds, picking up weapons to salvage and trying to find their sanity again after such epic devastation. Not many were speaking and as a new mist was rising, they tried to find peace in their hearts.

As the warrior made his way over to the mound, he saw Jacob. The boy was awake, but very delirious; lying in the filthy mess and writhing slowly in agony. He was muttering an old poem that his mother had taught him and the bag and mud that packed his stump was now soaked with blood. The wound still smelled fresh, but many men died from such trauma. The Scot pulled back the mud but left the honey sack around Jacob's wound. Tearing pieces of a cloth he had hanging from his belt, he tied them tightly around the bloody stump. It helped, but he did not know if Jacob's plan had worked. He could still die from the heavy bleeding and infection. The men were not well versed at fixing wounds. They did the best they could. Burning the open flesh would possibly save him, but not many survived such shock. It was unfortunately the only option for this young man who would lose even more blood once the dirty poultice came off.

The man bent down and pulled Jacob up throwing one of those thin arms over his own back. He hefted him up the riverbank to where the other injured men were being loaded onto carts. The smell was almost unbearable, but Jacob was, ironically, in no condition to be choosy with his surroundings.

Jacob was pulled up close to one of the fires and two other men were asked to hold him down. They were confused by Jacob's uniform, looking up at the Scot, but he grunted for them to do what they were told and they didn't argue. They placed a leather strap between Jacob's teeth and put all of their weight on either side of his body. The big Scot walked over with a red hot sword that he had sitting in the coals and after saying a small prayer in his head, he gently pressed it into the end of Jacob's gaping leg. Suddenly, Jacob's eyes opened wide and his body lurched two feet from the ground.

He was flailing his arms wildly and screaming. The Scot shouted at the two men. 'Hold him down you stupid bastards! Hang on tight boys, for God's sake!" The men bore down and Jacob's screams were heard across the field. In his mind he was in hell and the devil himself was burning him alive. His eyes widened with horror as his heart nearly beat from his chest.

After the sudden shock, he passed out and the men could release him. They looked up at each other and wondered what had just happened.

"I'm sorry, boys. This one needed to live. I only hope this worked. Please go get something to eat. I'll watch him for now."

They could see that he had good reason for doing what he did and they backed away slowly. Now the Scot sat beside the brave boy and made certain that he continued breathing. For an hour he waited and finally, Jacob Douglas opened his teary eyes to a new world. He felt pain and great stiffness, but there were also moments of numbness that kept him from passing out again. He was sweating profusely so the Scot gave him water and Jacob tried to drink it. It felt good, in his dirt filled mouth and refreshed his stomach. He looked up at the Scot and had no words. He just stared upwards. The Scot looked down at him and said in a deep voice, "It's alright, boy. It's alright."

Chapter Two
Salvation

Cheryl Alleway

Wallace's second in command, Andrew Moray, had been injured and was dying while he lay amongst his men, but he noticed Jacob's uniform.

"What do you have there, soldier?" he questioned as he angrily wondered what his man was doing with a young Englishman in tow.

"Sir, this boy is not of English blood. He is a Scot! He begged me to take his leg so he could be freed, sir!"

"He begged you to take his leg? Is he mad? You believe him to be a Scot? Did he say his name?" Moray was fading, but still remained in control.

"Yes, he is a Douglas. Sir, I have a boy this age. If this one is of my clan, I ask that you allow me to bring him with us. To do this, of his own accord, is surely an honorable act! He is of no harm to us in his condition and he may be of value. Sir, I believe him to be nothing more than a young conscript; a farmer's son not able to deal with all of this. It has been brutally enforced on the lowland people as you know."

Moray thought about it for only a moment and said, "He is your responsibility. If anything happens, you will be the one to pay for it. If he has blood family, find them. We cannot care for a legless boy or waste our rations of medicine on him.

Do you understand I am gone from this world soon for certain? What do I care if he lives or dies? By the look on your face, you surely do." Moray's voice was shaky now.

"Yes sir! I do." The Scot took Jacob to the carts and laid him down in the straw beside another man whose face had been chopped off on one side. This man would not live either. Jacob's head turned his way and even in his state, he saw that the man's eye was hanging out of its bloody socket as it lay upon the straw like a wet stone sitting in a slimy pool of his own tears and blood. His cheek was gone and the teeth of his mouth were shattered on the one side.

Jacob fell into a deep sleep and only awoke once they had made the main campsite not too far away on the other side of the castle. The smell was unmistakable after the stink of death had drifted far enough away. Jacob smelled heather now; sweet purple heather. It was the smell of home.

He opened his eyes and thought he was dreaming. Another soldier walked by and Jacob asked, "Where are we?"

The dirty soldier spat on the ground and stated, "Well, we're outside Stirling. Don't you know your own country, boy?"

Jacob was confused. He looked around and then at himself. He wasn't wearing his English uniform anymore. It had been replaced with some old clothing and he was lying amongst the rest of the injured men. He couldn't feel his leg, but it had fresh dressings on it.

There was nothing they could do for the injured but keep their wounds clean. These men that fought today for Wallace were farmers and the poorer class. They had nothing but their own rudimentary knowledge of dealing with wounds. Most men died, but some could be saved, if lucky enough. Jacob was one of the lucky so far. He pressed his eyes together tightly and then opened them again. Looking down, he saw the dirty thistle he had embraced was still within his hand. His fingers were numb from being in one position for so long. They felt broken as he tried to open his hand slowly. His knuckles were cut and stinging. He was with Wallace's men now. Jacob Douglas was free. By the hands of God, he was free.

As time went by, Jacob believed that his family was dead. The fighting had destroyed many farms. He had once hoped that they would not be able to travel through his parent's land, but in his heart he knew otherwise. Without hope, he took a position with Wallace. He stayed on not knowing what else to do and yearned for the day he saw his father's fields, even if overgrown. He could at least say goodbye properly.

"Bring that one over, boy!" As a Scottish soldier worked on a few weapons hammering them back into their normal state and fixing their grips, Jacob scurried over with his hobbled leg with sword in hand.

"Here, sir! This one is not so badly damaged as the rest. It is a good one indeed."

"You have good judgment, lad." The man looked the blade over and down its length. Only a few nicks and a bent edge were seen. He patted Jacob on the back and told him to go and bring the other swords over.

Jacob was a hard worker and at night he would get water, carry wood to the fires and help feed the men.

"So what makes a young man like you come to us?" The soldier's name was Donnan. He had been with Wallace for many months and had kept his eye on Jacob. He saw how lost he seemed and realized this boy was alone in the world. Even with one leg, the young prodigy was gaining the respect of the men. He went about his work quietly, without complaint day after day, and there was never a moment when Donnan didn't wish for Jacob to be able to go home. He fit in, but he didn't belong. He should be home.

"I came here through the hand of God, Donnan. No other reason," Jacob answered him.

Donnan smiled at him and turned to continue working. Jacob was not the only young man in the Scottish army by any means, but he certainly was one that stood out.

As the months went by however, there was something that would take him by surprise. Much to his disbelief, Jacob's father was seen on the west side of the Wallace camp. His parents had survived. His father had been traveling near the fighting all this time asking anyone about Jacob. Many called him a fool for thinking he could find his son. His health was not good, but he kept searching and asking anyone who would listen if they had seen his boy. It had not been easy. His wife begged him to heed the area. She thought she had lost her son and could not bear to lose her husband as well. He had prayed that somehow, with the will of God, Jacob would be trying to get home. His son was young and inexperienced, but his heart told him not to give up on his boy. He had to try until he knew where Jacob lived...or fell.

There were many young men who fit Jacob's description. Thousands of young boys and local people were mixed in with the more seasoned fighters. Manpower was at a premium during Scotland's fight for freedom and many that were able would, at some point, be involved. Jacob's father knew of other conscripts who had escaped the English army. Some had been killed in the process, but others had made their way across the border back to Scotland. It was this small glimmer of hope that brought him here. He was willing to take the chance.

On the day that he would finally find his son, Jacob's father had come across the man that had ironically saved his boy four years ago in that terrifying moment. The soldier told him of Jacob's plight on the battlefield and it made Jacob's father weep with images of the pain his son must have gone through. The soldier then took him to where Jacob was working in the camp. They would allow the boy to leave because he had given them information about the English and shown them that he had been of use. Other young men had joined the cause and could take his place; men that were stronger and faster on their feet; men that would sadly, be facing the fighting once again.

As Jacob knelt over a table of swords, he flipped his head up and to the side quickly as he heard a familiar voice. It was that of his father.

"Jacob, lad! God, be with me. Jacob, it's your father, boy!"

Jacob looked through the dust with eager anticipation and hoped he was not dreaming. He lunged forward and hobbled to his father who was crying and walking towards him with open arms. He was twenty years old now and his father's face was in shock.

"Father! Is it you? Is it really you?"

Donnan looked up and felt a sense of sudden redemption for the boy.

Father and son met and stopped only a foot away from each other. They stared at each other with wide grins, eyes open; breathing heavily from the surprise of it, yet each was totally speechless for only a few seconds.

"My God, Jacob you have grown!" His father's face was wrinkled and his back curved. He wore the same humble clothing he always had and he gripped Jacob's arms with his thick gnarled fingers from decades of hard work. Their crooked knuckles felt good to Jacob as their touch brought back that warm feeling when he was a child and his father held him upon his lap.

"Father, I thought you were dead!"

"As I thought you were, lad! But no! Here you stand before me! A man at that, Jacob Douglas, a man at that!" He had tears in his eyes and he couldn't control his happiness as his cheeks rolled into large waves of wrinkles under his joyful old eyes. His boy was actually standing before him. It felt like a dream.

The two embraced and patted each other on the back. Pulling back again to make sure they were truly seeing each other's face again; Jacob's was still the same to his father and his eyes glistened with joy.

His father, laughed now and patting his son on the back; the two made their way down the path talking. Jacob's father had already spoken to Wallace about his son returning to their family's farm.

Wallace gave his permission and Jacob was ready to go home. There was no argument on his part. With his feeble father by his side, young Jacob

Douglas entered William Wallace's tent to say his goodbyes.

Wallace sat writing within his journal by candlelight. He turned calmly after telling the two to enter.

Jacob politely stated while he held onto his father's shoulder, "I am grateful for my stay indeed, sir. God has seen it right to have me rejoin my people and now that my father is here, I am truly blessed."

Wallace rose and walked over to father and son.

"Jacob, I am a man who has seen much death and much freedom taken from our people. I know firsthand what it takes for a family to lose each other slowly. When my own father died, I learned hard and fast that this country needed men to take charge and save our families from a destiny not deserved. Your father needs you more than I, young man."

William looked to Jacob's father and added, "Your boy has paid his price through guilt. There is no anger in my heart for what he has been forced to do. He is skilled, sir and can offer a wife and family much needed hope and guidance. I want him to make babies and teach them what it is to be a Scot! He risked his life to come back to us and for that, I bid him a good life."

Jacob's father tried to kneel down in front of William to thank him, but William pulled him back up quickly, "No sir, I would rather look you in the face. I am not a king to bow to. I am a man like you. A man who is happy to give you back your son."

Jacob and his father left William Wallace never to see him again. They walked up the path towards the north edge of the camp. Pulling a tent door open, Jacob saw the dark bearded face of the man who saved him in such a dramatic fashion that faithful day four years ago. He had come to know him now as 'Robert' Douglas. They had spoken about each other's families over time and surmised that they were not of direct blood, but Robert had heard of some of Jacob's family in the past. Most of them had died in battle and Robert had now grown to care for the young man who had so bravely faced him. Still part of the Douglas clan, Jacob's immediate family had few survivors…another reason for his father's exhausted efforts to find his son. A family's name was a proud treasure. Robert had been given his. Douglas was the name given to his grandfather who had fought for a noble. Being so poor, they took the name gladly and joined the clan to continue their loyalty. And so it was, that years later, Robert and Jacob would meet under such remarkable circumstances.

"I am leaving now, sir." Jacob had the utmost respect for this man he looked upon and as he stood to say goodbye to the boy he had saved and once fought against, he stated, "You call me Robert, boy. I am your friend now, not your keeper. You will be all right. In time, we may meet again. I hope it is in an independent Scotland. Take care of your family. Make babies with a good woman and remember why you are alive."

"Yes, I will. I hope we do meet again. I am grateful to you, Robert. You've taken me in and shown me how to be a man again. If you please, my father would like to meet you before I go."

Robert nodded yes and they both came out of the tent. They walked down the path to a small cart hitched to a stout old horse. Many men were watching as the meeting took place. They kept working but left a smile of admiration upon their faces. They had grown to be fond of young Jacob.

As his father stood up and turned to see Robert's face, he hurried forward to greet him with an open hand.

"You sir, have a welcome place anytime in my home. Bless you for giving me back my son."

Robert, as grizzled as he was, returned the acknowledgement. "This boy is a man now. He has paid his price. He has been true to his name." Jacob took this as an honor because Robert had lost his own son to the fighting two years before and Jacob always felt as though his presence by his side was meant to be.

Robert and Jacob shook hands. The young man made a fist and held it to his chest. "Scotland forever." Robert handed Jacob something as he and his father were turning to leave.

"I want you to keep this with you, lad. It was forged by my own hands and it will serve you well, young Jacob."

Robert handed Jacob a beautiful dirk dagger that was held in a hand crafted decorative sheath. Its grip fit his hand well and the brown leather felt good on his skin. He laced it around his shoulder and put his hand out to Robert's again.

"Thank you. God be with you, Robert Douglas." Robert held out his hand and they gripped one another's fists with honor. As Jacob and his father rode away, he turned to see Robert watching them. He lifted his arm to them and a sorrow filled Jacob's heart. He was leaving his family for the second time in his life.

As the cart rumbled roughly over the bumps and stones of the path, Robert felt warmth within his heart. The fighting was taking its toll on him.

His body was sore and he had lost his son. The only thing driving him now was his will. Robert Douglas had fought for his people with honor and pride. If he and others like him were not willing, Scotland could be lost forever.

It was not over and Jacob realized that. He thought about where his life would take him now and if he would marry. He wondered if he would ever fight again.

The sun was setting as Jacob and his father drifted on and for a moment, they both felt peace. He closed his eyes and held his face to the brightness in the sky. The colors warmed his skin as autumn oranges and reds danced amongst the misty hills. He smelled clean air and saw the beauty of this place as if for the first time. He felt so lucky to be alive and Jacob promised himself that he would do what he could to make his life worth something.

His father told him of his family and who had passed on. There were not many of them left and this saddened Jacob. He asked himself why this was happening, but he realized that he had been allowed to live for a reason. This farmland would be safe for as long as Jacob was alive.

He swore to himself as he saw the familiar images. Before him stood the tree that he played under as a boy and the fence that he and his father had built together. The small stone croft that he and his family had been born in sat snuggled into a grassy knoll. Suddenly, elation overtook him as he saw his mother come from inside. She was feeble but her face lit up when she saw the boy she once held, coming toward her.

"Jacob! Jacob! Oh, Jacob!" She walked forward as fast as her legs would take her. Jacob jumped from the cart and hobbled over to her as well. They met embracing and holding each other tightly. She was red faced as her heart beat fast at the sight of her baby boy, now grown.

Jacob stood over both of his parents in height. They seemed so aged now. Taking on the farm alone must have been so difficult for them and Jacob felt guilty even though they would never want him to.

Jacob's mother held his face at arm's length so she could see him. "Oh, my boy! You have grown so much! I cannot believe your father found you! Oh, my God above!"

She realized his leg was gone as she looked down at his right foot and saw the wooden peg. She touched it lovingly saying, "I am so sorry, son. Your leg; does it pain you?"

"No mother, it is fine. I can walk and do most things except run. I am lucky that it is all I lost. I am fine, mother. Seeing you is all that I need right now."

He held his small mother in his arms. She was a gentle being. She had seen much death and lived through many things. One would not think that someone so fragile looking could endure so much.

Jacob's father joined them and they all walked happily into the croft to sit and eat. They had much to talk about and they felt blessed to be together again. As the fire crackled giving off warm flame, Jacob's mother scooped a simple stew into their bowls.

Jacob was careful only to tell them of certain things. He did not want to place any more fear into their hearts. He tried to reassure them that Wallace was doing well and that there had been much advancement to the Scottish freedom fight. They slept that night knowing that their son would be there in the morning. They knew he would never tell them of the true horrors that he had seen. It would be too much for them to bear.

Jacob walked outside after their hearty dinner. Alone, he went to the large tree that he once played under. He sat down and admired the night sky. The colours cast a dark misty blue upon the moors. Flowing clouds drifted slowly amongst each other in the evening darkness against the shining moon. The stars were out and the scent of heather filled the air. Bats dove high and low through the air hunting insects and they seemed to be like symbols of freedom to Jacob as they soared gracefully, silently and swiftly through the clean night air. If only the Scottish people could continue to do the same. Jacob prayed for this under the tree and as he leaned back against it, he fell asleep while enjoying the colorful moths and fireflies that floated in and out of the wavy, soft grass. He could not believe he was home and it felt so good that his body felt as though it were floating.

His father looked out the door and walked quietly up to him placing a blanket across his lap. He gently shook Jacob's shoulder to wake him. "We need to go inside now, lad. The wolves will be on their nightly move soon." Jacob placed a hand on the tree and lifted himself up. His father patted him on his back and smiled with a gracious, thankful grin. His son was alive. By the will of God, Jacob was alive.

Chapter Three
For Love It Will Be

Cheryl Alleway

Jacob's life changed when he finally met his future wife. Her name was Mary and she was the sister of one of Jacob's childhood friends. The families were pleased with the union and Jacob was a proud husband. There were however, many demons in Mary's past, but she was never able to fully explain them to Jacob. He knew her life had been difficult before meeting him as the scars on her body had proven. There were never any words spoken about them at first and Mary was shy to allow Jacob to see her unclothed.

One night before they were wed, Mary shuddered and pulled her skirt back down as Jacob entered the room in her father's home while she was changing. He went to her and sat down placing a gentle hand on hers. She apologized for her coldness as they had already been together once.

It happened one night during a gathering in Carrick. Mary and Jacob had stolen away together into a dark misty field. They were shy and awkward, but they were so deeply smitten that they could not wait. Jacob wondered after if they should have, because Mary was so uneasy. He wondered if it were his hobbled leg that made her uncomfortable.

Now in the room with her, his heart pumped quickly. "I only wish to see my bride and if you bear the scars of life, then I wish to bear them with you. They will be ours together, Mary."

She felt more comfortable and began to slowly pull her skirt down again revealing a beautiful girl. Soft pale skin riddled with scars but rounded into feminine curves made Jacob's heart beat just at the sight of her. While reaching for her night garments, Jacob noticed she had a large six-inch scar down the front of her right thigh that he had not seen the night they were together. It was too dark and they had hastily given in to each other from pure young desire.

He sat her down beside him again and as he looked into her eyes, he placed his hand on the scar and traced it down to the knee. Mary had a tear on her cheek and Jacob wiped it away.

"You are so beautiful, Mary. Do not fear what I think of you. You are the greatest gift I have ever been given. You love me as a man though I have only one good leg." He felt a familiar welt on her shoulder again and wondered, *"Who would do this to such a girl and for what reason?"*

Mary finally smiled shyly and as Jacob continued to caress her leg, she told him she had to share one thing with him that she could no longer keep inside. Jacob thought at least she was opening up to him and he tried to allow her to speak without fear of his reaction. She was demure and looked upon him from sad eyes that had trouble within them; looking at him straight on.

"Jacob, I have been carrying a secret for a month now, but I can no longer lie to you. I feared telling…" she paused and lost her composure for a moment.

"Mary, please tell me. You must not fear me."

She continued but now got up and went to the window crying as she wiped her tears and then said bluntly as she looked outside, "I am carrying a child, Jacob!"

She turned to him and went to her knees.

"Please Jacob, do not hate me! We were together only once and yet I fear this child is not yours Jacob. I fear it so! You do not know what a husband should know! It is my fault! I should have told you!"

Jacob was fearful for Mary now. Was she saying that another man had her as well? How could he not know? Who was the man?

"Mary! Settle yourself, lass. It is all right. Please calm down. Please, Mary. I must know. I will not forsake you!" He had his hands around her upper arms trying to steady her.

She went to the floor and Jacob dove to her side helping her put on her clothing. He held her up and as she wept she muttered through her tears, "They came for me, Jacob. They knew we are to wed and they came for me. I wanted to tell you, but men have died for seeking revenge on the English soldiers. I would not see you die, not for this! I am hoping that the child is yours, Jacob. I do not know for certain, but I know that if I lose you, I will surely not know what to do!"

Jacob looked up and gathered his senses. He remembered he had been away for a week one month ago gathering supplies for the farm.

Many husbands would, of course, lash out at such a desecration of marriage, but Mary had kept her attack secret as they took her when she was alone walking home from the village market. She feared losing Jacob and to her, the child should not be without a father. She thought about harming herself to make the infant die within her, but she could not, knowing that it may be Jacob's. Mary was so distraught, that Jacob had to lay her on the bench.

He hoped that her parents did not come home from their family visit and find them like this. He calmed her down and after a while he leaned on his good knee to shelter her face with his arm and hand; cupping her cheek.

He said in a soft voice as he stroked her face with his other hand, "My beautiful Mary. You are not forsaken and you will never be without my love. It is not a woman's fault when a man chooses his power over her soul. If anything Mary, I love you more. You are a brave lass and any man would be lucky to have you in his arms. Do not fear me. I am not the man who raped you. I am Jacob and I will be your husband. This child will be ours, Mary. This child will be loved. I will take care of you; you and 'our' child. No other man will ever lay a hand upon you again! I swear by my blade!"

Jacob lifted her face to his and said, "I love you, lass. No man will change it. I swear!"

Her beautiful blue eyes were filled with tears of pain, guilt, fear and love all at once. Her soft gown lay gently across her small frame and Jacob gathered it within his hands and laid it across her legs. He got her a blanket and placed it over her shivering body. With a soft kiss to her lips, he smiled and she began to calm.

Mary felt a sense of safety suddenly in Jacob's arms. She had been raped and now she was given a man who would never place such burdens upon her. It was hard to believe, but she felt it now and she softened her cries into a quiet sigh. Jacob held her for a long time, and then decided that being found in Mary's father's home alone with her would make matters worse.

He left her sleeping quietly, but sat on the hill watching over the croft until her father and mother rode down the path as the sky became dark and the moon rose. He got up slowly and sighed. Looking up to the stars, he prayed for strength. He would keep Mary's secret until his grave. He wanted to know who had done this and he vowed in his heart to find out someday.

As Jacob returned home late in the evening, his father noticed his troubled face and asked, "You are a man with many things on his mind, lad? You are very late. Your mother was worried."

"Yes father, but do not worry, I am to be wed soon and I just needed some time to think about a few things. I shall sleep now. I promise to do my share of the chores when I rise."

"That is fine, lad. That is fine."

"Thank you, father, and I am sorry to have worried mother."

A few days later, Mary and Jacob were wed and when they stood side by side, everyone was still unaware of Mary's condition. She was not showing much yet and she wore loose clothing to disguise it. They thought that they could fool everyone into believing that she got pregnant on their wedding night. It worked and even though she gave birth to their daughter Deborah sooner than normal, no one, not even the women were wiser as the baby was quite small and Mary did not become very large at all during the pregnancy.

The next four years, however were difficult for her. She was often ill and passed blood from her lungs two winters. The fourth fall saw her demise and Mary died suddenly in the night. She had taken it on too many times in a row and her body finally let go. As Jacob mourned the loss of his beautiful wife, he knew that his life was to be focused on his daughter. He remembered Robert's words and William Wallace's hopeful speeches and he also knew that Mary had been given to him so that Deb could be born. This was the only way he could justify Mary's death and the pain she had gone through.

He raised his daughter as if she were his own, not knowing the real truth. Jacob was unsure how to treat his daughter, however. His parents had both passed as well so his mother was not there to assist in raising her. Deb looked fragile, but she was full of energy and eager beyond her years. Jacob had to find it within himself to take care of his little girl alone.

As young Deb grew, he trained her physically and mentally. Her strength became very apparent. He taught her how to build and use the English long bow. Scotland was known for its formidable claymore sword and dirk dagger and Jacob's unusual knowledge of the long bow would be an advantage to his daughter who was being trained as if she were a boy. She seemed to like it that way, especially with no female influences to give her thoughts otherwise. The farm, being so far from others, was all she knew. Her father was her only family now.

Deb would sit and watch Jacob with great attention as he crafted each tool or weapon. He knew to use the wood of the yew tree for bows and could remember their six foot length very well as they were often taller than he was at sixteen on the battlefields. He would often have to hold it a few inches off the ground as far as his arms would reach. Having used his upper back and arms to the point that his bones had grown crooked, Jacob would never forget. His body was gnarled and bent. Many young men had deformities after the heavy use of the bow from a young age. Deb's shoulder bones on her right side were slightly bent backward by the time she was fourteen. It was not a concern however as in most cases, the bones ironically became perfectly positioned for the task they would need to perform with such repetition. With Deb's feminine form, it actually made her stand up taller and lean backward giving her a unique figure. She certainly stood out amongst other young women of her age.

Deb would sit with him at night by the fire as he entertained her with stories from his past. The croft walls would be flickering with orange and red as the warm flames of the stone fireplace danced on the wooden beams. The straw and dirt chinking poked out through each one. There was little decoration except for the handmade tools and weapons adorning the back walls. There were two beds built into the left side opposite that of the fireplace. They were rudimentary, but comfortable and dry, raised up from the floor should a snake or other creature decide to explore too closely. The table sat in the middle of the rough boarded floor close to the fire and the large cooking pot that Jacob's mother used and was still cleaned every night by Deb, readied for the next meal.

There were simple but beautifully crafted blankets draped on each bed. Jacob's mother was a skilled seamstress and had made a few outfits in different sizes for Deb before her demise. Deb also had her mother's clothes to adorn her frame. They were slightly short but did the job. Mary knew the young girl would need something while she grew and it was Deb's honor to wear them as her body changed. She would try things on from time to time to see if they fit yet. She held onto her grandmother's items as if they were gold. She could only guess as to how their voices sounded. Gentle; soft; caring; nurturing; it made her feel comforted.

Deb imagined her mother and grandmother sitting together sewing in front of the fire. She would daydream before bed as darkness would take over the walls of the croft.

As the sheep bayed, and the old mare sent out a hearty neigh, Deb would listen as her father's voice took over and began to weave another image into her thoughts. She would sit staring up at him, hanging onto every word he said. He sat in the oversized chair he had built for the two of them to sit in front of the fire. Deb often played on the floor by her father's feet as he spoke. Little trinkets collected by her grandmother and mother filled a tiny box that Deb would admire each night and put away neatly when she went to bed. There was a miniature stone horse, a three inch hand sewn patch of the Douglas clan made by her grandmother and a tiny cloth doll that her mother had made for her as a baby.

They had very little in the way of treasures, but their lives were treasure enough for Jacob. He would look down at his little girl as her long black shiny hair would fall haplessly around her thin, but lengthy frame. She was beautiful, just like Mary.

Instead of picking flowers or brushing her hair, Deb was content to listen to her father's stories night after night. She was not a typical girl and he felt that as long as she would hear him, he would treat her just as he always had. He wondered if he should teach her how to braid her hair or weave a basket, but she was always bored with such things.

She was like a little boy more than a girl and it suited Jacob just fine. The only thing she wanted was to see her trinket box each night. It may as well have been a box of coins. Even then, she would put it away and wait for the next tale from her father's collection of stories.

"I had heard of those whose forefingers had been taken as trophies by the French during battle. This was the English archer's worst fear, lass, but not because of the pain. If they lost their fingers, they could no longer use their weapons. Even then, I knew of one English long bowman who had lost his fingers, only to return to the battlefield after locking his remaining digits into place painfully with leather and stakes to continue his job. He put himself through unimaginable pain! This was to his great demise however, as the rapid continued force against his two smallest fingers snapped them in half! Only the thumb and middle finger were left to be held in the air to the direction of the French army with hatred, as if to say, *You have not won! To Hell with you all!*"

Deb starred wide-eyed as her father spoke. He often wondered if he should speak of such things with her, but she was not a fragile teary eyed girl. Yet, he tried to allow her to see that smart decisions were a warrior's best friend even if a decision meant losing a fight at the time.

"Battles are won by wins and defeats of smaller fights, my girl. Just because Wallace lost a few, he never quit trying; thus his battle was won in the end, even though they killed him before us all. He won the battle of Scottish pride and freedom and for that, he was a true leader; fearless, but never allowing his failures to allow him to quit! You must never give up hope Deb. Never give up hope. Fight with all you have inside of you and don't ever believe you will lose! You're as tough as any man your father has known and it is this that will take you through life, lass!"

Chapter Four
Balance

Cheryl Alleway

The days went by and Jacob lived happily with his young daughter who was becoming more and more like a woman now. There had been a few instances where the English came close to their home and they had been lucky thus far not be included in the raids. Jacob knew that would not last. The Scottish lowlands were growing more and more volatile again while the English pressed on and the Scottish nobles argued about the future and who would rule. There were traitors and conspiracies and men who were willing to give the English partial power in exchange for a title before their names. Jacob spoke of all of this to Deb. He wanted her to know that she would have to be alert and strong of mind. There would be a hard road to travel for her once he was gone and Jacob was not going to leave her helpless. Her mother had been helpless at Deb's age and Jacob would not allow his daughter to be that vulnerable. He wanted Mary to look down and see that her little girl was prepared for life and the demons she would, undoubtedly, have to face.

It was Deb's favorite part of the day. The sun rose and she knew her father would be rising to teach her the next lesson. Jacob could not offer Deb the ability to read as he was illiterate, but what he could do better than anyone, was teach his daughter how to protect herself and how to stay strong physically and mentally. He had to learn these things on his own. For him it was pure survival instinct, but for his daughter he wanted more.

"Alright lass, now run the field evenly ten times. Once you are back I want you to balance on the stone fence. Don't allow your beating heart and shaky legs to make you fall. You must take power over your body with your mind. When you quiver, calm your mind and tell your limbs to settle. Now off you go!"

Deb took off like a fox and Jacob would tell her to slow down a bit each time she passed him. "You must breathe more, girl! When you do not breathe, your body will not listen to you!"

"Yes, father!" She would pant and once done, up she went to the highest part of the stone fence. Jacob had her climb up and balance each foot on the two smallest rocks he could find. It would be hard and she would fall a few times before learning to stabilize herself. Today, she would not fail him. She ran faster on the oncoming hill this time and once she climbed up the stones, she braced herself and straightened her back. She was panting, but closed her mouth and her eyes. Jacob was worried for a moment, because closing her eyes would make it even harder, but Deb surprised him and she held her ground. She concentrated very deeply and calmed her breathing down. In an effort to impress him, she picked up one foot and balanced on just one rock. Jacob kept his tongue, because the moment he said something, she might fall.

He smiled and when she opened her eyes and crawled back down, he put his hand on her back and said, "You are really trying to make me grow old before my time!"

Deb laughed and said back, "Father, you will never grow old. You will live forever!" She embraced him and as she did, his smiles went to a realization that she understood many things he had taught her, but one thing he needed her to know is that life and death come hand in hand. It is what it meant to be human.

"Well, for now, you must practice your archery. Go, get your things and come to the oak stand."

Deb was fifteen years old now and she was becoming a young woman. She was fast and incredibly strong. Jacob had her carrying water, chopping wood and riding the old mare as much as she would permit. Milling the grain helped as well as the two went round and round in circles pushing the heavy quern stones against each other. The old mare actually got up a good gallop when Deb rode her. Jacob could tell she enjoyed it too. Most of her days were spent standing around being a guard, and so when her bones had enough, she slowed right down and headed for the gate. Deb loved that old horse and she would lovingly hug her as they ended their practice for the day.

At the forest's edge, Jacob set up targets in a different pattern each time he had Deb practice. He even made her run and roll over things to simulate being chased or chasing someone. He would throw clumps of mud and sticks at her to make her try and evade them. She would have to hit the targets or practice would not end. He enforced this with a stern yet caring tone to instill in Deb that it was fun, but it was also something he took seriously and she should too. When she got older, she would understand why he made her work so hard. She would end some practices with bruises and cuts, but she reveled in it. Jacob would stand with his sword while she held a thick stick in both hands. Repeatedly, Jacob would strike at Deb and she would have to defend herself. She was fast and in the end, he couldn't keep up with her guarding techniques.

Once she took a blow and spun around low to strike him gently on his waist. She laughed and he looked down in surprise saying, "Alright, I think we're done for today!" He would be slightly embarrassed, but he couldn't help but feel so much pride inside. Deb would apologize, "Sorry father, I got carried away."

"No sorry needed lass, just make sure you use this spit upon your enemy one day." He patted her on the head and they would finish their day walking back to the croft to eat. Jacob would watch her run ahead and shake his head. She was quite an unusual child indeed.

There were very few days that she gave him a fuss and would get up to practice without Jacob. He was content to rise with hot mint tea in hand and sit, watching from the croft door. She would turn with a serious look on her face seeking approval of something she had just done and Jacob would nod his head yes or no (try again). These days had come to make him proud and the feeling of satisfaction would make him raise his head to the sky and whisper, *"Mary, she's a force to reckon with. I hope you are proud."*

As time went on, Deb became more than anything Jacob could imagine. Her mornings were spent in peaceful moments breathing with her eyes closed as the sun came up. Once she opened her eyes, she was focused, determined, unstoppable. Her abilities to flip over objects, kick, punch and fight like a man with her fists was remarkable. She was slightly wild at heart and Jacob said she had the heart of a wolf. Her knife throwing skills had become unbeatable and the side of the mare's enclosure had the marks to show for it. Young men from the nearest farm would ride for a day to visit and challenge Deb. Not one could beat her. It was not a shameful thing though, because they had become like brothers to her and it was the best part of the day when they could all sit and discuss their techniques.

    They had never seen a woman fight let alone dominate the skill like Deb. While the young men were hoping to take their zest to the battle fields, Jacob wanted Deb to stay with him. He made them promise not to speak of her skills when sipping the drink. He wanted to maintain some anonymity in case the wrong Englishman heard about them. As any family in Scotland, they protected Deb as if she were their sister. Some had looked upon her differently though, because Deb was growing into a beautiful young woman. Jacob would give the boys the look if they stared too long. "Keep your eyes on the target!" He would say and they would humbly do so. Jacob knew it was time that Deb had someone else in her life. He did not want her to be alone, but the boys that visited were not to his liking and although he knew he could not stop feelings from growing inside Deb's heart, he also wanted to make certain that whoever caught her eye, would have to be someone Jacob held in high esteem.

Cheryl Alleway

Chapter Five
A Boy Named Liam

Cheryl Alleway

Not too long into her sixteenth year, Deb's father hired Liam Barne from the northern clan to help them with the crops. Liam was a welcome challenge for Deb's skills as he was not without fighting talents himself, although he had not expected to find what he did when arriving at the farm. He would work for food and lodging along with a very humble amount of coin at each month's end. Jacob could only give Liam so much. His real reward was right under his nose.

  The days were filled with working and training and with the blessings from above, Jacob's health and age had been kind to him, but as with everything, his time was not going to last forever. The days that Liam spent on the farm were wonderful for Deb. She felt as though he was a gift for helping with the farm and she could not fight the feelings that began to stir within her chest. She noticed Liam right away. It didn't take long. She was learning what it was like to love for the first time. There was certainly a different feeling between them than there was with the neighboring boys. Liam had grabbed on to Deb's heart before she even realized it.

  Each day they worked hard and they both began to feel the same surge within. Liam looked upon Deb with amazement at her beauty and skills. The first day he arrived at the farm he was stunned when he saw her, but brushed it off when Jacob caught his eye.

"Welcome Liam Barne! I trust your ride here has made you hungry lad? Come, let us fill your belly while I speak of your duties."

Deb looked at Liam openly, but slightly shy; very unlike the way she looked at anyone else. "I am Deborah. Thank you for helping my father. I hope your journey was not too long."

"No, it was fine. The last couple of nights were a bit chilly, but I can see you have a hot fire going. I would love a hot meal right now. I haven't eaten since this morning." His eyes widened as Jacob led them into the croft with Deb in tow. Liam noticed her long gait and flowing hair. He felt his heart beat a bit faster. How could he eat with her sitting beside him? He shook it off and sat beside Jacob instead.

"We rise at sunup and we work until sundown lad. No rest for the wicked. We break for eating and water refreshment. The field, you see when you rode up, is the one I would like you to work first. It holds the potato, a most valuable root for certain." Jacob said. "Your father tells me you are skilled with this and with the sword. It shall be a good thing to practice and keep you strong when we are not working. My daughter is quite adept in the ways of fighting. It will be good for her to have someone else to challenge her."

Liam choked a bit and coughed on his last bite when Jacob said this.

"Cuuu Cuuu! I'm sorry, you said challenge?" Liam looked over at the beautiful Deb smiling demurely as she sat at the table.

"Yes, she has been trained by my own hand. She is very skilled. We'll test it out tomorrow before we take to the field. It will be exhilarating!"

Deb swallowed and smiled again seeing Liam's surprise. *"It will be good for me to have someone of your skills take me on."*

All Liam could see in his mind was his arms around Deb in the grass at that moment. Fight her? Take her on? He wanted to kiss her, but if that was what Jacob wanted, that is what Jacob would get. He promised his father to do what Jacob told him to do and he was an honorable young man. The next day, he would oblige; with no argument now that he met Deb.

"Now remember your stance, lass. Liam! Take her on her left side. It is her weakest. She needs to work on it the most! Begin!"

Deb and Liam circled each other and the sparring began. They were clean fighters together. Strikes were thought about and motions were smooth, but then Liam started noticing her form again. He shook it off and gave her a challenging set of strikes to counter. She had to work hard to defend herself, but suddenly Liam's eyes lost themselves in her flowing hair. Deb stepped in and using both hands made a strike downward that Liam stopped with his sword horizontally. In doing so, he tripped and fell to the ground. Deb landed on him with her sword raised to strike again as she stopped breathing heavily over him with her legs straddling his chest. Liam looked up red faced and stuttered, "Well, I think she's getting the hang of it, Jacob!"

Deb looked down at him with her hair flowing down on one side. He knew that in that moment if her father hadn't been sitting there *watching like a hawk, he would have reached up and kissed her right there. It was torture. They got up and Deb knew by his look that Liam was seeing her the way she saw him. A budding love was beginning to stir inside of them.*

She was what any young man would desire. It was becoming difficult for him to watch her each day without running over and ravishing her even if Jacob was watching. It was like dangling food in front of a starving wolf at times, but he kept chivalry close by because Jacob could still send him away if Liam did anything disrespectful.

"Deb can you bring me the sickle!?" Liam shouted from the top of the hill. He had no shirt on and was sweating profusely as he worked in the hot sun. He looked so handsome to her longing eyes. She hollered back in acknowledgement and ran up the hill. Deb looked back to see if her father was watching and let her hair down a little more so that it fell upon her partly bared shoulders. Liam stood, stopped and starred. She was teasing him and he liked it. He smiled and took the tool from her hands. She shyly looked down at the ground and asked, "Do you need my help?"

"No, just maybe a little more time to look at you," Liam grinned down at her.

Deb's face flushed and she looked back again to see if her father was watching. He was not and with a quick surge forward, she reached up with her hands back behind her and kissed Liam quickly. He felt a wave of desire roll over his body and as she turned to run away again, he grabbed her wrist and pulled her in to him for a more substantial embrace. "You are beautiful, Deb Douglas," he whispered against her face as he felt her form.

They both looked down the hill and then at each other again. Liam placed his lips upon hers and held her tightly. They kissed deeply and slowly but then knew that they must not get caught. He released her and she smiled with a light in her eyes that only Liam could bring. "Enough for now, father may be looking."

She ran back down the hill turning her head to look at him. Liam smiled back and he knew in his heart that this stunning girl would be his someday.

The weeks went by in the same way and the two were balancing their urges with their reverence for Jacob, but Jacob was not blind to what was happening. In fact, he expected it and he made a decision in his heart.

On the eve of Deb's seventeenth birthday, Jacob decided that his daughter needed to be aware of her future...and his. His health was now fading and he was determined to prepare Deb for whatever fate was to come of him. He would not die until he knew she was ready for life without him. Although, in his heart he could see that she was.

"Daughter I need to speak to you." Jacob was sitting outside their croft as he watched her tend to their sheep.

"Yes, father. What is it?"

"I want you to know that you may have to take control of the farm yourself. I am not well and I do not want you to be alone."

He said this with a matter of fact tone. Jacob was a man of few words when it came to Deb. Without a mother to help raise her, he struggled with the more feminine methods of parenting.

Deb looked at her father with a furrowed brow and said quietly, "I do not like it when you speak of such things father, but I understand." She looked out at Liam and suddenly, Jacob knew that it was time he spoke to the young man about his daughter. He was not so blind to the looks that he had given Deb either.

Liam Barne was a fine young man. The full area that the Douglas family had owned was too large for Deb and her father to maintain alone as his body aged. Liam's father was an acquaintance of Jacob's and the two men had known each other for many years. Their clans were at peace with each other and many of the men had fought beside one another. Many ties bound them together and Jacob was hoping that the young Liam would take his daughter's hand in marriage before he died.

"Ride up to the hill and tell Liam I want to speak with him, lass."

"Yes, father." She felt something in her father's voice and if it was what she hoped, that night would be a turning point in all of their lives.

Deb returned with Liam riding behind her. As he came up to Jacob, Liam was noticeably curious. He had a rugged handsomeness. His dark hair reached his shoulders and his stature was strong and solid. His skin was dark from working in the sun. He stood just less than six feet and had green eyes that were wise and kind. As filthy as he was from working, he remained calm as Jacob eyed him up in the moment.

"Sir, you wish to speak with me?" Liam asked.

"Yes, lad." He gave Deb a look. She knew he wanted her to excuse herself so that he could be alone with Liam. She looked down gracefully and went into the croft.

"I am not well," Jacob stated. "I have watched you work now for quite some time and your father speaks highly of you. I have asked that we keep you from battle with purpose. I know that you have been torn between leaving for war and keeping your word to me. My daughter is the last of our immediate family. I will not die knowing that she is alone. I do believe that you may have thoughts of wedding her?"

Liam was surprised by the candidness of Jacob's words, but he obviously cared for Deb and he was not blind to the fact that Jacob had known it. He dismounted from his horse and walked slowly towards Jacob who motioned to him to take a seat beside him and as Liam thought of what to say, he knew Deb was listening from inside.

"I do care for your daughter, Jacob. She is a fine woman and any man would be lucky to have her. I have tried to be respectful of you and your daughter's dignity."

Jacob shook his head agreeably. "Then you will ask her for her hand? She is as beautiful as her mother was. I hope you agree." He added, "Liam, she is my only child and the last of this family. These times are harsh for our people and I have taught my daughter many things. She is however, not well versed in love. If you marry her, I expect you to honor her and protect her against all odds. In fact, I demand it before I give you my blessing. I hope that this is clear to you."

Liam looked at Jacob's face and said without question, his heart racing within his chest, "Sir, I give you my word as a Barne. She would be the very reason for living, if she were mine. You are a good man and I have nothing but honorable intentions towards your daughter. I have not been with another. When I met her, I knew that one day, she would be my wife; I must be honest with you. I would be blessed if you gave me your permission."

Deb was smiling inside as she hid behind the door listening. Liam was making sure that she heard him as well. He had long wanted to say these words and today was the happiest day of his life.

"Then it is done. I ask that you wed her before I die. She must be in the presence of her father and it will be kept quiet. The English will not know of this union." Jacob could not bear to see his daughter placed in the same position as his Mary was.

Liam wanted to pull Deb into his arms, but he had to restrain himself. Jacob called her back outside.

"Deb, my girl, this young man has something to say to you!"

Liam was a bit shocked. He didn't think Jacob meant to have him ask her right then and there, but he swallowed the lump in his throat and looked at Deb. Her face was bright and excited. Her eyes were wide and she too was stunned at the abruptness of the moment. As Liam looked at her, everything else suddenly disappeared. She was stunning, but had the humbleness not to realize. Her long black hair flowed as if curled by angels. Her eyes were as green as the fields. Deb was tall and strong. Her shape was feminine, but her arms and legs had muscle enough to work as hard as any man. She was mesmerizing. The thought of being with her was unbelievable to Liam.

Liam's palms were sweaty as he bent down on one knee in front of Deb.

"Deb, your father has given me permission to ask for your hand. I don't have a ring, but in time, I will have something for you. If you marry me, I do promise to make you happy."

It was short and sweet, but Deb had waited to say the next words for months.

"I will be your wife, Liam Barne." She turned to her father containing her excitement and he nodded.

"I will tell my own father and with your permission Jacob, I would like to marry Deb here on your land. If you are to honor me with your daughter and your property, I think it would be appropriate." Liam also did not want Jacob to travel and die while away at his daughter's wedding. He made the suggestion with this in mind. Jacob Douglas deserved to die happy and a free man on his own land. It was the safest place, and the family to the north would be asked to travel in smaller groups so as not to draw attention.

"This would be acceptable," Jacob answered. "We will have the wedding as soon as your family can arrive. You will leave soon to bring them the word, Liam! They are welcome in my home. Come then! Let us celebrate this union."

Deb made a delicious meal and the three drank raspberry wine and ate and danced while they played music into the night by firelight. The night was chilly and Liam took a moment to help Deb carry out some sweet biscuits and more wine. As Jacob continued to play his mandolin, Liam found his beautiful bride to be standing alone inside. She turned with a smile while she hummed along with her father's music and seeing Liam, their passion overtook them.

They fell into each other's arms and Liam kissed Deb deeply with his hands running over her beautiful body.

"We must be careful that father does not see!" Deb whispered.

"He is happy outside with his music. I just wanted to kiss my new bride. I won't see you for days while I travel north!" He gently reached into the top of her dress and caressed her breast.

Deb felt Liam's chest and kissed him harder. They knew they had to wait, but for now, they were content just to feel each other's warm embrace.

Jacob started a quick paced tune and yelled at them both to come out and dance for him.

They gathered themselves and obliged. There was never a moment that night that Jacob doubted Liam's love for his daughter. He knew now that he could leave this world.

Liam raced north the next day to bring the news to his family. It would take almost two weeks for him, and the rest of them, to return. Waiting was torture for Deb. She was full of anxious anticipation each day, but when Liam returned sooner that she expected, her heart felt as if it would leap from her chest.

"You rode quickly, Liam! How did you get back so soon?"

She ran to him. Liam dismounted and dove for his new bride. They were not shy about embracing any longer and Deb leapt into his arms wrapping her legs around his waist. They twirled around in a circle as they kissed and squeezed each other tightly. Jacob came slowly to the door with his cane helping him. He leaned upon the door frame and had a smile upon his face as wide as it had ever been. His life felt complete. It was one of the last good days he had. Time was ticking for him.

When the wedding day came, Jacob was not well. He managed to sit up straight in his chair but his cough was getting worse. His lungs were failing him. It was similar to what Mary passed from. Jacob accepted it now. His daughter was safe. He had done his job and now he wanted to see Mary again.

As the ceremony went on, Deb's happiness was being overshadowed by sadness for her father's state. He had done so much for her and she knew that he was not long for the world, but the party saw dancing and singing and a roast of lamb that adorned a bountiful table of food and wine. Liam's father gave him ten more head of sheep to ensure a good winter of food. They had ridden them separately in two large carts down the worst traveled path south in order not to be seen. It was hard going, but Liam's father knew that they must not draw attention to their destination. The last leg of the trip was done in the night by the light of the moon. It had worked, and when Liam's family had finally arrived together, there was much adulation indeed.

Though weak, Jacob kept smiling. He called Liam over and gave him a new bow that he had made himself.

"Thank you Jacob, but I need to practice so that I may be as good as your daughter!"

Jacob laughed and said in a fragile voice, "I have shown you enough skill, boy. Now use it. My body is bent, but at one time, I was a fine archer. Use it well and protect it at all times. The English did give me something of value, little did they know. You will see its value to you for certain."

Liam smiled and put his hand on Jacob's shoulder.

"I believe you may be right, Jacob. Thank you. I will cherish it always." Liam handed it to

Deb and she placed the bow beside the door to the rear of the croft. She stepped out back for a moment to gather herself. She remembered playing hide-and-seek with her father. The back door to the croft was smaller and came out the other side of the bank that the croft was built into. She smiled as she saw herself crouching and staying quiet while her father searched for her. She would never forget him. Liam gave her a moment alone and stayed with Jacob.

When the festivities ended, Liam and his father carried Jacob to his bed. Deb came to his side and sat with him through the night. Liam's father, Malcolm, told Jacob that he and his family would help the young couple in any way that they could. Before he closed his eyes to sleep, Jacob asked Deb to reach behind the bed frame.

"There is something I want you to have, daughter. I have never used it. It was given to me by the man who once saved my life."

Deb did what he said and pulled out the dirk dagger that Robert Douglas had once bestowed upon him. He had cherished it ever since and kept it hidden to give to her on just such an occasion. She looked it over and then at her father.

"It is wonderful, father. The markings are so beautiful. I will never let it leave my side." She began to weep quietly.

"Deb, don't cry. I am not leaving you. My body is almost gone, but I will never leave you."

With a shaky voice, Jacob coughed and continued, "Liam is good. He loves you. Hold each other and protect your name, child. You will be a Barne now, but you will always be a Douglas. It is all that we have in this world of hatred. Never forget that. Remember what I have taught you. Practice it and keep its knowledge close to you at all times." With that, Jacob started to close his eyes and he was soon asleep.

As dawn broke, Deb had fallen asleep in the chair. Her eyes opened at the sound of Liam's voice.

"Deb, love, wake up."

She opened her eyes more and as she looked from Liam's face to her father's, she broke down and wept over his now limp body. Jacob Douglas was gone and his daughter was devastated. She wept deeply into the blanket that lay on her father's body. Her fingers gripped it in pain as she felt him leaving her as she knew him. She had never felt such agony before and her stomach was tossing as her mind whirled with anger. She was inconsolable, so Liam left her alone and closed the door. He knew her well and realized that she required the time by herself. She spoke to her father and thanked him for her life and her husband.

Through tears, she muttered, "Father, you are everything to me. Why did you leave me now when we are so happy? I will mourn for you forever. Please know that I will be fine. I hope that you see mother soon. This is my only consolation for your loss. I will miss you, father. I will love you always." She laid her head on his chest and clenched his hand in hers. She did not want to let go. He had scars on his hands and arms from his days with the English and Deb stroked each hand, folding them neatly together on his chest. Her face felt hot and her eyes were sore and hard to keep open.

Deb sat with him for a while and when she finally came out of the room, Liam knew that his life was now dedicated to this woman before him, just as Jacob had. There was something about her that drew you in. He embraced her grieving, beautiful face and held her tightly in his arms. As he did, his own eyes welled up with pain for this girl that had come into his life in such a way. She was one of the most exciting young women he had ever met, but in her heart, she was a girl with feelings and loyalty beyond words. Liam could not believe he had been given such a gift.

"It will be alright my love. I am here." Deb wept in Liam's arms until she finally fell asleep and as he laid her down gently, he covered her with a blanket. He thanked God for her. Jacob's life had ended, but their lives had just begun.

In a small ceremony, Jacob Douglas was buried beside his wife Mary, his mother and father. Ten feet over were the graves of Deb's grandparents and their parents before them. They covered her father's grave with rocks and Liam made a cross for him. Deb placed flowers upon the stone shrine and whispered, "*I will never forget, father.*"

As her tears fell to the ground they moistened the rocks beneath and her eyes aged beyond her years in that one moment. She was now a woman and she stood with her parents' spirits driving her to go on. She could not believe Jacob had left her life.

She wept in deep sorrow for days before she could stop. Liam never rushed her. He understood the pain she was going through. He still had both his parents and he could not imagine losing them let alone his entire family. Deb needed him more than ever. Liam was learning what it was to be a man. He ached for her at night as she sobbed herself to sleep.

The days after were sullen, but Deb and Liam had to work at preparing the land for winter.

The Barne family had returned to the north to take care of business and get their own lands ready. Liam wanted to take his place with the Scottish army, but felt compelled to stay by Deb's side. Collecting wood and repairing the structures was quickly attended to. Only enough sheep were slain for the winter months and the rest were fed plenty to keep them fat and their coats thick. Root vegetables were harvested and grains were milled and stored in small batches.

    Life was fragile on the Scottish moors and war was a veil to some who would take advantage. Word was spreading of a renegade from a northern clan pillaging and raping farmland to the east. He carried the MacDonell name, but people were confused. The MacDonells were well known in the highlands for their leadership and contribution to King Robert the Bruce and his cause.

    Deb and Liam were hearing things they feared. Thanking God for their youth and strength, they prayed every night that they would not have to defend the farm, but time was not kind and the threat was real. They knew what they had to do. It was unbelievable that this would come to them while Deb was just healing from Jacob's death. She seemed to be dealt cards that held a dark fate for her. Liam could not believe the courage she was showing through it all. Still, she had fear in her heart. She'd never had to use her skills in this way, but realized in her heart that this was why her father had done what he had for her. He knew she would be tested. She knew she had to be strong.

    Alone now, Deb and Liam had found themselves in an all-out war of their own. The safety of Jacob's land had now been infiltrated by an unlikely enemy. Gully MacDonell had made his way west and people feared for themselves, their land and their daughters. If war was not enough, now they had to face one of their own. He was said to be merciless, taking anything he wanted. Some young women were taken from their families and everyone knew what their fate was.

Chapter Six
Madness

Cheryl Alleway

Gully did not listen when people begged for mercy. He did not bow down when people tried to fight him. He had somehow managed to do his bidding in a very short period of time, taking advantage of the turmoil that war was creating in the region. With most of the young men off to battle, Gully saw weaker prey in the small landowners who had little protection for their farms. His assemblage of rogue ruffians was gathered from all areas to the south. Some were disgruntled soldiers and others were simply traitorous men bent on tasting the power that Gully promised them. With him, they had money and women and people feared them.

    In time, Gully ironically touted himself as the future King of Scotland, a supreme commander that would rule with an iron fist. He was a madman. His father's position and money made Gully believe that it belonged to him as well. This was not the case. He was a crazed and unintentionally spoiled young man, disowned by his father after realizing the boy he had raised was volatile and uncontrollable. His criminal activities had given him great satisfaction and without being prosecuted. He did not respect law or superiors. His insane mind was driving him and his victims into a path of destruction. He took what he wanted because he could. He came from money and although his own father denounced him because of his bite, Gully knew he had power and he wanted more. His father was unaware of this new taste for blood and Gully was biding his time before his father found out. Then, it would be father against son.

He was forging his own rogue war through pillaging and fear tactics. He and his men stole weapons from small northern English villagers as well. He stole bows, swords and horses; anything he could take and get away with. The people kept their tongue with the authorities because Gully didn't always threaten only. There were stories of him stealing daughters and even killing those who tried to defend their land. They prayed for something to happen. There was no way Gully could continue to profit under the noses of lords and get away with it. Hoping he would cross the wrong person and meet his fate, the lowland farmers could do nothing but wait. Surely something had to happen.

His men trained by mock fighting. At night, they drank heavily and drove themselves further into Gully's mad world. Each time they succeeded with a raid they grew more lustful and their bloodthirsty lifestyle required men that had no conscience, no fear and no honor.

"Damn you! Yu cut my flesh, bastard!" Two of Gully's men were showing off their sword techniques.

"You should be faster then, pig!" They laughed and swilled their wine. They had made camp only two days from Gully's ill-gotten fortress. The smaller Castle Dominon was taken from its owner once Gully heard that most of his men had left to take arms with the Bruce's troops. With fewer men than Gully's band he was forced to flee. One of Gully's men took aim and killed him in cold blood. Word could not be sent to the Bruce as no one had survived. His men would not return for over a year and so Castle Dominon was now a dark retreat for Gully. It was remote and held its position beyond a boggy section of land, which was difficult to cross. Now driven by the taste of victory, it had been the beginning of Gully MacDonell's mad exploits.

The fire's flame lit the night sky and Gully watched the entertainment. He was beginning to get bored however, and decided to show them a real sword fight.

"Get back! I will take him on myself!" The man with a cut on his arm now backed away and the other looked confident, but curious. They knew Gully was crazed and when he drank, he was like the devil. Not wanting to look weak in front of the others, he took the challenge.

The man stepped back and readied himself. He eyed up the feisty Gully who stood five foot nine with red hair that was pulled back into a tail at the back. Bits and pieces of hair fluttered around his ugly face. Gully's eyes were so dark brown that they looked black. He had a partial stubby beard that led to each sideburn sprouting to his ears. He was stout but not large framed. The one thing he always had was crazed vigor, which his parents and fellow clansmen saw as vulgar at best. To his men, it was something they could not miss. It made him stand out and he loved it. Gully was loud and blunt. He was going to be a challenge.

He spat on the ground and let out a flatulent sound that made the men laugh. He took point and they flew at each other. The other man was holding his own as Gully's sword hacked at his. If he didn't know any better, he was thinking that Gully would take it one step too far and kill him if given the chance.

He forged on as they jumped around trees and dove into the dirt around the fire. The men hollered and shouted obscenities in jest. Suddenly, Gully's drunken motivation took a piece of the man's forearm and he reeled back looking up at the smiling Gully.

"What is wrong? Did you not think I would strike? This is not a game that can be played gently! In battle when someone makes you bleed, it should make you angry! Fight back! Come at me!" Gully's fighting techniques had no structure. He raged when he fought; that was his approach. There was no thought, just rage.

The man looked up; then at the men jeering and drinking. He would not back down even from one of Gully's tests or it could be the end of him. He said nothing, but stepped forward and lunged at Gully. They met swords again and this time they held onto each other's wrists, nose to nose twisting in a circle as they stared each other down. Gully sneered at him and the man realized he was up to something.

Not backing down, he made one twist that Gully did not see coming. With it came a shallow slice to Gully's thigh.

"Awe! Now that is what you should have done in the first place!" Gully didn't seem to even feel it. His grin was sinister and he seemed invincible to his drunken disciples. The alcohol had masked his real pain from the small wound. He stepped up to the man again, but this time with his sword down. They were both sweating and dirty and now bleeding. Gully stood there silent looking the man straight in the face and the others went silent.

In a blunt statement, "This is the man I choose to be my second in command. Take your place beside me Angus! These men now answer to you! Do you hear that? All of you will take orders from this man from now on unless I see otherwise. Do you understand? Now drink! Eat and we shall take our leave in the morning! Tomorrow we take the land of Jacob Douglas!"

A rider had given word of Jacob's land to Gully. Many had seen him threatening townsfolk to the south and forcing them to talk about anyone who had done business in the markets selling their goods. Jacob had done that very thing before his parents passed and he had logged many hours on the trails towards Stirling and beyond. Some of the helpless townsfolk could do nothing but talk if it came down to it and so they did very unwillingly. It made them feel like traitors to Jacob Douglas, but a blade to the throat would evoke anything.

"We are not certain if the man and woman seen there are alone or not."

Gully licked his lips and made a sinister face speaking with a snake's voice, "Let us toast the Douglas woman and her man on their last night as landowners!"

The men laughed and held their wine and weapons high in the air as they shouted and gloated while dancing around the flames. Gully sank back into his blanket on the ground and watched his men revel in his leadership. It fed his insanity to see his influence on them.

Before they left the next morning, the rider was seen approaching. As the horse neared Gully's camp, he could see it was a familiar face. The face of his informant came into view and Gully watched as the thin, evil looking little man dismounted and slithered over to him, weary of the large men all watching him.

He was filthy and wore nothing but disheveled clothes. He spoke quickly like a weasel and his language was bad. His stench was horrible and his teeth were broken and rotten. Gully paid him to travel ahead and behind him at times as a lookout. Because of his appearance, he was not noticed or threatening to anyone who may see him. For a tiny fee, he was Gully's eyes and ears. No one else would pay him any mind and so he followed Gully and his men like a starving animal doing as he was told.

"Sire, I see no one on the land of Douglas, all but the woman and the man. They is all alune! If there are anyone else, I can nut see 'em! Yer way is clear from here as well. No soldiers, no soldiers!"

Gully was happy with the news and he ordered his men to mount. As he got on his own horse, he looked down at the sniveling informant and said, "Here you are Mulden, you tick. Now off with you to the west! I need to know if there is any army activity there before I head back to the castle!"

He flipped the man a small amount of coin and a piece of bread. He grabbed them quickly, shoved the money in his pocket and swallowed the bread in one bite. "Yes, Sire! Yes, I weel go now!" He mounted his horse and took flight.

Gully yelled at him again, "If you sell your horse for anything, I'll have your throat! She's mine and you are just using her. Remember that, Mulden!"

Mulden looked back and waved his hand up and down. He had thought about doing so many times, but he knew Gully would track him down and kill him and so he kept his word out of fear. It was torture to him. The fee from selling a horse could bring him more money than he could ever imagine. As he disappeared over the horizon, Gully and his men went the other way towards Deb and Liam's land.

On the second night, they had made it to the hills above Deb's father's croft. It was far in the distance and they could see the difficult passage they would have to navigate. They were quiet as they approached cautiously, like wolves. Some men went to the left and some to the right. They stopped on Gully's command and held a straight lined position in front of the building once they reached a distance that they could shout at the dwellers inside. They were talking and arguing among themselves as to what to do next. They still didn't know for sure who was inside. Mulden was loyal, but he wasn't very smart.

As dawn broke, Deb and Liam awoke to the sounds of voices. They knew instinctively they were in trouble. No one they knew was expected on the farm, let alone to arrive that early in the day. For days they had been making arrows in anticipation of a fight. The same villagers who told Gully of their whereabouts let Deb and Liam know of their guilty admission. Deb felt for them. What else could they do? Gully wanted their land and he had finally come to take it. Liam was afraid of leaving Deb alone to tell his father. It would have taken him five days to reach the north and another four or five to return. If he had been gone when Gully appeared, he would not have forgiven himself. Deb wouldn't leave. Liam understood because she had just buried her father there and there was no way a woman like Deb would run from anyone. She would stand her ground and Liam prayed that it was the right thing to do, but now they were trapped. They would have to dig deep inside themselves to fight this enemy. He would not ask anyone else to risk their life either. They were alone. If anyone was able to come, it was too late.

"Liam!" she whispered. "They're coming from the left. Take your bow and I will watch the right."

Liam loaded his back pouch with arrows. In the dark, cold air his fears had come to fruition. "Listen to me, Deb. Do not leave my sight." He grasped his bow as she looked over to hear his words.

"I love you, Liam Barne," she mouthed back to him.

Suddenly the cry came from the mist. "Liam Barne!! You are on land that Gully MacDonell wants! If you don't leave now, we will take your wife, kill your livestock and burn your croft to the ground! What will it be?" The matter of fact voice was most disrespectful as it bluntly made the point.

Liam looked at Deb and she nodded her head up and down once. She grabbed the sword her father had taught her to use. "*Our land*," she stated.

"*Our land*," Liam repeated. He threw his voice to the men outside, "There is no victory for tyranny on this land! We own it! We will fight for it!"

No answer came, but with only seconds to brace their weapons, the first arrow pierced through the window and landed beside Deb. She pressed her lips together and damned them under her breath.

Liam watched with anger through the window as their precious lambs were being slaughtered and it fueled a fire in him that burned with the heat of a thousand hells. His strong, dark arms pulled with all their might and a forceful thrust sent the first fatal shot thru the air. It struck one of the assassins bringing him down into the dirt.

Deb was braced at the door when she saw one of them creeping up to its frame. "Liam," she whispered and motioned her head in the man's direction. Liam knew she was going to take him on.

"No, Deb! Stay inside!" he begged her. She saw only one and if she could bring him down, maybe the others would not follow his path. She had played out this type of scenario many times with the local boys since she was fourteen years old and she was ready to put it to the test.

"I'll not fail, Liam!" she stated. With that she lunged out of the door like a cat and took him by surprise.

The henchman smirked when he saw she was a woman, "Ah, this is what our catch will be?" he jeered.

She smelled his rank breath in the morning air and smiling back she answered, "Yes my boy, but this catch bites back!"

She forced her body forward and plunged her sword into his belly. He swung at her but only grazed her arm. His last breath seeped from his vile lips. She quickly swung back around and shut the door again behind her.

"You're going to make my heart stop, woman!" Liam spit out under his breath, but he knew this one well. He was energized by her bravery.

A call came again from outside. This time it was Gully MacDonell himself. "Barne! You're just a man with a small woman at your side! Do you think you can hold my men off all day?"

Liam embraced his anger. Gully enjoyed taunting and creating fear with words as well as with his blade. He would not make Liam bow down though. Deb motioned to Liam to bark back.

"You'll not take us quietly, Gully! My men are with me today as well. If you continue battering this house, they will show you the way off this land!"

Deb looked worried, but it was worth a try.

"Men? You have no men, Liam Barne! You have a meek wife and twenty dead lambs!" The men all laughed. "But if you say you have men, show me! Send out six arrows together. There is no way the two of you could do it alone. Your wife could hold but one and no man could shoot five all together! Show me these so called men of yours!"

Liam grinned at Deb. "You can do it," he said. "Just pull back and hold yourself against the wall until you get them loaded. Use your father's teachings to guide them straight, Deb. I can only hold them by strength; it is you that can make the mark!"

She took hold of a second large bow by the door. Liam loaded three in his own. Pulling hers back, Deb braced her arm on the window frame locking her shoulder. It hurt terribly and her body quivered, but she held strong and placed the arrows together in a row.

"Well, I'm waiting!" Gully yelled once more. Before he could finish, Liam nodded to Deb and suddenly they released the arrows in a rush of air that was heard by the men outside.

"Down, boys!" they cried as six powerful arrows lanced through the air. Two of Deb's hit their mark and Gully himself shuffled his horse to the left narrowly avoiding a shot. He steadied his horse and looked around at his fallen men writhing in pain on the ground below him. His face turned black. Now he was hard pressed to believe that Liam and his wife were alone in that house. He was confused by the display of firepower.

Deb fell to the floor in pain as her shoulder had come out of position. "Come here, Deb!" Liam whispered. "Hold still love, this will hurt a bit." He held himself tightly to her body and placed his hand on her shoulder. With a quick pull, he snapped it back into place, immediately grabbing her mouth to quiet her cry of pain. She looked up as he released his hand. "I'm alright. God help me, I'm alright!" she spouted back. Deb was even more determined now. They would not take them today. Not today. She shook off the pain that stayed with her now. She prayed that her breathing techniques would keep her mind off of it.

All at once, the arrows began. They bombarded the windows and pierced through the door when shot at close range. Liam and Deb fought back for two hours. Gully liked to wear his quarry down slowly.

Suddenly, in a brief moment of chilling silence, the thing Liam and Deb feared the worst happened.

"Deb, do you smell it?" Liam questioned. She bowed her head and closed her eyes for a moment. Opening them up again, she nodded. The realization was more painful than any wound.

"How about a little heat, Liam! Maybe you'll enjoy it on this chilly night!" Gully growled.

Fire was growing above them and for the first time, Deb and Liam grew weary.

"I'm not cooking like a piece of meat!" Deb stated. "If we're to die, I will die as I should; fighting for my land and my family!" Liam looked outside as the men laughed and Gully sat on his horse as pompous and evil as only he could. Crawling under the window to Deb's side Liam held her in his arms.

"I love you. You're my life and if you die, I die as well." A sullen tear ran slowly down her determined cheek as he kissed her lips and embraced her tightly. Out the back into the trees was the only way possible. Taking all they could hold for weapons, they quickly went to the small door in back and slipped out slowly. As they peered around the trees to make sure of their position, it came. A sharp blow to his back snapped Liam to the ground! With his club raised again, a henchman took a hit of his own when Deb threw a knife through the air piercing his left arm. He lurched in pain as she gathered Liam up from the ground.

"They're running!" the injured henchman cried as he pulled the knife from his arm. Liam turned and plunged his foot into his face knocking out three teeth and putting him out, but it was too late. Six more came around back. Swords sliced and shouts of anger filled the night air. The fight lasted only a few minutes this time as they overtook Deb and Liam. They had to give up. They would not win this fight. There were just too many of them.

They tied a rope around Liam's neck and fastened his hands together behind his back. His hair had come loose and was ragged and tattered around his face. He was kicking the entire time. They dragged him over to Gully's horse. Liam would not look him in the face. It began to rain and the only thing that would be saved was the croft as the droplets slowly put out the fire that had been started on the roof.

Deb was being pulled by her hair and dress. They threw her onto the ground beside her husband like an animal and tied her hands in the front. One of Gully's men tore her dress in the front and shouted, "I think this one should be saved, don't you?" The men all laughed and stared at Deb as she kneeled; stripped for all to see.

Liam lunged forward at the man and they landed on the ground scuffling in the dirt. "Get him off me!" Another grabbed Liam and threw him back over to Gully. Liam looked back and spat the dirt out of his mouth with fire in his eyes.

"Liam, these 'pitiful boys' are just surprised to see a real woman for the first time!" Deb jeered as she spat back. She glared at the man who tore her dress and he backed up slightly. She looked as if she would kick him at that moment. He sneered back at her and said, "There's fire in this one's eyes! Yes, she will give us much entertainment!"

"Silence!" Gully shouted. "I've had enough of this child's play. Tie the husband to that tree and place him on that beast of a donkey he calls his horse! Take his lovely wife and tie her to my steed. She is mine. None of you touch her!"

As Liam watched through the mud and blood on his face, they took her from him. They left him sitting on top of his horse; eyes filled with angry tears, hair soaking wet and muddy with his neck held within a noose. Deb watched her husband and her life fade into the night mist. Her chest was heavy with pain as she wept quietly struggling to break her hands free. Just as Liam's figure began to vanish from her view, she closed her eyes and vowed to never give up hope. The husband and wife locked eyes through the pain and tears as Liam mouthed, "*I love you. I will find you.*"

Gully shouted one last thing to his right hand man, Angus, as they left the scene with Deb, "We'll be back in four days to clean up my new property and bury Barne with his sheep! I don't want any rotting flesh on my land."

With that, he turned his horse around and Deb strained her head backwards to look at Liam. Her wet hair was wrapped around her and her face showed fear for the first time. It was the last thing Liam saw before he passed out.

Chapter Seven
Stolen Lives

Cheryl Alleway

They took her. The sun was rising as Gully's entourage rode up to his fortress miles away. Mud and thistle bushes surrounded the building. Its appearance suited its owner well and was very unlike his father's Inverness castle with its majestic peaks and well-built stone walls…nothing more than a memory to Gully. He was nothing to his father now; banished from the castle and the family. Gully had to be disowned and it fueled his devastating pain inside to rebel.

His father had known that if his wretched son had his money and his position, the highlands would be destroyed slowly by his son's hatred and lust for power. Thomas MacDonell was an honorable man. He was given a high position within the clan to assist the Lord of Islay and the other clan chiefs with protecting the northland islands and mainland regions. They were flanked by the large clan of Campbell and had their share of quarrels, but Thomas had been working hard at calming relations with some of the smaller clans in the north and his ability to fight and lead his men caught the eye of Lord John Islay. He was as much a hero in these lands as were many other men who had fought off southern enemies and tried to show his people and his family that their land was rugged, but proud and beautiful. It was a place detached from the rest of the world for a reason. This place was their home and no one could take it or tarnish their history. Gully threatened it all, and the shame was too much for Thomas to bear anymore. He had not heard of his only child for two years.

The sun was coming up over the castle as Deb opened her tired eyes to see the place that had become her prison. What Gully would do to her, she knew not. The only thing she did know was this; that when she got free from this place, Gully would pay for the pain he had put her and her family through. His father would know of Gully's murderous rampages and she would hand Gully to his father herself!

Slowly, the large castle gates opened with a low grim moan and the horses were led into the grounds. As the gates swung closed again, Deb looked back and noticed that only two men were guarding them. Above, four more watched from the top. She made a mental note of how everything was laid out: where the horses were, where the men were, how the door was latched and could she lift it. They had not expected her to be so strong after the day's battle and decided to have a bit of fun with her until she showed the weakness they were all thirsty for.

"Ah! This one is going to be my favorite," cried Gully. "She is the one that will possibly stay the longest if she survives. What do you think about that?"

Deb made no motion to him and no expression showed on her face. She knew from her father's teachings that if captured, one must never show emotion of weakness or strength. It was best not to entertain them at all, especially for a woman. If she showed the real spark and power she had, they would test her even more and possibly beat and rape her more than they may already be thinking of doing. No, she had to stay calm and quiet.

"I want to hear you speak, woman! I want to hear that fire in you that you showed when I beat your husband in front of you!"

Gully came down off his horse and walked over to Deb who was still silent. He touched her bare, bruised thigh and looked up at her. His smelly leather glove traced the rest of her down to her bare feet and she had to hold back the urge to kick his teeth out as he paused to admire her with a perverted, disgusting smile. She finally looked down slowly, without emotion, and she could tell he felt something for her even though it was repulsive. He was enamored with her. This would be his down fall. This would be her best weapon against this monster that had taken her life and family from her. This man, Gully, would die.

"Throw her in the cell and wash her! I want a clean dinner guest at the table tonight! Bring her new clothes and make her worthy to sit with me!"

He turned quickly and his black cape drifted behind him as he marched off with his servant to his quarters.

This was when Deb felt the most frightened. The low life men that worked for Gully were now alone with her and she feared rape and molestation. Yet, if Gully's treasure was found sullied at all, they all knew he would kill them instantly.

They dragged her harshly from the saddle and pulled her by the wrists across the courtyard. They took her boots from her feet so that it would be hard for her to run. Once in the dark hallway, she could see the stairs where they would take her. More mental notes as to the layout of the rooms were made. She noted how many candles were on the walls and what rooms were being unused that she could hide in temporarily while escaping. She saw an archer's corner with a small window looking down towards the river. It wasn't the normal narrow archer's slit and she noticed that she could probably slip through it with only a few scrapes from the mortared bricks. The drop would be about thirty feet however, and the river was at least that deep in itself.

She had to stay calm and clear headed. That was going to be her only weapon for the next few days.

As the man that was dragging her stepped down to a lower level in the hall, Deb began to feel the loss of her beloved Liam. She held back the tears and for a moment, she felt fragile. All she wanted to do was sleep to gain her strength back. But she could tell that it wasn't the way this night was going to go.

With a final shove, the dirty, foul smelling henchman pushed her into her room. Her hands still tied, she bumped into the far wall and when she turned to face him, he was glaring at her with a filthy lust. Her breasts were partially uncovered and although she was dirty, bruised and bloody, Deb's beauty was unmistakable. Her black, wavy hair fell around her shoulders and she sported skin that had almost a golden sheen. Working outside and practicing the skills her father taught her had made her very fit and strong. She stood taller than the average woman and could actually look many men in the eye.

"Hmmm…you are a fine catch. I wonder if Gully would notice if I took just a little bite!"

Deb still stared at him with a sullen emotionless face, but decided that this one was too stupid to succeed with any threats he might make.

She decided to play his game. "Well, maybe if you untied me, I could get cleaned up like Gully asked and if you help me, I might show you a little something for it in return."

She surprised him and he hustled over to her to cut the ropes from her wrists. Deb knew this one's weakness now as well.

"Well, do you have any clothes for me to change into?" she asked.

He stuttered at the thought of seeing her naked and rushed out the door locking it behind him and shouting, "I'll be right back!"

Deb realized that he had left the rope he just cut from her on the floor. She grabbed it and tucked it in the back of her dress. His footsteps were coming back down the hall and she sat on the bench in the room, acting as if she was just waiting for him to return.

He unlocked the door again and entered. "Here! Put these on and make it quick. I want a show, lassie!"

Deb stood up slowly and asked him to turn his head just for a second until she was ready for him. With nothing but perversion on his mind, he made his fatal mistake. Deb lunged forward with one end of the rope tight in her left hand and before he could turn to see what she was doing, the right hand came up on the other side of his neck. With that one hard, strong thrust backward, Deb snapped his neck back. He lurched frantically and almost released himself, but Deb held on tight and they both went to the floor. With everything she had, she tightened the rope's grip around his stringy neck.

She used her strong legs to grapple him. He punched at her face and made contact once causing yet another bruise under her left eye. They rolled as one in a flurry of arms and legs until he ended up face down on the dirt floor giving Deb the advantage to pull even harder on the rope. Her face contorted as she made sure she did not fail. His power faded as the oxygen was taken from his lungs and Deb crushed his throat. It was over for him.

Quickly, she grabbed the outfit he had brought her and put it on. She pushed his body out the door and watched for anyone coming down the hall. Dragging him feverously, she made it to the one room in the hall that was vacant. Shoving his body in and closing the door, she ran back to her room and closing its door tightly, she had to wait. This was not the time to try and escape. She had his knife and his keys now and there were several other keys on his ring that she knew would come in handy. She hid them under her torn corset and tied it as tightly as she could manage, pressing them into her skin to mask their shape as much as possible. The knife would be harder to conceal, but it was small enough to tie to her leg with a piece of her old skirt. She made sure it was low enough so that when Gully was fondling her at the dinner table, he wouldn't find it on her. She knew of his kind.

Washing her face and hands, she began to clean the blood and dirt off of her body as best as she could. With another torn length from her old skirt, she bundled her long black hair up and tied it on top of her head allowing it to drape down slightly here and there. Even with nothing to work with, Deb was sure Gully would be pleasantly surprised.

She was ready. Her heart raced and while she finished cleaning her feet, another one of Gully's low life men came for her. He was angry looking and not as stupid as the other one.

"Where is that idiot who brought you down here?"

Deb stepped forward suddenly acting ignorant and answered, "I don't know, he brought me these clothes and said he was going to find a pint somewhere. I haven't seen him since."

The guard took her by the wrist and pinned both hands together in the front as he lead her down the hall to a staircase that lead up to the next floor. The floor was cold and damp on her feet and the moon was now shining down through the windows in the castle hallways. The smell of food was floating in the air and Deb suddenly realized how hungry and thirsty she was.

With not another word, the guard pulled her into the great hall of the castle where many of Gully's men had assembled to eat with him. There must have been thirty or so and every one of them stopped talking and cussing as they turned to see Deb enter the room. She captured their attention above all of the other half-dozen girls that were there. They were all slaves and prisoners with an obvious weariness in their faces. Deb felt so much pity for them. She wished she could save them all from this evil, disgusting man. They were like fragile lambs in a den of wolves, but Deb stood tall and strong as she looked around and found Gully's ugly face sitting pompously at the head of the main table. He gazed at her like the devil, but in his face one could see that he knew Deb was a force to be reckoned with. The thought excited him.

She took a deep breath as the guard released her from the shackles. She could do no harm with this many men around. Deb thought otherwise, because the drunker they got, the weaker they became. This theory included Gully and Deb had a plan to get him as drunk as she could. If she couldn't beat them, she would have to trick them.

On the end of the table sat a young girl who watched the confident Deb stroll towards Gully. She must not have been more than fifteen years of age and Deb noticed her the most. This girl looked familiar to her. From that thought, Deb refocused. She needed to eat and she needed to try her plan. She was not going to escape tonight…no she wanted to weaken them and learn more about their ways. Her father had also taught her that to simply run from your enemy was not a battle won. You must make them less of their former self. You had to know how they worked so that you could cut them off at the ground they stood on. Tonight, she would put that plan into play. As she arrived at her spot at the table, Gully stood to make an announcement. He motioned her to sit and as his smelly hand pressed her down by her shoulders, she swallowed to maintain her constitution.

"Shut up, you filthy lot! Listen carefully. We have had a good day!" He was tipsy, but not drunk. His cocky tone made them all stop talking. "This lovely wench is Deb Barne. She's mine! She is off limits! These other gifts from our travels are yours to do with what you will. For now, we have taken the surrounding farmland, but beyond the river Tay, in Perth, is prime country. Farms there are said to have more heads of sheep than any!"

Suddenly, one of the men cried out, "But Gully, that's in your clan's territory. What about your father?"

Gully's snake like neck turned slowly, his dark eyebrows lowered and his crooked mouth twitching. "My clan's land is still mine as well! I will have what is mine! He is nothing but an old man who knows nothing of what it takes to be a great leader! He is soft! We will make our way there after we have gathered as much weaponry as we can! We will train and build our stores. If we must pass through the Grampian Mountains, then we will not take lands before them. Instead, we will save our weapons and forge through to the tip of land to Loch Ness. My father's land covers Inverness. If we take it, we will have bases to the north and south! The king will come to know me as a great leader! With my father gone, I will own the title of Earl MacDonell! It is rightfully mine!" His eyes were wild and his face was contorted from his rush of energy. He was rambling, the men could see it, but it seemed to be a drug to them. The more insane Gully became, the more they believed he could do what he claimed he could.

"We will revel in the riches that it will bring! Is there any man here that does not want to share in that victory as well?"

They all mumbled amongst themselves. Some were leery of taking on some of the harsh north-country, let alone Gully's father. Not to mention the fact that the king's armies would have to be evaded. If they knew of Gully's ambitious plots, they would surely hunt him down and imprison him. Gully seemed driven by the hatred for his father and the confident power in his voice pushed them into agreement. As one man shouted, others joined him, even with doubt still in their minds. It was greed that was clouding their judgment and with little knowledge of the highlands, they would blindly follow Gully to the ends of the earth.

In Gully's mind, the English would never actually take Scotland and it would be men like him that would be left to rule when the king's armies did their feeble part.

Ironically, he was a coward by heart. Like any tyrant, he preyed on those who were weaker than he was in order to prove his power to those who would blindly buy into it. If he cared about true leadership and victory, he would have fought by his father's side as an honorable man, but Gully was a vulture, an opportunist and a thief.

One large man stood to shout, "To Gully! May we all follow him to victory! He is the next Wallace!"

The men hollered back and a drunken party arose from the sweat and alcohol. They danced and fondled the women. They ate like pigs and wrestled on the dirt floor to see who was the strongest. Deb had her own problems at the table with Gully. He was looking at her closely now. His filthy hand began to touch her shoulders and he pressed his leg against hers.

"You are a beautiful woman, Deb. Why can't you see that I am more the man for you than your weak husband ever was? Look at what I can offer you. I have a castle, not a shack. I have many miles of land, not just one small farm. I am a man with a vision for greatness. What you don't admit now will become your destiny."

Deb decided that he was going to lose some of his power tonight. She would use what the heavens had given her and play him for the fool he was. She would play on his sense of control. It was obvious that if he didn't have it, he would not be the same man. Right now he had control over his men, his own fate and the poor women around him taken against their will. Yes, Gully's weakness was the very control he had over his world. She wanted to be the one to help him lose it.

Gathering her senses, she turned and looked him in the eye. "Well, you have hurt me and I don't know if I could ever forget that Gully, even though you do have more than Liam ever did." She then turned her head away and stayed calm trying to make her act seem real. She had to forget about today. If she didn't, she would die right here and now but nothing could please her more than to slit his throat. If she tried with these men around.... she would never see Liam again. Slow and steady. Just like her father had taught her.

Gully took her face in his hand and brought it back to his. "If you're playing with me, don't. I can kill you as easily as I did your husband. I do think however, that you will see that being at my side will be addictive to you, Deb. You are a strong woman; not like these other girls."

Deb looked in his direction again, but not in his eyes, "I am a strong woman. I won't be easily won over."

This was a risky thing to say. Gully didn't like to beg for anything, but he was becoming aroused by her willingness to speak to him. It was working in Deb's favor as Gully said back, "I see. What if I showed you just what a great man I am?"

She didn't want to find out what he meant by that.

Gully noticed the swelling around Deb's eye. It was obviously fresh and he hadn't noticed it before when they brought her to the castle. He knew someone had handled her.

Suddenly, he rose up from his chair and shouted, "Who touched this woman against my wishes!"

No one said anything. Gully's right hand man Angus stood up from the table and yelled, "Speak up now and you may live. If you are found out, you will hang in the courtyard! No one disobeys Gully!"

The guard who brought Deb to the room stood up and went over to Gully and whispered in his ear, "I think it was Kearney. He disappeared just before I went to get her from her cell and she was untied."

That was all Gully had to hear. He sent two men to look for Kearney and sat back down at the table. He leaned over to Deb and whispered with bad breath. "He won't live to see daylight. If anyone has the right to touch you, it's me."

She closed her eyes to try and hide from the moment as Gully's hand slithered down and squeezed her thigh. He swept his hand gently over the wound on her eye and she jolted her head away. Gully grinned like the devil and continued to eat and drink. This night was the first of many that she would need to keep her wits about her.

The drunken party went into the night and Deb had no choice but to go back to Gully's room with him. He closed the door and locked it behind him. She was terrified, but refused to show it. She wasn't afraid of 'him', she was afraid of losing her senses. Anger drove her now. When he touched her, the only face she could see was Liam's. She felt guilt and sorrow and pain all at the same time. If pleasuring Gully would help her fool him, she had no choice. She had to get back to Liam. She just knew he was still alive.

Cheryl Alleway

Chapter Eight
Redemption

Cheryl Alleway

F or two weeks, Gully and his men built up armor and supplies for the trip to the river's edge. During that time, Deb had given herself permission to do whatever she had to. Gully was a man of quick decision and a lack of romance or feeling. Servicing him each night was nothing but a moment of discomfort to Deb. It was her body, not her soul. There was no feeling in her when they were together. She was numb.

She was a prisoner, but one that would fight back. Deb closed her eyes each time and held onto her faith. The tears stopped after a while but sometimes, when Gully left the room, she would weep in silence. Even though he had killed many people, for some reason, Gully had not beaten her. She had not laid hands on him either. She did not want to give him reason to hit her. She needed to be in the best of shape and health to escape him. Sometimes she would catch a moment with one of the other girls and they would speak to each other about their plight.

Deb taught them how to make even an evil man treat them better. "You must use their animal instincts against them. They want your body, so give it to them. Don't struggle. The more you struggle, the more they will want to hurt you. Feed them wine with valerian root crushed into it. It will make them tired and less violent. It's the power they have over you that makes them strong. When they become rough, show them the woman you are. A man can't fight his urge to touch a beautiful thing or take the drink. They can only use you; they can never possess you. They can't take your spirit and they will never control your mind if you are strong. This place is not your destiny. I will see to that!"

The young girl that Deb thought she recognized that first night had come to her alone one day. Her name was Sarah. She was the daughter of someone Deb's father had known and as the girl sat and quietly told Deb of her captivity, Deb's heart grew larger and beat with even more revenge than before. She remembered seeing Sarah once as a child. This man had stolen her innocence.

"I was fourteen last year when Gully came. We had heard that he wanted our land but my father, like the others, was not ready to fight. My mother was ill and she was not long for the world. I had been sitting with her day and night until the day I had to let her go." A tear welled up in Deb's eye. This girl had seen so much already at such a young age, not unlike herself.

"My father tried to fight off Gully and his men, but they killed him and my brother. My mother's body was left in the house and then they took me and..." She suddenly stopped and bowed her head. She could not speak.

"Sarah, what did they do to you?" She took the young girl's trembling hand and held her small face with the other. "Did they rape you Sarah?"

She fell into Deb's lap weeping and Deb's back stiffened up straight. She was going to make these men pay for what they had done. They respected nothing but the sword. Deb had waited long enough. Her chance would come. She looked up and said to herself in her head, *"Now is when you need to remember. Remember your father, remember your mother. Remember your skills and the words your father taught you. You were brought here for a reason. You will save these girls. You will!"*

Looking at the limp young girl at her feet, Deb said with absolute in her voice, "Sarah, I need you to do something for me. When you see the other girls and no one is around, tell them that I am going to escape soon. Make them keep quiet. It is not to be spoken of after it is told to them. Go on about your days as usual. I will wait until Gully and most of his men are gone to the river. Steal as much bread and vegetables from the kitchen as you are able to. You can and leave it in my clothing. In three nights when the moon is high, you will know when it is time. I will blow out my candle and the smoke will be my signal. No one else must try to escape yet. They will beat you all to get the truth. If I do it alone, they will believe I was on my own because I am the newest one here. If they start to ask if any of you know anything, tell them that you hated me and that you were jealous that I got to be with Gully. They will believe you. Then tell them that you hope they find me and kill me."

Sarah couldn't say those things, but Deb convinced her to do it and before long, the other girls were given the instructions as well. They were terrified for Deb but they looked upon her as an angel that had been brought to them. They trusted her plan.

Sarah had dried her tears that day and looked up at Deb with great reverence. This strong woman had become a mother figure to her and the other girls and they could feel it in their bones that Deb was going to come back and save them.

That night, they all prayed for her. If something went wrong, they would never see freedom.

For the next two days, Deb prepared. She hid the food in a hole behind the head board of the bed and each night she would sit in her window and make notes as to the location of the guards and the times that they drifted off to sleep; all the while plotting against the beast that slept with her night after night. It would be difficult, but tomorrow night after Gully and his men were gone, she would take flight.

Nothing could have been more risky than what Deb was about to do. Gully left twenty men behind to guard the castle walls and keep the women and supplies in order. The only relief the girls seemed to get was when Gully left with the majority of his men on trips. The ones left behind were usually too busy eating and drinking to bother them very much. Instead, orders to clean and wash laundry were shouted at them. At least it wasn't the usual sexual indiscretions. These girls were young and naive and very battered mentally. Sarah, on the other hand, was changing her way of thinking. She had seen a glimmer of sunlight in the eyes of the more senior and worldly Deb. Sarah realized that Deb would not succumb to this life forever. She was tricking the beast into thinking he had won. She marveled at the woman's courage and ability to separate her mind from her body.

After nights of consoling and mental healing with Deb, Sarah was starting to get stronger. The other girls were still afraid to revolt in any way, but

Sarah could see something more than these filthy, demeaning walls. She could see herself again and she wanted to learn more and feel stronger.

Deb watched the sun go down that night. It was dark, cold and the water had an eerie mist rising above it. The guards that had been on duty during the day were now asleep. Some were eating supper in the great hall and five were guarding the front gate. The remaining four were at the castle's entrance path in the forest. They had four horses and two watchtowers. Two men were on the ground and two were above. All were now accounted for. The one thing Deb had to do was make sure the eleven guards inside did not awaken from their sleep. Hopefully, they had enough wine in them to keep that from happening. Nine men would be enough to deal with. She had instructed the girls to overdose the wine goblets with valerian root. No traces of it were to be left behind. Any indication that the girls had something to do with it and all would be lost. It had to look like a drunken lot and nothing more.

A single breath, deeply inhaled, brought her closer to action. She was ready. No one guarded the hallway to her room, but the men at the gate often took turns walking around the castle grounds to check on everything. The girls had to act like nothing was going on. They continued to clean up after the men and make the bread dough for the morning. Someone would notice Deb missing from her room eventually, so Sarah had volunteered to be her double. They would not likely notice Sarah missing as the other girls were like sheep to the men. Deb, on the other hand, was Gully's woman. She would need to be checked on for sure.

This gave Deb the chance to hide and take them one at a time. The more men she took down now would make it easier as she went.

Once Sarah arrived, Deb fashioned her with a wig made of black horsehair, painstakingly collected. Her body was cushioned to create Deb's full figure and blocks of wood under her on the chair made Sarah taller. In the night lighting, sitting across the room by candle, they would hopefully not tell the difference. They were too afraid to get any closer, lest Deb fill Gully in on it.

Now she would need to prepare her weapons. She had collected three more knives since the one stolen from the first guard. She missed having the dagger her father had given her. She had kept it in the same place behind the bed, but knew that one day soon it would be in her hands again. She strapped the others strategically to her body. One on the upper arm, one on her right calf, one tied across her back and the last on her hip ready to pull. She would need to use arrows on the men in the towers. Only four could be stolen by one of the girls and hopefully they would be enough. If Deb missed, they could take her. The two on the ground would be easy enough if she could take care of the five at the gate first. She would have to be quiet about it, which meant close combat. Darkness would be her best friend tonight. One woman against nine men would be a feat too unimaginable for most. But Deb wasn't like most women. Not only was she trained mentally and physically, she had a burning drive pushing her to take her life back and find her beloved husband Liam. She refused to believe that he was dead.

With the night sky full of stars and drifting clouds, it was almost too peaceful to believe what was about to take place. A long, tearful embrace left Sarah standing in the doorway of Deb's room praying for her and the lives of them all. Deb had gone to the window in her room and blew out the candle that would signal to the other girls that the moment had come, to stay calm and remember what she taught them.

Seeing the smoke, they all looked at each other with apprehensive eyes and continued to work. They had come to the courtyard to gather wood for the fires and watch the window's frame, but they went back to their places with anxiousness in their chests. Two of the guards were already making their way to the hallway of Deb's room and she would have to take them both silently. Sarah took her place in the corner by another candle on the table and pretended to be sewing one of Deb's dresses. She kept her face tilted slightly away but not enough to create suspicion. When the guard opened the door, she said nothing. He looked around and felt content to close the door again. Sarah's hands were shaking, but she held fast. She listened as his footsteps drifted down the hall.

Carefully, Deb took the handle of the knife at her hip and waited in the darkness of the empty room down the hall. The body of Kearney whom she had initially killed in her cell had been tossed out the window and into the moat by the other girls weeks ago, but Deb swore she could still smell him.

The first guard came around the corner alone and the other went up the stairs to check on the kitchen girls. Waiting cautiously, every muscle in Deb's body was hard and she was poised to strike. Her bow and four arrows were strapped across her back. She was wearing her old boots that one of the girls had found for her in the courtyard tossed in a corner and she had taken some of Gully's trousers and a jacket to keep her warm. She had sewn them to fit her better so that she could move properly in them. Her hair was tightly tied back in a braid with leather string and she had stolen a pair of gloves to wear upon her hands. The food she had managed to get the girls to steal was strapped tightly against her back under the bow so as not to hinder her. She was ready and she flashed back to the lessons her father had taught her over and over again. *"Never give up!"*

    The first man entered her vision and as his body stepped slightly past the dark doorway, she made her move. Grabbing his face and mouth tightly and pulling his neck back with all her might, Deb slashed his throat. She quickly dragged his body into the room and closed the door. Sarah came out for only a moment to help wipe the blood away from the floor and throw some ashes around pressing them into the stone floor to cover any scent and spots of blood that may have been missed.

    The second guard had gone into the great hall to touch bases with anyone who was still awake. All but one man had gone to bed and he was so drunk that he had passed out. As the guard turned to leave, he noticed a shadow outside the door. Walking slowly with his hand on his sword, he glimpsed carefully around the corner only to see Jessica, one of the girls holding a candlestick. She took a deep breath and said to him, "Are you the only one left awake?"

    He was puzzled by the question, but realized that she was propositioning him as she shyly gazed at the floor. He noticed her firm, white cleavage and slightly tattered skirt. She smiled gently and he answered, "Well, if you're the prize, then yes I am!"

He made his way over to her passing a doorway. Jessica pretended to drop the candle. "Oh, I'm so sorry! Let me clean it up!" He was a bit annoyed but she was so beautiful that all he wanted was to grab her and take her right there. Without warning the girl turned and bolted down the hall. "Where do you think you're going?! Get back here!"

Before he could finish, Deb drew her knife across his throat. Jessica had been the perfect ambush. She peeked around the corner at Deb and the grizzly scene. Deb looked up and said, "Very good, Jessica…now go back to the kitchen so no one notices. Stay calm. Act normal. Don't run."

Jessica nodded with wide startled eyes and did what she was told. Deb cleaned up the mess and moved down the hallway to the outside entrance. She whispered to herself with a powerful tone, *"Two down, seven to go."* Now was the hard part as there were three men left at the gate. If she tried to get out another way, she would not be able to get at the horses down the path to the towers. She had to deal with these three first. If they were left alive, they would hear her struggle at the towers and alert the others inside. There would be no way of taking them all on.

As Deb made her way outside she was careful to stay in the shadows. The men at the gate were focused on the outside of the castle, not the inside courtyard. She readied a knife and hid behind a hay wagon. One man was ten feet from her and the other two were facing the path. She started to whine like a puppy very quietly. The guard heard it and started over to investigate. Deb tensed up and buried herself in the hay and shadows continuing to whine softly. The guard peered around the edge of the wagon and as he did so, Deb plunged the knife up into his belly. She reached up quickly to cover his mouth and pulled his heavy body down behind the wagon.

The other two guards returned to the gate and were looking uneasy. "Where is that sloth?" one asked the other. They also commented on the length of time the guard was taking checking on the inside rooms. Deb was worried they were suspicious already.

Someone was coming out of the castle and walking towards the two guards. It was Sarah! What was she doing? Deb's heart raced as she feared they were about to be discovered. Instead, Sarah had a smile on her face as she approached the guards.

"What do you want, woman?" one guard asked her while the other had a smutty grin on his face.

"I was told by the other two guards to give you some wine. It is a cold night and they are gathering some warmer clothes to bring out. Here, I have warmed it for you. They said they will not be long. One is relieving himself and then they will be back out."

Deb was puzzled by Sarah's initiative, but Sarah had been watching the whole time and knew if Deb didn't kill these two quietly, she would perish. It would be very difficult to separate them undetected. They were already uneasy.

Then, as Sarah pressed her arms against her breasts showing their cleavage, one of the men finally said, "Ah, a wench that brings wine deserves a little reward."

Deb held back from rushing them. She knew what Sarah was going to do and it made her cringe to be responsible. Sarah slowly lured him away from the other.

"You can't leave me alone. If Gully finds out, we'll both be boiled alive!"

"Shut up you imbecile! Don't you see this ripe peach is ready to pick? Gully is miles away and the others will be here in a moment. Stay at the post and I will be right back. I haven't had any female for days!"

"You have five minutes! If you're not back, I'll boil you myself!"

Pitting them against each other was a fine move on Sarah's part. Deb was impressed and as Sarah led her quarry away into the shadows, Deb poised herself. This one was alone but he was at the ready now. She decided to try something different. Standing up, she pulled a burlap cover sitting on the hay over her body to hide her weapon and placed it over her shoulders like a blanket. Deb walked right out to the guard who stammered when he saw her coming.

"What are you doing out of your room! Gully will hear about this!" He was clearly agitated.

Deb approached him and answered, "I saw the other guard leave his post from above. Gully will be angry."

"You keep your tongue woman! I had nothing to do with it! One of those stupid wenches lured him away with her breasts! I should kill her!"

"Shhhh....don't worry. I won't tell Gully anything. That other guard is an idiot to think he won't be found out. When the others return, you should tell them of this. In fact, I think you should take a break and have some wine while you wait. If they deserve a break, so do you. It is freezing out tonight and you can't do your job if your belly isn't full. I'll get you some bread. Wait and I'll be right back."

He knew something wasn't right. The women were never nice to the men and Deb knew this would puzzle him. No one else had returned and as Deb drifted into the shadows, he drew his sword to follow her. She molded herself into the corner of the entrance throwing off the burlap; as the tip of his blade passed through she dove at him. This time her mark was slightly off and his sword grazed her leg. "You women are nothing but trouble! I told Gully to be wise of you all!"

Deb gave him a look that burned through him. He saw her weapons now and realized that he was not fighting a naive girl. "Are you surprised to see a female that doesn't cower to you, pig?" Deb circled him carefully watching the sword with one eye and his feet with the other.

"You will cower to me, woman. I'm going to make you pay for this treachery first!"

Deb was worried now that the guard with Sarah would hear them. "Fight with your sword pig, not with your mouth!" With that he lunged at her and she folded herself at the waist to avoid the blade. With a running jump she leaped onto a section of the wall and was now above him. He lashed his blade at her feet and she tossed herself onto the ground, rolling a few feet away from him. On the ground, she allowed him to get closer. As he poised to slam his blade into her, Sarah appeared behind him and threw a rock at his head.

As he flinched forward, Deb kicked the sword from his hands and plunged into his gut with her knife. Lying on the ground, with his eyes closed, he moaned his last breath.

"Sarah! What happened with the other guard?" Deb caught her breath and Sarah answered shaking, "He won't be a bother." She had a tear in her eye, but this tear was one of redemption. Deb stepped forward and cupped Sarah's face in her hands.

"Did you?"

Sarah raised her head and stood up tall as the tears fell. She kept steady and showed Deb the blood on her hands. Deb held her and looked her in the face, "You have seen and done too much for one so young. I am sorry that your innocence has been taken from you, but know this; you must gather yourself and go back inside. You have done well and I thank you for your courage, Sarah."

Sarah lunged forward and held Deb tightly. She looked up without saying a word. Deb knew what the young girl was saying. "It's not over yet, I have to get past the tower guards. Sarah, you must go back in. You can't go any further. It's for your own safety and for that of the others. Please, trust me."

"I'm sorry Deb, but I just had to help you."

Deb looked into Sarah's eyes and saw the desire she had to end this torture. It would be so easy to just let her come, but if she did, it would mean the end for them all. Deb's plan would not work and all would be lost. She had to make her stay.

"Sarah...once I have cleared the towers, I will howl like a wolf from the top of the hill. Go to your room and wait. When I am gone, you and the girls must act as if you knew nothing. Remember what I told you. You have to tell them it was I all along. Tell them I had planned it and threatened you if you had said anything. It will be the only thing that will save your lives. Tell them you all hated me. Tell them you wish me dead."

Sarah nodded her head and Deb turned swiftly. She made her way to the gate. A smaller single door was used instead of opening the full gate and she slipped through it silently.

At the halfway point to the towers, she fell quietly back into the bush. The horse that she needed was tied up at the base of the left tower. It was a good horse with strong legs. She had picked him out weeks ago and knew that it was the only one that could give her the speed she would need.

Once she was within range, she evaluated the position of the four men. The two within the towers had to be taken without them falling out. If they fell, the two on the ground would hear it and it would be over. Her aim would have to be perfect. Closing her eyes, she remembered what her father said. She remembered the targets he made for her and how he pressed her day after day to be nothing but perfect with her shot. He would blindfold her and ask her to concentrate. *"This will save your life someday, Deb."* He guided her even now when she was alone and facing her fate head on.

Opening her eyes she steadied one arrow within the bow. The other she stuck in the ground on an angle at her fingertips so that she could grab it within seconds of the other making both shots hit only moments apart. She measured the distance once again by tracing the path her hand would take. With a deep breath in and out slowly, she pulled back the bow and let it fly. Quickly she braced the other in place and with great control she released it as well.

Not more than a couple of seconds passed and she watched as the first arrow hit its mark.

Immediately the second hit the right tower guard in his chest. She raced forward to get close to the other two on the ground, but one of them had looked up just as one of the tower guards' body folded over and fell. He started to shout to the other when Deb leaped on his back slitting his throat.

The other heard the first part of the cry and ran to the scene. Deb picked up the dead guard's sword and faced the last man head on. This was it. He was the only person standing in her way. He lunged toward her and slit her upper arm. Deb's adrenalin kicked in and both blades met in a furry of steel. She was smaller than he was, and if she got too close, he could overpower her. He was good with a sword and Deb knew that he might beat her. She uncovered the knife on her thigh quickly and braced herself to use it. He chased her around the bottom of one of the towers and she dropped the sword in order to run faster. She gained a few feet on him around the base of the tower and turned quickly with her knife drawn, remembering his height and picturing his head as a target. As he looked down to see her sword on the ground she threw the knife and as the guard looked up in mid stride to see her braced on the ground below him, he plummeted to his knees. The knife had gone through his neck and he landed only feet from Deb.

All at once she burst into tears. She was free! With no time to ponder what she had just achieved, she leapt onto the massive horse she had chosen and raced into the night.

Cheryl Alleway

Chapter Nine
The Trip North

Cheryl Alleway

As she reached the top of the hill before the castle, Deb howled as loudly as she could. Satisfied that Sarah must have heard her, she raced the horse beyond his limits and did not stop until she felt she was far enough away that she could rest.

Nine of Gully's men were dead and when the other eleven awoke to discover what had happened, there would be a search for her for certain. Deb prayed that the girls would not be harmed but she believed in them. She knew they were grasping onto her and praying that she would return to them.

Sarah got rid of her disguise and went back down to the kitchen to finish her work. As the girls fell asleep that night each one cried for Deb. Sarah sat in her window and watched the night skyline hoping to catch a glimpse of her on her horse, but Deb was long gone. A tear fell from her face and it landed with a splash in the dirty, still water in the moat below. Sarah gripped a bracelet that Deb had made for her. "God speed, Deb. God speed." She lay down on her bed and tried to sleep.

In the morning there were shouts and curses throughout the castle. The body of one of the guards was found and then the rest. The head guard called the men together in the courtyard and he ordered every girl to be present.

After tossing them to their knees and slapping some to the ground, he stated with fury, "Any one of you will be killed right here, right now! I want to know where Gully's woman is? Who helped her! Speak up now, or I will kill you all!"

Sarah looked up and spoke. "We want you to find her and kill her!" The girls were shaking. Sarah continued, "She was nothing but a spoiled bitch that kept Gully to herself!! I hate her! She told us she was leaving last night, but we didn't believe her! She said if we told anyone she would slit our throats in our sleep!"

The head guard slapped Sarah so hard that she fell to the ground. Her mouth was bleeding and another girl shouted, "No, she is telling the truth! We all hated her for having more than us. She always got the best clothes; the best food and she didn't have to do half the chores we did! She called us whores and spit on us when she passed by!"

He didn't believe this. How could one woman kill nine men? Jessica spoke up this time. "She didn't do it alone!"

Everyone was shocked. What was she doing? She was going to ruin it!

"She had help," Jessica proclaimed.

Sarah looked at Jessica with fear. What was she doing?

"I watched her making love to the guard you call Hamish. I heard them talking about leaving together! She told me that if I told anyone, Hamish would beat me and take off one of my fingers for talking. They must have taken on the guards themselves. She was good with a knife. We heard of the fight she put up when Gully captured her!"

The head guard grabbed Jessica's hand and yelled at her. "If you are telling the truth wench, you will lose that finger now to prove it!"

The girls gasped and Jessica's face fell. Her heart suddenly jumped a beat. She trembled with tears in her eyes but seeing them all down on their knees with only her bravery to save them all, she looked up at him and said with a cold trembling voice. "Take it then, for I am telling the truth! She left us here to deal with Gully's wrath when he sees what has happened! We will all be blamed for this!" She wanted to vomit she was so terrified. Her face went red as it flushed with fear. Jessica knew he would do it.

She shocked him. He did believe her now, but he cared nothing for her and to show his power to his men, he gripped her small hand holding it precariously over a piece of wood and sliced off her pinky finger. She lurched in pain and fell to the ground screaming. The girls all stood with tears filling their eyes. They were shaking uncontrollably. The blood trickled down Jessica's wrist. Sarah rushed to her side and tied her apron around Jessica's hand. She looked up at the men and shouted defiantly, "Are we finished here? This girl needs to be bandaged properly!"

The head guard looked down at the two girls. They were obviously no threat to him or his men. "Five of you come with me. The rest stay here! Get this girl away from me! Get Hamish's body and the others out of my sight."

Sarah helped Jessica to her feet and two of the men rustled them all out of the courtyard.

After loading up on arrows and swords, the six men took to the path and went after Deb. They did not know Deb was long gone.

She knew the ways of the land and the horse she was on was one of the fastest that she had ever seen. He was saving her life.

For three days the men looked for Deb. They ransacked several village homes and threatened anyone that might help her.

Deb had made it safely to her homestead and found no trace of Liam. She had a plan. After seeing his body gone and the ropes that had shackled him still hanging from the tree, she knew he was alive. She found her father's dagger and promptly placed it on her side where it belonged. Deb took a moment to look at their home. The croft was still intact. The now disappearing carcasses of their sheep peppered the field, but nature was seeing to it that they were disposed of. Only bones were left. Gully never intended on coming back to bury Liam or do anything with the land. He just wanted Liam dead and Deb in his bed. Most of all, he wanted his reputation to grow. Because so much time had passed, Deb knew that Liam would be devising his own plan. He wouldn't give up on her either. He couldn't.

To find each other would be difficult, but as Deb asked along the way, she found out that Liam was alive and that he had headed north.

Liam knew that taking on Gully's men alone would bring another victory to him. He needed to hit Gully where it hurt most; his father.

Deb knew Liam and she had to find him before he reached the MacDonells. She was taking a chance, but it was her only option.

On the third day of the search, the men headed back to Gully's castle. They had failed and were now trying to figure out what to tell him.

Someone was going to pay for allowing Deb's escape. Not to mention the loss of men.

When they arrived back at the castle, they made a pact to stick to Jessica's story, but to make it sound more believable; they told Gully that Hamish was with her. They burned his body so there were no traces of him and kept the other bodies to bury as proof of the fight. This way, Gully's attention would be on the man who took his woman. Nothing hit a man harder.

This held true for Liam as well because he *was* alive and he *was* planning to meet with Gully's father and tell him of his son's rampages. Liam would be with Deb once again, or die trying. No one had been brave enough to mention Gully's name to Thomas MacDonell because he had ordered the strict silence and dissolve of his son's existence. He was dead to him. Thomas had no idea of the pillaging his son had done in the south. Gully's father held much of the land in the northern territory and was among some of the finest Scottish leaders of his time, but he was aging and the threats from the south were making him weary. Liam knew that if he could just make Thomas see that Gully was threatening the future of Scotland, he might be able to take him down. One card Liam planned to play was treason. He would tell Thomas that Gully was fighting for the English. The fact remained that Thomas and Anne did not even know that Gully was still alive.

On the morning of the fifth day after Deb's escape, she had made her way back up north, past the main lowlands and through to Stirling. On the northern outskirts, she took shelter that night with a family on their small farm. She told them of her journey and quest to find her husband. They had not heard of Liam, but said that one of the other villagers had remembered seeing a man riding alone along the riverbed one day. He did not stop and they said he had been riding hard.

"You are the daughter of Jacob Douglas?"

The head of the household was asking Deb questions. If she had something to do with Gully, he wanted to know everything about her. He knew about Gully's foul ways and if Deb was telling him the truth, he would know for sure as he questioned her. He wanted to be certain she was Gully's enemy and not someone sent to stake out his land. There were more women on the wrong side during these times. They could be used like a sheep in wolf's clothing and although he could tell she had been through something horrific, he had a family and they were his first priority.

"My father died recently. My mother died when I was a child and I am alone except for my husband. Liam and I lived on my father's land and we wanted a family, but I knew the battles were getting closer every day and I needed to stay strong and ready to take a stand along Liam's side. We didn't think it would be someone like Gully that threatened our land. We expected English soldiers."

The man noticed the beautiful leather quiver that held Deb's arrows.

The family was as lovely one. The father was a dark haired, stout man in his forties. His wife was a quiet woman with red hair and beautiful green eyes. Two boys in their tenth and eleventh years sat across from Deb and their parents. Their eyes were glued to her not only because of her beauty, but of the fact that she carried weapons they had only seen a man use. Her story continued and they were compelled to listen.

"I can tell you right now, that I am not your enemy. I must find my husband. I believe he is riding north to the MacDonell clan in Inverness. I only stopped to ask if you have seen him."

The mother asked gently, "You look injured. Are you all right? Do you need anything? I can get you some clean clothing."

The husband cautioned her with his eyes.

Deb noticed and said quickly, "I am fine, but the clothing I will gratefully accept. I cannot pay you, but I can leave you this as a token of my appreciation."

Deb reached around the back of her neck and unclipped the necklace she was wearing. It was a gift from Gully. Although she hated taking it from him, she now felt that by giving it to this woman, she was giving back something that was probably stolen from a family such as this in the first place.

The woman was very thankful and said, "Any woman that would give up something so beautiful, must have even greater inner beauty."

She went out of the room and returned with a warm shawl, an extra pair of boots for Deb's feet and a dress that was a bit weathered, but of good quality.

"Please take these, I have another shawl and this dress is old, but it is warm. It will help you at night."

"Thank you very much ma'am. You are very kind."

One of the boys was looking anxious and their father could tell they had questions of their own. Having spoken to Deb for a while, he decided that it wouldn't hurt for them to be in on the conversation now.

"Go ahead, lad. You look like you are going to burst."

They laughed a bit at the boy's attentiveness. He was being polite and keeping quiet until he was given permission.

"Did you fight with those knives? How did you learn how to use them? Have you seen battle with any of the English?"

He was very anxious and excitable. His father added, "These boys are full of energy to fight. I have told them they must wait until they know more. I try to prepare them for anything. These lands have become a place of treachery and blind lust for power."

Deb bowed her head respectfully and answered, "Well lads, I have had to do my share of fighting, but it was only for defense of myself and others. Fighting is not something to look upon as a thing of glory. It should only be used to protect. Aggression against others is not honorable unless for this reason. My father did not have any sons, and he knew that I needed to be strong in case something happened to him. He was a great man. I can show you some knife skills if you like, with your father's permission."

Deb knew that by taking this small amount of time to bond with the family, they would tell others about her and keep a protective trail of secrecy behind her from Gully's men. She had to move on, but she knew a bit of rest and time with such kind people would do them all good.

Their eyes widened and their father smiled with an accepting nod. Deb looked at the boys and smiled too. They followed her outside to the fence and she got them to place a piece of wood standing vertically against it. The wood was three inches wide and she marked the center with some mud.

She began to walk away from the board and when she reached a distance they could not believe, she turned around and poised on the ground, she began to meticulously fire each of her four knives at the target. One after another she hurled them with great accuracy hitting the target so closely that it appeared to be one large knife from their location.

The boys ran to the target and yelled back, "Father! Did you see that? She hit the mark every time!"

They all chuckled at the boys' wonderment. Deb said thank you and bowed as they ran back to her handing her the knives. She placed them back into their sheath and as she did so, the other boy asked, "Father, can I get the sword? Can she try the sword father?"

"Why not?" he shouted. He was enamored by Deb's skill. The boys ran back out with a stunning sword that was one of the finest that Deb had seen made by anyone.

"Did you make this yourself, sir?" she asked as it was quite impressive.

"Yes, I did at that. My father had a great skill in blacksmithing. I am teaching the boys as well. If not to fight, they may make the swords that will someday."

"I am honored that you will allow me to use it." She took the sword and got the feel of it. She held it up to the sun and looked down its length. It was very straight and had a solid grip. It was one of the finest Claymores she had ever seen. The boys set up a training dummy out of straw bound in twine that was in the shape of a man and Deb laughed at their excitement. At the same time she realized how sad it was in some ways. Their beautiful innocent faces may someday turn cold and black from battle, but Deb knew the value in a stout and determined attitude.

"Here, Deb! I bet you can cut it in half!" One of the boys ran over and drew a face with a chunk of mud. Deb thought he should have the honor of the first strike.

He gripped the blade with both hands and could hardly lift it. Turning around and away from the target, he lifted as hard as he could and swung to strike only grazing the wooden post it was attached to.

"That was marvelous!" Deb praised. He looked a bit disappointed, but he was anxious to see what Deb could do. "A little more force and it would have been cut to pieces! Use your whole body, not just your arms," she added.

"I bet you could cut it in half Deb!" He bounced around her with an anxious smile on his face.

"Well, if you really want me to, I'll try my best." He handed the sword to her and she focused on the target, its distance and height. She then turned away from it and walked ten paces further. They could not figure out what she was doing. With a deep breath, Deb turned and ran straight for the large target. A few feet before it, she did a backward twist and came from the other side with the blade in full force. Bracing her legs into the ground she sliced the wooden post in half and sent the dummy flying through the air in two pieces. The boys' faces lit up and the father laughed, "Well done lass, well done!"

As the youngest now stared at the bow and arrow on her horse, Deb could see that he knew what he was looking at. The English long bow was well known as being a frightening weapon of war. He was very curious and Deb asked his father if she could show it to them.

"It is very odd that a young Scottish woman be so skilled in weaponry, especially that of the English as well."

Deb told him about her father's life and how he was forced to fight with the English and the man was not aware of a lot of it even though he had met Jacob. He only knew him as a quiet farmer and merchant. He felt for Deb. He felt for Jacob.

With pride, Deb took the bow down from the horse. She asked the boys to set up a target for her. They watched with great curiosity as she set the arrows in the ground to make them ready for their fast journey. Six in total were placed in a row. She braced herself and slowly aimed the first arrow at the center. With a rush of speed Deb drew all six arrows one after the other and each time they hit directly beside each other's point forming a mass of feathers looking back at them.

They all stood in wonder and the boys wanted to touch the bow and try it themselves. Their father politely pointed out that it was late and their guest was tired.

"It was a pleasure to practice with you!" Deb stated. The man's wife called them into the croft again. She had prepared meat and some bread for the evening.

As they walked to the entrance, the father commented, "Jacob has taught you well. Come, let us have food and drink. You must rest. I am grateful for this time with you especially knowing what hardship you face. There is much angst in your eyes my dear, but you hide it well. With your horse rested now, you should have a faster trip north."

Deb settled in with the family and they allowed her to stay overnight to get the much-needed rest she would require for the journey ahead.

She spoke of the girls left behind. The man had judged well when he looked into her eyes. All of them were saddened and wished that they could help in some other way.

The man's wife sat and looked at Deb with a mother's eye. She knew terrible things had happened to this young woman. She noticed the scars on her hands and face. The way she sat indicated that her body was sore. She could see it in Deb's face that more had happened than she was telling them and for this, her heart sank for this beautiful girl with the black hair that was all alone and facing such a challenge. How could such a young lady exist? How could she go on after everything that had happened?

When morning broke, Deb was ready to ride again. Her horse was in good shape and he seemed to know that he needed to be his best for her. He snorted and pranced with excitement when he saw her come out the door.

"I like your horse." One of the boys was petting him.

"He is quite a nice lad, isn't he?" She smiled as she stroked his gorgeous black mane. He reveled in the attention and pranced gently on his hooves as if showing off his girth and prowess.

"Does he have a name?"

"Actually, he does not. What do you think I should call him?"

The boy paused and stated quite clearly, "I think he should be named Finnean because of his white head."

"That is a beautiful name and rightly so. I chose him because he looks as though he wears a uniform. His golden body is like his armor. His black feet are like his shoes. His white face and black mane are like his helmet. I rather fancy the name Finnean. He'll live by it proudly."

The boy smiled and Deb rustled his hair. The others came out and they helped Deb pack Finnean for the ride. He was so tall they had to use a small stool to reach the top of his back properly. Deb had to mount him by grabbing onto the reins and his mane tightly, hurling herself up from the side. Finnean was as large a horse as they had ever seen.

The father came up to Deb with a serious look on his face as he knew what she was headed for. He and his wife were praying for her safe travel.

"When you reach the Firth of Lorne lass, it will narrow into a valley. You may be able to find your way without taking too many of the mountain trails. You will pass through clan Cameron territory alongside the MacDonell's of Keppoch. Take the valley northwest until you see the forest's edge. You will find Thomas MacDonell's castle to the west within Inverness before you hit the sea. His land in Glengarry will be a straight line from the forest. You will know it when you see it, as a large open piece of rolling field will fall just before the castle grounds. There won't be many places to stop for a while for water, so make sure your horse has been refreshed before finishing your journey. The Grampian Mountains will make him work harder."

"You have done more than you know, sir. Thank you for everything. Keep yourselves safe and if asked if you saw me, tell them you heard of a woman who was killed to the south. Tell them it was said that a girl with black hair was killed and a man that was with her also. They must not follow my path north any further."

"We will do what we can to help you. Go and find your husband. God speed to you, lass."

With that, Deb mounted Finnean. She sat so high upon him that up close, they had to look up bending their necks. As they waved goodbye to her, she couldn't help worrying about them. With time she hoped that the man's sons would grow to be strong men who were free to live on the land their father had worked so hard for. She couldn't bear to imagine another young child having all of that taken from them.

Time was of the essence now. If Deb could catch up to Liam before he got to Thomas MacDonell, she could make his plight sound even more convincing.

She would tell Thomas about what his son had done to her and about the girls that were being held to service his men. It was hard to believe it had gone on as long as it did, but the turmoil of war took many from their homes to concentrate on the battles and with this in mind, men like Gully would swoop in like vultures.

Deb hoped to meet Thomas' wife as well. She was a lady that was well respected among the people in the highlands. She was a pioneer of her time for women. Her strength of character had won the hearts of many and she and Thomas were nothing short of royalty in Northern Scotland. They came from money and Thomas was a friend of King

Robert I. Robert himself had endorsed giving Thomas the title of Earl. The Lord of the Isles had agreed whole-heartedly. He had fought many battles and made his name by heading some of the fiercest defensive wars that Scotland had ever seen. His people were men of honor, who would die for the clan and its name. They were Liam and Deb's only hope now.

When the sun began to fall, Deb knew that she would have to make one more rest stop. Finnean was feeling the burn in his legs and she made sure that she slowly brought him down to a trot at the river's edge. He drank well and she wiped his coat down before she washed up, ate some bread and bedded down under a pine tree. The smell of flowers was in the night air and Deb dreamed of Liam's face. She wanted to get up and keep going, but she knew that she had to maintain her strength and that of Finnean's. He was her lifeline. Without him, she would never make it. The Scottish landscape began to change as the highlands came into view. Slightly colder temperatures at night, the Grampian Mountains and wide expanses presenting a rocky lay of the land made for a long journey. She was getting her first real look at where Liam had grown up and she would close her eyes as she rode to feel him in her heart. *"Come to me Liam. I'm here. I can hear your voice within me."*

As they came to a stop, she dismounted and took in a deep breath of air to relax her weary mind. Finnean snorted and nibbled on fresh grass nearby. As Deb lay down, he slowly walked over to her and putting his head down to hers, one could see that he too was enamored with her.

Deb used to sneak pieces of food to him when Gully's guards were not looking. She wanted to bond with him so that when she needed him the most, he was there. His long eyelashes tickled her face and she sat up to hold his muzzle in her hands as a small tear trickled from her eye. "You are a brave boy, Finnean. Thank you for saving my life. Keep the wolves away tonight. Tell me if you smell any close by. You have come to me from the heavens."

He knew her love for him and stood up tall above her sniffing the air and looking as if he were guarding her. He was a massive stallion standing eighteen hands high. She had never seen such a beautiful horse. His large, dark brown eyes looked striking on his white face and Deb's legs barely fit around his back when she sat upon him. She looked up at him one more time and said, "Goodnight, my beautiful boy. Rest and we will ride when the sun breaks."

The night was cold but Deb was well equipped. The thick wool dress that the farmer's wife had given her was very well made. It was very rudimentary; its wool outer shell laced at the sides with leather strapping and a tie around the waist, but it was a gift of warmth. She could put it over-top of the rest of her clothes like a blanket. The boots were of soft dark brown leather and laced up to her shins. They were helpful as her other ones had gotten wet a couple of times and having two pair to switch back and forth between was a godsend in the cold weather. The leather straps holding her various weapons were thick and worn slightly so they were quite comfortable around her shoulders and limbs. She threw the extra shawl the woman had given her over it all and covered her head. With Finnean near, she knew he would alert her of wolves or riders and so she was able to drift off to sleep. They had tucked themselves into a tree stand that had pine trees to lie underneath. The softer ground was just what Deb needed.

While she slept, she began to dream. Nightmares were flooding her mind. She dreamed of fire and war and Liam's face. At one point she was flailing wildly and it made Finnean uneasy. As she slept, the image of her father on his horse came to her. He was at the top of the hill alone when he suddenly leapt into a great stride. He was coming toward her yelling her name and telling her to get inside. Like devils from hell, Deb saw an army of men raging across the field chasing after him. His sword drawn and still yelling; she watched as they caught up to him. He turned knowing that they had outrun him and with anger in his face, he charged back in their direction.

Deb screamed for him. "No father! No!"

He collided with them fending off as many as he could when the dream suddenly halted into slow motion as Deb watched her father be cut down by one of his assailants.

She ran to him with tears in her eyes and a sword drawn. Then the dream froze and she was looking at herself as a young girl. She could barely hold the sword in both hands and in the dream, she could do nothing but watch herself fall into the hands of the soldiers as they overcame her home and carried her away screaming for her father. His bloodied body lay dead on the field and Deb screamed so loudly that Finnean had come to her side and was nudging her to wake up.

Sitting up quickly and breathing heavily, Deb brushed the sweat from her brow. "It's alright, Finnean. It's alright, lad. It was just a dream...Just a dream." She fell slowly back into her bed of pine needles and looked up at the stars with tears in her eyes. As she wiped them from her cheek, her hand clenched into a fist and she held it tightly to suppress her rage. Her heart was heavy, but she took a deep breath and gathered herself. Her hair was draped all around her like ink on the ground. She closed her eyes again and did not awaken until the sun broke over the hill.

As Deb woke up, the mist was rising on the rocky fields and Finnean was ready to go again. They both had a cool morning chill in their bones. She drank water and ate some dried fish from the farm that was wrapped within a brown satchel. Finnean had his fill of fresh river water as well. Deb filled a small jug with just enough water for the day. She settled herself on top of Finnean's back and made sure to position her weapons properly. She may have to use them at a moment's notice.

"Ready, boy?" She tapped Finnean's side gently with her boot and off they rode to the hilltop where the valley was beginning to narrow. The forest would be visible before the day was out.

Pacing Finnean, Deb kept a steady stride. For hours they would take only momentary breaks for water. She ate more fish while she rode to keep her strength up and as the day began to end, she saw the first sign of trees.

In the distance was the forest that the farmer had told her about. She was close now. As Finnean came over a small knoll, he whinnied and stopped dead in his tracks. There was some fog, but Deb could make out a form moving within it. She smelled smoke as well. This was no small fire that stopped Finnean. This was a large one and Deb could smell the rancid scent that she knew all too well. Someone's home was burning.

She pulled Finnean to the left and found shelter behind a small grove of trees. Dismounting, she led him slowly through them to get closer. There, amongst the mist and smoke, she could see it. Five men were burning down a small homestead. There were two people on the ground dead and another man fighting them with a young boy by his side. The boy was small, but he was fighting like a cat. The man was holding his own against one of the assailants on horseback while the others were busy throwing torches onto the remaining buildings.

Deb tied Finnean to a tree and grabbed her bow and arrow. She ran about two hundred feet ahead to get closer.

"My God, did they get this far north?" she asked herself the question that made the hair on her arms rise up. Her worst fear had come true. Some of Gully's men had made it all this way.

She couldn't believe they had not run into her, but she thought they must have been ahead of her the entire time passing her in the distance as she had made her stops along the way. They were a second group sent out the find her for sure. Gully was not giving up.

She braced herself and let the arrows fly. From the cover of the bush, three of them sliced through the air like missiles. They killed two of the men but the third missed. Quickly turning in her direction, the men still could not see Deb. She ran further along the bush line and fired two more arrows. This time, a third man came down from his horse and slammed into the ground.

The farmer and the two men who were fighting him paused only for a second and as one man turned to see who fired at them, he met his fate as well. Deb ran forward from the bush now. The farmer saw her and not knowing where she had come from, lunged at the last man on his horse. He missed and by that time, Deb had arrived on the scene. The boy backed up in astonishment as the farmer grazed the leg of the remaining soldier. He turned to swing down again and as he did so, Deb leapt onto the back of his horse. She gripped the horse's belly with her legs and braced herself as she flung the soldier's head back slicing his throat and snapping his neck.

They both fell to the ground and the farmer with his boy stood in shock. Breathing so hard he could barely say anything, he belted out to her, "Who are you? Where have you come from?!"

Deb gathered herself and stood up. Her leg had been bruised, but she was alright. Wiping the blood from her knife upon the grass, she placed it back into its sheath and walked toward the man and his son out of breath herself.

"I am Deb Barne, sir. My horse and I are traveling to the north. I won't involve you and your son, but know that I am a friend. Are you alright?"

They were still in shock that a woman had saved them. On top of that, this woman was laden with weapons and could send an arrow through a man's heart as easily as any man they had seen.

"We are alright now, but my brother and my eldest son are dead. This boy is my last. I am grateful for your help. Where did you learn to fight like that?" His clothes were torn and his face was soiled with blood and dirt. He was shaking slightly, but could not help to pose his question.

Deb took a deep breath and told the man that she had been on her way north for reasons she could not explain. She was in a hurry to continue on and this man and his son had been through enough.

"It is of no importance, but sir do you know who these men are?" She asked quickly.

"They were looking for a woman and a man." Just as he said it, he realized that Deb could be the one they were looking for, but where was the man?

Deb looked at one of the men she had taken down and opened her eyes widely as she recognized his ugly face.

"Sir, I want to tell you more, but please trust me. These men were looking for me. I escaped from them and now I am looking for my husband. I can't tell you where I am going but you must tell me if they said anything to you!"

Deb took him by the shoulders and looked him in the eye. "Sir, was this man's name Hamish that they were looking for?!"

Her insistence frightened him as she grasped his arm. He answered her immediately, "Yes lass, I believe so. I heard them arguing and I believe they used that name. They thought we had given them shelter and that we knew something of it, but we knew nothing! I swear!"

"Did they mention a man named Gully?!"

Deb was like a raging bull now, she was piecing the scene together and her worst fear was coming true. She had to find Liam or get to the castle quickly. Once Gully knew that she and the 'pretend' Hamish were still alive and more of his men were killed, he would stop at nothing to stop them from getting to his father's castle. Gully knew that the only thing they could do was get to his father before he did. If there were five men here, there would surely be more in the area searching. They were not more than thirty miles from Thomas MacDonell's castle and now it was a race against time. Deb feared that Gully was going to make his move on his father now and she was the catalyst for it all.

Deb changed her mind quickly. "Sir, Gully MacDonell tried to burn my home as well. He kept me captive and left my husband to die. You and your family have met a similar fate. You must know now that I am on my way to find my husband. We are both on our way to find Gully's father. You must keep quiet about seeing me. You must!"

The man realized the connection of events and was well aware of Thomas MacDonell. He did not know that Gully was his son. "This Gully is Thomas MacDonell's son? I did not know that Thomas had a son. He has forsaken his father's name indeed then."

"That is why you must not speak of this to anyone. You must leave here for now and take shelter with others. Sir, I respect you, but you are an old man with one son left. If they return and see these men dead, they will know you had help."

He agreed and he and his son packed their horse and took to the southern path to shelter with friends. Deb knew that if they saw the arrows made by his men, they too would be a clue as to who had been here. She collected them all but the one she snapped off in the chest of the man who led them. She mounted Finnean to continue her ride north.

With speed and fury, the two rode as fast as they could both handle. Deb's body flowed with Finnean's gait each time he rose and fell. There were times that they blended together as one and Finnean barely knew she was on his back at times. She was so strong that she could withstand the constant pounding on her hips as she braced herself with her muscles tensing and relaxing with

Finnean's. Within an hour they had made much ground. The castle was so close, but Deb was not sure how close she was until she spotted three men.

On the ridge, riding swiftly the three men rode in single file. She waited until she could make out more detail and then she saw him. It was Liam! His father and his brother were with him! Quickly, she raced toward them. Liam had his back to her still and was too far away to hear her, but within minutes, Finnean had caught up to them. Deb yelled out Liam's name, waving her scarf in the air.

Liam turned to take a fighting stance until he saw her. "Oh God, you are with me today!" he shouted. His father's eyes lit up. Liam's heart beat like a drum as the realization of who was riding towards him became clear. His eyes welled up with tears and his hands shook as he braced his own horse's body so as not to fall off with anticipation. He could see her beautiful hair dancing in the wind. He and his father and brother were elated beyond words and they all looked up to the heavens to thank God for bringing her back to them. They were without words. None of them, including Liam, could believe it. How did she get away? How in God's name did she find them?!

"Deb!" Liam raced toward her not wasting any time. He saw men riding behind her within sight. More of Gully's men had caught up with them.

"Deb! Ride lass, ride! They're behind you!" His heart raced. There would be no way that they would harm her. Not now! Not after she had returned to them! They would not take her from him again! Never again! His brow furrowed into the deepest anger.

Deb pointed Finnean north on the hilltop and he dove into top speed. No horse could catch him easily, but they were gaining ground slowly. Liam's father and brother took their weapons off their horses and hid behind some trees ready to take the men by surprise.

Quickly, Liam and Deb met but there was no time to embrace. They turned their horses and traveled down the other side of the hill until slightly out of sight. The only thing to do was take shelter and fight! They had only three minutes to ready themselves and when the men came over the hill, they assaulted them with a barrage of arrows.

Liam had many arrows with him as well and with both he and Deb firing, the men had no choice but to dismount. They were hard pressed to get close to Deb and Liam because there seemed to be no end to the stream of arrows. Liam's father crept around the right of them and his brother to the left still not being seen.

One man got off his horse and made his way along the brush line. Liam's brother made short work of him and struck his face with an axe. The man screamed with pain and fell to the ground as the blood spilled like a fountain into the grass below.

The other four men that were in the group were on the ground as well, crawling through the grass to avoid the arrows. It was by luck that two of them made it close enough to Deb and Liam that they had to put the bows down and pull their swords. Liam was an expert swordsman and he took down one man immediately. His power was unbelievable and Deb saw the rage that he had held in for so long. She took the other and shouted at Liam to get one left hiding in the grass. Liam's brother and father attacked the fourth from the bush and ran screaming as they swung their weapons. He got up and tried to run, but Liam's brother pounded on his back and took him down. His father followed with a blow to his head.

While Deb dove and missed each swing of her own assailant, she realized that she could grab the knife on her hip quickly. She raced away from him far enough to get around a tree and continued to fight with the sword. He was having a hard time maneuvering around the tree, but Deb noticed that it was working to her advantage again just as it had at Gully's castle. She tried the same tactic on this man and urged him to chase her around another larger tree. She managed to get down and in front of him and with one powerful underhand shot, she buried the sword deep within his belly. Once again, her technique of coming from below had saved her life. Her father's teachings were proving to have been efficient and as she sat there on her knees smiling, at long last, as Liam and his father and brother raced to her, she stood and ran to meet them all.

She was magnificent. No man could resist this woman who could take on a man and win. He raced to her and she leapt into his arms kissing him ravenously. "My love! My love! Liam, my love! You're alive! My God, you're alive! I knew you were alive!" She kissed his face so many times, he could not see until she pulled back. She had her legs wrapped around his waist and they were twirling around until they fell together into the grass.

Liam held her so tightly that he nicked his wrist on one of her knives. He jerked back and they both laughed at each other crying between every breath as well.

"My God, Deb, I can't believe you are in my arms!" He was looking her over feverously. She was so beautiful and he grabbed her face kissing her over and over again. Liam's father and brother were tearing up and grinning from ear to ear. They lowered their weapons, putting their arms around each other.

She told him that there were other young girls being held and that she had promised to return and free them somehow. She would not leave them there. Liam listened as Deb told him about the castle and of the details of her miraculous escape.

He told her about his plan to use treason as a way to make Thomas MacDonell help him to stop his son. It would be one thing to hear about Gully's plundering, but for him to be fighting with the very enemy that Thomas fought against would be more than he could handle. He would not allow his son to damage his military standing or his clan name. This is what Liam and Deb hoped.

"I would have died were it not for the poorly tied noose. When our horse decided to move, I was left hanging for only a few seconds until I fell to the ground. I cut my hands free on the blade of one of their own swords left behind. Once I regained my strength, I made my way north immediately to find my father. I thought we could find Gully's castle, but with an injury to my arm, we knew that we could not fight them all ourselves, not knowing how many they had within the walls. We tried to convince some of the locals to help us, but they too were afraid of Gully's sword."

Deb told Liam exactly how many men Gully had at his side, but besides the men she killed, he must have at least seventy men and some that she may not know of on the outskirts of his land patrolling. Who knew who else he had contacts with? The only way she got free was to wait until most of them were gone. Otherwise, she would still be there. Liam was smart to wait as well, there were too many to take on in full numbers.

As the final hours went by, the four made their way into the site of the castle. The horses were almost spent and were wet with sweat. They needed to stop soon or they would drop. As they finally got full view of the castle walls in the distance, Deb breathed a sigh of relief. Upon entry to the watch towers, the guards asked what their business was and when they said they had a message from King Robert I himself, there was no hesitation. It was a ploy that would only get them through the castle gate however. To gain the attention of Thomas MacDonell, it would take much more work when they stood in front of him.

Cheryl Alleway

Chapter Ten
Trust

Cheryl Alleway

They were asked to wait outside the great hall. Deb's heart was pounding and Liam could see she was incredibly nervous. She paced back and forth staring at the floor. He stopped her gently with his arm finally and smiled to calm her. His gaze snapped her out of her thoughts and she smiled a faint grin of acknowledgment.

This was the father of the man who had raped her and left her husband for dead. Liam did not know the entire story. In his mind, he knew she had been through something she did want him to hear and because he trusted her, he decided to let her take the time she needed. If she wanted him to know everything, she would tell him. Right now, they had to stick together and be strong. Liam's brother and father stayed in the hall and waited as they prayed that this was the right thing to do.

"Earl MacDonell will see you." The guard led Liam and Deb down a smaller hallway and into the earl's personal chambers. He took all of their weapons and as Deb handed over her father's dagger, she wrenched her hands together feeling naked without something on her body for protection. She turned to her training and felt her power within. Taking a deep breath, she focused on the task at hand. She could fight without them if needed and she trusted herself again. Right now, she had to be truthful and slightly vulnerable as she told her story to the Earl.

"Earl MacDonell, I am Liam Barne and this is my wife Deborah. She is of the Douglas Clan. My father and brother accompany us. We ask that you hear us on a most imperative matter."

Thomas sat quietly in his chair. There were ten guards in the room with him. The chamber showed his wealth with its bountiful adornments and tall stone walls. Silk and embroidered cloth covered his short but burly stature. He was a man in his late fifties and was quite handsome, with thick red hair and a solid jaw line. Thomas MacDonell suited his position well. He sat up straight and had a calm, proud demeanor.

"What is your business with me? I have been informed that King Robert himself has asked you to come to me. This is very unusual." He asked the question with a suspicious tone and Liam knew that he may not have believed them already. The king would not send a man and his wife with imperative news. Thomas was curious as to why they were really there.

"Earl MacDonell, we must inform you of something that you have forbidden anyone to speak of. We feel that if you don't listen to us, there will be many strikes against your house. These include the suspicion of treason."

Thomas was shocked by the word 'treason' and it gave Liam the reaction he was hoping for.

"Treason! My family will never be associated with treason! I am the Earl of these lands and King Robert is a close confidant of mine! We have fought against the English devil for years together. You dare to speak of treason within these walls?"

Deb was uneasy and decided that a feminine voice was needed. "Sir, I beg of you to allow us to discuss someone that you have decreed as dead. I will respect your wishes and not speak that name, but if you do not allow us to tell you what has been happening to *your* good name, it will only bring further injustice to your cause and that of the king himself."

Earl MacDonell stayed quiet for a moment staring at Deb. He was taken by the fact that she stepped forward to support her husband.

He placed his thumb and forefinger on his chin and leaned into the arm of his chair toward Deb.

"Young woman, am I to assume that you are speaking about my son?"

The room went silent. Deb began to breathe heavier but as the visions of Gully touching her in the night and the voices of the young girls came to her, she straightened her back and looked back at Thomas.

"Yes, Earl MacDonell, I am speaking of your son."

Thomas briskly pulled his hand away from his chin and sat back firmly in his chair. He looked as if he would burst. His face was angry and he stood up. "Men! Leave us at once!"

The men all exited the room and Thomas paced up and down until he came right up to Liam's face.

"I assume that what you have to tell me is worth more than your life? I assume that what you have to tell me is worth this disturbance of my day and that you realize that I could have you both killed immediately if this is a rouse to harm anyone within these walls?" He paused to gather himself and added in a slow, loud, dominant voice, "What has my son done?"

Thomas MacDonell was a strong man; merciless against his enemy, but he could sense now that Liam and Deb did not march into his chamber alone with frivolous words for him.

Liam blinked and said politely, "Earl MacDonell, your son Gully has been plundering the southern territories; he has burned down villager's homes, killed some and taken young women for him and his men. He has stolen land from some of the small families that fought for William Wallace and now King Robert. Earl MacDonell, he attacked my wife and I on our farm in Carrick, killed my livestock and left me for dead. What's worse, he captured my wife and has kept her as a prisoner with other women at Dominon Castle. It is said that he took possession of the castle after killing Baron MacDubh. There was not enough of his party to fend your son off. Sir…there is more." Liam paused and mentally prepared himself for the lie he was about to tell. "Gully has been seen speaking with the English."

Thomas was walking around by this point listening to Liam. He had his back turned when Liam finished and as the rage built inside of him, he turned like a bull and roared so loudly that some of the guards heard him down the hall.

"You have spoken a name that I have banished from my lips! Why am I to believe you? No MacDonell would deal with the English pigs. Gully's mouth would have gotten him killed by now and if what you say is true, it is cause for death!"

Deb knew that she had to tell Thomas something that neither he nor Liam would want to hear. It would tell Liam what had really happened to her and it would prove to Thomas that they had been telling at least partial truth. She looked at Liam and he furrowed his brow seeing the look on her face. He knew she had something to say.

"Earl MacDonell? May I speak again?" She was trying to show him respect.

He looked at her and tears were building up in her eyes. She stood tall but he could see she was dead serious. "Speak up," he said in a calmer voice.

"Sir, I have spent weeks as your son's prisoner. My body is no longer solely my husbands." Her hands were shaking and Liam touched her shoulder. Thomas walked over to her and looked in her eyes.

"What did he do to you?"

She took a deep breath and steadied herself. "I slept in his bed to stay alive. His men raped the other girls as well and they are nothing but slaves to him. They are the daughters of men who fight for Scotland. They are innocent and before I escaped, I vowed that I would return and put my own sword through Gully's belly!"

Deb was enraged as she spoke and emotion overcame her. "I beg for your forgiveness Earl MacDonell, but your son is forsaking his name and his people! His greed has consumed him and if you don't help us to stop him, he will be your worst enemy sooner than you think. Your own son is, at this moment, working his way towards your land and is plotting to steal it from you!"

She swallowed and took a deep breath and added, "I know of the mark on his body that no one but a parent or lover would know of!"

It pained Liam to listen to Deb's story. He had a lump in his throat now. His fists were clenching, his face was flushing and he wished

Gully was in the room so that he could choke him to death with his bare hands. Thomas' face went white.

"On the small of Gully's right thigh is my proof! It is in the shape of a snake, the birthmark that you and your wife bestowed upon him with love is now a symbol of what he really is!"

She was crying and shouting uncontrollably. She had held it in for too long. She was getting physically agitated pacing and stomping her feet as she made her point with each sentence.

Liam restrained her and with his hands on both of her arms, he pulled her back slowly and said, "It's alright, Deb. I don't blame you for your words." He looked at Earl MacDonell and added, "I don't think anyone would." Liam felt so much anger inside that he had to turn away for a moment to contain himself. He wanted Gully dead right there.

Thomas did not know what to say. His face went whiter and he walked stunned over to his chair collapsing into it with a blank look. His large hands slammed down upon the arms as his fingers wrenched with anger around the ends and all became silent.

He sat there and neither Deb nor Liam said anything else for a few minutes. They sat down together on the ledge nearby while Liam helped Deb gather her senses. He placed one hand upon hers and squeezed it while looking into her distraught face.

When Thomas had composed himself, he stood up and stated, "If what you say is all true, this is a black day in my house." He had to believe them.

He walked over to the window and added, "This will not go any further if I have any say. My son was supposed to be the heir to a proud family."

Thomas was pursing his lips tightly. He would have shown his shame as a tear appeared in his eye, but a man of war and leader of such a great family, did not display such emotions. The years of humiliation had finally hit him. Thomas knew what he had to do.

"Please, leave me now. I need to think. You may take shelter here until I decide what to do about this. Tomorrow, I will summon you and my men and I will discuss this matter further. How far north do you think he has come?"

Deb stood up and moved toward Thomas, "I believe only a few of his men were forty miles from here sir, but we fought them off and killed them. Gully had taken his men to the west over toward Selkirk and vowed that he would travel this way and to the Grampian Mountains to make camp. He will be hard to find. He hides like a fox and he knows the lay of the land well, as you must know. We may be smart to travel towards him. His weapons are well stocked and he will not make himself known as he travels. He will stay away from the towns and take cover by night. Sir, I think he may be gathering more men along the way. He is mad, Earl MacDonell. He is taking advantage of the wars and his name. He is using it to cloak his own path to power. I don't know how he thinks he can continue. You must know that he is not your son anymore. I am sorry, sir. I am sorry to be the one to have to bring this to you."

Thomas nodded and with that, Liam and Deb left him alone. They had pushed his emotions far enough. He walked down the hall to his private room where his wife, Anne, was waiting.

"What do these people ask of you, Thomas?" She sat in a beautifully painted chair. She was an attractive woman with fine white skin and attire fit for a queen. Her hair was blonde and her eyes green. Her hands were adorned with rings of various design and decorated with large jewels. Her face however, was plain and quite demure. She was the lady of the house and held much respect. Thomas approached his wife with a sullen look of disgrace.

She stood at the sight of his expression and as he walked away from her struggling to say the words, he felt there was no other way than to just say them. He gave her a gentle gaze and slowly stated, "I have word that Gully is alive and has been on a rampage across the southern territories. These people have proof of his crazed actions. He is said to have his eyes set on Perth and Inverness as well. The pair that brought this news to me is legitimate, Anne. The woman told me that Gully had kept her prisoner along with other girls. He has been holed up in a small castle in the south."

Thomas' wife listened intently to her husband dumfounded and then he added, "She knows of his birthmark."

Anne MacDonell's face dropped. She began to cry as her sweet face began to contort with pain and as Thomas went to her, she pulled away and rushed to the window.

Through her tears she cried, "My son is a criminal? How could he become this? How could he shame his mother in this way? How could he shame this family?" She vibrated when saying the last words. "I thought our son was dead!"

Thomas quickly spoke again.

"Anne, we knew of his madness. It was in him as a child. We should have done something sooner. We were stupid to think that he would not survive on his own."

"I don't care what you have to do now!" Anne turned in anger. "You must not allow him to continue this treacherous path, Thomas!" She fell onto the bed. "My son...my son, I have lost you forever." Anne wept and Thomas finally went to her side and held her.

Bowing his head and speaking as the man in Anne's life, not an Earl, "My dear, do not cry for someone that is not a part of us any longer. We are good people. We will stop him. He is like a vulture taking the leftovers of war for himself and thinking that he will become a man by doing so. I cannot involve King Robert. No one else must know of this. Our name will be sullied and my future with the Scottish army jeopardized. He will not attempt to take on the Scottish army in any way, his party is too small. No, he will continue to hide and take what he can from those who do not have a voice. This Liam Barne gives me the impression that he is using the capture of the young women as one way to keep the families quiet of his actions. The threat of a daughter being harmed is more than any father could bear, I am sure. God, help me. It will not last! I swear to you. It will not last! When I find my *'son'*, he will pay for his insolence. It will be a moment that he will well regret!"

Cheryl Alleway

Chapter Eleven
A Storm Cometh

Cheryl Alleway

That night was a privilege to Liam. He had not held his wife in his arms for weeks. The passion that should have engulfed them was overshadowed by their deep exhaustion. Their bodies had endured so much and they had not eaten nor slept properly for days. For now, they were content to hold one another and be as one again. They fell asleep quickly knowing that they were safe for once, dreaming of the farm and the life they had only just begun together.

As Liam's father, Malcolm, and his brother made their own effort to sleep, they got down on their knees together and prayed. So much pain and so much agony were raking the hearts of their family. The blessing of rejoining Liam and Deb was almost too much for them to comprehend and Liam's father wept for their young hearts.

Thomas MacDonell's castle was a fortress that could not be easily taken. It stood atop a large ridge overlooking the hills and valleys deep within the Inverness Highlands. To the south were the Grampian Mountains. Loch Ness was to the northeast with a small piece of land separating it from the Firth. The MacDonell clan was large and powerful, and at present, Thomas MacDonell had the loyalty of other clans to the north. Thomas did not take his son for granted though. If Liam and

Deb were right, Gully would find a way to do just what he planned on doing.

In the morning, the castle was an active place. Thomas and his wife employed many. In quiet, he summoned his men to his chamber and prepared himself for what would be a humiliation he would have to bear. It was burning a hole in Thomas' heart. He would trust that their respect for him would overshadow the shame he was about to endure. Thomas was going to order a defensive battle to protect the castle and endorse the death of his own son.

"Today, I must speak of something that I have ordered a silence upon. The four people that are with us have traveled far. They are from the south and they claim that my son has been committing acts of war and treason against our people. Today I ask that you all find it in you to understand the decision that I have come to. You know of my son's problems in the past and that he was banished from my family and this clan forever."

Thomas gathered himself and continued, "Gully has been pillaging and raping the southern lands with a group of men that he has gathered somehow. There is proof of this that I will not divulge, but his criminal activities have included theft, rape and the murder of innocents. To add to it, he has been accused of treason by these people."

The room sounded like a beehive as the voices muttered amongst themselves in surprise at the accusations. Gully was insane, but no one would have believed him to be the leader of a group of renegades. They were surprised and they could all see that Thomas was pained by his own words. He stood there with a facial expression that was unlike any of them had ever seen. His name bore such honor that to have a son so traitorous was more than he could manage.

One of the knights spoke up and asked, "Earl MacDonell, what do you want us to do? If this is true, he could be hanged, or worse, if the authorities catch up with him."

Thomas lowered his head and poised himself for what he was about to say. The men looked at themselves when they saw the look on his face and were puzzled.

"This is worse than you all know. As we speak, Gully is preparing to make his way toward our land. He has stated that his intention is to take this castle and I am afraid to say that he will not stop before killing as many of us as he sees fit. I will not see my wife look upon her son's face again in horror. She must be taken along with the other women and children to the high north. The rest of us will prepare a plan. There will be no involvement of the king. I ask for your devotion to silence in this matter. The MacDonell name will not be dragged through the dirt and dishonored. This will end before it becomes anything more than a spoiled lunatic's empty attempt at gaining power. He must be stopped and I give each man in this room the authority to do what he must to make this happen. We must contain the fighting within our own lands. To do this, we must allow him to reach the Grampian Mountains and take them on the other side. It must end there."

Thomas lowered is head and turned away to the window. The men looked at each other with sullen faces as they realized the magnitude of their task. This was not a battle against the English, where the line between right and wrong were clear to them. They felt Thomas' pain now. He was a good man. His wife Anne guided their families and the women and children revered her as their matron. They had been disgraced and the men knew that they had to protect Thomas and do what was necessary. The fact did remain however, that the enemy this time was his own son. No other clans must be involved. This had to be something they faced together; alone.

As they talked quietly amongst themselves, Deb and Liam asked if they could enter the room. The guards let them in after an approving nod from Thomas and they walked through the men toward him. Deb saw his angst. The men stood in awe of the graceful girl that looked as if she had been at battle. Liam walked proudly beside her and the two stopped just before the earl.

They both kneeled down before him; swords by their sides held tightly by one hand and the other bracing the other knee. In unison, they looked up at him.

"Earl MacDonell, my husband and I are your devoted servants. This is something that has touched us deeply but we cannot imagine what our news has done to you and your wife. We only hope that you see it in your heart that we honor you and your name by coming here and risking so much. This is why we have come to you. We stand by your side in whatever you wish to do."

Another knight spoke up as well stepping forward and added, "We all do, sir. We fight for you with honor no matter what the enemy may be. You have our loyalty!"

Thomas took a deep breath and stood up tall. He was touched by the respect he was being given. He grasped his sword and looked around at his men.

The shame was now biting his heart less and he felt as though the years of Earldom had shown at that very moment. They were by him no matter what; no judgment.

"We will discuss the details of this tonight. I want three men to ride south now in either direction from the castle to search the area towards the mountains. Take heed and be watchful. Gully is said to be skilled at hiding his presence. Go now! Ride!" Thomas motioned to three of his best men to go and they left immediately after a quick bow.

Liam and Deb turned and as the other men left the room ahead of them, Thomas' wife entered from another door. She and Deb met eyes and Anne walked over to her. Deb's face flushed as she realized who it was in her view.

She asked Deb to sit with her. Liam left them to their discussion, joining his father and brother in the hallway. As Thomas left the room, Anne spoke to Deb about the situation. Deb was honored that she wanted to speak to her, but felt very intimidated at first. This was Gully's mother!

"Your name is Deborah Barne?" Anne asked.

"Yes, I am of the Douglas clan before marrying my husband. My father passed some time ago; my mother, when I was a child. My husband and I were running the farmland of my family to the south on the west coast near Carrick."

Anne sat with a regal presence. Her clothing was fine-looking and her demeanor enamored Deb. She was a true lady.

She saw honesty in Deb's rugged, beautiful face and that made her trust her. Anne was barren, but she had wished that a daughter would have blessed her and Thomas after Gully was born. As she looked at Deb, she saw a young woman of strength, resilience and grace. Immediately, she feared the images in her head and what Gully had done to this girl. She ironically felt responsible.

"I believe you have been through much pain." Anne had shame on her face as she continued. Deb felt so deeply sorrowed for her. This majestic woman did not deserve this.

"Yes, my lady, but I am fine now. This world sees fit to protect those who should carry on. Sometimes, it takes pain to see the good in life. I lost my mother many years ago, but my father raised me to be strong. It is the one who chooses the path of peace that will eventually find redemption and truth. Your son has chosen otherwise. You are a gracious woman. You and your husband are respected more than you know. I am sorry to have brought back the pain you once thought you had been free of. For this I feel sorrow and guilt, but I believe that we meet the ones we are meant to in life for different reasons. These times are harsh and unpredictable. We must find friendship and alliances with people we least expect to."

Anne marveled at the wisdom in Deb's words. She was young and not raised around nobility, but she seemed to hold herself as if she had been. Anne thought of her father's name 'Jacob of Douglas' and she felt as though she knew Deb somehow. It was strange. She looked like a woman that Anne once knew. That woman was connected to Jacob somehow. The thought left her quickly and she continued to speak to Deb.

Wringing her hands in thought, "I am the wife of a wealthy earl. I try to guide my people towards peaceful ends. The events that have transpired have troubled me deeply. My son could have been a good man. I feel that my husband and I failed in some way to make that happen. I see in your face a woman who must do what she must do. For this, I do not blame you." A tear came to her eye, but she held it back turning her head gracefully. "Young lady, I want you to take this to heart when I say that I give you permission to take whatever action you must. I am not a stupid woman. I know that my son has hurt you and taken something from you that only another woman could understand."

Deb took a quick breath in when she heard these words. Anne knew what Gully had taken from her without even being told.

"I trust that you are joining my husband when he rides?"

"Yes, I am. I must." She paused looking Anne straight in the eyes. "I do not blame you. I have accepted what has happened and now I choose to move forward. If you are saying what I think you are saying, then I must be honest with you." Deb stood up and walked slowly to the window. She looked out and took a deep breath before turning back around. "If fate sees fit that I am the one to take your son's life, do I have your permission as a woman and a mother?"

Anne stood up as well; her beautiful dress flowing behind her as she walked over to Deb. She took Deb's hands and held them tightly looking into her eyes. She felt the strength and the scars that were raised upon her skin. Deb felt like weeping, but stood still as Anne spoke. Her words made her heart beat and her body quiver. Anne's eyes were full of pain and glistened with moisture as she forced herself to say the next words.

"My dear, I will weep the day my son is dead, but I will not weep the loss of his evil. If *you* are the one who is meant to rid him of that, then so be it. His mother I am, but I refuse to feed the pain he is causing."

She began to shake and Deb held on to her.

As the tears filled Anne's eyes, she stated very bluntly, "Do what you must do. I will not fault you. I would rather you take his life than have my husband do so. It would break him inside. I hope that we meet again, Deb Barne. When we do, know that we will be at peace with each other, no matter what becomes of this."

Deb knelt before Anne and bowed her head touching the lady's hands with her face. Still holding them she looked up at Anne's tormented face and said, "We will make the pain stop, my lady. You will find peace again. I swear it!"

As Anne looked into Deb's eyes, she saw the soul of a woman she once knew. The resemblance hit her.

When Deb left the room, Anne's heart raced. Walking to her private chamber she thought hard. The woman's name was Mary! Anne had known her around the time that Deb would have been born. It was strange, but Anne remembered Mary quite vividly. Mary's father had done business with Anne's family while he was a farmer on their land. Anne's father was a lord and Mary's family lived and farmed a piece of his land. Now she remembered. Mary died and had left a daughter and husband. Was this girl Mary's child? She had to snap herself out of this. Could she possibly be wrong?

Her mind was filled with something much more personal. Anne MacDonell's son and husband were about to meet each other on the battlefield.

Her heart sank into her stomach as she lurched back to the thought. She was delirious with heartache and fell to the bed from the exhaustion of crying. Later, Thomas ordered Anne's room not to be disturbed except for her personal lady in waiting. The castle was quiet that night. Everyone felt the tension. It blackened their hearts and their lives were about to change in a way they never expected.

It would take the riders at least a day to sweep the area and return with any news. That evening after organizing the horses and weaponry, Thomas called everyone to the great hall. Gully was surely close by now. The alternative was that he was crouching like a wolf waiting on the edge of the mountains. This was what his father was hoping.

"If Gully is on his way, we will know it, but I don't want him to get passed those hills. We must be ready to ride at any moment. Hopefully, time will be on our side. I would like twenty men to guide the women and children to the north of Inverness. Take shelter with the Barne clan. Your lead is Malcolm Barne. Stay with them and protect them against all odds."

He turned to Liam's father and asked, "I ask you, Malcolm Barne, if you and your son will take this responsibility. I ask of your loyalty in this matter. I will compensate you for your assistance."

Liam's father and brother nodded a definite yes and responded, "We are here to help in any way, but no coin is necessary. This is not a fight that you asked for. You shelter my son and his wife. For this we are in your debt."

"Then, I do wish you to have my weapons and armor at your disposal," Thomas stated.

"So be it. Thank you, Earl MacDonell." Liam's father looked at his sons and they gave him an agreeable nod.

"You will leave soon then. They are gathering them now. There will be food and water for your journey."

Liam's father and brother turned to leave and Liam placed a hand on each of their shoulders saying, "Thank you to both of you. Be watchful. I do not know how long this fight will last. I do know that you will see us again. Go now. Be safe, and pray that this ends well."

Liam's father placed his hand on his son's shoulder and pulled him inward to embrace him, "Don't worry lad, stay strong and God be with you." His brother followed suit by embracing him and patting him hard on the back. The young man feared he would not see Liam again, but he honored his brother's valor.

Deb arrived and Thomas asked her to come to the front of the room.

"Young woman, I trust that you will put up a fight if I do not allow you to come with us?"

Liam grinned respectfully and Deb smiled proudly back as Thomas looked down at her. He could tell Deb had a will of steel. She had already proven it.

"I wish to hold a position at the front, Earl MacDonell. My horse is powerful and I am confident that my skills will serve you well."

"So be it then." He turned to the men and addressed them now as well. Deb stood with her back straight and her father's hand upon hers. This is why he died a proud man.

"As you know the riders should be arriving back some time soon. We do not know exactly how many men Gully has with him, but the Barnes believe him to be at least one hundred men strong and possibly more. Whatever the number, we will separate our men into three groups. One will take the left flank and the other on the right. They will be cavalry only. In the middle, mounted knights will gather behind an infantry of spearmen with twenty more men behind the horses with bows and arrows. Our two guests are more skilled with the English long bow, if I understand the rumors correctly. I expect you to take their lead and follow their instruction as to direction and timing. I will ride forth alone to show Gully my face."

Thomas slowed down and said in a quieter voice, "It will be the deciding moment. I doubt very much that he will flee. If he charges forward after I give a warning, I want everyone to hold their ground. Wait, and once they are within range, the archers will strike first. As they reload, the infantry will force forward and take down as many men on horseback as possible. Don't spare the horses. They are noble beasts, but they carry on their backs men that must be stopped at all cost. All mounted riders shall then drive forward from both sides and center. It will be harder for them to focus on three different oncoming groups. Use the element of confusion against them." Thomas added, "We will not allow this land to be dishonored. You must put away the idea that these men are of our own country. Put aside that it is Gully. We are taking the law into our own hands. They have chosen a path that is criminal and disgraceful. They do not have the knowledge of fighting that we do. They fight for blood and will be formidable, but their lack of experience will bring their defeat."

He bowed his head slightly thinking about his son, but held it up again with a purposeful gaze, "I authorized you all to do what you must." He looked directly at Deb and she nodded respectfully.

As the men filed out of the room to assemble the horses, Deb and Liam took a moment to be alone. They walked out into courtyard and into the garden area. As they sat down, Deb noticed the sweet smell of heather planted amongst other beautiful flowers. The lady of the house had created a lovely spot. She and Thomas had been married there, the stories said. The castle walls were fashioned from the finest stone available so thick; it would take a fleet of serge weapons to breech them. At its peak height, one could see for miles and although it was by no means the largest castle in northern Scotland, it had seen the presence of King Robert and many other figures of nobility.

Liam was visibly uneasy. Deb took his hand and spoke to him gently. "Liam, I know what you are thinking. I want revenge on Gully as well, but we must keep our thinking clear. He is not the only one that we will be fighting tomorrow. To get to him, we will have to fight with the others as one. He will not stand still and allow us to take him easily."

"I know, Deb. I just can't stop thinking about his hands on you." He turned to her. "I do not blame you my love. You did the right thing by deceiving him and I am prouder than you know that I have a wife who had the fortitude to escape those walls. But I can't get your father's words out of my mind. I feel as though I have failed him."

"Don't say that!" Deb whispered loudly. "They took me that day after you risked your life to save me and my father's land. Liam, he had more men than we could handle! It was not your fault that I was taken. You must be thankful that we are both here together and know that all of this was meant to be! We are the ones who have beaten him so far and we will be the ones who keep him from continuing this mad path."

She looked into his eyes. "No one else has had the courage to stand against this man, but you did. You thought clearly and kept faith that I was strong enough to stay alive as well. Don't you see, Liam? This was meant to be. My father often told me that our life is in our own hands. God guides us and shows us the path, but we have the power inside alone. You have proven that to me."

Liam still sat quietly as he listened to her words. He finally stood up and pulled her closely to him. "You don't know how I yearned to see you. A man is not a man if he cannot protect his wife. The anger that I have felt has often turned to rage, but I know that a man who has no control has no power over his enemies. I do not wish for you to be there tomorrow."

He sighed and gazed at her longingly and added, "But if a walled castle of men could not hold you, then how could I?"

They smiled at each other realizing that they had come to terms with their situation and they would stand by each other's side. Liam gently pushed her hair from her face and she felt his strong arms under her hands.

Liam held her closer and finally said, "Tomorrow we will fight side by side as fellow warriors, but tonight I will make love to you as my beautiful wife. I have missed you, Deb. I have missed you so!" His hands traced her shape.

Passion and emotion filled them both. They kissed deeply and she embraced his strong muscular back. Liam felt his wife's beautiful form; her strength, her curves. He never wanted to let her out of his sight again.

Deb whispered as her breathing became heavy from Liam's attention, "Our path will not end tomorrow." She paused. "It will begin, my love!"

He kissed her again and led her to their room. That night, Liam and Deb made love as if it were the last time they would see each other. They threw themselves into the lustful waves that they had held back for so long. Deb was dizzy with emotion and she felt as if her heart would burst for this man. He loved her like no man loved any woman. Liam gazed into her face and became aroused like he never had before. She wrapped her legs around him and they rolled into the large bed as two souls intertwined together in young passion, becoming one entity. Deb felt as though she would cry as Liam showed her how much he had missed her. He was raw and so deeply excited by her touch. He rolled her over onto her back and looked down at the goddess who had married him. He was in heaven and felt the greatest rapture on earth. Deb reached up and kissed him so deeply, he almost lost his breath.

For an hour they were engulfed in the sweet apex of their powerful love and they both collapsed at the same time. As the climactic emotions of being together and physical pleasure grew higher and higher, they buckled in each other's arms panting with a wildly satisfying release.

Liam pulled a blanket over them and they lay cradled in each other's arms quietly. He looked down at her soft, warm face. She was so beautiful. His hands held her tightly.

The moon glistened through the window and a peaceful wave fell over them. Deb took a deep breath and sunk into Liam's chest. She closed her eyes but Liam stayed awake just long enough to watch her as she fell asleep. His eyes slowly shut and exhaustion finally overwhelmed them both.

As Thomas tried to settle himself on the other side of the castle, his heart weighed heavy. With Anne and the other women and children gone and safely on their way north, he took a moment to release some of the anger that he had bottled up for the last two days.

In pain from the angst he was feeling, he walked around his private chamber and bedroom. The table to the left of him had books and a candle lit upon it. His rage built up within his fists and in one powerful sweep, he slammed everything on the table to the floor. He gripped the table with tears in his eyes. Looking up he asked the heavens, "Why? Why is this disgrace upon us? Have I not given my life to this boy? This shame must end! It must end!"

Three rooms were bound together by doorways and a long hallway. One was Thomas and Anne's bedroom chamber, one was a sitting room with a grand fireplace and the last room was where Gully had been born. Thomas felt sadness as he walked into the room and remembered the day Anne gave birth to the child who had become a monster.

The instruments that Thomas had given Gully to play as a young man and the hand crafted wooden toys that one of the carpenters had made especially for Gully were now put away in a box in the corner. Anne could not part with them even after

Gully was banished from the castle. She and Thomas had not spoken for days afterward, but Anne finally realized that they had done the right thing. But the right thing did not stop Thomas from remembering...

They had brought in a man of medicine and potions to try and settle Gully's agitated behavior as a boy. He would throw fits of rage and throw things at times. A few of the knights who lived and raised their families within the castle walls had boys that were Gully's age and they had complained to their parents that Gully would hit them when playing, steal their toys and run.

As Gully grew into a young teenager, he would take one of his father's horses and race him through the field until the horse could barely breathe. One day when his father and mother were away visiting family, he was seen beating it in the stalls because it would not allow him to mount it again. He struck it over and over again and screamed at it saying that he would teach it a lesson for being disobedient to him. It was said that Gully finally gained a seat on the horse's back and slashed its hindquarters brutally with a whip to make it run. As no one would do anything about it out of fear of repercussion from Gully, he left the castle and ran the horse so badly that it stumbled and broke its leg. Gully himself had injured his face in the fall; a fitting gift for his treacherous behavior. He brought the horse back limping and ordered the blacksmith to put it down and bury its carcass so his father would not see it. He then threatened him and told him not to speak a word of it, but if asked to say that the horse simply ran away and could not be retrieved. The man feared losing his position and did as Gully said.

His parents had the hardest moments just before Gully was told to leave by his father. One cold night, Gully had been drinking to extremes after dinner had been served. His father asked him to retire to his room and Gully angrily sauntered off claiming that he was nobility and did not have to be treated that way. He went to his room and got his sword. He made his way quietly past his father's room and down into the courtyard. There, a guard that had shown distaste for Gully in the past was on duty at the main gate.

As Gully approached him obviously intoxicated, the guard tried to maintain his composure. He hated Gully with a passion.

"Can I help you, sir?" he said respectfully to Gully who was dragging his sword behind him while swilling wine. He looked crazed and the guard was prepared for anything.

"Ah! I am bored! My father has said I have been drinking too much! Do I look like I have had too much to drink? Nonsense! I am perfectly of my own will and, in fact, I wish to have a little swordplay! You! You will join me!"

Gully shabbily dragged himself and the sword closer to the guard. He threw the wine flask on the ground and it sprayed all over him. His eyes were mad and the guard did not know whether to leave or fight him.

"Sir, I cannot as I am on duty." He tried to stay calm. Another guard heard the commotion and came over. He looked at the other guard and then at Gully and knew right away that Gully was crossing the line again. Everyone knew him well, but held their tongue out of respect for Thomas.

"Ah! Yes! Two men to take me on at once! It is a perfect match! I think this will be interesting!"

Gully stepped up to the first guard and held his sword up to him closely. The guard stood still and left his sword at his side. Gully became angered at being ignored and swung his blade just enough to nick the man's cheek. He was now very serious and the guard had had enough of his behavior. There was little reaction except for grabbing his cheek and glaring at Gully while looking at the other guard for direction.

"Sir, I insist that you stop this at once or I will have to defend myself!" He raised his sword to Gully who shouted, "I am Gully MacDonell, man! No one ignores me! No one orders me!"

He lunged forward again and this time the guard held his sword high and Gully's blade came down on it. The other guard stayed back and waited to see what his role would be, if needed. They were far enough away from the main castle that not many could hear them, but as Gully raged on loudly, one of Thomas' head guards heard them and came running.

"What is the meaning of this?" he yelled at them both and the guard that was watching spoke up and told him that Gully was drunk and having words with them.

"Stop this at once!" He saw the blood on the cheek of his guard and as he stepped closer, Gully went into a hysterical rage. In his mind they were all attacking him at once and he started to curse and swing wildly in all directions.

"Stay away or I shall kill you all! Damn you to hell, you bastards! Back off!" They tried to stop him but he was becoming dizzy and flailing like a lunatic.

By this time, Thomas had finally heard of the incident and came rushing to the scene as well.

His cape flowed behind him as he made his way to the men with his sword held upon his side by his hand. His face went red with anger and he screamed, "Stop!"

The guards stepped away upon seeing Thomas and as Gully continued to swing his sword and mumble obscenities; his father looked on in horror. What had his son become? He was like an animal. The guards stood there feeling their Earl's embarrassment. Thomas looked mortified beyond words.

"Gully! I am your father and I order you to stop this insanity at once!"

Gully stopped swinging now only because he was started to lose his footing from the spinning and the alcohol. He spat at his father one last impudent phrase before falling down on his backside.

"Father, you wouldn't know what to do with me either! Come and have a drink with me, you old sop!" He was sweating and slobbering and angry that his fun had been interrupted. "Father! Oh yes, I was just showing the men how to fight like a man!" He was slurring his words.

"Get up! Get up and go inside!" Thomas finally got close enough to take his sword away from him. In doing so, he took Gully's only means of stability left and he plunged down face first into the dirt. Thomas shook his head in shame and motioned the men to take Gully to his room.

As he watched his son being taken away he took a deep breath and made his way back to his private chambers. That night, Anne and Thomas spoke for hours. Neither of them slept and it was the break of daylight that ended their conversation. Gully had problems too large for them to handle.

He needed to go off on his own. Thomas could not allow this crazed dog to become heir to the MacDonell castle; let alone be part of the clan. Since he was twenty years of age and a man now, Thomas and Anne decided that telling their son to leave the castle was the only thing they could do.

The next morning, Gully sauntered into the dining hall looking for food. Thomas and Anne were sitting alone at the end of the table. They said nothing and just watched as he slithered his way into a chair grabbing a piece of bread from the table and shoving it down.

"So," as he slopped his food. "I think today, I shall take a few men and go hunting, father."

Thomas and Anne sat silent and Gully added, "Do you hear me? I would like to use the black stallion father. He is the best horse for the job!"

Thomas finally spoke up calmly and stated, "Your mother and I would like to speak to you."

Gully grabbed some water and drank it down. He was very dehydrated. His face was white and his eyes had dark circles around them. He looked like death sitting there like a spoiled brat in his silk tunic and leather boots. He took a flower from the table and poked it through a notch in his vest. He was pompous and arrogant beyond belief.

"About what?" He said with an indifferent tone. He wasn't even looking at his father.

"Your mother and I feel that you have been troubled and I will not stand for your attitude any longer."

"What? What are you talking about, father?" He seemed to remember nothing of the night before and went on eating and drinking.

Thomas had had enough already and he instantly stood and shouted, "You will speak to me with respect! I will not tolerate you any more, Gully! You are shaming this family and you show no remorse for yourself! Last night was the last straw! You will leave the castle and find your own way! My word is final! I disown you!"

Gully sat stunned finally hearing his father but still not remembering what had happened the night before. He didn't care. As Anne kept silent, she got up and walked away from them to the other side of the room trying to contain her tears. She was devastated.

"Leave? You want me to leave? I am your son!" Gully was angered as well and stood up leaning down the table at his father who was staring back at him.

"You heard my words. They are final. You are to leave this place by tonight. You are not to return. I've left you enough coin to feed yourself until you can find employment."

Thomas looked Gully straight in the eyes and added finally, "You are disowned from this family and I do not want you to ever return." These last words were spoken with a deep, absolute voice.

Gully's face went red, and he got up and stepped toward his father. He picked up a chair and threw it against the wall and pushed everything off the table with a swoop of his arm.

Food and drink went flying and Gully raised his voice to his father, "You can't do this! I am your son! My name is Gully MacDonell and I am the future leader of this clan! You can't take that from me! I don't care if you are my father! My blood is my blood! I should have killed you when I had the chance!"

Suddenly Anne turned with fear in her eyes. What had Gully just said? Had he meant it?

She was terrified by the words and screamed at her son, "How dare you say these things to your father! How dare you shame your mother! How dare you speak of this! Get out now! Get out of my house now! You are not my son anymore! Leave now!"

She was frantic as her hands trembled and her tear filled eyes widened. Gully was fuming as Thomas pulled his own sword to defend them. Gully was without a weapon and at that point the guards had come to the door. They pulled their swords as well.

Thomas stood shaking while he said, "Guards, my son is to be led to his room and given a few moments to gather his things. I then ask that you lead him off the castle grounds. He is not to be allowed back in the gate for any reason...ever." The guards were confused, but they had heard the argument and realized that Thomas was serious.

Gully screamed at the guards realizing that his father was not backing down. "Keep your hands off of me, you swine! Get out of my way!" He stormed out of the doorway and he could be heard slamming doors and throwing things around his room.

When he finally came out of the hallway and met the guards at the main door, he had fire in his eyes. They stared him down and were careful of his sword. He could give them trouble if he wanted to, but he mounted his horse with the few things he had gathered and spat on the ground. "That is what I think of my father! You will all pay for this! You will see me again!"

With that Gully MacDonell rode away from his father's castle and his life. Thomas stood in the window of his room and watched as his son rode into the distance. Anne was weeping and when Thomas went to speak to her, she asked that he leave her alone for a while. They could not speak to one another for days and when they finally did, Anne thanked her husband for dealing with it as he did. She just needed time to gain her composure and realize that they had done the right thing.

Thomas could have sent word of Gully to the authorities and warned them of him, but he didn't. In his mind, Gully would not survive the world on his own. He would insult someone who would not take his tongue and it would be the last time he did. This is what he had hoped.

Cheryl Alleway

Chapter Twelve
A Father's Pain

Cheryl Alleway

Now on the eve of battle with his own son, Thomas sat and pondered his son's life and what had now become of it. He felt guilt so deeply that he could not make sense of it in his mind. It was a heavy weight to bear thinking of the suffering that Gully had caused. His men would have to fight Gully's men and there would be loss of life. They did not deserve this. They should be defending themselves against the real enemies of Scotland, not a crazed, spoiled man who had wasted his life and damaged so many others. It could have been avoided. He should have thrown him in the castle prison, but then they would never really have been rid of him. Why had it come to this? He heard the voices of the young girls that Deb had told him about. He thought about the pain his son had caused their families. He wondered how many good people Gully had killed or stolen from. It was too much for him to think on anymore. Thomas; a man of strength and character, a man who had lead soldiers on the battlefield now sat and wept alone in his room. It was his darkest moment.

As the sun came up, everyone in the castle of Thomas MacDonell was preparing for battle. The men were organized outside the castle walls. Deb and Liam joined Thomas and the three rode out to the front of the men.

As Thomas turned around to address them, he seemed more determined and resilient. The night before had given him the chance to justify this day and he felt that it was meant to be. His hope was to end it as favorably as possible, but he also knew that he could be facing the sword of his own son.

Deb and Liam sat upon their horses listening to Thomas' words. Deb felt that today was the day she would need her own father the most. She touched the dagger he had given her before he died and she asked for his guidance and the strength for what she may have to do.

Liam was focused and prayed silently for a safe end to the day. He did not want to let Deb out of his sight and although killing Gully would take no thought if given the chance, she would be his first priority.

The air was cool and they could see their breath as morning dew coated everything like liquid silver. The smell of clover and sweet grass filled the air. Smoke from the fires was still lingering from the night before. It seemed too peaceful a place to be the arena for battle. The landscape was massive with high peaks and low valleys rolling with grace like waves on the sea. It was however, a formidable landscape to travel upon. This worked to the advantage of a defending army who could hide their numbers and spread out amongst the dips and curves. The only problem was that it was at times difficult to see clearly at a distance. It came down to the most skilled commander and his ability to follow the right path and make his move at the right time. The skill of orchestrating defensive war maneuvers was something that Thomas was well known for. His riders would be his eyes and ears.

Thomas spoke with diligence as he walked his horse slowly amongst his men. He would, at times, tap their shoulders as he strolled by.

"Today, I ask for your strength and courage. I wish that I did not have to ask you to fight this battle, but it is with pride and appreciation that I look upon you all now. I do not need to explain why we must do this. Most of you have been with me for years and you are not just soldiers to me. We will end this day with our best intentions, but if we experience loss of life or injury, I swear to you all that your families will be well taken care of. I pray that it does not come to that. The riders have seen Gully's men riding north toward the mountains, but they have not cleared Perth as of yet. Therefore, we will use the element of surprise. They will also be worn from their journey. The path towards the Lorne is the most desirable one for them. Gully knows this. I hope that this will help our cause however, as their route will be narrowed and they will not have a clear view to their right. We must align our three groups accordingly. We may be able to trap them against the waters before they can get past the mountains. To strike them there will be our best chance to weaken them. We must keep the third group free and holding position at the base of the mountains. If Gully's men break through our first and second groups, they will have to engage us again and they may not expect it. They will be weaker and have fewer men at that point. We must be strong and ready to finish them off. They must not gain access to Inverness. There are only twenty men to guard our castle walls and they are hoping that the first men they see again are us. Let us ride now!"

He looked at the two men who had initially sighted Gully and said, "I would like you to continue riding as lookouts. Your job is very important and you will be our first set of eyes. Go now, lads. Ride fast!"

They took to the valley and Thomas closed his eyes briefly to embrace his emotions. When he opened them, the determination could have burned a hole in the sun. He turned his men in the direction of the south and began making their way toward the mountains. The thunder of horses raced across the ground and a flurry of weapons glinted in the early sun against their masters. Dust was kicking up behind them and the visual of Thomas' men on foot was formidable to say the least; spears drawn marching in unison like a wall of doom.

As Deb and Liam sat upon their horses there were no words spoken. Deb's father had taught her the skill of concentration and he had instilled a determined drive into her to keep her mind clear. Liam had seen it as they practiced archery with her father. She could turn the world off around her and he admired her focus. He turned his head to look at her as she rode with her back straight and head high. She had allowed herself to show her anger and hatred for Gully at the castle and now her renewed energy was forging her forward to do what she must. Liam's heart raced when he looked at her. Her flowing black hair, her strong form and dignified presence would surely be a surprise to Gully when he finally laid his eyes upon her. Even more shocking would be the sight of Liam sitting defiantly beside her.

As they passed through and cleared the Firth of Lorne, the first group of cavalry turned toward the waters. The center infantry followed their path and flanked their left side. Thomas led these two groups. Deb and Liam rode with him to coordinate the archers when needed. The role of these few men would be an important one as they would strike first, hopefully taking a few of Gully's men and creating confusion amongst the rest. In the process they would lure the enemy to fire their arrows as well, forcing them to use their supply up quickly.

Thomas' men were armed with huge battle shields designed to layer together over the soldiers and protect them from the shower of arrows. Deb had warned Thomas that Gully's men, although not the best archers, could be carrying twice as many as they had. This could be one of Gully's advantages, but she pointed out that they were not going to be useful if they could get close enough to take them out. They were not well trained to fire from moving horses, but Deb and Liam were and Thomas was counting on them to take the lead when the time would come.

Riding slowly toward the mountains was the third group of Thomas' men. They would be the final defensive line and Thomas asked his long-time friend and right hand man, William, to take the lead. William had the battle scars on his face to prove his devotion to Thomas. He was a short man, but his shoulders were wide and strong and he rode a horse better than anyone Thomas had ever seen. His hand to hand combat was unwavering and his swift agility made him a hard target. He turned and waved to Thomas as they rode away from the other two groups.

Suddenly Deb noticed something on the ridge ahead of them. She wondered if it were one of the riders that Thomas had sent ahead, but as they all seemed to noticed him, Liam stated, "That's not one of ours!"

Quickly, Thomas halted the men and Deb made the comment, "If he is scouting for Gully, we must take him now!" She added, turning to Liam, "I can do it Liam. I just need you to get me closer!"

Liam had no time to argue with her. He knew she would go anyway. Thomas' own riders had not been sited yet and Liam assumed that Gully was not close enough to be an issue. They had to take the rider down now.

"Come, lass. Let us do it quickly!"

"Ride then! Swiftly!" Thomas shouted agreeably.

Deb and Liam took flight. Liam's horse was not fast enough to keep up with Finnean and so he took to the right of her to distract the rider's attention to him while she flew around the hill undetected. Finnean raced like the wind and Deb held tightly to him holding her body low. She had readied her bow closely by her side and three arrows were sitting within inches of each other, freely within the sheath.

She rounded the corner of the hill and as she did, her sight became clearer as the ground was becoming flatter. Liam was racing straight for the man who now made the mistake of turning in Deb's direction to flee him. She met up with him only seconds before passing each other just thirty feet away. The rider was confused and riding erratically now.

It was Mulden. Deb recognized him.

He had been sneaking around the area for two days looking for something to tell Gully. He was not strong enough to take on the landscape of the north and he had become lost in the mountains trying to find his way back toward Gully.

Suddenly, Mulden turned and almost fell from his horse. Deb had caught up with him and she had him in her sights. He saw her face and she terrified him. Her black hair looked like a flowing cloak as she came down the hillside after him. He turned south and ironically headed in Gully's direction, but within seconds, he felt the warm flow of his own blood filling his organs. His eyes rolled back into his head as Deb's arrow thrust through his rib cage. With his horse still riding, he looked down and as he saw the arrowhead, he spun backwards and fell to his death. The horse had to be taken as well. If it made its way to their enemy, Gully would know they were close.

Deb centered Finnean with the path of Mulden's horse and she said out loud, "I am sorry, old boy. You must not give our position away." She came up beside him and carefully placed an arrow into his chest. Instantly the horse fell and Deb pulled Finnean's reigns back to stop him. She leaped off him and ran to the horse's side.

"It's alright, lad. I am sorry. Sleep now. You are free." The horse stopped breathing and she mounted Finnean again and rode swiftly back to Thomas. Liam met her halfway and they both turned and kept riding.

Thomas' men had finally seen first-hand, the skill that Deb held within her. They had no problem accepting her as one of their own and they stepped their horses aside to let her move up beside Thomas.

"Well done, lass. Thank you," he said to her.

"It is my duty, sir. Riding by your side is an honor," she stated.

Deb looked forward again and Thomas looked her way. Anne had spoken highly of Deb and Thomas trusted his wife's judgment. He was beginning to admire this young woman who came to him so humbly only days before. As he and Liam met eyes, they nodded to each other respectfully and Thomas knew without a doubt, that fate had brought them together.

As the end of the day was nearing, Thomas' riders came fast over the hills and told him that Gully had at least one hundred and twenty five men. To Thomas' relief, they were moving in one solid group.

One of the riders spoke up and said with caution, "Earl MacDonell, they are close and not more than five miles away. They saw us, sir. They are riding swiftly."

Thomas nodded his acknowledgment and turned to face his men. Deb and Liam took their places.

"We must move swiftly to the water. When we get there, every man find your position! Deb, Liam, ready the archers! Everyone else wait for my command. Quickly now!"

They rode ahead and not minutes later, they saw Gully's men come into view.

Gully slowed down and they came to a halt after seeing what was ahead of them. They had sighted Thomas' party. Thomas took his horse forward slowly and it wasn't long before Gully could see who was approaching.

Thomas gazed at his son and his heart raced. He rode slowly toward him but stopped within yelling distance. Gully stood his ground and said nothing at first. Thomas now saw the animal that his son had become. His face was dark and cold. He felt nothing upon seeing his father but hatred.

At long last, he shouted out to his father, "What shall I make of this? My father has come to fight me?" His tone was sarcastic and insolent as usual. "What a picture of a man you still are, father! I thought you would be dead by now!"

Thomas said nothing and kept staring. His hands gripped the reigns of his horse as if they would tear through them.

Gully spat out one more insult but this time with vengeful hatred frustrated by the silence his father was displaying.

"You are not going to stop me from what is mine rightfully! You misjudged me, father! When you left me for dead, I vowed to come back and kill you! Today, I will do just that!"

Now Thomas broke his silence. The years of rage were building inside of him but he held back just enough to give Gully one more chance to realize his mistake in his warring approach.

"If you continue to move forward, you will lose many men! This will not end well, Gully!"

Gully kicked his horse forward and he rode toward Thomas alone. Their eyes were burning with anger for each other as he and his father came face to face. Thomas held himself steady as Gully came up to his side only a couple of feet away. The men on both sides watched as father and son met. Thomas was disgusted by Gully's boldness and realized that he would have no other choice. Thomas readied his blade and kept his eyes on his son's hands; all the while, noticing the men who sat ready to fight with him. Thomas knew Gully could very well have an archer ready to take him out at any moment, but he could bet on the fact that Gully would want that opportunity...he'd kill his own father himself.

"I'm not your child any longer. If you resist now, there will be a bloody end." Gully was speaking in a low, grizzled tone as he circled his father looking at him like the mad dog he had always been.

In the distance, Deb caught his eye sitting high upon her horse and Liam by her side. It was not hard to see her from that far away with her long black hair mounted regally upon *his* large, tan coloured beast.

Gully ground his teeth, looked back and sneered at his father. They had come here and won his father's trust to join forces against him.

He turned quickly with rage and barked out as he rode back to his men, "Prepare yourself old man! You, the bitch and her useless husband are about to meet God!"

He wanted to take his father down.

Angus sat in the front of the pack. He too had become a dog of hatred; losing his sense of loyalty through his tarnished vision. These men were a black mark on the highlands and Deb prayed, as she sat upon Finnean, for her strength to prevail.

"There she is; the black-haired bitch. I will finish that one myself. I do miss that body though!" Gully sneered with confidence.

Then he thought about the embarrassment that would come if he took her on and lost in front of them all. Truth be told, he feared her. Gully MacDonell was intimidated by the very woman he had abused. He showed nothing on his face, but in his gut he realized that this was the one woman that could possibly take him on and win. He knew what he had done to her and even though he cared nothing for her feelings, he was smart enough to recognize her power. Seeing her there at her best and beside Liam was like salt on a wound. He was humiliated. He was filled anew with jealousy and hot rage. It was a cocktail that fueled his insanity even further.

He changed his mind quickly, hoping to save his reputation. "But, if you can put a blade into her, do it! She means nothing to me. I'm more interested in seeing this old man dead today."

Deb and Liam were visibly anxious. The sight of Gully made Deb so enraged that Liam had to settle her again. "Steady, Deb. Come to the center, we must prepare." All the while, he was burning inside his own chest and he felt his hands on Gully's throat in his mind squeezing until there was nothing but a final cough of death. He wanted to rip his eyes out and feed them to him. If they hadn't been with Thomas and his men, he would do just that. Unlike Gully, Liam knew the consequences of an unharnessed rage and it was his only saving grace at this moment. He never hated anyone with such passionate vengeance as he did Gully. The man had kidnapped and raped his wife. Liam was sick with the thirst for blood in his gut. Then he looked at his young wife's face again. He pleaded with her to stay behind.

Deb did as Liam requested and they organized the archers in a formation that would cover the entire width of Gully's entourage. With twenty-two archers, including Deb and Liam, they could release approximately one hundred and fifty arrows each minute. Every archer had with him a sheath of twenty arrows. She did not want to waste all of them at once. When they did release, it had to count.

"Thomas! We need half the men to go farther back! We need a second line of archers!" Liam saw a flaw in their plan and he quickly tried to adjust it.

Thomas was concerned about this, but Liam spoke up and stated, "Sir, if we keep them all together and Gully's men overwhelm us, we will lose our distance for the arrows to be of use. If we pull half the archers back, the spearmen in front can move forward as the first strike of arrows fly. Then we will have a second round to fire upon them while the horses move forward!"

Jacob had described such a strategy to Deb while he trained her as a young girl. Remembering the rocks in the dirt, the lines drawn with sticks, she knew Liam was right. She prayed to her father that it would work again.

Thomas motioned quickly for the men to do as Liam and Deb suggested. He steadied his horsemen up front and they armed themselves. Thomas turned and shouted to them, "When you are certain of position and distance, you have my command to fire!"

Gully's men raced forward and his archers began firing at once. It was not organized and although the shower was tremendous, the shields that Thomas' men had with them kept the arrows from being efficient killers. They were wasted and as their adversaries were reloading, Deb, Liam and the first line of archers fired back. This batch *did* do harm. Gully's men pressed back and even his archers could not fully reload before a second wave of arrows came upon them. Ten men fell from their horses and a handful of Gully's archers went down as well.

The scene became dramatic as Gully raged forward with his men streaming in behind. He'd never followed his father's path. He'd never learned from him because he didn't care. Gully had never fought beside his father in battle or even sat in on the meetings with the other men. He would 'play' fight, but never learned the finite skills it took to be like his father. He hated authority and could never follow instruction. At twenty, Gully had learned that he was nobility and nothing more. The fighting skills he had were learned from the desire to look bigger than he was. Bragging in pubs, making bets and seeking out men who were less of a fighter than he was with no money was his game. This was how he gained a following. Gully was nothing more than a thug.

Thomas called for his spearmen to start moving ahead and they rode behind them in a solid wall of cavalry. Deb and Liam's group continued to fire and then stopped to move to the left and right to try and strike the vulnerable sides of the field. More sets of arrows were released into the sky within minutes of each other and like rain they came down on Gully's men again and again. They took down more horses, but now the two militias were about to clash. Thomas held his sword high and dove toward Gully and his men. Screaming as the blades began to swing; the spearmen took down fifteen horses whose riders were thrown to the ground.

They got up only to be advanced on by Thomas' infantry who had come from behind the cavalry and spearmen to do their part. With axe and sword, they fought heavily. The bloody scene created a storm of enemies that no one could stop. Both sides were fighting hard.

The men on the ground were now intertwined. One man stepped backward tripping over a body and impaled himself on the knife blade of his fallen comrade.

Deb ran to Finnean and Liam yelled back at the second line of archers, "Prepare your arrows! Ready yourselves! When they break through, take your mark and fire! Do not stop until you must retreat!"

The eleven men ran back towards the water and prepared their arrows within the ground in front of them just as Deb had shown them. Deb and Liam were right to have pulled them back. Thomas now had another line of resistance even if it was not large.

Deb and Liam were in the fighting zone and the remaining first line of archers was aiming in close range but they were getting overtaken by the horses. The main battle was getting close to them and some of Gully's men had broken though to their side.

One of them raced forward and took out two of Thomas' vulnerable archers. Liam turned instinctively and let an arrow go. It pierced the man in the back of the neck and he came down from his horse. Liam yelled at one of the archers on the ground, "Take his horse!"

The young man leapt onto the horse and pulled his sword joining Liam within a few seconds. Deb flew into the fighting and wanted to get closer to Gully, but he was making his way towards his Thomas. Liam made his way to Deb and together they fought their way through the black sea of men.

Finnean was kicking and snorting as the men swarmed. He bucked heavily with Deb trying to hang on, but it was to his advantage as he was a hard target indeed. With one hard snap, he knocked the teeth out of one bloke and broke his jaw bone. He flailed on the ground in pain and looked up at the horse that had just injured him. Finnean's prowess was showing and some of the others were afraid to get too close to him.

One of the men nicked his thigh but Deb quickly made short work of him. Her blade came down on his head and cracked his skull open. He fell to the ground bleeding and twitching like a fish out of water.

Gully's men were falling, but as the fighting continued, Thomas noticed that some of his own were also dead. He shouted to Deb and Liam that they must pull back. They agreed and slowly, they forced their way out of the pack. Gully was not letting up. He ordered his men at the rear to go around the side and most of them made it through. They were headed straight for the second line of archers.

With determination, the soldiers waited for proper range and then began releasing their arrows. The oncoming riders were being showered by surprise. There was chaos and now there were two battle scenes.

Thomas looked up as he swung his sword and saw the eyes of his son. As if the fighting froze for a moment, Gully raised his horse up and pushed toward his father. They met in mid stride and as their blades slammed into each other, Deb saw what was happening. She made her way around the men and found herself watching Thomas fighting his own son. Neither would give in. Each swing of their blades was met with a scream of angst. The blood and dirt was covering both of their faces and the years of hatred exploded into a dance of death.

As they became engulfed in their vengeance, Gully suddenly realized that his men were losing strength. He abruptly pulled away from his father. For the first time, he had backed away from a fight, but he wasn't finished yet. He still out numbered his father's men and in pulling back he thought he could regroup and take them again while they were down in numbers and fleeing back to the castle. Gully didn't count on William however, who was still poised behind the hill waiting to have his chance.

Thomas shouted to his men to retreat to the valley if able and they followed him. He gave Gully one more look as the sweat streamed down his face.

Deb wanted to follow after Gully, but Liam begged her to fall back as well. They had to follow Thomas' strategy.

It was all she could do to pull away and as Gully's men took themselves back away from the water, she caught his eye. He glared at her with a sick combination of lust and contempt. She shouted a scream of frustration out loud and pulled Finnean away, aggravated by how close she was to killing him.

Gully shouted back at her as he turned as well, "You'll not live to the end of this day either, little bitch!"

He and Liam met eyes just as he said it and Liam's look required no words. He was losing his will to remain calm as well, but he knew that to do so would cause the plan to fail. They must remain clear and follow through as a team. He spat on the ground when Gully stared at him and raised his sword defiantly warning the man that because he had laid his eyes on him and his hands on his wife, the villain would die.

As the two groups separated and the field began to clear, Thomas met up with Deb and Liam again. They still had half their men, but Thomas looked back at the bodies lying on the ground and felt guilty sorrow. There was nothing he could do now, but move on and continue with the plan. They rode toward the second line of archers who had survived and were falling back toward William and his men. Thomas had not expected any of them to survive, but he was thrilled there were still ten archers left.

As they found their way in the direction of William, they were met by one of the men that he had sent ahead. Thomas informed him of what had happened thus far and cautioned him to let William know that Gully was going to strike again. From his experience, Thomas knew that they would be only minutes or so behind them; just enough time to regroup and gain some strength. Gully could not allow them to get too much further away. He also wanted a win before reaching the castle. He did not know how many men his father had left, but judging by the size of his troops there couldn't have been many. He wanted as little resistance as possible.

William came forward and spoke to Thomas. "How many are left?"

"We have maybe half of us. He outnumbered the first group, but at least fifty of his men went down. Gully still does not know of your presence. We still have the numbers advantage. If we move again to distract him, you could take him by surprise once we've worn them down."

"It will be done. Men! Ready yourselves!" William walked over to Thomas who had dismounted to take a drink of water.

"How are you, my friend?" He placed his hand on Thomas' shoulder.

Thomas thought a moment and then answered, "I looked upon the face of a man that I once held as a suckling infant. When he looked at me, there was no feeling. I am his father, yet he has no emotion, just hatred. How am I, you ask? I suppose I am numb. He is insane William; utterly insane."

"Perhaps you should have something stronger than water?" William pulled out a flask of rum from his coat and Thomas grinned sadly accepting it with thanks. He had just enough to warm himself and no more. He would have to be ready to fight again.

The riders took to task once more to see where Gully's party had taken rest and they returned within fifteen minutes. They told Thomas and William that Gully had taken his men only ten miles or so south again and had been seen preparing to leave. With the news, Thomas mounted alongside Deb and Liam and took his remaining men southwest, close to the water again. His aim was to keep Gully's attention away from the mountains where William's men sat waiting. One thing he did know: Gully would be even more determined now.

As Deb and Liam rode side by side, Liam tried to talk her out of going back toward Gully with the smaller group.

"Deb, I think we should take our place with William's men. Thomas can do this without us. He knows what he is doing. If we stay with William, we will be fresh and more useful to hold them back from the castle."

Deb thought about it and said, "Liam, we brought this to these people. We could have gone to the Bruce, but we chose to allow Thomas to take care of this by himself. What if we made the wrong decision? If we have, it is our duty to be front and center with him. He allowed us into his home and chose our word over that of his own blood."

She thought for a moment and saw the anxiety in Liam's face. As he began to defend the idea to her, she suggested something that even Thomas may not have thought of.

She asked Liam to ride up front with her to Thomas. As they came up on his sides, Deb had a look of epiphany on her face.

"Liam, wait."

She turned and spoke to Thomas. "I have a suggestion that may help us even further. What if Liam and I take some of the men to the very edge of the mountain and come around the rear of Gully's men? We can flank them following the base of the mountains and we can help you and William actually shut him in. He won't be able to go forward or backward."

Thomas and Liam were unsure of the idea. How would they get past Gully without being detected? They would have to go over the lowest point of the mountain running into the valley. It would be difficult and it would take too long.

"I don't see how it could be done. There is no time," Thomas said.

"Then let us hide halfway between you and William. Once he breaks through your men, he will have not one, but two more defensive lines to get past. You will wear him down and take out as many horses as possible. Even if the men are still alive on foot, they cannot fight our remaining cavalry and win. We will take all of the remaining archers only and wait in hiding. The grasses are high and will make good cover. We will have to leave our horses here and go on foot. When we see them coming, we will shower them with what arrows we have, crippling them even more. William and his men will then have a real advantage."

Liam looked at Thomas and they stopped the men for a moment. "You would be vulnerable and on foot at that point," Thomas stated.

Now Liam spoke up believing in Deb's idea. "Yes, but we can stay close to William who would be only a few hundred feet behind us. When our arrows are gone, we will fall back immediately to our horses, joining William and his men."

Thomas was worried it would not work. It would happen so quickly that there would be no time for error. He thought about it and decided reluctantly to attempt it.

"Ride back and tell William of the new plan, then make it so. I will carry forward with the other horses and we will proceed as planned. If there are any of us left, we will wait and pursue Gully and his men from behind if he breaks through. Once I see that you have engaged them, we will come back up to assist. This must not fail."

Time was standing still as they took their places. Deb, Liam and the other archers poised themselves within the tall grass. William waited pensively for the sign. Thomas and his remaining men rode ahead to face Gully one more time.

As they came across an open section of land they moved towards the waters of the Firth of Lorne, Gully made his bold move. He pushed his men to ride madly toward his father. One of Thomas' men was heard saying that they looked like devils riding across the field. Thomas looked at his men and they knew what they had to do. As they kicked their horses to gain speed, they shouted and held their swords high, approaching with the same fervor.

When the two groups of men finally met it was with a blow that shook the earth beneath them. The fierceness of Gully's command was greater than before. He wanted to kill as many men as he could. In his mind, this was his last chance to gain access to Inverness and take his father's land. Raging, forcing their horses to their limits, they came.

As Thomas made his way through the fighting, he and Gully met eyes once more. They charged each other and met with a thunderous wrath. Each of them was swinging at the other with only one goal; to kill. Gully would not be satisfied with injuring his father.

Both blades struck over and over. Gully's horse was jolting around with fear. The horse Thomas was on was ramming into the other horse as they twisted and turned. Thomas swung a heavy blow and Gully jumped from his horse. Dismounting quickly, Thomas ran toward his son on foot. Their swords hit so hard that it dislocated one of Thomas' shoulders but he did not stop. The pain was intense, but the cause was pushing him further into the fight. Gully was holding his ground and his father was shocked at his powerful swing. He lunged in too closely however and Thomas took a piece of his ear. This only made him angrier. With blood dripping down his cheek, he went into a frenzy that Thomas remembered all too well.

"Draw as much blood as you want, father! You will not win this fight! I will have your land and your life!"

Thomas' arm was growing weak and he could not hold his sword properly any longer. Gully dove at him pressing him closer and closer to the ground. Thomas held on as Gully cut his wrist and they tumbled down in a heap of armor and weaponry. He had his father on the ground.

"Kill me, Gully. I am not a man that begs. You know not what you have done to yourself! I am not the only one who has come to stop you and you will not succeed!"

Gully was baring his teeth like a wolf and breathing heavily as he looked down upon his father. Something held him back but for only a moment. He could see some of the men watching from the corner of his eye and the rush of defeating his father in front of them took over. He raised his sword and plunged it down into the belly of his own flesh and blood. As he felt his father's rib cage crush and break under his weight, it was like a foreign power claimed him. The blood boiled up and out of the Earls' chest and his wrinkled eyes widened. Gully pulled the blade out and looked up at his men with a look of a crazed animal.

"No! My lord!" one of Thomas' men screamed and two others joined him as he ran toward Gully. Three of Gully's men met them before they could make it to the scene. Gully had just murdered their beloved leader and they too had suddenly found themselves fighting for their lives. There were not enough of them to defend themselves and the remaining men that were able, retreated to the north towards William. Gully's men fell back to his position and as the air began to clear of dust and debris, they too realized that this second fight had taken its toll on them.

As Thomas lay moments away from dying on the field, Gully walked away from him coldly to his horse thinking it was over. For only a moment, Thomas had enough breath to send one last message to his son as he watched him shrink before his eyes.

Shaking and bleeding he said in a deep voice as tears welled up in his eyes, "You could have been so much more. You have disgraced this clan and your mother. Enjoy my death. It will be your last taste of victory for you will never lead our family!"

Thomas closed his eyes and his body went limp sinking into the muddied ground; his head lying rested upon a round stone.

Gully turned as the last words were spoken. His neck twisted around like a serpent and he said to himself under his breath, "Neither will you, father!"

As Thomas' men rode feverishly to the safety of mountains, two of them looked at each other with utter pain in their eyes and saying nothing. They knew what each other were thinking. Thomas MacDonell was dead. It was all they could do to ride on.

The sun was almost gone and as the remaining men found their way to Deb and Liam's location, it was clear that Thomas was not with them.

They stopped just long enough to tell Deb and Liam how far behind Gully was and then they held their heads low and stated, "Earl MacDonell was killed by the hand of his own son. We will retrieve his body when the way is clear. He must not rot on the spot of his murder. For now, you have a least fifty men on their way toward you. They are protecting Gully by keeping his horse within the center of them. He is like a devil. Be warned, he is determined to take us."

Deb and Liam took heed and readied their few men, but not before Deb wiped a heartbreaking tear from her cheek. Anne's husband was dead. Liam gave her a look of despair and sadness, but they had to keep going.

At that time, William had shown himself to the rear of their position and as Thomas' men found their way to him, he let out a cry of anger that was most certainly heard for miles. William's friend and leader was gone. With a deep burning fury, he sat tall upon his horse. William would not fail his friend. He grasped his sword thinking of the years that Gully had wasted and his frustration was getting the better of him.

"Deb! I see them on the ridge!"

Gully's horses were coming and coming fast.

Deb shouted at the men to stay low and ready themselves. She held up a large reed from the grass and waved it twice from side to side. William kept his men out of sight. They must strike when the archers needed their escape route. It would have to be timed perfectly.

As their nemesis rode toward them, the men listened to every word Deb and Liam said. They became numb, focused and on point. With stealth and skill, they readied themselves and as Deb gave the order to rise, they did so with a rush of arrows that stopped Gully's horses dead in their tracks.

"Load again. Quickly! Quickly!" Liam shouted. Each round was pushing Gully back and some of his men were forced off their horses. Gully ordered any remaining archers he had to fire back, but they had only a few left. Deb and Liam had extra men with them to hold shields up protecting them each time they had to make themselves vulnerable and rise from the grass.

As William watched, he knew the time had come to strike. Deb and Liam had very few arrows left and they would have to retreat any moment. Liam stood up and waved to William lunging back down into the grass, narrowly avoiding an arrow.

William charged and Gully's men halted abruptly, shocked. Gully was surprised as well, but he yelled at them to ride forward. He was suddenly looking as if he were confused. He was blinking his eyes repeatedly and his eyes were wide; pupils dilated.

Deb, Liam and the others raced back toward William who passed them, giving them the shelter they needed to gain access to their own horses. Finnean was leaping on the spot and pulling at the rope holding him to a tree as Deb made a running jump to mount him. Liam had already mounted and was riding swiftly to join William. Deb followed and quickly caught up with them.

This was the moment they knew would come and as they pulled their swords, one of the men screamed, "For Thomas MacDonell!" The cry fueled them all and they rode toward Gully and his men in a wave of passion.

As Gully realized that he had been ambushed his mind began to drift within the madness of his own insanity. Just enough of it was like a drug, but too much and Gully's demented brain could not handle it. He heard voices and the scene began to spin. His men noticed that he was falling back and they became confused, but continued to ride. Gully's mind had finally been broken. The reality of the moment was rushing in and he was snapping. The image of his father's face as he killed him was sucking him into a dazed moment of disorientation.

They kept looking back at him and one of them finally yelled, "Gully! Pull your sword!" The voice jolted Gully's attention back and he regained his position just as William and his men met him head on.

The bloodshed was extensive. William dove into the fight as an unstoppable force. One of Gully's men looked up and saw William swinging his sword with one arm and his axe with another. No one could get to him.

On the right side of the pack, Deb and Liam were fighting beside each other until Deb caught sight of the beast she had come to slay.

It was then that Anne's words came back to her and she forced the images of all of the girls at Gully's castle into her thoughts. She was justifying her reason for being there. It was not vengeance, it was justice she sought.

To the left towards the water, Gully was fighting off a few of William's men. He made his way towards William, but then was pushed back in the direction that Deb was coming.

She broke free of the mass of men and rode Finnean around the outside towards Gully. Liam had only seconds to notice that she had left his side and he feared the worst. He yelled and screamed for her to come back. He swung his sword one last time and sliced the arm off one of the men; not pausing before bolting his horse in Deb's direction. She made it to Gully's position and shouted at him to come to her.

"This is what you wanted isn't it, Gully? You killed your father and now you have the chance to kill your slave as well! Fight me, Gully! Fight me!"

As Gully turned to see her; there she was; the girl with the black hair flowing behind her as she forged a path straight for him. She was magnificent upon Finnean and Gully, for a moment, felt that urge within him to admire her.

Once again, Deb could see that he was falling deeper and deeper into his irrational world and it would be as she promised; he must die in the end. She had to play her strategies right.

Gully saw nothing but Deb as he beat his horse into a fast stride toward her. She poised herself and as he rode past her to strike with his sword, she ducked down at the last second and cut a large gash in his leg. Gully screamed in pain and turned with fire in his eyes. The blow had shaken him out of his daydream.

"I won't fall by the blade of a slut!" He dove at her again and she pulled back on Finnean's reigns turning to the side where her bow sat. She had four arrows left and with a clean motion she let one fly as Gully drew almost too close for a shot. It pierced through the top of his shoulder, taking a chunk of muscle with it.

Liam had raced around the outside of the battle scene to Deb's position and as Gully sauntered around in a circle on his horse, it was clear that he was losing blood quickly. He looked up, dizzy and delirious from the rush of battle. There before him he saw Deb and Liam sitting high upon their horses staring him down. He was seeing double at times and as William made his way to the edge of the fighting where Deb and Liam sat, he saw what was happening and pulled up close to them. They just watched Gully. He was like a rabid animal. His eyes were wide and his face soiled. He was mumbling and breathing hard. He was losing control while circling his horse in a feverish swirl. The horse was whinnying with confusion and didn't know what Gully wanted him to do.

Deb thought to herself. *"I told you this is the position you would be in one day!"*

"You are all going to join my father!" Gully screamed in a mad confusion. He could barely see properly as the dizziness overcame him. There were cries from within the fighting that Gully needed someone to get to him, but William's men made certain that no one got through to save Gully.

Most of Gully's men were dead or dying and he sat upon his horse crippled, filthy and defeated. Even then, his evil soul would not quit. He screamed out loud one last time and struck his horse's sides making it bleed. The horse rode forward and as Gully came within fifty feet of his conquest, Deb raised her bow one more time holding her aim while asking William's permission to fire. With a voice of certainty, William said, "Finish him, lass."

She focused as she gave Finnean the familiar squeeze with her legs telling him what he needed to do. He stood still and she braced herself high. The arrow flew silently though the air and Gully fell back on his horse as the dust drifted from its hind quarters surrounding Gully in a slow motion spin. The arrow entered his chest and cut through him like hot steel. His bloody face fell to the side and the horse continued to ride through the men that were left on the field. As he did, the fighting stopped and everyone watched. The horse finally halted in front of a tree and Gully's body slipped off, falling to the ground.

As his remaining men realized they were horribly outnumbered and without their leader, they bolted. Some were cut down as they fled, but at least eight men were able to flee on horseback. Angus was one of them. William told everyone to stop and hold position. This fight was over.

After gathering the wounded and salvaging what they could, everyone knelt down amongst the bodies of their fallen men. William ordered that anyone killed was to be taken home. No clansmen would be left on the field. William rode with Liam and Deb to the site where Thomas was last seen alive. They walked through the bodies carefully and within minutes, William saw his long-time friend lying lifeless on the open field his noble blood spilled carelessly over the bright green of the grasses.

William ran to him and bent down beside Thomas' body. He was overcome with grief. Surrounded by the stench of death, William fell onto Thomas' chest and wept.

"I will not allow your death to be in vain, my friend! This clan will be strong!"

Liam stood back and as William gathered himself, two men with a cart came to his side. They loaded Thomas onto it and they all slowly made their way back toward Inverness after saying a prayer for his soul and the souls of the other valiant men who had stood by his side. As the wooden wheels moaned over the rough ground, it was a fitting backdrop to the day's events. Gully's body was left on the field with the others for the wolves and ravens to dispose of. He deserved nothing else.

As Deb rode by, she did not look at him. He deserved nothing more from her, not even a glance.

Chapter Thirteen
Reclamation

Cheryl Alleway

The trip back to the castle was dreary and quiet. The wounded were in pain and everyone's hearts were weeping for Thomas and the men lost. They were bloody, soiled from head to toe and the horses were spent. They sauntered into site of the castle on their last fumes of energy. William was dreading the thought of facing Anne. He was devastated, but Anne…she had lost it all. No son and no husband would ever look upon her face again. The Barnes had brought the women and children back after a rider had given them word that the battle was over. He told them nothing else. When they returned safely to the castle, Anne was at the front of the group and jumped from the horse she had been riding. Her lady in waiting caught her to protect her fall as she could injure herself.

"Thomas! Where is Thomas!" she cried. As William met her eyes, she knew what he could not say.

He removed his sword as Anne ran to him. He said nothing but held his head low and took her hand, pulling her into him to hold her. Deb and Liam were walking up to them and decided to stay back out of respect. Anne noticed them and as she and Deb met eyes, the tears flowed freely. The ladies that were with Anne took her gently into their embrace and led her into the castle courtyard and to her private chambers. Anne's crying was heard and spoken of throughout the castle. She had suffered the greatest loss any woman could; her husband and her child were gone.

William spoke with his wife and they vowed to do whatever Anne wanted. They had to take care of the castle and the land for her for she was in no condition to do it. Her pain had to be deeper than the sea itself. William's wife feared for Anne's sanity and spent many hours checking on her.

Deb and Liam had stayed on for only a couple of days afterwards and William offered a few of his men to accompany them back down to Dominon castle. Liam's father and brother had wanted to go as well, but Liam tried to explain that they were needed more at home. His mother was ill and Liam's father realized their place was by her side. It was gut-wrenching for Liam to watch them ride away. His mother was on his mind for certain, and once again, he was facing the many emotions of separation.

On the morning before Liam and Deb were supposed to depart, many of the people that lived and worked for Anne and Thomas had gathered to see them off and wished them well on their journey. One young girl had made a necklace for Deb.

She looked up at her and said quite innocently, "This will keep you safe."

"Thank you so much. It is beautiful." Deb put it on and the girl's mother smiled as she took her daughter's hand to lead her off.

As Liam watched Deb's face, his heart weighed heavy. The night before, William and some of the other men had spoken in private. A messenger had arrived with news from the king. It was addressed to Thomas, but in his absence, William had the power to read it and act on it if necessary. Deb had begun to get ready for the next day but Liam joined William and the others.

"There has been word that King Edward of England is planning on an attack in the Lothian region. King Robert is aware of it and he has told the people there to clear the land and leave it as desolate as possible. He does not want Edward's plan fueled in any way. When Edward arrives there with his army, Robert wants him to find nothing. It should throw him off."

Everyone, including Liam, was listening closely as William continued.

"We are hoping that the lack of supplies will curb his eagerness to continue into Scotland further. King Robert seems confident that Edward will not succeed, and has not yet revealed what he will do next, but we do know Robert has his eye on the area near Carlisle."

William took a confident breath and added, "For our king and the protection of Scotland, I ask for as many of you as we can supply to join the trip south to the King's location. We would leave within two weeks. We cannot take every man because of the need to secure the castle, but I ask that we take part in a drawing of straws to see who will go. With Thomas gone and the naming of the next earl for this territory not completed, I cannot enforce it, but in the name of honoring him alone, I ask for your loyalty to the king."

Some of the wounded men stood or sat while listening to William. One man looked around at the men who had fought so bravely for Thomas. He stood leaning on the makeshift crutch he had to help him and shouted, "I stand behind William. This leg can still ride on top a horse and my arms can swing a sword!"

The other men looked over at him and saw his determination even being wounded. Another stood and shouted as well. "Right then! I won't stand by while the English attack our king! I too shall fight beside William and the Bruce! Thomas deserves our loyalty now more than ever! Honor him and join us!"

The men all shouted agreeably and as Liam looked around at them, he felt the strongest feeling of loyalty he had ever felt. These men had muddy faces and wounds on their bodies. Their leader was dead and yet their hearts were so noble and so loyal that he felt humbled in their presence. He had grown up thinking that his life would be by his wife's side, raising a family, and now he was feeling compelled to join the men before him to fight with his king.

Liam and Deb were only nineteen and eighteen years of age, but their lives were quickly becoming filled with decisions that forced them to be stronger and wiser before their time. Deb thought about what her father had gone through when he was even younger than she and those memories of him brought a swelling of pride within her. They were following the example he left behind with his physical body.

There was no doubt that William would honor his word to send a few men with Deb as she made her way south, but Liam was still feeling distraught at the thought of leaving her to go and fight with the army. He made his way to their chamber, Liam closed the door behind them and Deb sat on the bed closing her eyes for a moment to focus. She was exhausted and both of them still smelled of battle. Liam sat beside her and gently embraced her. They looked at each other and even though they both wanted to cry, they had no tears.

Liam pushed Deb's hair back off her face and said, "Even when you're filthy, you're beautiful."

She smiled and said back, "I am sure that right now, I am not *beautiful*."

Liam took her by the shoulders and looked her straight in the eye, "You are, lass." He bowed his head and stood up, walking back and forth slowly in front of her, his mouth in a tight line and she knew right away something was wrong and he was about to tell her.

"Deb, the meeting…it was about…the king needs men and we drew straws and…"

She stopped him by taking his hand and making him sit again. "Liam, what was said by William?"

He looked at her and closed his eyes a spell. When he opened them, he answered, "Edward is forging on into lower Scotland and William has asked for a group of us to join Bruce to stop him."

She looked at the window and back at his face, "And you are one of the men going?"

He sighed and took her hand. He was being asked to leave her again after all they had been through, but how could a young man deny his support for a leader when he was just given the greatest gift of freedom and his young wife back in his arms. It was a debt that Liam was compelled to honour, but looking at Deb and knowing that they would again be apart was breaking him inside.

She stood and brushed his face with her hand. She walked to the window and gazed out upon the castle grounds.

Turning with a tear in her eye and her voice faltering she whispered, "Liam, I know what you are thinking and I am thinking it as well. We fought so long to find each other and now that we have, we are facing the thought of parting again. I can't tell you what to do and I refuse to make you feel guilty for whatever choice you make. I do want you to know that I will ride south and I will free those girls. I will fight for them if I must. Sarah, the girl I told you about is the oldest one among them and she is only fifteen years. I am only three years older than she, yet we have so many similarities in this life. She needs me, Liam. I can't turn my back on them and break my promise. It is not who I was raised to be. Father would want me to finish this."

"What will you do if you free them? If you take the castle, how will you get them back to their families? These girls may not even remember how to get home. Some of them will only know the region they are from."

She paused, "I will talk to some of the families along the way to the castle if I must. I may be able to find some of them. Once word of Gully's death is known, it will spread fast. If the girls can at least tell me where they were taken from, we can find their families. If I have to take some back to our home with me until their families can be given word, I will do it."

Liam looked at Deb and took her in his arms. She knew he had to follow his calling as well. She understood. She was content that time was standing still for them both, yet they had to face reality.

"I will return home as soon as I can. I must stand alongside William. He stood by us and is giving you the safety of his men as companions."

He took a deep breath. "I am your husband and I *will* be by your side again. We have been given this story for some reason. We must finish it and in the end, we will hold each other finally for more than a day."

Deb pulled Liam close and held him. She wept and squeezed him tightly. He was a caring young man. She knew the guilt of not going with her was killing him, but Scotland was at war and she wanted him to know that his choice was clear and unselfish.

She kissed him gently and said, "Don't forget my face, Liam. Let it guide you through difficulty. Stay strong and hold my heart close to you. I love you so deeply. We are both needed in places that have been chosen for us. Go with pride, husband and believe that we will see each other soon."

Liquid sorrow spilled from her eyes yet she stood without wavering. Liam put both hands on each side of her face and stared at her with an admiration so profound that he could not believe she was his.

That night, they allowed themselves the pleasure of each other's bodies one last time before the morning came. There was never a moment that they let go. Waking up in the comfort of the arms they loved so deeply, Deb and Liam rose together to face their demons head on.

Morning dawned and Liam watched as Deb and William's men road off toward the south. She turned as she rode away, blowing him a kiss. She was like an angel as her flowing garments danced atop Finnean's great stature. William walked up to Liam and placed his hand on his shoulder.

"She is quite a surprising young woman, lad. She will do us proud so do not fear for her. My men have strict instructions to protect her for I know the importance of this one. Many people will someday know her name...and yours. You have my greatest appreciation, Barne. A man that can capture the heart of such a woman and watch her ride away from him must himself be blessed. Come, we will drink and have dinner. Two weeks from now, we will be riding into battle with one of our greatest leaders. You should be proud, Liam. You are doing the right thing. We will take control of our own destinies together."

Liam nodded politely but with sadness behind his eyes. They turned to walk back into the castle courtyard. The night was calm and the air still smelled of the same lavender that Deb had tied into her hair. Liam closed his eyes for a second as they walked and took the very unique fragrance into his lungs making him feel rapture and sorrow at the same time. With his eyes closed, he could see his Deborah. When he opened his eyes, he saw the faces of the many men that would be his comrades in arms. They mingled with his visions of Deb, but she remained at the center of his thoughts.

He gained his composure and accepted the fact that his wife would have to give all of herself to the girls. Liam understood at a different level than most and he was so proud of her will. He knew she could not leave them there. He looked out at the men in front of him again. These were his people and they would fight together for Scotland's freedom. For this, Deb would be proud of him, he knew it. He held on to that thought and allowed her spirit to push him forward.

On the edge of the Grampian Mountains, Deb was feeling Liam in her very core. She wondered if they had truly made the right decision. She missed him already, but they had agreed to press on and fulfill their promises. Still, Liam's voice was in her ear and there was emptiness within her. She wanted to hold him. Steeling herself, she fought back tears and told herself to keep going.

Deb and her fellow riders stopped to rest. She wanted to know more about them if she was going to be with them for the next couple of weeks. She sat down on a stone beside the man who led them. He looked to be about forty years of age. He was wise behind his eyes and he held himself with a calmness that William knew would help Deb and her group. He was very stout with years of fighting under his belt. His name was Alexander and he had vowed to protect Deb and her crusade above all odds. He witnessed her skills first hand during the battle that killed Thomas and there was no question in his mind that she had earned his respect.

"Do you think we will make good time, Alexander?" Deb asked.

"Well lass, with Finnean leading the way, I dare say that we will be making very good ground!"

The others chuckled and agreed. Finnean was a good match for his beautiful rider.

Deb laughed back and said, "Yes, I do believe he will keep us working hard."

"How did you find a horse of such girth and strength?" Alexander asked.

Deb smiled again and stated, "We were brought together by angels, I suppose. He was one of the poor animals Gully decided to steal from someone. Although he cannot talk, he and I both know that our hearts we were meant to be together.

I am sure wherever he came from, someone misses him dearly, but he saved my life and I am forever bonded to him."

There were fifteen other men with them. Two men were of a similar age as Deb and two more were in their twenties. The rest of the group, she could not tell their age but they had been with Thomas and his family for years.

One of the men, David, walked over and sat with Alexander and Deb and asked, "How many do you think we will be against when we arrive, Deb? We had twenty or so, on the run from us, but how many do you think are still at Dominon?" David was not looking at her directly. This was unusual for any man to pull off around her, but he was polite as he fumbled around trying to find a place to sit.

Deb smiled at his slight awkwardness and thought about his question. She surmised, "Liam, his father, brother and I killed at least eight men before we reached the earl's castle and with the help of a local farmer and his son, a few more were taken down. I recognized some of them. I don't believe there will be many there. I do know however, that we will still be outnumbered. Their lack of experience and Gully's death will create confusion. Gully's second in command survived the battle, if I recognized him properly. His name is Angus and he will be the one I am the most concerned with when we arrive. I know not if he will be rebuilding Gully's tainted legacy. I can only say that he is not a man of honor. He followed Gully's same lust and it was he who tied the noose around my husband's neck. We must identify him first and kill him. The others are pathetic creatures that will fight hard and without skill. We must use our discipline and knowledge against them. When we reach the area, we will see the hill that will give us a vantage point without being seen. From there, we should be able to tell just how strong our enemy is. Bear in mind, Alexander, I may need to get closer to fully see what we need to in order to be victorious." She paused and added quite determinedly, "Those young girls deserve to be rescued as if they were of nobility. Most of them come from good homes and their families do not deserve the pain of losing them. I promised them, Alexander. I promised them I would return."

She bowed her head and placed her hand on his. "Thank you for helping me." She looked at everyone there. "Thank you to all of you. I am honored to have you by my side."

One man walked over and knelt down, placing his hand on Deb's shoulder. "Lass, you need not doubt our loyalty to you. We stand by you. You are one of us now."

Deb nodded and they all decided to keep on riding until the sun went down. Alexander reminded them to keep a watchful eye. Although they were far from the Lothian region where Dominon sat, the English may have riders on the lookout.

Upon reaching the River Tay, they watered the horses and decided to turn towards Fife and rode along the edge of the sea. Once close the Firth of Forth, they would ride down past Stirling, Glasgow and into the outer region of the Lothians past Falkirk. Beyond that, they would have to be very weary of the English army. Dominon Castle was then southeast on the edge between Selkirk and Berwick. It would be hazardous traveling, but Deb knew that the location of the castle itself was remote. This would be their saving grace.

On the journey past the River Tay, Alexander decided that they were making good time and they should stop and rest. Deb agreed, as it would do them no good to push themselves or the horses to exhaustion. They would need their strength when they arrived at their destination. Still, she was anxious to get to the girls. Who knew what fate had come to them after everything that had happened. She tried not to think the worst.

While in her thoughts, David walked over and handed her a vessel of water.

"Keep yourself watered as well, lass. It will keep your mind clear." She graciously accepted it and noticed his hand lingered upon hers for a moment after handing it to her. He walked away with a kind smile that held purpose as he checked the horses and spoke with Alexander.

They found a place to rest and one of the men heard a sound in the distance. It sounded like music. As they listened, it came closer and when they saw where it was coming from, they were surprised. On the edge of the hill ahead came a man leading two horses. He was alone and he was playing a flute as he approached. He didn't seem concerned with Deb and her group and he rode up slowly, a smile on his face at the sight of other people.

"Aiee! I be wondering when yu would all stop. I've been following yur path for an hour now!"

He was a strange looking man. He had a hump on his shoulder, his eyes were offset as if looking in different directions and his teeth were rotten. His clothes were humble and his horses were old, but sturdy. Their backs were laden with objects like kettles, spoons and jars of strange mixtures. A rope was wrapped around some odd looking papers and he had coloured ribbons and pieces of string bound together with straw. His feet were crooked and pointed outward and even though he was a sight to see, he smiled as he walked up to Deb and addressed her. His speech was cumbersome to say the least probably because his jaw and teeth were so out of sorts.

"Iee was hopin' to meet the lass that is said to have killed Gully MacDonell!" He was gracious despite his appearance and Deb looked at Alexander with confusion. How did this man know?

She dismounted from her horse and faced him. "How does someone find out about something that only happened days ago and so far away?" she asked.

The little man was surprised that she was unaware of her fame and he asked politely if he could approach her closer. She obliged but made him stay back. The men with her kept a watchful eye on him. David placed his hand upon his sword and moved toward Deb to protect her if needed. The little man appeared to have no weapons of any kind other than a small knife that was probably used to eat with and carve wood.

"Why lass, yu are becoming quite well known around these parts. I heard yu took him out with that fancy bow yu have. There was some that say they saw from the high ridges. A watchin' the battle they was! Some say yur quite the archer. Others say yu're the devil in a woman's dress!"

Alexander was becoming annoyed with him already and he shouted back down at him, "Mind your tongue man! This lady will not hear things of that nature against her name!"

The little man was frightened by Alexander's scolding and quickly apologized with an explanation.

"Oh sir! I mean no disrespect! It is just that some have the idea that she is a powerful one indeed!"

"Who told you of this? Where did you hear of it?" Deb asked.

He smiled excitedly and said, "Why it's all over the south. Families of the girls being held know of yer return. They have prayed for yu to arrive, lass. Oh yes, they have prayed."

Deb had had enough. She stepped forward into the man's face and yelled, "How do you know about the girls? How do you know that the families are aware of my return! Speak the truth now or I shall cut out your tongue!"

Alexander and the men sat back. They smiled knowing she could handle herself.

The little man bowed down whimpering to the ground and said in a fearful voice, "Ahhh, lass! Please don't harm me. I am a humble medicinal peddler. I mean no harm. I only know of this because the families I visit every month. Ah, please lass. That is all I know. I only know from the families! Well, and a few pub stories by sume bad men. I am tellin' yee the truth! I have spoken to no one else! I have heard it in my travels only, miss! I know of the dread that yu yourself must have been through because sume bad men talk loud on the drink! My travels give me many nights to talk…many nights to listen, ma'am! I listen a lot and I talk a lot. That's why I em a peddler, ma'am. Just a peddler with a big mouth to talk and big ears to listen! I mean no harm."

He was cowering and Deb knew that if he knew more, his fear would have made him say it. This one was nothing but an innocent traveler; a busy body peasant who made his life on the road. She still wondered how the families knew about Gully's death already, unless someone *had* been watching from afar that day. This little man must have a big mouth and travel fast over much ground. It seemed impossible, but maybe he didn't sleep very much and was constantly on the move...it was strange to say the least.

Alexander stepped in and said, "I believe that when men such as Gully's come from a battle as they did, there would be a lot of tales told, Deb. Surely it has spread amongst the people in this manner. Drunken nights make men speak of things they should not. They would have stopped quite a few times to taste their poison of choice. I think our plight may be better known than we think."

"Yes, I suppose this may be true."

She looked at the man that was in awe of her and yet terrified of her at the same time. He looked up at her and asked, "May I offer yu and yer friends something for yur journey?" He was obviously trying to make amends and asked for no payment in exchange. He was holding out a sack of something.

"Roots to make yur sore muscles better, lass. Please take it as a gift from me. Just mix with water and place on yur aches and pains."

He seemed sincere and Deb asked, "What is your name?" She took the bag, slowly looking inside carefully.

"I am Henry, lass. But me friends call me the Hen. Yes, I am said to walk like a chicken with my crooked legs, miss. Yes, I think 'tis quite a curious thing!" He seemed slightly insane Deb thought, as he pranced around on his crooked legs smiling and sweating. David was hovering, still uneasy, and watching over Deb as if taking on the role of her body guard. Alexander gave him a look to relax and David let his sword sit easy.

Deb thought about Mulden the slinky man who worked for Gully, but this poor soul before her was stricken with more than bad teeth and for him to do any wrong doing would be a contradiction to his demeanor. He had less courage than a flea. He seemed quite harmless; almost sweet and innocent.

"Alright, I do believe who you are, but if I catch word of you speaking of *this* meeting, I will track you down myself. Do you understand? You are not to tell anyone else!"

She knew that she would never harm such a person, but he needed to know that his silence was no joke. Stories passed down from person to person often became unclear and false. She did not want word of their presence getting to Gully's men either. Henry the Hen bobbed his head up and down and went back to his horse.

"I weel be keepin' to meeself, miss. No talk of this in the towns. Yes, I weel be a friend of yurs yu weell see! Yu weell see! Shhhh. I weel be quiet, miss. Yes, I weel. Good luck, miss!"

He hobbled back to his horses and continued to walk on. He kept looking back with a smile on his face, waving his hands back and forth saying, "I weel always be at yur service, yes? Until we meet again!"

He waved his crooked arm goodbye and Alexander and the men chuckled watching Henry hobble away. David finally relaxed.

They started riding once again with small breaks until they came to the area of the Lothian region. Deb wanted to enter the town of Dunbar as that was where Henry the Hen had heard of Gully's men last.

Alexander spoke up. "We need to find out more, but we can't risk being seen. Most of the men should make camp outside the town and I think it is David and I who should make our way in. You should not be seen yet, lass. We'll act as travelers, visit the pubs and stables. They may have tried to have repairs done to their weapons or even tried to get more. David and I will find out if there have been any recent sightings of them. We'll see if our little friend Henry was really telling the truth."

Deb was anxious and she tried to convince Alexander that she needed to be a part of it too. He knew she would be a difficult one to hold back as she stated, "My friend, I must come with you. They will not know me if in disguise. If these pigs have been here, I want to find out myself. I cannot allow you to do this alone."

"What if we find ourselves speaking to someone? You will stand out, lass." Alexander asked.

"I will be mute; injured in a fight. My tongue cut out. It will be believable and I will not falter. You can pass me as your son if needed."

Alexander thought about it and David agreed that it might work. Deb would have to tie her long hair back and dirty her face. Her beauty was noticeable from even long distances away. They tore a cloth and draped it over her shoulders with layers of straw underneath to make them look wider than a woman. She wore the boots of one of the other men and gloves on her hands as well as a well-worn hood that came down a bit over her face.

Alexander and David also made themselves look slightly more disheveled. They all stood back and looked at Deb. The men snickered and one chuckled, "Deb, you look almost as dirty as Henry the Hen!"

David smiled at her as well and chuckled but there was that strange look on his face again. It was like he was uneasy around her, but his loyalty so far was unmatched. He grabbed the reigns of his horse and mounted with a straight face while everyone else was still smiling.

Deb grinned and scratched her behind jokingly before mounting onto the back of Alexander's horse. "I will be in good character then! Come, let us go."

Alexander, David and Deb made their way into town on only two horses. Deb left the handsome Finnean behind as he too would draw attention to them. He was not a horse owned by poor travelers. The ones they rode were stripped of their soldier's gear and left with only a plain saddle, a couple of burlap bags, and a blanket attached. They rubbed dirt on their legs and hind quarters to make them look less cared for. A few muddy twists into their manes helped with the rugged look they were after. They would get a bath in the river later; for now they played a big role.

On the outside of town, the three friends noticed a local drinking hole right away. It was an important business to people who had nothing. Men would sit for hours drinking pints, brawling and telling stories. The drunker they got, the more money the owner made. Some nights, winning a fight won you a pint. It was also filthy; chickens walked the grounds and the path outside was so thick with mud they sloshed through it like it was quick sand.

Dunbar sat just south of Edinburgh. The area itself was dangerous at best with English close and war taunting the faith of everyone on both sides. Small pockets of rebels on the side of both good and treachery flowed through the seaside towns on the east coast of Scotland. You never knew who you would find sitting in a corner enjoying a drink while having a seedy conversation.

Treading lightly and keeping your mouth shut was a good idea in places, like the one Deb and her friends were about to enter. Many stains on the floor from the blood of those who did not heed this rule were a sign that this particular place was just the spot that dogs like Angus and his men would stop at. To see anyone of nobility walk through the doors would be unheard of. This was a place where the loud and rough frequented. As Alexander, Deb and David walked closer, they looked at each other and reminded themselves of the dangers. In full character, they sauntered like locals toward the door sloshing through the mud and walking through the few chickens that were picking away at the bits and pieces found at the doorway from crumbs and refuse flung out the door.

They made it to the door the owner came out with a bucket and threw its contents out onto the road. It reeked. They didn't want to know what was in it. The chickens and a couple of dogs showed up to fight over it. Alexander stepped into the doorway and Deb kept her head down as David opened it for her. She kept silent and did not make eye contact with anyone. Dust was thick in the air and smoke from pipes and the corner fire pit filled the room. It smelled rank and one could tell that these poor souls spent many nights and days drowning their sorrows here. It was far from the life of the MacDonell clan and it was easy to see how men like Gully could build a following. These were men cast aside from the rest of the world. Many of them were criminals and thieves. They were only interested in survival. They more than likely had no loyalties, or so Deb and the others thought.

As Alexander came up to the owner, he asked quietly for three pints of ale and took them over to a small table in the corner where David and Deb sat down. No one seemed to pay any attention to them yet and so they decided to stay quiet and just listen for a while. There were many people in the small room that day and the characters that were entertaining themselves were boisterous and obnoxious at best. If something were to be said of interest to Deb and her friends, it would surely be heard here.

David and Alexander leaned into each other with Deb in the middle and pretended to have a conversation. One man that was causing a lot of commotion in the corner stood up and challenged another that was with him to a wrestle.

"Aeee! Get up, yu fat bloke! I think yu weel be on the floor before I can sip my next pint!"

Everyone was laughing as they watched the two large men stand up and bend forward, ready to grapple each other to the floor. The other man laughed and his teeth were so rotten that they looked as if they would fall out right there. He reached out and the other man grabbed his arms so they were locked together. They pushed and pulled one another around in circles as the on-lookers cheered. They pushed over one of the small tables. One of the men flew down and grabbed the other's right foot bringing him crashing down on the dirty floorboards.

He shouted, "Awww! That was a dirty trick to pull on ye but I had to do something to bring down yer fat arse!"

Everyone laughed and as the dust settled they got up and shook hands but not before swatting each other around a bit. As they sat back down, another man started up a conversation. He was very drunk and as he spoke, he ground his knife into the table using it to emphasize his story's high points. His face was wrinkled and his beard, unruly. His fingernails were dark with dirt and Deb could smell his rank breath wafting to them on the still air. He was flatulent and belched as he spoke. No one seemed to care. None of them were much better off than he was.

"Yes, I think we Scots are goin' to kill off those English pigs! We won't let em' take Scotland! We won't!"

Deb, Alexander and David were surprised. The people in the room shouted and cheered. He had his audience for certain now. These were the types of men who once fought for William Wallace when most of the nobility were being held as English prisoners. It was men like these that stepped forward to take arms with their most decorated leaders. Although unskilled as soldiers, the farmers and poorer class of Scotland were made of grit and pride.

David whispered to Alexander and Deb, "Should never have judged them so quickly."

Unfortunately, in the case of Gully's men, some were also lured by coin and a lust for women. This was also the type of man that Deb thought to find here. They listened to the man as he continued his rant.

"So what should people such as us do? What can we do? We can stand beside our king! Robert is said to have amassed an army near Carlisle. I, for one, weel join him soon!"

Someone in the corner did not agree with the speech and he spoke in a low tone disrespecting the man's opinion. It was not taken well by people in the room.

"What shall we do if the Bruce fails?" The room went quiet as all eyes turned on the voice. The man sat forward and came into the light from the window. Deb was shocked and held her hand over her mouth to avoid her deep breath of surprise being heard. It was Druggan; one of the men who had been with Angus and Gully since they started their insanity.

"What do yu speak of? Do yu dare to disrespect the most noble of Scots in this room in front of us? He played the game with the English, but his true loyalty is with us now! He will not fail!" the very drunk, very loyal man snarled.

Druggan stood up and everyone could see his large stature. He was wearing a claymore by his side and he had on high quality leather gloves. His face was slightly cut, but healing and Deb, Alexander and David knew where he acquired those injuries. They remained calm and the three of them placed his rough face.

The man who was defending Robert the Bruce stood up too and looked as if he would strike Druggan, who moved forward a bit and added, "We need our own leader. I am not going to stand by and wait for the political gesturing of kings to determine my fate! Bruce has held hands with the English! What's to say he won't again?"

Druggan was not gaining friends in the room because Robert the Bruce had made enormous ground in the fight for Scotland and he had developed an iconic image with the poorer class. In the days that saw the end of Wallace, Bruce realized the ties between the English and Scottish nobility had to be severed even more. There was no reasoning at that point. It was known amongst men that Bruce knew this in his heart and it ached for some of his earlier decisions, but it was clear now. Robert the Bruce was fighting for the Scots. No one could dispute that.

Deb wanted to know why Druggan was still this far up north. She wondered why he had hadn't gone back to the castle. His speech was confusing. Was he trying to gain their support? Was he attempting to use their poor situation to pull them into his way of thinking? He was almost as insane as Gully, it seemed. His stupidity certainly showed.

The man who had started the conversation was also confused, but he stood his ground in front of his friends and answered back, "The Bruce was once a man of our breed! He too has worked the land and strived ta be who he is to us now! The Bruce weel not fail us! He is the King of Scotland. Yu say such things against such a man in this place? I should slit yur throat for such words of treason!"

Then another man looked at Druggan and he seemed curious. He stood up and got a closer look at the stranger and blurted out, "I know yu. Yu're one of Gully MacDonell's men. Ahh! Yu are no hero. Yu're a criminal! Yu're the one who took the farm from my friend in Dumfries! I was there! I was there! I saw yu're ugly face!"

A turn in the scene made Deb, Alexander and the others realize that maybe some of these men were not of Gully's brood after all. Some of them may be on the right side.

This man was drunk as well, but he knew what he was talking about. He was right and as the others in the room realized who Druggan was, they began to get agitated. The alcohol was making them braver than usual and this had not been a good place for Druggan to tout himself as a mercenary after all.

Realizing that this man had just endangered him, he turned and motioned to three other men that had been sitting in the shadows. They stood and drew their swords. The locals were feeling a sudden sobering amongst themselves as they realized who these men were.

The man who had identified Druggan was now regretting his sharp tongue and he backed down toward the door, but Druggan was no Gully. The others followed suit not knowing that he wasn't as big a threat as he appeared to be. Druggan seemed almost embarrassed, but his twisted logic made him turn and spout one more comment at the small group of villagers. He leaned toward the man who had recognized him and his face looked as if he would slice him right there. It was completely false but he couldn't leave with his tail between his legs.

In a commanding, deep voice Druggan said, "If yu were there when I took yur friend's land, small man, then yu know what we can do to yu if yu don't hold yur tongue! I weel not allow myself to be bothered with the garbage in this room. Yu speak of the king and pray for his success. Yu are all fools! You'll be knocking on our door for protection! Likely, when the time comes, we will leave you all to rot for your stupidity!"

Druggan's logic was looked upon as lunacy. He spouted of being part of the true leadership of Scotland while pillaging the very people he was standing in front of. Nothing he said made sense.

Even though not all of Scotland supported their king totally, these people were behind him and they felt as though Druggan was a wolf in sheep's clothing. Here before them stood a man who was a kidnapper, a rapist and a thief. Alcohol would always be a fuel that cemented a man's fate if not under control. Druggan's tongue would be his enemy tonight. His attempt at mirroring Gully's path was a failure at best. He picked the wrong watering hole.

He turned in anger and added, "If I hear of this conversation beyond these walls, you will soon regret it!" The people were cowering slightly and even the man who had started it all was sitting down and giving no resistance.

Deb, Alexander and David got up slowly after Druggan had left and they followed the enemy slowly as Druggan made his way to the edge of town. His horses were laden with bags and parcels. He had come for supplies and at first, he most likely thought Dunbar was a place where he would find no opposition. Most of the farms Gully had raided were so far from other people that they were almost easy to take. Stepping into a room full the followers of the Bruce was surely a mistake that Druggan couldn't repair. If Gully was alive, he would have, ironically, killed him for his idiocy. For now, it was back to Angus. One thing Druggan *did* know was that he couldn't survive on his own.

Deb mounted one of the horses and asked Alexander and David to make their way back to the campsite where the other men were. Alexander did not like this, but he knew that he had to trust Deb and her logic. She was the least likely to be noticed and she knew where she was going.

She followed slowly, far behind them, and dismounted as she came to a series of rolling hills. From behind a tree, she watched as Druggan and his men made their way south toward the castle. She made a note of their tracks and their exact direction.

Back at the camp, Alexander was readying his men. They would be four days out from the castle according to Deb and when she came back into sight, Alexander met her.

"Are we in good shape, lass?"

"Yes, we will be following clear tracks if we move now. We must be careful to stay back. Druggan made many motions to look behind him as he rode and he appeared very weary. He'll be rethinking his ranting. I think he will simply run back to Angus once he realizes what he just did while under the spell of ale. When he sobers up, he's going to be sorry."

"Alright then, let us take our leave. Remember that we will move in a straight line. We don't want to appear as a large group if sighted from afar. Be swift and stay alert. Keep your eyes on the area around us at all times."

Deb cleaned her face with a cloth and let her hair back down. She wanted a bath terribly. They were all smelling like death after the riding and traveling, but the men didn't seem care and she readied her weapons as they did. She took her place behind Alexander and in front of David at the beginning of the line. They had been instructed by William to try and keep her between two of them at all times. Alexander would not allow harm to come to Deb if he could help it, but he had the feeling she would not be easily reigned in. He could see why one would become enamored with her charm and intelligence. His feelings for her were growing into that of a father figure, but he did notice her beauty. He wondered how proud her father must have been. He vowed to himself to be her guardian through anything that came upon them. Alexander caught David's gaze as well, but his was far from a look of fatherhood. It was no secret how David's demeanor around Deb changed and it made him slightly concerned. David had always been loyal, but he was acting a bit strange. Alexander furrowed his eyebrows trying to make sense of it, but he pushed it aside as his attention shifted to fall upon the view in front of them. They had been on such a long journey already. He must keep them all focused.

Almost two weeks had passed since Liam had said goodbye to his wife once again and William had ridden his men south to meet with the Bruce's army. When they arrived, William had given notice that he would like to address the king with news from Thomas MacDonell's castle. He knew that telling him the entire truth may not be to his advantage, but he also felt the need to be worthy of the king's trust. He thought about what he would say and how he would say it. Robert the Bruce knew Thomas well and the news would be disturbing to say the least.

As William rode among the men, he saw the mass of soldiers that Robert had brought together there on the fields outside Carlisle. It made his heart race. A sea of Scottish soldiers were preparing weapons and practicing their fighting skills. The hills were filled with horses and tents. As William made his way toward Robert's location, he looked down and saw a young boy working. He must not have been more than twelve years of age and William's heart weighed heavy as he thought about what he was really seeing on these fields. This country would not fall before its enemy easily. This was not a war for one piece of land. This was a war to secure their children's future. This army was taking its place as a defender of the Scottish way of life and the freedom that came with it. Scotland needed its nobles to make a stand. William was honored to be there defending the highlands that he called home and his lowland neighbors who would soon be connected to the highlands forever in his mind.

From his horse, William could see the tent in which the king was waiting. He dismounted and walked respectfully the rest of the way. He caught the attention of some of the soldiers as he walked up to the entrance. William was a man of great stature despite his physical height. He carried himself like nobility. The way he dressed and the beautiful sword by his side let the other men know that this man was a leader. They stepped aside and as William asked for permission to enter the tent, he heard a voice that drew him in.

"Come, enter!" Robert the Bruce sat on the other side of the tent. He was surely the King of Scotland and as William drew the attention he did, there could be no mistaking Robert amongst the men as well. He was a strong, dark man with a brow that was stern and steady. His eyes were determined and wide. William was standing before his king.

He knelt on one knee. "King Robert, I bring word to you as my men and I join your forces. It is not news that I am pleased to have to bring."

The king was impressed by William's presence. He knew of his place beside Thomas

MacDonell and was looking forward to meeting with him one on one, but when William spoke, Robert's mood changed.

"What do you have to say?" Robert sat forward curiously and as William began, he grew troubled.

"Sir, Thomas MacDonell is dead. It took place only a couple of weeks ago on the fields outside Inverness."

Of course the king would not accept that as the entire story. He said quite bluntly, "How did he die?"

William was nervous and decided that to lie to the king would come back on him in the future. No, he had to explain the situation as best he could.

"Thomas and Anne MacDonell had a son. Had you known of him?"

Robert stated, "Yes, but he was not heard of for years. The earl and I hadn't spoken about it. I often thought he was dead. What are you trying to tell me?"

William took a deep breath, "Thomas' son's was a troubled man in his youth and it became apparent to Thomas and Anne that their son was too much to deal with. He was banished from the castle, your majesty. Thomas demanded that no one ever speak of him again. It was a cold day however, when it became known to Thomas that Gully's dealings were of a criminal nature."

Robert wanted to know more and he asked quite sternly, "What had he done?"

William could see the king's anger and he quickly denoted that Gully himself was also dead.

"Gully was angered by his father's decision to disown him and he took revenge. They met in combat and neither survived."

William was hoping that this would be sufficient to Robert as he did not want to draw attention to Deb's plight. Even though he knew that the king could bring swift recourse to Gully's men, there was more to the story than hunting down a few men and punishing them. If the king sent his men to assist Deb and Alexander, it was sure to be noticed, risking the rescue. It was too much to explain and William felt the need to keep silent about the girls. He knew that if Deb and Alexander could be given the chance, it could mean redemption for them all that came well deserved. William had carried his friend's body off that field. Not only was Thomas' body broken but his spirit had been as well. William was trying hard to tell the truth, but protect Thomas' good name at the same time so he held his tongue. A spoiled, rejected son was easier to depict than a thieving, traitorous rapist; a young, insane man who hated his king would be more than just a disgrace to Thomas. William's main purpose and intention was to defend his country and support his king.

Robert was saddened by the tidings and he stood up, walking over to a table to pour a goblet of wine for himself and William. He asked for the men to leave so that they may speak further in private.

"You stood by Thomas' side when it happened?" Robert was still asking questions and William was hoping to change the subject toward him and his men.

"Yes sir." William did not divulge much more. He wanted the conversation to end now.

"I see. Thomas MacDonell was a good man. Their clan has given of themselves loyally to fight the English. The Lord of the Isles endorsed it years ago and I have never regretted it. I believe Thomas has chosen a man of honor to be by his side." The king was making reference to William and he knew it nodding respectfully.

"Sire, I have ridden from Thomas' land with fifty of my best men. We are not a large group, but we come with the intention of giving you our loyalty. We are of your company now, King Robert. We fight for Thomas MacDonell to honor his name."

"We are always in need of good men. You can take your place up the center and with the men on the top of the hill. They will give you instruction. I thank you for your presence, William. You will be given a high rank of course, and your men will be given the standard wage. We break camp in three days."

"Thank you, my king. We are honored to join you and your men." William backed out and Robert sat back down to think about what he had just been told. There would be talk of a new earl for the MacDonell clan to the north now that Thomas was gone and no sons were there to lay claim to the title. Talks with the Lord of the Isles would be included in due time. He sipped his wine and thought about his old friend but King Edward of England was moving into the Lothian region and King Robert and his men had much to plan. There was no time for reminiscing.

Liam rode to the top of the hill where most of the horses were being held. He and William met with their new commanding officer and as the sun set on the men, Liam had but one person on his mind.

"*Where are you Deb?*" he said to himself. Liam gazed out on the open fields and could picture her riding over them toward him. His chest burned for her. His eyes were sodden with tears and he wished that she was there in his arms. He dreamed of her beautiful face and calmed his beating heart. Before he knew it, he was in a deep sleep. The long journey to Carlisle had made them all weary.

The night was calm and while they could, the men rested. Their new life for the next while had just begun and Liam prayed for Deb and the others.

Further north, Deb and Alexander were still following Druggan. It was getting too dark to see any longer. They had managed to stay back far enough, but now the area was changing to swampy open land and Deb remembered it well as they came upon it.

They bedded down where there was shelter and slept as much as they could. It wasn't easy to stop, but lack of sleep would be their greatest enemy. David was the last to lay his head down, but before he did, he walked over to Deb and placed another blanket upon her.

"So that the dampness of the night stays away, Deb. And the mornings can be damp as well. This will help."

Deb looked up and thanked David. "What about you?" she asked.

He just smiled with a sullen grin and answered, "I'm fine. You just get some sleep."

She wondered why David had been so serious since they left. He wasn't usually this way, but she was grateful for his kindness. If anyone should be this way right now, it should be Deb. She rolled over and made sure Finnean was settled before closing her eyes. She pictured Liam's face once again and this time, she could not hold back the tears.

It woke her up and she caught herself before making too much noise. She wiped her eyes and took a deep breath, gathering her senses. She missed Liam so deeply and the quiet of the night just made it worse as she felt alone. At least when they were travelling, she had the girls on her mind. She finally laid her head back down upon a blanket she had rolled up.

As the crickets and frogs sang them to sleep, Alexander had been watching the whole thing. He glanced between David and Deb, and then the other men, and wondered about the interaction he had witnessed. He felt confident that Deb was still holding herself together. He knew her heart was aching and he felt a great admiration for one so young to be able to carry on. As for David, Alexander saw a pining within his eyes. The young man had lost his own wife not too many years before and Alexander felt it was possible that David was taking pity on young Deb. He knew what it was like to lose the one you love and Alexander realized that he would have to keep watch on the two. They must stay focused.

In the morning they continued on without missing a step.

"We must stay further back, Alexander. There is a path that will show itself soon through those trees. There will then be a hill that stands quite high above the area of the castle. The land curves up from a valley into another hill where the castle sits. It lies above very boggy ground and we must leave the horses near the entrance where the two towers stand. The guards keeping watch must be taken without noise. If they have the chance, they will ring a bell that will signal Angus and the others inside."

David spoke up and asked, "Deb, how can we be certain that Angus and all of his men are there? I know we followed Druggan, but we cannot be sure that they did not see us and are waiting to ambush us."

"You are wise to wonder, David." Deb thought this would be a move of caution well recognized and added, "Come, let us keep the men back and you and I will take three others on foot to scout the castle. We can get within site of the main courtyard from the hill over there."

Alexander was content to go slowly and make certain that they knew what, and whom, they were attacking. He wondered if taking them by night would be better, but for now, they would at least see where they stood. He trusted Deb's knowledge of the castle and gave her his best men.

"Be aware, lass. David could be right. If they *did* see us following them, we must be ready for anything."

Deb, David and the others made their way quietly through the trees and down into the valley toward the castle. Deb knew a place on the wall that did not have a clear view in one direction. It was not a very large gap, but it would be enough for them to get closer undetected. Deb was wondering more and more as they went if she should get inside somehow to find the girls. She wondered if it were doable knowing that if found, she could ruin everything they planned.

"David, I can't see much movement." Deb was concerned. It was hard to hear anything and although she noticed two guards at each of the towers, she had not seen anyone else yet.

Along the first wall was the great hall. There were two tall windows that gave it light. It was located on the second floor and the windows were twenty feet up or more. Deb decided to see if there were enough vines up to them that she could climb to look in. It was going to be very risky. If she fell or made any noise at all, they would be discovered quickly. What made it worse was the fact that she would have to cross a small moat.

"If I do this and succeed David, it will mean a great advantage and I must try to find Sarah. She is the one that will know what I need to know. She is the eldest of the girls and I trust her to be steadfast when we attack. She could organize the others and make our task much more efficient."

David looked at Deb's determined face and remembered it well when they were on the field the day she killed Gully. He could not help but believe in this girl. She was driven and he agreed to stay back, but not before speaking with Alexander.

"Deb, please. Allow one of us to tell Alexander. He must know of this change in plans. He has given William his word to protect you and in Alexander's absence, it is I who is responsible for the task. We can't do this without telling him."

"I know. I am sorry for putting you in this position. I will wait, but we cannot afford to lose much more time," Deb stated.

As they waited pensively, one of the men slithered quietly backwards until he could stand up again to run to Alexander. As Alexander saw him approach, it made him uneasy. He thought that something was wrong.

"Alexander, Deb would like to make a change to the plans. She feels that she needs to get closer to the castle." He paused, as he knew what Alexander's reaction would be.

"She wants to try and gain access to the great hall by climbing a group of vines. We believe she can do it. There is some cover for her there and if she can find the girl named Sarah, it will be most beneficial to us."

Alexander was not happy with Deb's idea, but he realized that they might not have a choice. They needed to know more and the only way to do so was to gain access within.

He looked at the young man and said with apprehension, "Tell David that he must be cautious. He must watch her and be ready to pull her quickly. She must not take a lot of time. It must be done swiftly and she must get out as soon as she finds out anything."

"I pray that this will work as well, sir. If we are found out, we may need to be ready to fight sooner than we thought."

"Yes, tell David that we are at the ready. If there is any sign of trouble alert me at once with the horn."

"Yes sir. We shall for certain."

At the riverbank, Deb was breathing deeply and calming herself. She was nervous because she would be responsible if she failed. What was worse, she was putting them all in even more danger, including the girls if they were still inside.

When the soldier returned with Alexander's acknowledgement of the plan, Deb readied herself. David placed his hand on her shoulder and said, "Take it slowly, lass. We'll be right here. Tread lightly."

David and the others stayed low as Deb slithered on her belly through the grass. She was the smallest and quick with her movements making her the best person for the job. David knew that he could not hold her back even if he tried to. She knew this place better than any of them and so he gave her full support with the men at his side ready to protect her if needed.

At the top of the hill, Alexander's lookout managed to catch the sight of three horsemen riding slowly along the edge of the forest. He rushed to Alexander and stated that they didn't look like any of the men they had seen in Dunbar. Still, Alexander was reluctant to be seen and motioned for his men to hide. As they did, his gut felt an uncontrollable urge to warn David and Deb, but he knew that he could not risk being seen or heard. They stayed back keeping watch over the three riders coming nearer. Once closer, they appeared to be slowing down. When they were within range of Alexander and his men, they dismounted and walked cautiously along in the shelter of the trees with their horses walking behind them in single file.

In the middle of the line, Alexander noticed a figure that seemed familiar even at the distance they were away from them. With a gasp of surprise, he noticed the strange gait of the man. Suddenly, Alexander realized who it was. Henry the Hen was with the other two. They didn't look anything like Druggan's crew. He kept his men back and decided to meet them himself, but he too stayed in the cover of the trees. He walked on foot and made his way, ducking in and out from the trunks with his sword drawn. As the three men were about to approach Alexander's position, he came out from behind the tree and held his sword out to caution them. When Henry saw Alexander, his face lit up. The other two men tried to keep him quiet. It was as if they did not want the men in the castle walls to see them either.

Henry trotted off ahead a few feet keeping his exuberance at bay, but when he met Alexander face to face, he was jumping around as he had done the first time they had become acquainted. Alexander quieted Henry, and the little man stated quite bluntly, "Sir! I have two men with me to help yu!"

Alexander was puzzled. He wondered how Henry knew where to find them. As well, he was warned not to speak of their meeting. It angered him. One of the men walked forward as well and addressed Alexander.

"Sir, I am Patrick Murray. This is my son, James. We ask that you pardon our presence as we are aware of your journey and ties with the lass, Deborah Barne."

The man put his head down and with a look of determination in his eyes finished with, "My son and I have come to assist you, if you will accept it. We have heard of the death of Gully MacDonell and my silence could no longer be controlled. My daughter, Isabella, was taken from us a year ago. He beat my son and I before tearing her out of her mother's arms. Before he left, he promised that my son would be the next if I spoke to anyone. He had many men with him and I was helpless to save her. Henry knew that I was looking for my daughter and told me of the woman who could save her. He knows that you have silenced him, but I have known Henry for years and I forced him to tell me what he knew…if anything. When he told me that he saw you on the trail, we started following your path immediately. We have told no one else, I swear it."

Alexander was trying to take in what the man was saying while being angry with Henry for speaking of their meeting. They explicitly told him to stay quiet. Just when Alexander was about to scold Henry, Patrick spoke again in his defense.

"Sir, please don't punish him! He is a simple man who means no harm. He has been quiet about your presence here. I am the one who pried information from him. He sees many things in his travels. He was terrified to tell me anything, but I told him that if he guided us here, I would make certain that no harm would come to him."

Henry was cowering under Patrick and Alexander's strong brow began to soften. He believed them and could see that they were there to help.

"Have you spoken of us or any of this to others?"

"No sir, I have not. I wanted to, but I know of the damage these men can do. I did not wish to bring it upon anyone else, or to endanger you. I only came to find my daughter."

Alexander figured that the man didn't comprehend how many other girls Gully had stolen.

"Our mission here is not only to take down the remaining men who worked for Gully, but to rescue five other young girls. Deb Barne and some of my men are scouting the castle as we speak. We must stay in the cover of the trees until they return. I will accept your help, but you must know that there will be confrontation. Can you and your son fight?"

The man signaled for his son to come closer. He pulled back the blankets around the sides of their horses to reveal many weapons.

The boy spoke very clearly, "I have come to save my sister, sir. My father has taught me in the ways of battle even though I am only fifteen years of age. The man named Gully MacDonell beat me, but I am here to show them that I am now a man who will not stand by and allow this any longer."

The boy was a bit shaky, but his father placed a hand on his shoulder and Alexander could tell that they had been waiting for an opportunity to break their silence. He could not take that from them and they deserved it.

"So be it then, lad. There is a fine line between revenge and redemption, I hope that your sister sees what a brave brother she has, and I pray that she is there with the others."

Alexander then looked at Henry. "You are an honorable little man, Henry. Do not fear me. If you wish to assist us, you shall."

Henry looked relieved and nodded his head up and down as Alexander spoke.

"You will need to go to the castle towers for me."

Suddenly Henry's face looked white. He was terrified of getting closer to the castle. He had heard so many stories of Gully recently, that he begged Alexander to allow him to stay back with the men.

"Pleeeeeese sir! I am afraid. Yes I am! I only come to bring these men. Eeee! Please sir, please don't make me. The men are bad, sir! Yes, they are bad. They weel chop off mee crooked legs!"

Alexander put his hand on Henry's bobbing head and said, "Henry, calm yourself. They will not harm you. I only want you to pretend to be offering your goods to them. They will not harm someone such as you. You can show them your medicines. Just be yourself. I am sure you will have a story or two you could tell them. I just need you to distract them."

Patrick and his son smiled a bit as Alexander was making light of Henry's awkwardness. They knew he was only humoring the little man who seemed proud when someone recognized his strange, but valid talents.

Alexander made his way back with his three new recruits and the other men held steadfast as they approached. Alexander introduced them all and explained his plan once Deb and David had returned with what they had seen. Now it was time for patience and they waited quietly in the cover of the trees.

At the moat's edge, Deb was making progress. As she crept slowly, she could finally hear some sounds. She would pause every few feet and listen carefully. Deb found her way to the edge of the moat and made certain to look in all directions, including up. She saw no one and decided to slide into the water. It was unclean to say the least and the smell was not something she expected. On the edge of the moat was a patch of reeds and cattails. Deb thought that putting most of her head under the water, it would help to keep her wake minimal. She broke a large reed off and placed it in her mouth. Submerging most of her face, she started swimming carefully.

Halfway across, she had to stop and take a breath of fresh air. The water smelled worse than she thought the closer to the castle wall she went. Continuing on, the disgusting thought came to her. She was swimming where they had thrown out their feces and urine; not to mention Kearney's body. Deb closed her eyes and fixed her energy on the faces of the girls inside. She had to be strong. She could not fail them now. As she neared the wall where the vines were growing, David made certain that there were no threats to her as she climbed. They signaled each other and when David replied that he saw nothing, Deb started up the thick vines.

There were some sharp shards of rock sticking out as her hands felt for a spot to grab and she cut the skin of her hands more than once. It did not bother her as she neared the window's edge. Looking through the opening, Deb listened carefully. She wanted to hear a familiar voice, see one of the girls cleaning or anything that would tell she had not been too late.

Suddenly, a loud male voice was coming into the room. Deb ducked her head down below the window opening and waited. David and the other men were shocked to see one of the men come right to the window and look out. Deb clung precariously to the vines and stone, trying desperately not to move. Her hands were sore from the cuts of the stone and it was all she could do to hang on as the dirty vines dug into the wounds. She winced and pressed her lips tightly to quiet herself. She breathed slowly and held on.

The man that had come to the window was none other than Angus. Deb listened to him being angry about the incident in Dunbar with the town's people and he was acting as Gully had when something did not go his way. He slammed his fist onto the window ledge. There were some damaged stones around the frame that fell and hit Deb on her head. She shook them off and as David became restless to watch, Angus left the room. David signaled Deb again that the room seemed clear and she looked in slowly.

With a good grip, she waited and shortly after his departure, she heard Angus shout at someone. "Get in there and clean that mess up!"

Not moments later, a small girl ran into the room with her rags and broom. It was Angelica. Deb remembered her. She was not more than thirteen years of age and her timid face made Deb's heart ache.

For a moment, Deb thought that she would just observe, but the vines were beginning to be difficult to hold onto and Deb wanted inside more than anything. The window's ledge smelled horribly. It had remnants of the refuse that had been thrown out the window time and time again. Deb's stomach was telling her that if she held on much longer with no clean air, she would vomit for sure. Wrapping the vine around her wrist and getting a decent hold, she let go with the other hand and tapped on the window with a chunk of stone.

Angelica looked around wondering what the sound was. Then, she noticed the figure at the window. She gasped! She could see Deb's face from where she was standing and she rushed over to her looking back at the room's entrance. Opening the dirty window fully, she was frantic at the sight of Deb.

"Shhh lass, it's really me. Help me in. Keep yourself together!" Deb whispered to the girl and as she helped pull Deb in and over the window ledge, she began to weep and wrapped her arms around her. She then noticed how badly Deb smelled.

"Don't worry, it's not me. I had to swim through the river's filth. It was the only way I could gain entrance. Are you alright, Angelica?"

The girl's face was elated but confused. Deb tried to calm her down and explain that there were others outside in the area waiting to take the castle. She cautioned Angelica to be quiet and hold her tongue. She did not want to draw any attention. Deb stepped back behind one of the large hanging curtains and told Angelica to continue working while she spoke to her and asked questions. If anyone entered the room, Angelica would tell them, she was singing to herself.

"I need to know if Sarah is still here."

"Yes, she is here, but she is injured."

Deb frowned and asked quickly, "What is wrong with her?"

"She was saucy with the man at the gate and he slapped her. She fell onto the ground and broke her wrist. We wrapped it up tightly and it seems to be getting better, but it pained her so for a long time. They make her continue her chores even though she cries out in pain. She often spoke of you, Deb!" She lifted her voice with emotion and Deb calmed her again.

"Angelica, you must stay quiet and think clearly. Remember what I told you a long time ago?"

"Yes."

"What was it I had said to you?" Deb was trying to make her think to keep her steady.

"You said that if you breathe deeply and focus on the task at hand you will never lose control."

"And what else?"

"And if you stay calm, you stay strong."

"Exactly. That is what I would like you to do. Finish here and go to Sarah. Do not tell her about me yet. Just tell her you need help in the hall. Inform her that Angus ordered it and she'll come right away."

"Alright, I will."

Angelica finished her work quickly and ran down the hallway. Five minutes or so later, she returned with Sarah. As she walked into the room, she was confused by Angelica's request as the room appeared fine. She continued to look around and then Deb stepped out from behind the curtain slowly holding her pointer finger over her mouth to quiet Sarah's reaction.

Sarah's eyes opened wide and the smile on her face said it all. She ran to Deb and embraced her tightly. Deb looked at Sarah and examined her wrist.

"Are you alright, little sister?" Deb was happy to see Sarah as well.

"I am now, Deb. I knew you would come back! I knew you would! After we found out that Gully was dead, we didn't know what was going to happen! Deb, we have lost two girls to fever. I prayed night after night that you would come. Some of the girls wanted to try and escape, but I told them that they would only perish."

"Well, this will not be easy, lass. I have men outside in the forest waiting, but we must be smart about our plan. I cannot stay. I must go back with them, but I needed to know what we are up against. How many men have you seen in the last few weeks?"

Sarah thought carefully and said, "There are at least forty men. Some of them came back from the highlands with Angus and the others have been here with us. When Angus returned, there was chaos. The men argued about what had happened and what they wanted to do next. Angus told them all that he would continue to pay them if they stayed on. This is all that I know. Angus has made a few trips to the north. I believe he was not only finding supplies, but he must be trying to get more men. So far, I have not seen any new faces, just those of

Druggan and his few men who returned shortly after Angus. Angus was angry with Druggan for not bringing anyone else back with him. I think he feels weakened."

Deb nodded up and down as she listened. "This is good. Sarah, you must inform the other girls of our presence, but there must be no recognition of it in front of Angus and his men."

Deb realized that she had so many questions for Sarah. She wanted to know what happened after she left. Were any of them harmed and how were the rest of the girls? But she did not have time to satisfy her curiosity for details. Only the basics must be known and then she must leave and take her place with Alexander. He was probably sick with worry while wondering what was happening.

"Sarah, is everyone alright and able to flee if necessary?"

"Yes. But there is a young girl named Isabella who has been ill. I fear she has taken on the fever as well, but I have been by her side caring for her. I think I can encourage her to be strong. She will need help if you need her to run or ride a horse."

"Alright, keep her with two other strong girls tonight. When the men want their dinner, bring them all much to drink. If you can place valerian in the wine as I showed you before, do so. We will strike when you hear me howl from the hill. Do you understand? Listen from your window and get ready."

Sarah nodded yes. Deb added, "You must try and get the girls to the front of the great hall once the fighting begins. The men will not have time to watch you. Tell the girls to be quick on their feet. There will not be time for crying or carrying on, Sarah. They must be strong! You must make them strong!"

"I will, Deb. I will make sure of it. When they hear that you are back, they will gain strength they have not felt in weeks. None of us has ever given up faith. You taught us that."

Deb held Sarah tightly and said softly, "I am proud of you, Sarah. Do not have fear in your heart. Fill yourself with power and courage."

Sarah looked up at Deb and she nodded. Deb turned and said goodbye to her, made her way out the window and down the wall again, slowly. She wasn't looking forward to the wretched water, but her mission had been successful and it drove her to get back to David.

On the other side of the moat, David and the other men were relieved to see Deb as she reached their location. They all crept quietly away and made their way back to Alexander.

As Deb rode back up to the main group of men, she had a few moments of deep emotion. She felt an enormous emptiness without Liam by her side and yet the anger that raged within her for Gully and his men was pushing her forward. It was as if she would burst if she didn't find an outlet for it all. As they approached Alexander and the others, she saw Henry and the two strangers. Alexander rode forward to Deb immediately to explain quickly. Henry was bouncing on his spot at the sight of Deb. She and David spoke to Alexander in private to the side and the others stayed mounted and kept quiet.

When the three joined the group, Deb went straight for Finnean. He nudged her but seemed a bit annoyed by her scent. So she went behind a tree and put on some dry clothing. She brushed her hair as best as she could with the wooden comb she had with her and rubbed her skin down with mint that grew sparsely beneath the trees. When she regained her composure, she spoke quite bluntly to the other men.

Addressing Patrick and his son first, her voice was stern and serious. She was focused and everyone could see the energy building within her.

"I am sorry for the pain you and your family have been put through, Patrick. I can tell you that your daughter is alive if her name is Isabella Murray."

Patrick and James opened their eyes wide and their faces became tense.

Deb continued, "She is ill with fever, but the others have been taking care of her. She will be feeble to move when we strike. I was able to climb the wall and find two of the girls in good health. One of them will organize the others and they will be ready in the great hall while we take on Angus and his men."

She lowered her head and stated, "We have a large job to take on, my friends. There are forty of them inside the castle walls and we are a mere twenty. I do believe that we must do this in an organized manner. If we make our move in a couple of hours, it will be our best chance. It is getting dark and they will be settling in with their regular food and drink. The girls have been instructed to give them as much as possible. My hope is that it will dull their senses."

Alexander spoke up and added, "We must find this *Angus* immediately. He must not be allowed to flee again."

Deb looked over to Alexander and said, "Yes, but I know that he will have men around him.

It will be difficult. My bow and arrow will be of no use in close combat, and I must be with you within the castle walls. I know of the castle's rear escape route that was built for clergy and nobility that stayed here. There is a tunnel in the north side of the castle. There is a small door that leads off of the main hallway toward the great hall. That is where Angus may try to retreat, should he decide that fleeing is his only chance once again. He knows we will be after him. He is evil, but he is no fool. I often thought that he was more cunning than Gully at times. Be watchful of him."

David spoke up and said, "I will take on the task of finding him. If I must I will follow him if he flees. Two men will need to stay with me for this task."

Alexander thought this to be a good idea, but it would be difficult for them to gain access to the inside once the fighting began. He agreed nonetheless. David was a great fighter and his ability to track was even better. If Angus did flee and was able to gain ground, David would find him.

"How will we get past the guards at the gate?" another man asked.

Alexander stepped over to Henry the Hen who had been standing off to the side wriggling in his boots with wide eyes. He was terrified.

"Why, our good friend Henry will play an integral part in that task," he announced.

Henry smiled nervously with his rotten teeth showing. His bulging eyes were looking everywhere. He looked at Deb and mustered the courage to say, "Yes, I weel help. If me lady Deb can face the bad men, then I weel too. Awww!" He swallowed, "Then I weel too." Henry looked petrified and everyone was smiling as the scared little man stood up as straight as his crooked back would allow. He walked over to Deb and looked up at her humbly.

"Miss, Henry weel help. I em smart with me tongue and I weel do ya a very good job. Yes, I weel."

She smiled down at him and he lowered his head as if he were her dog. He was an innocent, ugly little man, but he had heart. "Thank you, Henry. You will do just fine. Do not be afraid."

Henry smiled again and walked back over to his horse. Patrick and James stepped forward. "What will Henry do then?"

Alexander looked at Henry. "I ask that you take your horse and peddling items up to the men. They will see you coming and know you are of no threat to them. Let them say what they will to you, Henry. Show them potions, your medicines and your roots. Offer them a deal because you have been nearing the end of this trip. Tell them that you are the only peddler of this nature in the area. Keep them talking and take their attention away from the right side of the castle's path. There, Deb will be ready with her bow. She will strike the first man and I will come from the left among the trees to strike the second. You must stay quiet, Henry. No screaming. You must get out of the way quickly once Deb hits the first man. Take cover up the trail and join the group."

He put his hand on the gnarled shoulders of the little man and said calmly, "You will no longer be known as Henry the Hen."

Henry looked up curiously and Alexander added, "You will be known as Henry the Brave."

Henry smiled so widely that the largest crooked tooth in the front of his mouth stuck out over his bottom lip. "That would be nice indeed! Yes, it weel be nice indeed."

"And now men, I ask for your bravery and your clarity of mind. I would like half to come in behind Deb and half to follow me on the other side of the path. Once we reach the gate, you will hide tightly against the walls." He did not like what he was about to say, but it would be the only way they would open the gates.

"I am going to act as Deb's capture. I will tell the guards that I caught her and brought her back for Angus. Once they open those gates, we will have to rush within. It will be messy and you must take as many men down as you can. Hold nothing back. Remember Thomas. Remember your fellow soldiers and friends who were cut down by the men within these walls."

Everyone was morose but a look of determination fell upon the group. Deb stepped forward and looked at the men. She too showed signs of anxiousness.

"You are my friends now. I do not look upon you as strangers. I am honored to have you with me. Without you, I could not attempt this on my own. Thank you for helping me."

Patrick and James stepped forward and Patrick said, "If you weren't here lass, we would not be either."

Deb nodded in respect and they all tried to stay calm and think about the task ahead. Soon, Henry would be making his move and Deb and Alexander would have to succeed in killing the two guards without being heard.

The sun was falling quickly and the evening brought on a light fog that rolled along the ground like smoke. It would be beneficial to their plight.

Deb stood below one of the trees preparing for the first blow. She was holding in so much emotion that it was beginning to wear on her. For a brief moment, she was not there at Dominon Castle. She was holding Liam and he was safe and as she closed her eyes to picture him, a tear wept slowly down her sturdy cheek. She wondered why it had come to this. The child within her wished that she could go home and be with Liam, but the woman inside knew that life was not that easy. She heard her father's words telling her that she could defeat her fears if she could see them clearly and understand that each time she faced them, she would become stronger.

Chapter Fourteen
Eyes Wide Open

Cheryl Alleway

The sudden hand on her shoulder made her open her eyes quickly. It was Alexander.

"Lass, it is time."

Deb nodded and wiped her face. She straightened her back and walked toward the path. Alexander motioned to Henry and he too made his way toward the castle towers.

The men separated and moved slowly and quietly to their positions as well. They all watched as Deb and Alexander drifted into the trees. They stopped and lowered themselves into a ready position. They could see the guard towers and as the faint sounds of two owls calling within the night were heard, they knew that Alexander and Deb were ready to strike.

The fog was rolling thick around the tower bases and Deb and Alexander watched as Henry approached the men guarding them. As he came into sight, the two guards readied their weapons. Once they saw him clearly, they relaxed. Approaching him slowly, Henry put on his acting face. Slightly quivering, he began to set the trap.

"Ieeee gentlemen! Good evening to ya. I was hopin' to get meself some food and shelter for the night. I woont take it for nothin' though. I have in me sacks sume of the finest medicinals in this area."

"What are yu thinkin'? This is nawt an inn for dirty beggars!" They both laughed at the ragged sight of Henry, whose feelings were a bit hurt, but unaffected knowing where it came from.

"Why, I knew that for sure!" He laughed along with them. "I am only seekin' one night. I'll sleep in the hay if ya should see fit. I am at the end of me trip yu see and a fine castle such as this should have fine medicines! I've sold me things to kings and queens, gentlemen!"

They looked at each other and were not impressed. Henry needed to act fast.

"Well, yu see, there is talk of an illness coming north yu see. It gives yu bumps on yer weely and a fever that makes yu see more than one of the same thing. Iee! Yes, it's a nasty thing, gentlemen, indeed! Some say yu get it from rolling around with whores. Yu can also get it from eatin' bad meat." Henry was hoping that his story sounded believable enough. He made it up on the spot and prayed it didn't sound too stupid.

The men looked at themselves and were now curious, but seeing the sight of Henry, they wondered if he himself wasn't infected. He was quite a sight and one of the men said, "Yu don't look so good yerself! Why do yu look so funny?"

Henry again had to swallow his pride and remember why he was here.

"Well, yu see, I am a healthy specimen indeed! Don't let me body fool ya! I dun't catch much because of me potions! Iee yes, it is me who works among the sick and it is me who makes the medicines to cure em'. I have never been sick a day in me life! Why, I have been to towns that have sickness aboundin' but I dun't get it. No sirs! I am a man of greet knowledge of these things despite me appearance!"

The other man was not completely convinced and because they wanted proof that Henry wasn't sick with this illness he was speaking of, he asked a question that almost made Henry ruin everything.

"Well then, if yu dunt have the sickness yu speak of. Show us yer weely and prove it!"

The two men laughed uncontrollably and Henry was mortified. He was a simple man, and he held onto his humble side tightly. He did not want to do what they asked, but if that was what they wanted, that was was what they would get. It was the only way to make them believe him.

Deb and Alexander were ready and waiting. At any moment, Deb would strike. Alexander was poised anxiously under a tree.

Henry blushed and the men continued to laugh. One man said, "He probably dusent have a weely!"

The other was hysterical now and Henry was a bit angry at the taunting he had taken so far. He pursed his lips together and pulled open his coat. Grabbing the rope that held his pants up, he yanked the ends and as they fell to the ground, the two guards were shocked. They didn't think he would do it.

"Awww! Damn it man! That is the ugliest weely I have ever seen! Are those yer balls? They're as small as a new born! God help any whore who tries to find those to play with!"

The other guard was almost out of breath laughing. "Oh, God be with ya boy! It's as tiny as a sprig of straw! Hooo! Haaa! Haaa! It surely doont have any bumps on it! Why it's a bump all by itself!"

Henry was mortified and he angrily pulled up his pants. Just as the two men were engaged in heavy laughter, Deb rose from the underbrush. Alexander steadied himself and as she released her arrow, Henry fell to the ground and rolled under his horse to avoid the scene. The arrow struck the first guard in the back of his head. Blood trickled down in a warm stream as the point came through his forehead. As the other man turned in shock to a grinding halt from laughing, Alexander bounded from the trees and plunged his sword into the man's back. At the same time, Deb had lunged forward and as the man opened his mouth to scream in pain, she grabbed it with one hand and slit his throat with the other.

Henry was shaking terribly on the ground and Alexander pulled him up quickly pushing him in the direction back up the path. He whispered, "You did well, my small friend. You did very well! Now go!"

Henry hobbled along swiftly and disappeared into the night. He was to wait a couple of miles away with extra horses when needed. He feared for his new friends and it would be torture for him to wait, not knowing what was going to happen. He had a tear in his eye as he looked back. Henry felt as though he had finally found the only friends he ever had in the world.

Everything happened quickly and Deb was hoping that the girls were going to be able to handle that moment when they would have to run for their lives.

They concentrated on getting the men as close to the castle as possible without being seen.

Deb and Alexander put their plan into action once they knew they could get the gate open. Castle Dominon was not a huge castle. Its moat was more functional than a protective barrier. As Deb could contest, it was a partial sewer and in its disgusting waters, there were some fish and amphibians such as frogs surviving, which surprisingly were caught and eaten with no thought to the place they came from. Inhabitants relied on the difficult terrain to slow down their assailants and as Alexander's men worked their way toward it, the mud and boggy ground was continuously pulling their legs down. It was tiring work and horses would have made it worse.

The castle itself sat within the bog. Its foundation was built on some of the only solid ground in the surrounding area besides the forest, which sat much higher above it. It did not have a very deep underground level. In fact, most of the castle was above ground. There was a partial lower floor, which held sleeping quarters for the servants and a cold room where root vegetables and grains were stored. It was a damp sleep at best.

This was the private home of Gamelin MacDubh, a man given the title of Baron within the region of Fife. He had very little immediate family and his men were few, but he gave what he could to the fight for Scottish freedom. As he lived a semi-autonomous life, Gamelin did not seem to be missed and the few men that had left him to fight against the English had not been heard from in months. Most of them were likely killed in battle and if the pay was more than Gamelin could have afforded, they would have opted to stay with the king's army. They were not wealthy men and some would have had no choice.

Angus knew that someday he could possibly see their return however, and he would have to make short work of them, but as time had passed, Dominon castle had seen no other claimants other than Gully. One would surmise that it was less than desirable in location and stature.

Alexander and Deb now joined each other at the entrance bridge. Alexander had tied Deb's wrists together but not so tightly that she could not easily break free. They made their way toward the gate and over the small bridge.

The guard on the top of the gate had already sighted them but they stayed calm and Deb moved as if defiant of her capture. Alexander pushed and pulled her often to make it appear as though they were not friendly with one another. The lone guard had drawn his sword and shouted to Alexander to stop halfway across the bridge.

It was tense. All was quiet now that the guard could see who the girl was down below. As he made certain it was Deb, he shouted loudly for assistance. Three more men came running to join him. He stood up and looked down at Alexander and Deb.

"Who you be that brings this bitch to these walls?" The other three men ran back down to the gatehouse door and opened the small single man entrance to get a better look.

Alexander stated, "I am Alexander from Galloway. Gully MacDonell hired me a month ago to track this wench should you all fail at killin' her and her husband! I'm not stayin', I only want food and compensation for bringin' her back! I know Gully's dead, so it be Angus I'm askin' for! She is worth a lot of money and I'll not hand her over until I am paid by Angus himself!"

The men seemed to believe Alexander, but they were concerned as to why he was alone. They didn't believe that part. Deb had killed enough of them as proof that she could not be held easily. Alexander was concerned that they would not open the gate or that Angus would come out and have her killed before they could enter the walls.

Deb looked up and then at Alexander. She whispered under her breath, "Strike me."

Alexander was surprised. Then Deb said again, "I'll struggle and then you strike me."

Deb pushed her body into him trying to break free and he raised his arm. With as little force as he could use he struck her in the face trying to make it look real.

Deb shouted at him and spit on his boots, "Let me loose! Let me loose so that I may kill you all!"

The men were entertained by Deb's tenacity just as they had been before. The only difference was that Gully wasn't around to stop them from laying hands on her. Deb knew this and she enticed them more and more. She allowed her shirt to fall from her shoulder revealing her skin and one of the guards said, "Don't call Angus yet! Let's enjoy her ourselves first!"

Alexander now realized what Deb was doing and it was working. He acted angrily shouting, "I want my money or I'll slit her throat here and now. You won't have no fun with her then!"

The man above now came down as well. All four men were at the single doorway. They were chattering and arguing amongst themselves and finally one of them said, "Alright, you may enter with this prize, but you will allow us our time before we call upon Angus. If you are who you say you are, you will enjoy this as much as us! You'll get your money, if we have our fun."

"So be it. But you have only ten minutes before I call attention to you. Angus won't be pleased to know that you soiled his prize before he could taste it."

"Fine! Enter!"

As the gate opened, Alexander's men on either side of the trees began creeping forward. Alexander approached the gate slowly with Deb. The four guards had to back up to allow them entry. Alexander had brought the tower guard horses with him and spread them out across the opening forcing the men to backup and lose sight of the bridge. Within seconds, his men stood up and raced towards it. They made it half way across as Deb burst free from her shackles. Alexander drew his sword and the four guards lunged forward to protect themselves. The others pushed their way into the gate entrance and filled the courtyard.

David took his two men with him off to the side and tried to find the entrance to the interior hallway.

Alexander and Deb pushed their way passed the four men and ran to join them.

The four guards found themselves under siege. They fought feverishly against Alexander's men, but they were overcome. As Deb met with David, things went drastically wrong.

There were guards running up the hallway to meet them. They had heard the fighting and were rushing up the narrow passageway toward Deb and the other men. David managed to make his way down another hallway and gain access to a room off the kitchen, but Deb and Alexander were pushed back into the courtyard. Down the hallway and on the second floor within the great room, Angus and the rest of his men heard the ruckus. The girls heard it too and those that were in the hall with the men looked at one another. They knew this was it. The men were not paying attention to them and this was what the girls needed.

Down the hall, Sarah could hear what was happening and she gathered the girls that were working in the rooms near her. She knew that the rest were still in the great hall and she prayed that none of them would panic.

Angus and his men leapt from their seats and he ordered the men to head outside. Half of them were drunk and half were well on their way, but it did not stop them from charging down the stairs to join the fight.

With a look of pure anger, Angus grabbed his sword and just then, one of the men from outside came rushing in.

"Angus! It's the woman Barne! She is here, Angus! She is here! She has men with her!"

With an enraged face, Angus twisted his head around to look at the man and said, "She will die today. I am sick of this bitch!"

One of Angus' men whispered to him, "Angus, if she has anyone that represents the king with her and you are caught, they will hang you for certain. Gully's name must be known well across these parts by now. They will know of you as well. You must leave here, Angus. If we leave now, we stand a chance of making the Firth of Forth without capture."

Angus thought about this. If he ran he would look weak to his men. If he stayed, his days were numbered, even if his men were successful in warding off Deb and her men. He was enraged to think that she was the cause of it all. He was angry with Gully for becoming so blind to her wiles. She was nothing but a whore to him who had become scorned. He could not think clearly. The alcohol was not helping his plight, but he decided that his own survival was more important than killing Deb. She would not survive this time and he ordered her death above all others. He himself would run like the coward he was.

"Get her! Do not allow her to live today! Kill her!" Angus screamed as he turned to flee.

He raised his eyebrow on one side and stated, "As much as I wish to smell her blood on my blade, I will not rot in a piss infested cell by the hands of the king's spoiled guards! Come, let us ride!" With that three of Angus' men joined him as they made their way to the secret corridor.

Outside in the courtyard, the fighting became unorganized chaos and it was taking a toll on Alexander and his men.

Deb swung with all her might as the men within the castle came pouring out. Alexander was fending off as many men as he could and everyone's surging energy was at its peak.

As the screaming and shouting got louder the bloody brawling ensued in full power. Alexander could not see Deb well as the dust was swirling and the fighting became worse. She turned to find her bearings and protect her right arm from a large sword coming down. As she did so another sword deflected off of someone's shield and sliced through her leggings. It cut her badly on her left leg and she dropped suddenly to the ground. She took deep breaths as the scene slowed down. Everything was whirling and Deb had to shake her head to recover.

Down in the cloud of dust she ripped her legging off at the sight of the wound. Dragging herself over to the wall, she wrapped it around the leg quickly. With a short tight pull, she knotted the material around the cut. It was deep, but she stopped the bleeding. Alexander could see her at last and tried to make his way toward her. They were being overpowered.

Patrick and two more of Alexander's men could also see Deb's plight and raced toward her. Patrick was injured on his face and as he made his way, trying to see through his own blood, Deb looked up and saw the blade of another coming toward her. She had to regain her stance. Then she remembered her knife. The blade that her father had given her slid out of its sheath and glistened through the dust. She gripped it tightly and thought of her father's face. She saw Liam and Sarah and her anger overtook her pain. She raised herself up slightly on an angle and held her knife in front of her. The man came down hard upon her. Deb screamed a defiant 'No, not yet!' and rolled low to the ground lunging up toward and underneath him. He pressed back slightly at the rush of her blade and tripped over a body. Deb threw herself over him and plunged her knife into his throat. She was enraged and was not going to give in. Taking deep breaths as her father had taught her, she pressed down her emotions and tried to regain her senses.

Alexander and Patrick reached her finally and the three turned together to take on the approaching men. Deb stood up now and stood between her two friends. Alexander held his long claymore sword outward and Patrick's son James joined them. He held a shield before him and the four now pressed their way together through the men. As Alexander and Patrick swung from both sides, Deb would lung in and out with her knife while low to the ground. Patrick's shield masked her arms as she dove down to slice their ankles while they attempted to match Alexander and Patrick's swings above. It was working. They stuck together like a machine. Angus' men were losing ground as they were finding it difficult to strike them. Some of Alexander's other men had gained access to the gate above and Deb yelled at them to fire their bows downward. They were not the best marksmen, but the few arrows that they could manage to release were distracting Angus' men. Some were striking limbs and weakening the intoxicated henchmen. Deb and Alexander were now gaining ground.

Seeing their progress, Alexander yelled to his men to create more courage and motivation amongst them.

"Fight, fight, fight for our clan! Fight for Thomas MacDonell! Fight for the innocent!" His men shouted in unison and Angus' men were beginning to believe that if they did not flee, they were going to die even though they had already killed four of Alexander's men.

As Deb stood up, she grasped her sword. She took her place between Alexander and Patrick. She was weak, but the shock was beginning to take over as well.

"Can you continue, lass?" Alexander yelled.

"I've not come this far to leave these girls! We must find them, Alexander! We must make our way in now!"

There were many of Angus' men also on the ground, far more than Alexander expected so soon.

The four remained tight together and rushed toward the doorway. They could see that some of Angus' men were fleeing, but there were some that still remained intent on continuing their defense.

Enough of Alexander's men were taking charge of the courtyard and this gave Deb and her friends the moment they needed to duck out of sight and into the castle walls.

By this time, Angus had made his way down the long tunnel that led outside to the back of the castle. What he didn't know was that David and his men had been following him and his guards in silence.

David stopped and signaled his men to stay quiet and freeze. They were in the shadows at the end of the tunnel. Angus and his men were in sight and attempting to mount their horses. If David did not strike before they took flight, he may lose them.

With only a second to think, he and his men dove from the shadows. Angus and his men turned quickly to see them bearing down on them. Because they had not fully mounted, they struggled to get up onto their horses, but it was too late.

David threw his knife in mid stride and struck one of the men. Angus was in front of him and turned to flee. One of the men with David had made it forward enough to throw his axe at the horse's legs. Although it pained him to do so, he had no choice. As the axe blade struck the left hind foot of the valiant beast, Angus was thrown from above. He landed on the ground and rolled to a stop. He rose to his feet stunned slightly by the blow of the landing.

The last man on horse took flight and Angus yelled at him, "Coward! Come back, coward!" That man was Druggan and he wasted no time fleeing without any thought of Angus.

David thought how ironic it was that Angus was calling Druggan a coward when he was about to flee. He was pitiful. David and his men surrounded him as he snorted profanities wielding his sword.

"Kill me, and my men inside will not allow you to leave this place. You'll all die!"

David and his men did not know how Deb and the others were doing and they knew that Angus' words could come to fruition, but they had sworn their allegiance to this day. Unlike Angus, David was a man of honor and he would not back down.

"Do you wish to live or die at this moment?" David shouted to Angus as he circled him. Angus was covered in dirt and his eyes were on fire. He was trapped like an animal and he knew it.

"I'll not go quietly! You know not who you fight! I say you have not the guts to take me on alone!"

Angus was clearly trying everything he could, but this was no time for games and David wanted desperately to return to the inside to help his friends.

"You will not walk away Angus! Put your sword down now or I will kill you!"

Angus was not backing down. He spit some dirt out of his mouth onto the ground and lunged forward at David like a mad dog. David turned and lowered himself while swinging his blade. He hit Angus in the thigh and as he turned, one of the other men swung at Angus from the back. He struck him in the arm and now bloodied and injured, Angus stood losing his strength. He continued to speak as he pulled his sword up clumsily to hold his ground.

As he wobbled on his feet he was still threatening David and his men.

"You think you are men of valor? You are nothing without your precious nobility. You hide behind their money while the rest of us have to fend for ourselves!" His eyes were rolling into the back of his head as the heavy flow of blood covered the ground around him.

"You had a choice, Angus! You could fight for more than just yourself! You chose to follow a madman and now look at you! You are as lost as he was. You just won't admit it and the only way you know how to survive is by preying on your own kind. You're like a vulture!" David was disgusted by Angus and his insults.

Angus shook his head and he lunged one last time with what little strength he had, screaming. David could see the same pain in his eyes as Gully once had. These men had lost themselves. Like unloved children, they had hardened inside. They were damaged forever and had lost the ability to feel compassion, or anything for that matter. Everything was spinning and Angus' drunken injured body was giving up. David suddenly pitied him for a moment, but he stood his ground and easily plunged his blade into Angus' heart thinking of what these men had done to Deb and the girls; let alone the loss of Thomas and his good men.

He held onto the blade as Angus went slowly to his knees still muttering. He fell onto his back and David finally pulled his blood soaked blade from Angus' body. It was over. He looked one last time at the face of Gully's right hand man muttered, "You could have run with us Angus, but you forgot who you were."

With no time to waste, David turned to his men. "Come, let us join the others!" The three men ran swiftly back through the tunnel. Angus was dead with his eyes still open and his sword still clutched within his hand. Before following David, the man who had struck the horse with the axe went over to the animal and sadly finished him off so that it would not suffer any longer.

"I am sorry lad, but you would not have wanted to live if he were your master."

Inside the small fortress, Deb and Alexander were finally on their way to the great hall. Deb's heart pounded and she prayed that when she opened the door, she would see the faces of the girls.

As they reached the door Alexander and Patrick stayed back to watch for danger. As Deb approached it, she pressed her ear to it to listen. She heard nothing but a faint shuffling. There were no voices and she could barely stand it. Looking back at Alexander, he nodded up and down. They had to move. With a deep breath, she lunged forward grabbing the handle and pulled hard to open the doorway. As she did, a man jumped out and dove at her. She was knocked down and rolled onto the floor with him. They struggled as Patrick's son dove onto the man. He pulled him off Deb, struggling to keep the assailant's knife blade from hitting his own throat.

Deb held her leg in pain as the man had come down on it hard. Just then, someone else jumped out into the hall and plunged a sword into the back of the man who was attacking James!

As Alexander and Patrick made it to the end of the hall to help, they all looked up and saw the cloaked face of Sarah standing over the man. She had his blood on her face and she stood shaking and breathing heavily with fear. She froze as James looked up at her. When Deb made eye contact with her, she fell to the floor weeping quietly at what she had just done.

Deb rose up and went to her. She held Sarah tightly and as Alexander and Patrick flew into the room to see if the other girls were there, Sarah said, "We are alright, but Isabella is very ill."

James and Patrick looked up when they heard the name.

"Isabella! Isabella!" Patrick raced into the room and saw his small daughter lying down with a blanket on her. She was sweating and the other girls were huddled around her. They all went white when they saw the men enter the room. They had waited so long for rescue and in the moment, they were in shock.

Alexander said calmly, "You are alright. We are with Deb. You are alright now…safe."

The girls rose up and embraced each other. Patrick had tears in his eyes as he lowered himself to see his daughter. She looked at him and said in a feeble voice, "I knew you would come."

James now joined his father and sister and he kissed her hand. She looked at him and he said, "You're safe, lass. You're going home with me and Pappa."

Isabella was delirious and Patrick and James picked her up to carry her together. Patrick had steady tears streaming down his face and as they met with Deb in the hallway, he said to her. "God bless you, Deb." He turned to Alexander and said, "God bless you all."

The other girls now raced to Deb and embraced her together. She looked down and held back tears as they wrapped their arms around her as if she were their mother. She could not believe she was seeing them again.

Alexander nodded politely but added, "We are surely blessed to have found the girls, but now we must be weary of these walls. We are not quite safe yet. When we are free from this place, we will be liberated."

David and his men came down the hall and he rushed to Deb's side when he saw that they had found the girls.

"Deb, lass, are you alright? Are the girls all here?"

"Yes, my friend, we are all fine, except Patrick's daughter Isabella. She will need to be handled carefully. She is sick with fever and we must avoid the fighting in the courtyard."

David spoke up right away and stated that the tunnel was their best option. Patrick and James started taking the girls down the corridor.

Sarah stayed back while they all made their way and Deb turned to see her look of determination. She knew Sarah wanted to go with her to the courtyard, but Deb could not put her into any more danger.

"I can't risk you getting injured, Sarah. Please go with them. Everything will be fine. I will meet with you soon."

Sarah looked frustrated and said in a raised voice, "I can't watch you leave again, Deb! My mother left me, and then you did! Now just when we've found each other, you're going to leave me again! Please, Deb! Please let me stay by your side! You've seen how I can fight!"

Alexander looked at Sarah. He saw the same thirst for survival in her face that he saw in Deb. Her fragile exterior was deceiving. He did not say anything. This was for Deb to decide.

Patrick's son, James came back down the hallway as he was wondering what was keeping Sarah. He was concerned and Deb saw Sarah's eyes light up when he came into view. They were obviously smitten with each other even though they had only just met. The young at heart were always stirred by another that caught their eye in a moment of passion. They were the same age and Deb felt for them both as she knew this feeling all too well.

She experienced it when she met Liam. Young hearts are overwhelmed with emotions, when they have not yet learned to harness them, but to Deb, it was a good thing. Anything that could create the sweet look now on the faces of James and Sarah was beautiful, especially in a world that was ravaged by war and death.

The passion that the fight for survival creates is unlike any other. It can evoke emotions that one may have never truly felt before. When one is faced with their own mortality, they become an open book. Deb could see it clearly with Sarah because the only true feelings she had ever shown a man were that of hatred and fear. When she looked at James, it was different. This look was gentle and shy and her cheeks were blushing slightly. She had a brightness to her expression that Deb had prayed to see one day.

Sarah looked over at James and she politely said, "I would like to go with Deb. I want to help her."

James looked at Deb who was trying to show him that she had no desire to take Sarah into danger. James knew that he had to convince Sarah to go with him.

"I have seen your bravery and I believe that if it weren't for you, these girls, including my sister, would not have gotten this far. I owe you my life as well now. Please come with me and help us. Deb will be safe with Alexander. I need you to help me with my sister. Please, Sarah."

Deb nodded to James with thanks. Sarah looked at her just then and she said, "Sarah, my sister. I need you to be with the girls. Go with James. We will rendezvous with you as soon as we can. Don't worry. I won't leave you again, Sarah. I promise."

Sarah was wearing thin and her senses were even clearer after James spoke to her. Deb had also said the word 'promise'. It was not a word Sarah took lightly and to this point, Deb had never broken a promise to her. She bowed her head with a slight tear and looked up at Deb.

"I will go with James. I just don't want to lose you again." She rushed forward and wrapped her arms around the woman who was now like family to her. She remembered losing her mother and being dragged off by Gully's men. Sarah had been traumatized so badly, that she could not bear to leave Deb's side once more, but knowing that James would be with her, she seemed to be more willing.

"Good girl. Be strong. You have men with you who will protect you."

Sarah nodded and James held out his hand for hers. Deb gently handed her over to the young man and Sarah shyly obliged. They turned down the corridor and were on their way.

Deb sighed heavily and Alexander put his hand on her shoulder.

"Off we go, lass. We have some business to attend to. Is your leg alright for now?"

"It pains me, but it has stopped bleeding. I don't believe it to be very deep. I can still use it. Soon I will have Henry attend to it. Let us take this castle and finish this bloody day."

She was tired and Alexander wanted this to be over as well. As they approached the outside courtyard, they could not hear the fighting. In fact, they heard hardly anything more but a few voices shouting back and forth. Carefully they looked out and saw something that shocked them.

In the middle of the courtyard amongst the dust were eight of Angus' men in shackles. Around them and above on the walkways lay the bodies of the rest. Most of Alexander's men and someone they least expected to see were standing guard.

Turning around to look at Deb was Liam's father, Malcolm. On the other side, she noticed the face of her brother-in-law as well. They had brought with them ten other family members all the way from the north and a few men that Deb did not recognize. Henry had given them the information they wanted only after they told him who they were. He knew that Deb could not be angry at him for that. They were only hours away from Henry, Patrick and James when they first came upon Alexander at Dominon Castle.

Henry just knew that he had done right by talking this time and he had proven himself to be an invaluable friend to Deb and the others. He was intelligent and thoughtful with his calculations of the situation and it was impressive to say the least.

There was much more to this little man. He had skill that went unnoticed by most…until that day.

Deb was overwhelmed and ran to Malcolm who also made his way toward her. As they met in a warm embrace, Deb's eyes began to well up. She was exhausted. He was like an angel from the heavens.

Malcolm took her face in his hands and said, "What kind of a father-in-law would I have been if I did not come to help? Liam's mother is alright, lass. We tried to get to you for days and were forced to take a different and longer path to avoid the English army. We passed them finally and found out where you were from your little friend, Henry. I am sorry I did not get here sooner, lass. If my son is fighting for us all, it is the least I can do as his father to come to the need of his young wife."

Deb smiled so widely that everyone else felt her joy. She kissed Malcolm on the cheek and said, "God brought you here in due time. We are blessed by the heavens!"

She looked over at her brother-in-law and everyone was standing over the scene with a look of victory and pride. It had finally ended. They were bloodied and tired, but it was over.

"These pieces of garbage will be living in the dungeons, lass. They won't be hurting anyone else. The girls' families will see some justice indeed," one of the men stated.

"It will be so," Deb answered. "Thank you my friends."

"Lass, we must get you some treatment for that leg." Alexander said and as they gathered themselves together after such a harsh and bloody journey, Deb looked up to the sky and thanked her father, Jacob. She closed her eyes briefly as the men went about gathering the wounded and salvageable weapons. She wanted to see one more person now…the one face that would calm her most; Liam.

"Where are you, my love?" she asked inside her head. The dust was clearing and Deb joined in.

They gathered themselves and made their way out of the castle walls to meet the others. Henry would be with them and Alexander wanted to make sure that everyone's injuries were attended to first and foremost before leaving the area. Infection was everyone's enemy. If an injury itself did not kill you, a rotten wound certainly would.

He looked over at Deb. "It's over, lass. It is really over." Alexander said.

"Yes, my friend. Now I have to find the homes that these girls miss so deeply. I will be keeping Sarah with me. She does not have any family alive that she is aware of. I will try to find any that may exist first, but she is my responsibility."

"You care for her very much don't you?" Alexander asked.

"It is a strange connection we have. It is as if I were her mother although I am only two years older than she. Her mother died when she was young, as did mine, and I believe she sees a maternal image in me. I worry for her future though. She is very troubled and will need time to heal."

"You have also gone through quite enough for one young woman, Deb. Don't under estimate the power that life gives us. Look at yourself. Sarah will be fine. She is strong within as are you." He paused. "She has you now doesn't she?"

Deb smiled and answered, "Yes, I suppose we have each other. My hope is that we will be reunited with Liam. I fear for his life although I know he is a great fighter. I pray for them all. Someday soon, I hope to see their faces. I just hope that if that day comes, it will be a day of peace."

One of the men riding beside Alexander looked over at Deb now and added, "Don't worry, lass. William is a great leader. He will be by Liam's side for certain. He will have high standing with the King's army. They are cavalry soldiers; the finest in Scotland. Your husband Liam is a man of great skill. Have faith, Deb. Have faith. It's all we have." Deb looked over at the man whose face was dirty and bloodied.

"Yes, it is," added Alexander. "When you are faced with danger, you must fill yourself with power from within. Your father obviously instilled this in you. Without it, you would not have come this far. Be strong, my girl. You have done a great thing here today. The stars will guide you now, and I will not leave your side until you desire so. It has been ordered by William himself."

Chapter Fifteen
The Journey Home

Cheryl Alleway

Deb sat up straight and looked to the sky again. She believed their words. Their friendship and kindness had given her confidence, but what was beyond the hills was still unknown. There was goodness in the world, however. There were good men and destiny forging her path. Now, she had to open her eyes and follow her heart. What would come next was uncertain, but she was not finished yet. The young girls that surrounded her, needed to be returned to their families. She thought about it, and decided that they should make camp when they reached a safe area. The other ominous entity looming over the hills was the English army. They had still not quite reached the Lothians and if not careful, Deb and her friends could have even more trouble on their hands. Caution was a must. David and three other men would scout the land before the others rode each mile. They could take no chances.

Malcolm rode over to Deb's side. She looked over to him and reached out to take her hand. They rode in this way for a few moments and Malcolm was overwhelmed with pride. His son had chosen a woman of great honor and he would die protecting her, but he feared for their future. Scotland was ravaged by war and families were separated constantly. Only the strong would survive and he prayed for Liam and Deb everyday. To lose his son would be a dark day in Malcolm's heart and he prayed for protection as he held Deb's hand.

As they rode, their journey was calm and they passed only a few small stone crofts and farming areas. They stopped to rest and gather themselves before nightfall. It would be much needed rest for all and Deb would need to find her courage once again for the next leg of the journey. She wondered if it would ever be over and if she would ever see Liam again.

When the morning light broke, Henry finished tending to wounds and administering medicines as best he could. He had little left, but his small crooked hands worked diligently and as he finished, he noticed Deb sitting by Finnean alone. He walked slowly over to her and was careful as he could be sitting down beside her.

"Excuse me, miss Barne, but yee need a new dressin' on yer leg."

Deb turned her head to him slowly and noticed the dirty little man who had helped them so much. She smiled at him and it made him lower his head.

"Don't bow down so much, Henry. I am not to be feared by you. You have proven yourself to me. You don't need to bow down to anyone." She looked back out over the hills.

"No one has ever said that ta me beefur, miss." He looked away from her and added, "I em a monster to most. I em not beautiful as yu."

Deb suddenly heard Henry's tone and looked him straight in the face.

"Henry, don't you ever think that you are a monster! A monster would not have helped us save these girls. A monster would not be tending to the wounds of men he just met. A monster would not ride for miles to bring medicine to strangers."

He looked up at her and his sad face made Deb realize that he had been a tortured soul for so long that kindness was almost an oddity to him.

"Miss, I weel be yer friend no matter what happens. I have no family and yu have made me feel like a person." He handed her some fresh cloth for her leg. "Thank yu."

She held out her hand and took the cloth. With the other, she patted Henry on the back. He almost flinched when she touched him, but realized that she didn't care about his bony stature. She was the kindest person he had ever met.

Deb began to change her dressing as Henry stood up. He walked away and Deb suddenly felt a sense of strength come over her. She felt good about talking to Henry. She stood back up and stretched her leg carefully. It was feeling better and the flesh was sealing itself cleanly. She would have a large scar, but at least infection was not going to start.

Alexander now approached her and said, "Lass, we should gather ourselves and discuss our day. David's riders will return soon to tell of what they have seen. Two of the girls say they are from the area on the outskirts of the Dumfries. We should find their families first. It will be the most difficult portion of our journey. Two more girls are from Galloway. James and Patrick will be taking Isabella home. They know of a safe way south. Their land lies twenty-five miles west on the tip of the Dumfries region. They will lead us until we must turn northwest toward Carrick. If we are successful in finding the families there, we can make our way west. It should be less treacherous."

"Alright then, we ride as soon as everyone is ready and the riders have confirmed a clear path."

As Deb and her group readied themselves, Sarah sat quietly under a tree. She was crying softly as the realization of her freedom came to her. The view of the land before her made her heart soar and ache at the same time. James noticed and walked over slowly. She could see him out of the corner of her eye and wiped her tears away quickly. She turned and smiled gently as he approached.

"May I sit down, Sarah?" he asked.

"Yes, I'm just watching for the riders," she said.

"Well, if there is anything I can help you with…" He was feeling clumsy and didn't know what to say.

Sarah looked away shyly and said, "Thank you James. I am ready to go."

The two sat awkwardly for a moment and then James took a breath and said, "Sarah, may I be open with you?"

She was nervous and answered, "Well, I suppose. What is it?"

"I…I just wanted to say…" James found he could not speak in the presence of such a beautiful girl. Sarah knew he was nervous as well now and cut in.

"I am very glad that you and your father are here, James. Isabella is someone I have come to love as a sister. I think she will be alright now that you're here. I believe her fever is breaking." She paused. "You are brave to have come."

The young man blushed and he knew that Sarah noticed him the same way he noticed her. He had just enough courage to say, "You should also be proud, Sarah. For someone so young and beautiful as you to go through what you have, you have my respect." He turned his head away slightly.

Sarah's heart was racing a bit at the attention she was getting. She had never felt this way before, but somehow, she knew it was a good feeling and her tears were fading just sitting with James. She was the happiest she had been in a long time.

"James...I hope we see each other again after this."

James looked back at her and smiled, "Yes, I do as well." He reached down the hill they were sitting on and picked a small bunch of heather. He bundled it and tied it with a blade of grass and handed it to Sarah.

"For you."

Sarah put her hand out and as James placed the flowers in her palm, he wrapped his fingers around her small hand. Looking into her eyes, he said, "A girl that carries a bundle of heather will always have the affection of another."

She wrapped her hands around his and they sat embracing one another for a moment. The call from Patrick ordering James to saddle his horse broke the spell and James stood to leave.

"Thank you for the flowers," Sarah said.

"You are welcome." James hurried down the hill to his father. He had a special bounce in his step. He looked back and Sarah was still watching him.

Deb noticed the exchange and felt a great joy for Sarah. She was finally learning how a man should really treat a woman.

As the sun began to fall in the sky, the riders returned. They had not seen the army, but a villager had told them that puffs of dust too large for a small party were seen in the distance just thirty miles to the south. They were clearing out and suggested that David and his men tell Deb and the group to do the same. There was word that the King of England had met nothing but a desolate Lothian region upon entering it only days before and now, he was angry and deciding whether or not to turn south for England again. King Robert the Bruce had judged his opponent correctly and he hoped the lack of food and supplies was going to drive the English army back home with nothing to show for their efforts.

Alexander and Deb called for everyone to get ready and before long, the group was on their way once again. David rode two miles ahead with his men. Henry suggested that he join them as he knew of various trails to travel on and could help James and Patrick navigate the safest path. They needed to get Isabella home and it would take the group at least a day and a half to reach their land. Traveling at night would be harder to do, but it gave an advantage over being seen in the daylight, and Henry knew his way well after having traveled these lands for so many years.

As the group rode on, time passed quickly. When the horses were traveling in a straight path, Deb would close her eyes and meditate, allowing Finnean to keep his stride and follow the others. She was clearing her mind and trying to build up her inner strength. It was something that had been a part of her since childhood. Her father had known one thing for certain; that if he was to instill the strength in her that she would need as an adult, he would have to start teaching her ways of coping with life at a young age so that it came easy to her and something that she didn't have to think about.

His wife had been able to share her vision of Deb's future with Jacob before she died. Deb had four good years with Mary who gave her the ability to listen and learn. She taught Deb how to be quiet when someone was speaking and to really listen to what they were saying. This gave Deb the ability to feel people's emotions and read their faces. Mary also taught Deb to speak honestly and clearly when she had something to say, but to never disrespect her elders or those who knew more than she did. This taught Deb the value of knowledge and to learn as much as she could when she was being taught something she had never done before. It also gave her courage because she was comfortable with new ideas and trying things she may not understand or know how to do at first.

Deb's mother influenced her more than she knew. As she rode upon Finnean, she opened her eyes to see the night sky turning a beautiful, blue gray with very few clouds and a moon so bright that it lit their path. It made her feel as if her mother was there, showing her the way and comforting her. She missed both her parents dearly, but at that one moment, she felt them there with her. She spent a moment inside her own head, remembering times and stories from her past.

Jacob Douglas had spent many loving moments with his daughter when the day's work was done, after Mary had died. At first, playing with makeshift wooden swords and such was just a game to spend time with Deb, but as she grew, Jacob realized that those games were becoming valuable lessons. With his daughter's eagerness, he began training her more seriously in the ways of battle and fighting. She was thirsty for knowledge and he sometimes had to hold her back. Deb pushed herself and became an excellent student. She was far beyond even young boys her age and Jacob was hard pressed to keep her curiosity curbed.

He knew she would have to deal with the normal feminine issues, but was hoping that her strong physical prowess would help her through. She said little, but he told her to come to him if she needed him. At times, he would feel uncomfortable finding the words to say or comforting to do when she suffered through female ordeals, but Deb seemed to handle it quite well and would not complain very much. She often went through times where she did not experience much physical pain at all during menstruation because she was so fit and exercised to such a high degree. She did the best she could to keep herself clean and would lay down in the croft if her body pained her. Jacob would leave her alone and when she was ready, she would return to her chores. Jacob would tell her not to fear it each time it came. "It will pass, lass; no worrying now."

Jacob did make certain that she did not feel alone with the changes in her body and he tried his best to give her a sense of compassion when he felt Mary should have been there to do so. Life on the Scottish fields required a strong constitution and a matter of fact attitude when it came to life's daily experiences. Just like life and death, everything else had to be dealt with at some point and so there was no reason to fear or be embarrassed of changes to one's body. Jacob was becoming increasingly weak and that was a change he was not looking forward to, but realized it to be a reality.

When Deb began to grow into a woman in appearance, Jacob took it in stride and knew that she was eventually going to be noticed by men. He *took as much time as he could to protect her however, and was not looking forward to the day when she was no longer his naïve, young daughter. She would one day become an adult with purpose and a need to venture out of the safety of his arms.*

The many days spent on the farm were joyous to Jacob. He reveled in passing on his skills to his daughter and it gave him a sense of purpose he did not know he would achieve at that point in his life.

He had learned such things from Robert Douglas and others who had taken him in after escaping the English army. Robert had traveled to the mainland in his youth and had seen the skills of the French. He had listened to many stories over wine about men from even further east that rode camels with skill and used weapons as extensions of themselves rather than a separate tool. These ways of thinking made a human being far more accurate and skilled as an individual fighter. Tales from China and beyond would be muttered in dark corners and on the streets of the large cities where trade and adventure was becoming like a drug to those who wanted to travel and learn more about the world they only heard of. It fascinated Jacob and Robert would light up as he told the tales from his life.

"Ayee, the ships will become more and more laden with goods and traders of all kinds Jacob." Robert lit a pipe as he stoked the fire that he and Jacob sat at one night. Wallace and his men were resting from battle only days before and Robert had been in the mood to talk.

"Do the English think they can conquer these places where men are so vast in numbers and

hold such knowledge of battle?" Jacob was amazingly curious when Robert spoke.

"I believe they do, but many of we Scots have obliged the challenged. The killing is something I am growing tired of. That is hard to break from a man's head, when it has been engrained in it for so long. From the days of Viking invasions, this has been upon their shoulders. They had their own burdens to bear when the invasions began and in time, men learned to live with violence as their only means of survival. We too have had to turn to this. The world is vast, lad. Land has become a commodity that is priceless. With land brings power and resources. It entices men to kill others for it and give in to the allure of it all. I know Scotland. I know it is my home and I want to stay right here. William Wallace has this sentiment in his heart. He is known as a driven man, but a man of vision. His knowledge of Latin and French shows that he is more than the scorned ruffian the English claim him to be. He wants to see more for his people; he wants this killing to end as vicious a fighter as he is. It has been a part of life since the dawn of time, lad and I fear his dream may never come true, but he believes in us. He is one that will not give in; he does not believe the past has to continue. He sees peace in our futures. I do not know if it will come, but God be my witness, I'm willing to try and find out with him!"

He continued to speak of places he had seen. "The holy land itself is teaming with men of education, artists and radical thinkers. It is far too large a world, Jacob, to lose sight of. I do believe that the things I have seen outside of Scotland have made me even more determined to protect its beauty and innocence. I am grateful for my time away, *though, because it makes me love this place even more; just like Wallace. I am not alone. Many more of us are now determined to stand by his side. This country is destined for greatness if we keep our faith."*

"Scotland's beauty is easy to see, but innocence? I do not understand, Robert."

"Jacob, we are a people who have existed for hundreds of years because we continue to protect our way of life. Yes, we've been just as violent in our quest to protect this place; we must admit, but we want nothing more than to be free; to live our lives and raise our families in peace. These lands are harsh to some, but to us, they are lush, mysterious, and wild. This is the innocence I speak of. We must protect this rawness. It is untouched in so many ways; especially by the hands of those who wish only to use it for glory and power. This is all that the English armies see."

"How can men feel so little for each other; for women and children? We cut each other down like animals, Robert."

Robert's face fell sullen and he looked directly at Jacob. He looked down at the young man's leg and up to his naïve face. "Lad, I know it is hard to understand the brutality that we have inflicted on both sides. It is the greatest pain that we have given and taken, but understand that when laws are enforced upon men that are blatantly unjust, there is no choice but to fight. It is for those who cannot defend themselves that we do this. If it is not us protecting Scotland, Jacob, then who?"

Jacob understood slowly and then he realized what Robert was saying. He one day hoped to travel and meet some of the kinds of people

Robert was speaking of and learn more about what was at the heart of his beautiful country.

"Now you understand why we fight for our country, lad. You'll learn more in time. For now, just keep it in your heart."

That night was ingrained in Jacob for all eternity. Robert would fight like a demon on the field, but was still able to sit and speak with such clarity of thought and purpose. Jacob could see why he fought so passionately. He was a simple man, but one who knew exactly what he wanted and what he had to do to get it.

This was something that Jacob would try to emulate as he lived his life. It would be his duty to pass its power onto his daughter.

Deb held on to the stories her father told her and she vowed as a young woman to never forget his words.

As she opened her eyes on the trail to see David, Alexander and the others, she knew that she had to keep going at all costs. She looked back at young Sarah and James who were riding together and saw herself and Liam in their young faces. They needed people to teach them and push them forward as well. How could she deny them of that when she had learned so much and been given such love? How could she break the chain of freedom now when her father, and others before him, had worked so hard to keep it strong? She could not. She would not. This was the Scottish faith that drove the battles that surrounded them all. She understood now too.

As she turned around again, Alexander was motioning for them to stop and make camp in the safety of the hills. They were close to the lands where Patrick's home lay. Caution and open eyes were imperative. The English army was probably closer than they thought.

The next morning, as the group rose from a much needed sleep, Finnean was restless. Deb walked over to calm him, but nothing she did seemed to work. Suddenly, a call came from one of the riders. The English army was seen only five miles to the north. They were obviously heading back to England, but in their wake, they were leaving their mark as much as possible. They wanted the Scottish people to pay for their embarrassment of a failed assault. The riders had seen them attacking a church only fifteen miles away. It was said that they burned it to the ground with nothing more than a sneer on their faces. If they came across Deb's small group and saw the young girls, they would take their liberties for certain. They would not even think twice about murdering Alexander and his men in the process. There were far too many of them for Deb and her party to take a stand. They had no choice but to run and hide.

"We must take cover, lass. Come quickly!" David hurried the girls and the rest of the men behind a small group of hills that sheltered a stream. Beyond the water was a grove of trees. It was their only hope.

They took the horses as deep into the trees as possible and Alexander told the men to keep them quiet. Deb stroked Finnean's nose to settle him. He knew danger was in the air as well. When the last rider returned, they all stayed calm. The girls were huddled down with Patrick and James and as the sound of horses in the distance began to get closer, James put his arm around Sarah and she held onto him tightly.

"I'm frightened, James," she whispered as her hands began to quiver. James knew all too well, that her fears of being raped were getting the best of her. It was a real nightmare that she had been living. He felt for her. No one should live with such fear, but taking on the few men at Dominion castle was so far from the thought of and English army that James was shaking a bit now too.

"It's alright, Sarah. The angels have protected you this far. They will not see any more harm come to you. I won't either."

She put her head down and peered out from the branches with wide eyes. Deb was poised with arrows, ready to defend if needed. She knew she could not win this battle though, but she would face it, prepared to die, if she needed to. She wouldn't just stand there while her friends were slaughtered.

Alexander was keeping his wits about him. He noticed that they would be down wind of the soldiers when they came close. This would help, as the English horses would not be able to pick up their scent. It would be about their only saving grace; that and the fact that their tracks were buried in the river's water.

Alexander prayed, as the sound of horses was getting closer. Fear was in all of them. Bravery had been their driving force, but the reality was that they were too small a group to fight and win this time.

"Quiet everyone! Do not move." David whispered harshly.

As the dust was seen in the distance, they finally could see the lead riders. Slowly, the English came closer. They were staying on the other side of the river, but one of them stopped as he noticed the water. As he raised his arm for the rest of the army to halt, Deb and her friends held their breath. One of the men dismounted and went to the water to drink. He ordered the men to fill their deerskins and Alexander watched with barely a breath as hundreds of men dismounted and walked towards the water. The fear they all felt in that moment was so great. It was cutting a hole in Sarah's stomach. Patrick's chest felt heavy and he breathed in and out to calm himself, closing his eyes and praying silently. Alexander stood stoic and strong, but inside he was terrified of what would happen should they be found.

David flicked his gaze to Deb and he watched as she held onto Finnean, clutching him so strong you couldn't pry him from her if you tried. He felt a burning in his soul for this girl and what she had accomplished. He had not left her side through it all and he wasn't about to now. He stood proud as he knew that if it came to it, he would shelter her and Alexander above all. David's eyes were changing. His gaze was deeper and his emotions were beginning to show. He was letting down his guard just enough for Alexander to notice again and this time, Alexander wasn't uncomfortable with David's look. It was one that he knew well. With no time to think about it, he turned his attention to the girls and then to the massive army that was threatening them all at that very moment.

Isabella couldn't help that she had to cough. Patrick slapped his hand over her mouth and Alexander's eyes had a look of horror as he turned to make eye contact with Patrick. He slowly dragged a blanket over Isabella's face and as Patrick braced for her chest to heave, he made the sound of an owl as loudly as he could. Any other animal probably would have prompted them to send someone into the trees to kill it for food. By now their supplies were most likely extremely low and an owl wasn't the best catch. If Patrick had howled like a wolf, or bayed like a sheep, their hiding place would have been compromised for certain.

Alexander looked back at Patrick and as he blinked his eyes slowly with a stressful gaze, they knew it had worked. After a tense ten minutes or so, they all breathed a sigh of relief when the soldiers finally began to mount their horses again. Finnean was getting restless and Deb was worried. He would not settle and as the English army turned south to leave the sight, Finnean whinnied.

"No boy! No!" Deb whispered. It was too late. Without hesitation, Alexander and Deb met eyes. They both knew what had to be done. She leapt onto Finnean just as two of the English soldiers started toward the trees to investigate the sound. At top speed Finnean and Deb broke free from the trees on the other side of the river and took flight like the wind. She had to lead them away from her friends. Alexander and David looked on in horror, but motioned for the rest of the group to stay quiet and still.

"God be with us now, Finnean! Ride boy! Ride!"

Six men were sent to chase Deb. "A spy! Catch them before they escape to give our position away!"

At the distance they were at, they obviously could not tell that Deb was a woman yet. She had tied her hair back that morning and all the English knew merely that someone was trying to get away from them in a hurry.

They raced side by side down river until Deb turned to the west. The soldiers dove across the river and chased her like devils. The water splashed loudly and she didn't even turn to look back.

Deb did look back, some time later, to judge the distance and paced her beast accordingly. She wanted to stay a safe distance from their arrows, but give Finnean the longest riding time possible. There was no way to know how long she would have to run.

Her heart was pounding and Deb was frightened. These were English soldiers, the ones in her dreams chasing her father and then killing him in front of her. She had to gather her senses. These were just men. They were just like any other she had confronted and she must not allow her imagination to get the better of her.

Finnean was clearly the fastest of the horses, but Deb did not know how to lose them. She tried zigging and zagging up and over hills, but they did not let up. They had tried to hit her with a few arrows, but they were just not able to target her. Finnean was so agile, he was creating a terrible bulls-eye. Deb decided to take a chance and try her own shot. She set Finnean up in a straight line for only a few seconds, holding him tightly with her thighs and pressing him into position. She turned at the waist and released three arrows one after another, but it was all she could manage because of the bounding motion of Finnean's gait.

Two arrows made their mark and took down two of the six men, but not before one of theirs' struck Deb on the outside of her calf. She screamed in agony, gripping her leg to find it had only cut through the skin. She could not stay this close anymore or she would soon feel the rush of an arrow through her back.

As the four remaining riders pursued her, Deb knew she had to do something. They could not ride like this forever and the men would not give up until they caught up to her. She made her way around a hill that had a clear path around it. Racing Finnean like the wind, she gained enough speed and distance that the soldiers lost sight of her for a few moments. It gave her enough time to take position and ready herself for the most difficult target practice she would ever face.

Down on the ground after smacking his rump, Finnean ran ahead out of range and Deb readied herself. She placed as many arrows in the ground in a line as she could and braced her body and mind for what was about to face her. Her time was out.

From second to second, her heart pounded so heavily that she could feel it in her throat and heard it in her ears. She could smell fear, but embraced it as only she could. Then, they came. Heading straight for her, the men did not realize she was at ground level and her black flowing hair that had now fallen from its hold was the last thing they saw as Deb lanced them one by one taking down two immediately while wounding another. He fell from his horse but the final soldier was able to get an arrow away in Deb's direction. Just as it made a clear path toward Deb's body, her own counter arrow flew striking the assailant's hand in mid-air.

As if in slow motion, the two arrows passed one another and the stunned soldier allowed it to take his attention just enough for Deb to strike him with another. He fell to the ground only feet from her and as his eyes blinked through his own blood, he saw her standing over him panting with her dark hair and beautiful face gazing down upon him. He left the world thinking that a female devil had taken him down.

The last man that Deb had wounded lay writhing on the ground and tried to stand when he saw her approach him. He was dizzy from pain and as he arose, Deb walked toward him as well. He did not know what to think. She held an arrow tightly in her bow aimed at the man and she ordered him to get on the ground and drop the sword that he had taken from his horse.

He did so and Deb proceeded to ask him if he wanted to live. The man was puzzled by her question and confused by what he was seeing; a beautiful woman with raven hair who had just killed five men on horseback.

He looked up at her in a daze and said, "I know not of what you are or who you are, but no woman could have done this. I think you to be a devil from hell! I...I..." The man fell to the ground and Deb lowered her arrow. He would not live and she was not an animal. She ironically marked his chest with her arrow and sent the final blow to stop him from feeling any more pain. She could not allow him to live even if she wanted to. He would tell the King of England about her and in time, she would be found and hung for killing the King's men.

Deb tried to decide what to do next, but as Finnean came trotting into sight where she had last seen him, she knew that returning directly to Alexander and the rest of her party was not an option. She would have to lay low until she knew the English had given up and were heading south.

As luck would have it, they would not wait around for six men to find one enemy scout. By now, she was hoping that King Edward had made a swift motion south. He had pillaged the area until they had nothing left to stay for. He had no choice but to head back to England. If Deb had been a scout, he knew his men had driven her far enough away that there was no immediate threat. Even if they did not return, he did not care. Six martyrs dying for an army of English was nothing to him. As long as they gave him time to get further away, he was satisfied.

Deb was unaware of her stroke of luck and had decided apprehensively to have faith that Alexander would hold to his position for a while longer. As it was, he sent David and two men out to see what was happening, if anything. They made camp in the forest that had sheltered them so well and they prayed for Deb to come into sight with David.

For two hours Alexander paced back and forth waiting for news. Just as the mist was rolling in and the night air was beginning to get too chilly for Isabella to handle, he saw them.

Across the field and riding in front of David, was the woman who had just saved them all from certain death.

Alexander suddenly felt emotion he had not felt yet and he ran toward Deb as if she were his own daughter returning. She smiled as they met eyes and after dismounting and showing him her injury, Alexander embraced Deb warmly.

"My God, lassie, I thought it was over. I thought we had lost you for good! Are you alright? Blessed be the angels that brought you back!" He looked at Finnean and added, "And God bless this old boy! Your fast legs have saved us as well, lad! Well done, Finnean!"

Deb looked as if she was still surging with energy and said, "Well, the bastards have wounded my other leg and now I'm afraid Henry isn't going to be the only one who walks with a limp!"

Just then, the crooked little Henry ran up to Deb with bandages and ointment.

"It's mee last bottle, lass! The heavens made mee save it for a reason! OOOh yees indeed! Sit down while I help yu clean that up miss!"

Deb gladly sat down with the help of David and Alexander. Everyone had come over to see her with faces of grand elation. Sarah rushed passed everyone else and bounded toward Deb falling on her knees and hugging her tightly.

"You kept your promise, Deb. You didn't leave me!" She was tearing up as she held the hand of her beloved Deb.

"Come now, Sarah. We have much to do before you get rid of me so easily!" As she spoke with a light tone for Sarah, Deb was still shaking inside.

Everyone forced a nervous laugh, but as the fire was lit finally, and the warmth calmed them, Deb fell into a deep exhausted sleep. Alexander looked over at her. She was still and it was such a mystery to him as to why she was so driven. He wondered if she longed for a child and if she and Liam would ever be together again. It saddened him. She was so young and beautiful, yet here she stayed risking her life time and time again for but one thing…freedom; her freedom, Liam's, the girls, her people.

As Alexander dozed in the gentle flames of the fire, David too was thinking about their plight and the young girl who had been at the front line of it all, but while Alexander thought about Deb with the reverence of a proud father, David was feeling differently. He sat and watched her sleep. Once in a while he would tell himself to stop thinking about her because she belonged to another. Liam was a man of honor and for David to have the thoughts that he did was wrong in his own mind, but he had been through so much with Deb who all but a month or so ago had been a stranger. Her passion and courage was unmistakably alluring to him. He could not help it and he feared his feelings. He had never met anyone like Deb before and as most of his days had been spent fighting for Earl MacDonell, he had had little time to find someone to court. David was a highly trained, dedicated man who felt deeply for his Scottish homeland and the desire to roam its fields without fear of the English or any other enemy. He prayed everyday for an end to the hatred and the bloodshed, and as this woman had entered his life so dramatically he could not help but wonder if it were more than just coincidence.

David shook his emotions off as sleep began to lull him as well and as the last of the girls nodded off, Deb and her friends got some much needed time under the stars. The moon was out and the flames had taken the dampness from their bones.

Finnean took in a deep breath and released a sigh that was unmistakably one of relief. He blinked slowly as did the other horses who for now were also feeling peaceful.

An owl hooted his haunting song on the night air and as Deb slept, she began to dream again. This time, she dreamt about a man who wore fine clothing and spoke in a deep voice. She must have been an infant in the dream, because she was looking up at him and he patted her on the head, but it was not done in kindness. She looked down at herself in the dream, and she was very small. She tried to speak, but she could not make words yet.

The man did not seem good to her and as she saw him more clearly, she became afraid. In the mist of the dream, she heard her mother calling and she turned to go to her. As she turned however, the man became enraged and tried to grab her arm. Deb struggled, but was too small to defend herself. Her mother came to her and the man slapped her in the face. She tumbled backward and Deb began to cry. She heard her own tiny voice and the screams of her mother. Then the man suddenly released her arm as he bolted backward from the blow of an arrow. Deb turned to see another man; a man with one leg. It was her father! He ran to her as best he could and scooped her and her mother up. They all turned together to see the man's face one more time. He was evil looking and Deb could see that he wore the clothing of English nobility. She was terrified. He seemed so large and frightening to her and as the dream began to fade, the last thing she saw was her mother's face. She saw the look of disgrace in her mother's eyes and Deb left the dream with a feeling of shame.

When she awoke, she pieced together that the dream was associated with many things she had just gone through and in an attempt to cope, her mind created a scenario that left her feeling empty inside. She cursed the night at times for it left a confusing wake the next morning. Alas, without it she would not be able to carry on.

When the sun came up, the group began to rise once again and as they wiped the sleep from their eyes, Alexander noticed one of the riders approaching. He had left in the early morning hours to check the next few miles of their journey south. He approached slowly, which was a good sign at first. As he dismounted, he had a long face and walked toward Alexander with a look of despair.

"Sir, I fear that I have troubling news."

"What is it?" Alexander asked.

"Ten miles south, sir. There is...or there was a church. Sir the English are ahead of us and so it is our saving grace, but those of the church sir...they are all dead. There were at least ten men of the cloth and three women." He cleared his throat and said with a sullen tone, "They are all hanging from the trees outside of the church walls sir."

Alexander and Deb looked at each other with foreboding expressions. David was listening as well and approached quietly. The English were leaving the country alright, but they were not leaving without some satisfaction. If they could not fight the Scots, they would punish them on their way back to their own lands; like spitting in their faces and walking away.

Deb stepped forward and looked at the rider, "Thank you for your efforts. Do you think we are far enough behind the English that we may make safe passage for a while?"

"Yes ma'am, but I suggest that we do not hurry. They will be at least twenty miles away by now, but we must still be leery. If a church of unarmed people were hung for being in their path, we would all surely see a worse fate if they saw us. I fear that we may encounter similar devastation."

"We will have to carry on. Isabella will begin to fail again if we do not end her treacherous journey soon," Patrick spoke up.

"Yes, he is right." Alexander stated.

"Pack up the horses and take on as much water as possible. We must return Patrick and his children home by tonight. The damp, cold night air is keeping Isabella from gaining her strength," Deb added.

"Ride then. We will forge on while the sun is warm," said David.

The horses began to line up and follow one another. Deb looked back at David who had been keeping his distance from her. He usually rode beside her. She turned back again and looked forward wondering about it but decided not to worry on it.

David looked up at her just as she turned her head and his eyes told exactly what he was thinking, but he straightened his back and galloped a bit faster so as to catch up with Deb and Alexander again. Deb looked over to him and he smiled and nodded.

Deb smiled back and suddenly wondered if she had not seen that look before. She suddenly felt strange in her stomach as she thought back to the times that Liam had looked at her that way when they had first started to admire each other. She was a bit surprised by her revelation and kept her head turned forward while she tried to justify her suspicions. Was she reading David right or was she just feeling the loneliness of being away from Liam? Whatever she was thinking, she knew it was not the time, nor place. It was buried and she vowed to stop the thoughts she was having immediately.

The journey along the path the English army had made was grim. The ground was torn up fifty feet wide and the mud was making the horses hooves cling a bit more with each step, but they carried on slowly as was suggested. It was a walk of great doom looming over them as they made their way.

The group made it to the church that the rider had described and as they saw the peaks of the steeples rising above the rolling hills, they all fell silent and rode very slowly toward it. Alexander wondered if they should not leave the path and take another route, but the landscape was harsh and it would take a toll on them all to struggle over stony riverbeds and rock-cobbled fields. They must take the easiest, quickest way. He instructed the girls to cover their faces while they passed by and as they did so, Patrick placed a gentle hand over Isabella's eyes. The scene was gruesome to and although the girls had seen such a thing before, this was particularly disturbing.

Deb tried to look away as well before she felt that these people deserved acknowledgement, even if it were difficult for her. She turned her head in the direction of the bodies now hanging limp and ragged from the tree branches. The church was smoking behind them, the birds were beginning nature's cleanup and the smell of charred wood filled their nostrils. While the birds pecked the eyes out of one of the women, Deb said a prayer for their souls and as she finished softly whispering, a tear trickled down Sarah's face even though she was not looking. Deb's words were enough to evoke the wave of emotions that they were all feeling. James noticed and came up beside Sarah.

He reached over as they rode and took her hand. She turned away from the scene even more so and he said gently, "Look at me, Sarah. You do not need to see this. I'll talk to you until we have passed. Just keep looking at me."

Sarah sniffed and nodded with a sullen motion.

It was difficult to escape the visual sight of it all when the smell of the rotting flesh was permeating the air. Alexander picked up the pace to get them clear of the scene and he was relieved to see a hill coming up. They crossed over it and made their way, free of the churchyard.

No one spoke for a while and Alexander found he was at a loss for words. He had seen so many people killed in his life on the battlefield, and many of them his comrades, but the ominous message left by the English was disturbing to him in a different way. Burning a church and its occupants was more than a fit of vengeance; it was a clear warning that more was to come.

"When will it ever be over?" Alexander thought to himself.

Steadily, they made their way into the valley where Patrick's home stood. Isabella's face showed a sign of great relief as she recognized the landscape at long last. She thought about her mother's arms holding her and how good the food would taste. She was finally home and free of her torture.

Deb and the others watched with grateful smiles as Patrick, James and Isabella were greeted with loving arms as Isabella's mother and grandmother ran from the house with tears in their eyes. They were screaming Isabella's name and the family embraced so tightly that everyone else could feel it from their horses. Deb dismounted with Alexander and they walked politely ahead to meet Isabella's family.

Patrick turned and introduced them to his partners in arms.

"Iona, this is Deb and Alexander." He then pointed to everyone else and added, "And their brave friends. Our daughter is alive because of these people." Patrick's wife, Iona, walked forward with tears in her eyes and took Deb's hand.

"God bless you, lass!" She looked at everyone and said louder, "God bless you all! Thank you for bringing my daughter back to me. Thank you so very much." She was weeping through her words.

Deb patted Iona's hand and said, "She is fighter ma'am. She didn't give up. She has the fever, but it is getting better and now with you, I am sure she will improve and be on her feet soon."

James looked over at Sarah, who was looking a bit sad that she would have to leave his side. He walked over to her.

"Sarah, I will visit you when I can at the Barne farm. It is not but three days of good riding away from here."

"That would be lovely, James. I wish Isabella good health. She is my friend always," Sarah said.

Isabella looked up at Sarah and smiled. She could tell that her brother was enamored with her and felt sad for their parting as well. Sarah had taken care of her and she too was sad to see her go.

Patrick's wife whispered to him, "Who is the lovely lass that our son is speaking to?"

"That is Sarah. She was one of the girls that were held captive. She is quite the young lady. Our son saw that right away as well. I feel for them having to part."

Iona gave Patrick a look that he understood but was surprised. He gave her a look back as if to agree with something. Iona then asked Deb to come with her into the croft for a moment.

"Miss Barne, does the young lady Sarah have family to return to?"

Deb shook her head to the negative sadly and said, "No, I'm afraid she was left an orphan when Gully raided her home. She is to live with me until I am certain she is alone in the world. After that, she will stay with me."

"I am wondering lass, if you would consider something? You see, my mother is aging and Isabella is quite weak still and may be for some time. It would be very helpful to have another woman here to help me with chores and I would feed and shelter her as best I could. These children have been put through hell and the look on my son's face pains me as he is seeing the young lass off. If you see it fit, I would take care of Sarah as if she were my own. Given the way James and Isabella feel about her, it just seems like fate that she stays. Would you consider it?"

Deb was surprised as they had only just met, but Iona had been alone for some time trying to take care of things with just her mother. It must have been difficult and Deb realized that her motives were part desperation and part sympathy.

"I would have to speak with her first of course, but I understand your logic. You have a real family here and I can't offer that to her. My husband Liam is fighting with the army and I was concerned about Sarah and what I would do if I had to take leave from the farm again. She would have been lovely company for me though. She is a young lady that has a lot of fire in her heart and she deserves a future. I also understand the ways of young love. I've been separated from my Liam far too often lately and for me to stop Sarah and your son from being together out of loneliness for myself, would be selfish of me. If she desires it, I won't stop her from staying."

Iona answered, "I am sorry, Miss Barne, I did not realize that your husband has been away as well. I am sorry to ask this of you now. With no husband at home, how will you take care of your land without Sarah?"

"I have thought about that, and I am going to request assistance from my husband's family to the north." She put her hand on Iona's. "I will speak to Sarah. The Lord only knows that a family is just what she needs."

Iona smiled and the two women walked back out. Everyone was a bit curious, including Patrick.

"Sarah love, would you dismount?" Deb asked.

Sarah got down a bit confused but figured that she was just going to be introduced to the family. Instead, as Iona and Deb spoke of their idea, she realized what was being offered to her. She felt utter elation and hugged Isabella and Iona with gratefulness. James was as bright as the sun, but knew that by his father's glances, he would have to be a gentleman while Sarah stayed with them. They were a bit young for a coupling in Patrick's eyes even though younger had wed before, but he was happy to have such a fine young lady join their family. He also knew all too well what Sarah had been through.

Sarah suddenly turned and looked at Deb. They both started to tear up, but Sarah knew that Deb would not allow her to give up such an offer.

At the same time, she felt as though she was losing Deb again.

"I am afraid for you," Sarah said to Deb. She had to be firm with Sarah, or her guilt of leaving Deb would keep her from accepting Iona's invitation.

"You need not worry about me, little sister. My life will be my own again now that Gully is gone. Do not fear. We are not leaving each other. We are both free now Sarah, and you will flourish here. We will be in each other's lives forever now. You will never be alone again."

"Promise you will visit, Deb. Promise me. You are my best friend and I think of you as my sister now and forever."

When Deb heard the word 'promise', she knew that if she did so with Sarah, it meant the ultimate truth to her. She had never broken a promise to Sarah yet and with a deep breath she once again gave her solemn vow to the young girl.

"I promise, little sister. We will have many happy visits."

Deb knew they needed to continue on and deliver the other girls back to their families and as they parted with Patrick's family, Sarah stood staring after them as the horses rode off.

Deb turned on her horse and raised her arm to Sarah. Iona walked up behind her placing a gentle hand on her shoulder watching Deb leave as well.

"No worrying now, lass. Life has given us all a second chance. Come now child, we must eat and get rest."

Sarah turned around and looked into Iona's kind eyes. She bowed her head as they walked and knew how blessed she really was. She could be dead by now, but instead, she was warm and safe and cared for. She turned one more time as they entered the front door of the croft and she prayed for Deb and the others. She would be forever indebted to Deb Barne.

Chapter Sixteen
Bittersweet

Cheryl Alleway

One more day of riding and speaking to the locals gave Alexander, Deb and the men a chance to give the other girls their freedom and return them to their families. It was a joyous day and one that was filled with many thanks and embraces from families who thought they had lost their children forever.

Once news of Gully's death became widespread, it finally got back to everyone in the area who had not known of the terrible story. William put high rewards on the heads of the last two of Angus' men who fled that day at Dominon castle and Deb felt as though she could return to normal life. She returned to her father's farm and knew that it would take her time to bring it back to what it was before, without Liam. Deb didn't despise the thought however, because to her, it would be a privilege to be home again.

Alexander, David and their men, made their way back to MacDonell castle and everyone awaited news of William, Liam and the others.

David rode away with mixed emotions. The time passed by so slowly that it felt like forever. Anne sent word to King Robert the Bruce that she and her clan had met with great confidence and motioned to have William become the next Earl of the MacDonell Clan in their region. King Robert would support it for certain. Anne had met with the

Lord of Islay and the decision was agreed upon. There was no other better suited to rule the people to the north. Anne was confident that William would make them proud and uphold the MacDonell name. At present, there had been no clan feuds in the Perth and Inverness regions and with talks underway with two of the neighboring clans; they too were pleased with the choice of William as Earl. When quarrels did strike up, it would be by the grace of God that William's presence would surely calm the situations.

Eight months had passed and Deb had settled back into farm life, but without Liam.

Her first winter without him had come and gone. She prayed he was still alive. Liam's second brother, Samuel, had joined the fight and Deb's father in-law had no choice but to send his last two teenage boys to help her on the farm until Liam and Samuel came home.

Young Sarah and James had come for a few visits and while she stayed with Deb, they worked very hard to help where they could. Deb would send extra food back with them to Patrick's family.

The farm was looking lived in once again and the grain had started to grow thick and plentiful. Liam's father had sent down six sheep to help get Deb going and he made sure that one was a good ram and the rest were ewes. When mating season came, Deb was pleased to see a few of the ewes pregnant and she began to put the last few months behind her. She felt lonely for her husband, but took comfort that her life was finally stable. It was a blessing to her and now all she needed was for Liam to return.

One morning, she saw a rider coming from the north. As he approached, she could see that it was a familiar face.

"Deborah!" The voice shouted as the tall grass separated in waves from his quick paced horse.

Deb smiled widely at the sight of her friend David. When he dismounted, she ran to meet him, but then realized that his visit was quite unusual be it that he was alone. The boys kept working in the field when they saw that it was a friendly visitor and Deb waved to them to continue with their chores.

"Be it the face of David all the way from Inverness alone? What brings you here? Is it Liam?"

He dismounted and walked toward her.

David was fighting to keep a smile on his face for Deb, but she could tell something was wrong. He kept looking down and up at her again. Her body turned into stone and a cold fearful pain hit her hard in the chest. David tried to step forward to her and Deb's eyes filled with tears. She couldn't move.

He had practiced what to say to her the entire way, but now faced with her pain, he lost his courage and simply hung his head managing only to say, "I could not be more sorry Deb. Liam, he...he was by William's side and..." David bowed his head before Deb and went to one knee, holding her hand while looking up at her.

The boys came running as they saw that Deb was crying. They rushed to her side and she looked at them as a sister would; embracing them both at each of her sides. Deb pulled them close and whimpered, "Your brother has died fighting for us all, lads. I am so sorry!" She comforted them and held them tenderly.

Although a strong lass, Deb lost her legs and fell to her knees and the boys wrapped their arms around her squeezing her tightly as they all braced themselves on the ground. David moved over and placed his hand upon one of the boys.

"Deb, are you alright?" One of the boys asked with innocent concern.

David felt as though he would be ill.

He spoke in a deep, soft voice, "God be my witness, he was a man to be reckoned with on the field. He was a great man, Deb! You must hold on to that! Your father would not want to see you like this. It's going to be alright, Deb. I promise you!"

David and the boys tried to help her stand up and as they did, David continued, "William and Anne have requested your presence at the castle as a show of support and they want to give you a proper burial for him. Liam was given knight's status only weeks ago. Your husband was an honored young man."

One of the boys looked up at David with tearful eyes and said, "Are mother and father alright? Have they sent for us? What of our other brother Samuel?"

David touched his head, "Samuel is fine lad, and of course, your parents have sent for you too."

"What about the farm?" The other boy asked.

"Henry has been sent to watch over it while Deb and the both of you join your families. No worrying now lads, you just think about your brother and sister-in-law now. You need to be strong and help us get Deb to Inverness as quickly as possible."

David's calming, matter of fact voice settled the boys and they shook their heads agreeably while wiping away the tears from their dirty faces. Deb released them from her tight grip and asked them to go to the house to prepare their clothing and some food for the trip. It was early in the day and there was no use in wasting time. She had regained her composure too after listening to David's voice and changed from stunned to numb. She was feeling empty now. Her emotions were black and her mind was still. It was as if she could not think and felt nothing.

David and the boys packed the horses and Finnean was brought from the back for Deb. He nudged her as she caressed his face saying nothing. He could sense her pain once again and this time he too was greatly disturbed. She was not herself and she was quiet. Finnean knew something was wrong and he was pacing back and forth beside her while pressing against her gently.

They were ready to leave within an hour or two. Deb knew the sheep would be fine until they returned in the evening from the fields. They usually worked their way back around the same time every day. They would need to be guided into the pen for the night, but Henry could do that without problems as there were not more than ten. The new pregnant females would be glad to listen as their growing bellies made them tired by the end of the day. They all knew a warm bed of hay awaited them.

Henry had left shortly after David and he was close. It took days to reach Carrick from Inverness and it would be quite a site to see Deb's croft pop into view.

The craft door was closed and the small windows were covered as the boys had pulled the wooden shutters in to close them. The fire was filled with wood to keep things warm for Henry. The thatched roof was dry and there had been no rain for a few days giving Henry a comfortable place to arrive to. He liked it here. Although Henry would need help once the grain was ready, his job for now was to keep the animals fed and the croft cared for. The wind and rain wreaked havoc on the roof at times in the past and the base of the croft had to be constantly repaired so that rain would not seep in. The boys had piled plenty of wood out back and it seemed as though something had made them prepare for the journey at the right time.

Jacob Douglas had a good piece of land and not having a lord to answer to, he had done quite well for a man without a title to his name. There were not many who could claim that. For some of Jacob's old friends who worked another's land, life was difficult to say the least. Deb grew up without a mother, but she had so much more than the average Scot. People were struggling for enough food and Deb's propensity to share her bounty in the winter months was a blessing indeed. She helped one family through the last winter by giving them two lambs and a large bag of grain. It wasn't much to Deb because she and the boys were able to mill plenty for them as well. She had no qualms about helping.

For now, she had to hold herself together and make the long trip north, but the fact remained…Deb had no time to grieve. Liam needed to be buried and she hated the thought of not being with him at that moment.

Everyone was awaiting their friend's arrival at the MacDonell's home. Liam's body would have to be embalmed to the best of their ability. It was going to take time for David to ride south and back with Deb. There were few that would embalm as a specialty, but Anne had actually seen it done and had called upon her knowledge to make it so. Two men volunteered and with Anne's guidance, Liam's body was given treatment. There was no other way with Deb being days away. Liam's body was filled with spices and mint and wrapped in pieces of cloth soaked in wax. The wax would seal the body long enough for them to arrive and bury him. He was placed into position as best they could as rigor mortis was their greatest challenge from the delivery of his body. They had to break a few of his bones in the process, but he would look much less damaged in the end once clothing was added. His face was left exposed, but a coating of wax was applied to the inner ears, mouth and nostrils. He was then placed in a private room while he awaited his young wife's arrival. Anne added the final touches to the room. She and two of the other women along with her lady in waiting cleaned Liam's face and tied his hair back. They made certain his clothing was lying upon him properly and said a prayer over his body. Once they were finished, they pulled a lovely blanket over him up to his chest and left the room for Deb to see him next.

This journey was going to be the most difficult one yet for Deb. She and David were quiet except for the occasional mention of stopping for a break. David did not know what to say to her and his mind was racing. He was feeling confused. His loyalty to Liam was burying his feelings for Deb who was riding beside him trying to come to terms her husband's death. David's stomach felt sick with emotion but he tried to concentrate on getting Deb and the boys to the castle safely.

When they reached the halfway point through Perth, they could see Henry rounding the water's edge on the river Tay to meet them. He was riding alone as usual, but had obviously been laden down with as many extra supplies from Ann MacDonell as possible. She had given him extra food, clothing, flour and a couple of extra lambs in tow. There were bags of salt and dried fish along with a satchel of coins in case he needed something else. She did not want him bartering his supplies away and Henry was appreciative for the generosity.

As they met in the late misty afternoon, everyone had sallow faces and Henry stopped to get off his horse to greet Deb. She dismounted and the two embraced gently.

"Hello, old friend, how are you?" Deb asked Henry.

"Lassie, I 'em worried more about yu. I don't know what to say, other than, I 'em so veery, veery sorry. Liam was said to 'ev been by William's side on many occasions and it ees because of 'im that many an arrow missed their mark on the his leader's chest."

Deb smiled and tears filled her eyes. She hugged Henry again and felt the warmth of his small heart. His humbleness was enamoring to say the least. He was bowing his head and tearing up himself as she touched his face with her right hand and held his crooked shoulder with the other.

"Henry, your offer to watch the farm for me is most generous." She placed a large key around Henry's neck. She had it tied to a string so he would not lose it. Door locks were futile on the farms, but Jacob had used it to keep the door from flying open in storms. Deb just simply continued to use it as it reminded her of her father.

"Thank you, my friend. I am worried that the work may harm your legs, so please do only as much as they will allow you. Rest your bones each day and let the lambs roam. They are strong and very independent. They have a large stream to drink from and plenty of field to feed on."

"I know lassie, I believe I weel keep the thatch good and keep the rain away from the root cellar. I promise I'll du ya proud. I am older now aneway, and I doont think that travelin' ees best fur me anymore. I 'ave been asked to do this from above indeed."

"Well, I am in your debt, sweet Henry. Are you alright to make the rest of the trip alone?"

"Ah ya, lass. No worryin'. I 'em fine. Lady Anne has given me plenty of supplies, and this horse as ya can see, is a fine one. He's no Finnean, but he's a loyal laddie."

Deb stroked the horse's face and thanked him too.

"Very well, we shall continue on. Liam's brothers are going to be grateful to see their father and mother. God knows they have all suffered."

"Yes, 'tis true lass, 'tis true."

Henry mounted his horse once again and Deb did the same with Finnean. They wiped their tears away and nodded a goodbye. David took the lead and as they rode away, Henry looked back with his sad, crooked face. He wondered how so much pain could come to such a young woman. He held his head down low and said to himself, "Well Hen, we 'ave a job to do. Let's not let the lassie down."

Henry's back was crooked as he rode slightly to the left of the saddle and his small shoulders tilted a little to the ground, but his expression was steadfast and he prayed that Deb would find solace in the fact that she still had friends who cared.

The hours went by quickly as David led Deb and the boys up the last leg of the journey to MacDonell Castle. They did not even wish to rest. Deb just wanted to get there. Rest would come when her mind allowed it.

Anne had prepared a beautiful room for Deb. Liam's parents had warm clothes and a small gift ready for their youngest boys when they arrived. Liam's mother stood waiting at the entrance pensively as someone announced that they saw David and his party in tow. She was weeping quietly as she anticipated seeing her daughter-in-law after such a long time. It was a terrible homecoming, to say the least.

When the call came from the watchtower that their horses had been sighted, everyone in the castle came to the courtyard to greet Deb and the boys. Anne had asked for a quiet welcoming to show their respect for Liam. It was a tradition for the MacDonell castle to honor the passing of anyone of the clan. Deb and the rest of the Barne family were considered just that. She sat in quiet contemplation before going down to greet the young lady who had become as a surrogate daughter. They had more in common now than they ever had. Anne's heart ached for Deb and she could not wait to see her sweet face.

The gates were opened as the tired group made their way through to the faces of so many people. It was as if a princess were arriving as young girls stood with flowers in hand for Deb. The women had created a beautiful hand-made blanket for her bed. It was lovely with its hand dyed cloth and yellow threads so lovingly sewn throughout. One of the women held it tenderly and neatly folded in her arms, ready to present to Deb.

Anne had arrived in the courtyard, as did William and his wife, Margaret. Anne had requested that Margaret take her place beside William. She knew that William's wife would ask for her advice when needed it and the people knew her to be honest, and caring just as Anne herself. Anne had other things on her mind. She was hoping that Deb would spend some time at the castle after Liam's funeral. She still had so much to share with her.

There was something telling her to guide the young girl. Something told her that Deb was destined for a different path and to farm for the rest of her life may not be the one that was chosen for her. Anne saw something in the girl that had a different purpose. She wanted the chance to show Deb her true potential as a woman in Scotland. Having lost Thomas and the son that left her heart broken, Anne MacDonell was feeling the need to change her own story as well. Deb was part of it. Her money meant nothing more to her than the dirt beneath her feet. It would be used to help her people and to provide Deb the things in life that so many did without. Her maternal emotions had built up with nowhere to go and she ached to have a child. It would never happen now, but this young woman who had come into her life so abruptly, had stirred her soul again.

Liam was a young man of immense courage and determination. He survived a hanging and the rape and kidnapping of his wife and still managed to gain his senses, getting control of his life. He had such faith in his wife that he believed she would survive her ordeal and they would be as one again. A man of such faith in himself and his partner would surely be a leader on the battlefield when he was called to duty and Liam would never be forgotten. His only regret as he lay dying on the field was never again seeing his young wife's face. Liam died with that guilt on his conscience, but he died knowing that he had her heart.

"Yes, I see great things for these two. If they want them," Thomas commented.

Anne had replied, "We shall have to see if they want to travel a similar path as we have, my love. I know you are a visionary and that you see leadership in unlikely places because of your time fighting for our people, but please realize that someone must want to devote themselves to leadership."

Thomas had smiled at his wife's insight and as he kissed her cheek, they fell asleep in their beautiful room within the walls of their castle, believing that destiny awaited the arrival of people like Deb and Liam Barne."

As Deb was settling herself in her room, Anne walked through the long corridor and gently knocked on Deb's door.

"Please enter," Deb answered in a sullen quiet voice.

Anne did so slowly and as she opened the large, heavy door, she saw Deb sitting on the edge of the four-posted bed. She was just staring into the flame of the fire that one of the servants had lit for her. Her hands were crossed on her lap and the blanket the ladies made for her was draped over her knees. She was painfully morose and Anne did not say anything at first.

Anne found her way to the side of the bed where Deb was sitting and she was surprised when Deb suddenly jumped from her seat and embraced her in a trembling hold. She was shaking and she began to weep...finally.

Anne's heart sank as she felt the pain in her face. She stroked the long, dark hair that fell around Deb's shivering shoulders and held her tightly. Anne's own eyes welled up as she tried to give Deb comfort.

"Take solace in your tears, child, they are the river that carries your pain away. They hold onto the hurt and carry it away from your heart. Your pain is real, Deborah. Allow it, embrace it and do not be ashamed. I cannot bring him back for you. I can only tell you that you will stop crying eventually and when you do, I will be there just as I am now."

Deb pulled back and stood by the fire. She turned with a face so deeply wounded, that Anne had never seen it in her before.

"Why is this happening, Anne! Why have our husbands been taken from us when everything else has as well? Is it some cruel punishment that we should feel such pain and be forced to live with it? I have seen so much death and I have even caused it with my own blade! So why should I now feel so helpless and weak?" Deb was shouting over tears and her words were, at times, slurred.

Anne stood and went to the fire as well. "Deborah, child, this is not punishment! Do not feel guilt, my dear! What you are feeling is what so many women and children have been feeling because of this fight for freedom! It is not punishment, but a cruel reality of our lives at this moment in time." Anne took Deb by the shoulders and sat her down gently again. Deb went silent.

Anne tried to calm her more. This girl before her was about to see Liam's lifeless body and Anne feared for the girl's ability to deal with it. She had been so strong for so long, praying for her husband's face to come across the fields of their home and take her into his arms. This would never happen and Deb was finally realizing that she truly was alone in the world. She had poured her soul into the lives of everyone else around her and now she faced her own fears head on. Like anyone who is pushed to their limits, Deb was not infallible and she was feeling it more deeply now than ever. Torture, battle, and even the death of her mother and father had not defeated her, but now she faced losing the young man who had captured her heart. He lay in the next room cold and lifeless and Deb Barne was not so resilient anymore. She was broken inside and Anne could not bear to see it happen. Not now, not ever.

"Deborah, take my hand and we will do this together. Fear not what you will see. It is not Liam. He is with you as we sit here. He is with you as you sleep. When I said goodbye to my Thomas, I embraced him in my heart. He held me tightly and gave me the courage to realize that life is not only what we can touch. Life is within us and if you truly love someone, they become a part of you when they pass. Instead of making you weaker, they make you stronger. They enter your soul and lift you up. You may not feel that way right now, but I promise you that you will be alright, my dear."

Deb looked over at Anne's kind face and through salty tears she answered back with tension and sorrow, "My father told me once when I was small, that mother would sit upon my shoulder as I grew. She told me that she loved me often and that she would not allow me to be harmed, even if she was gone. Sometimes, I think about what has happened, and I believe her words. How else would I still be here?" She put her head back down and closed her eyes, causing a tear to fall to her lap.

"No need to rush, my dear, but are you ready?" Anne asked.

Deb nodded and the two women stood together. Anne put the blanket around Deb's shoulders and added, "We are all here with you. You are not alone, my child."

As Deb walked with Anne, she remembered the funeral that had been held for Thomas and his men who had died fighting Gully. It was a day she would never forget.

Anne had her servants help her create the most beautiful memorial Deb and Liam had set eyes on. It was far more than a dirt grave and a few prayers said. Many bodies were burned while their families said goodbye, but burial of the body close to them was a sacred preference to many. There were so many candles lit that evening that the castle was seen for miles in a low glow of light. A massive stone cross bore Thomas' name under a large oak where others of their clan had been laid to rest. A young girl sang a traditional song in honor of Thomas and his men while her father played the flute. The priest said words so beautiful that Deb never forgot them. He spoke of bravery and family. He spoke of the men who had died before them in the fight for Scottish freedom and he spoke of a time when all men, women and children of the Scottish Highlands and Lowlands would live in peace. His name was John McGuire and he was there on this day as well to say a few words for Liam. Deb took comfort in the fact and tried to remember it all. She was not alone in her pain here. These people felt every tear that filled Deb's eyes.

Step by step Anne and Deb walked past the stone fireplace and through the main room door. The hallway was not long that separated the second room from the first. Anne had asked that each guest room be built with an adjoining room for families with children who came to visit them. The next room was smaller, but quaint and also had a fire lit within it.

As Anne opened the second door, Deb braced herself. Her heart was pounding, but she held tightly to Anne.

The room was blue and dim, but calming. There were candles lit and the walls were decorated with a few pieces of magnificent artwork that Anne had purchased in Paris. There was a small table with a water vessel and beside the fireplace was a pile of wood, neatly stacked. The bed that filled the right side of the room was laden with fine linen and draped with a beautiful MacDonell tartan hanging from all four posts, which fell from ceiling to floor. Though Liam's family name was Barne his father wished for the MacDonell tartan to be used in honor of the clan that Liam died for.

There was a large wooden chair and sitting beside it was a green wool blanket lying across one of its thick arms. The flickering candle flames illuminated the walls and added to the warmth of the evening light that was still entering the single window. Purple thistle sat gracefully in a simple vessel beside the bed on a small wooden table. Alongside it was a bible and a cross.

As Deb came to the edge of Liam's bed, she stood on the right hand side. Her shaking suddenly ceased and her entire world hushed. The curtain was pulled back and there, laying silent unlike he did months ago, was Liam.

Deb began to weep quietly as she let go of Anne's hand. She slowly made her way to Liam's side and leaned over to see her young husband adorned in knight's clothing. He was dressed in the colors of a Barne with a freshly sewn jacket and tunic. On his hip was a handsome leather sheath, holding a beautifully crafted Claymore. It was polished to perfection and he had been shaved neatly with his hair combed back into a clean tress. On his chest lay lavender, thistle and oak leaves. In his hands he held a book of Scottish poetry his mother had read to him as a child.

Deb noticed his hands were damaged and had the black marks of old wounds. He had a scar on his face that flowed from his left eye down his cheek to his chin, but he was still handsome. Pale as he was now, Deb still traced his strong jaw-line and stroked his forehead, dark eyebrows and long eyelashes. She would never see his eyes again, but Deb placed her hand on his and turned to Anne.

"Thank you for doing this for me. He looks as I would have imagined him upon coming home. You have gone to so much trouble. I do not feel worthy of this effort, my lady."

"Ah, but you are worthy. You are a part of this family now, my child. This is something that we do for family. Do not feel unworthy, Deborah, for it is one with such valiant grace as yours that deserves such treatment. I would not have it any other way."

Deb put her head down and wept quietly with a profound amount of pain. It was all too overwhelming. Anne cradled her hand to calm her. She had been through this very moment when Thomas had been brought home. It is an ache that feels almost unbearable.

As cold and stiff as Liam was, seeing him was still good for Deb. It was closure. Anne stood back for a moment and allowed the young girl the release that was burning her heart from within.

Through her own tears, Anne finally came to Deb's side. "You are giving him what he needs right now, Deborah. Your presence is helping him to leave this place and be free. He would want you to go on, my dear. He would want you to go on!" She embraced her and the two fell into the moment as two lost souls that had been brought together through the horror of death.

Deb looked up at Anne and turned from Liam's body. She fell back into Anne's arms like a child and held her tightly. Anne's tears colored her face with lines. She squeezed the young girl tightly and felt such warmth from Deb's attachment to her, that she was speechless. It was as if their husband's deaths had brought them together for a reason. Anne now had the child she had so longed for and Deb had a mother in her life once more.

John McGuire stood in the hallway and as Deb finished her time with Liam, she exited the room with Anne. John met them in the hallway and took Deb's hand.

"My dear, your life has just begun. Do not fear this change in your journey. Your husband wanted me to give this to you. He had carried it with him in battle and now it is yours."

Deb thanked him and took the piece of paper that was wrapped in a sheet of thin leather. She clenched it and sat on a bench outside the room. Anne and John sat with her and as they did so, David came slowly down the hallway. Deb looked up at him and he saw her pain. He knelt before her with his sword swaying back behind him.

He bowed his head and said very reverently, "Deborah, lass, I held onto this note from your husband as if it were a jewel. I did not wish to have you read it until you were amongst us all. Liam wanted it that way as well. Please accept my deepest sympathies to you."

Deb touched David's face and said, "I am blessed to have friends such as you in my life, David. Thank you for your valor and chivalry."

David's heart suddenly skipped a beat as Deb spoke to him. He was half mourning for the loss of Liam and half fighting his own inner pain as he watched Deb suffer. He wanted to grab her and hold her tightly.

Anne saw something in David's face that made her curious. His face did not just hold sympathy alone. David's face held affection, she was almost sure of it. For that brief moment she shook off the thought as everyone's attention was on Deb reading the note from Liam.

She opened it slowly, revealing a brown piece of parchment that was hand written in dark ink. It was a small passage, but Deb could not read it. Not only were the words so difficult to see, but she had a difficult time understanding the writing itself. She had never really learned how to read. Liam would have helped her with it as his father had taught him. She shook her head 'no' and handed it to John McGuire who kindly patted Deb's shoulder and took on the task of putting a voice to the words on the paper.

John read: *"I, Liam of Barne, give my wife, Deborah of Barne, any worth I have made as a soldier and all of my worldly possessions. I wish for her to carry with her my sword, my daggers, my bow and arrow for she is the one who will make them do what they should. May they protect her and keep me close to her if ever she needs them. To my wife Deborah: I love you and you should have any happiness that should come to you. Do not be afraid for I, and your father, cover you with a shield. Live on with your grace, your beauty and your power to be as strong as any man. You have been given all of this for a reason. The war is subsiding for now, and the treaty of Northampton has been signed by our King Robert the Bruce. Use this as a sign that better times will come and your future will be as a strong and free woman. Deborah my love...live, laugh and fight on, sweet lass. I love you. ~ Liam of Barne*

Deb cried gently and David was hard pressed not to weep at her side. Anne placed the blanket around Deb's shoulders again and John McGuire closed the paper, wrapping it back up in the leather.

They all stood for everyone would be waiting for Deb in the courtyard and Liam would be carried out of the castle walls and brought north to his family's burial grounds. Deb was fine with the idea as she felt Liam should be close to his father and mother.

The men took Liam's body and gently placed it on a platform that was carried from all four sides. There were 4 simple posts at each corner, which held a cream coloured sheer material to cover him slightly. They walked him out of the room and down a set of stairs away from Deb to the courtyard and out the gate to the carriage that was awaiting his body.

As the day went on, Deb felt empty. Floating in a sea of darkness and blind emotion, she drifted through the hours without feeling; without anything inside. She was like an empty vessel stripped of all that she was.

When it was over, she went north for a day or two with Liam's family and spent time with them until she returned to the castle. While she was there, Liam's father had spoken with her and told her that he hoped she would move on, but she should always come back to visit them. He would prefer that she stayed, but he knew her better than that. Deb thanked him again for everything he had done for her and saw them off with a final wave from her horse.

Malcolm stood in silence watching her leave. What would her life bring now? She was not unlike her father, destined to lose the ones she loved at a young age and make her way in the world on her faith alone. It seemed cruel, but it was not uncommon in the life they led. Forging on they struggled through these losses and rose again.

He whispered under his breath, *"Good luck, my dear, God speed to you."*

Deb made her way back to the castle with a blank expression. David and his brother had accompanied her and made sure she saw safe passage in her grieving state. She was not herself and David's respect for her independence was overshadowed by his feelings. He would not take *no* for an answer and Deb did not argue. Her mind was not as clear as it should be. Anne would not have her alone on this journey. Not this time.

Upon her return, Deb made the effort to take some time to stop and gather herself. She spent the next week or two walking Finnean and sitting by the stream. She was in mourning and everyone allowed her the space she needed.

Anne spent some of that time teaching Deb to write and to read. She was improving quickly and spent her nights before bed with a quill and inkwell writing down her thoughts. It was good practice, Anne had told her, and it was therapeutic as well. Anne thought that if Deb wrote her feelings down, they may begin to subside in bombarding her thoughts every day. Deb needed to clear her mind and repair her body and soul. The castle was the place to do it.

April 5th, 1328: Today, I sat by the river and saw your face in the water. It stayed for a moment until the wind shattered its image. Liam I miss you. I ache for your touch and I do not know of any other ache so great. I will try to live on. I will try. There must be something more in this life than this pain. – D.

Silence. This is what the night brought. Night after night, the silence came to her. It was supposed to be comforting but it allowed for too much thinking and she would rise often to go outside and spend time with Finnean. She was seen riding at midnight once, but no one, not even Anne nor David stopped her. She would return and fall asleep from her fatigue.

Anne was quite content to have the girl there and as time went on, there was a bond being formed unlike that which Deb had been unable to form with her own mother. It was simple with Anne and uncomplicated. It was maternal and valuable beyond what she ever expected. Anne was enjoying their time together more than she ever. It was a beautiful relationship given to them both from above.

David did not mind Deb's presence either and had pledged his loyalty to the young girl. When she ventured out with Finnean during the day, David was at her side to protect her if she would allow him. Anne worried about her, even though Deb was as good a fighter as any man. She could still not shed the maternal feelings that were building inside for the young woman.

"David will help keep the wolves at bay should they find Finnean an interesting treat," Anne would say to Deb, who would smile and chuckle at Anne's sweet concern. "Well, they are quite large up here in the highlands."

"I have seen them run deer. One was so large that I almost could not believe my eyes. It was a demon with its dark eyes and mouth wide enough to take a ewe in one bite!"

"Exactly! And my Thomas could prove it as he once slew a wolf that was almost the length of his horse, or so he said." Embellished or not, it was partially true.

Deb laughed, "Oh my! I would say that is a large one indeed!"

The days went by with every conversation. Anne had sent a few men down to check on Henry at the farm and he was doing wonderfully. He had never been so happy.

"He was filthy from the chores and laughing and playing his flute," the men told Deb and Anne.

Deb was so grateful and she hoped to return soon. She just needed to separate herself from the memories there for a while until she could deal with them better. As it was, she was doing as well as could be expected. She had teary nights and dreams of Liam, her mother and father, but time was at least helping Deb to cope with her loss and to see that she still had so much to do in her life. Liam's face however, seemed to never leave her. Like a haunting reminder when she placed her head on the pillow at night; her young husband was always there.

    Anne noticed this more and more because Deb did not realize the gaze of another who had been by her side through it all. Someone else who was wishing for Deb to picture his face at night just once; just once to show her he was there. Time however, had not passed enough for him to get over the guilt of loving her.

Chapter Seventeen
A New Road

Cheryl Alleway

Deb began working her body back into shape as she was beginning to gain herself back. She rode Finnean everyday and ran the same route over the hills that surrounded the castle. She practiced her fighting stances and the flips and kicking techniques her father had taught her while sword fighting. She often wondered how he had learned them. She had not seen many with the same type of combat style. David tried to learn from her and they had many moments of laughter when she would twist a certain way and evade him so easily. He would just shake his head and they would try again. She adored his energy and willingness to humour her. She saw something in him that was honest and loyal. It made her feel comforted inside, but she still did not see the truth behind his eyes.

At night, she would dream of her family. She remembered her father's stories and the moments that she learned something new about his life. She thought about the days when Liam first arrived and how they were so happy.

She wondered how her father's life must have been when he lived with his parents; even before Mary came into his life.

Deb had heard her father speaking at times about some of the interesting people he had met, but he divulged only small tales to her. Much of his traveling remained a mystery to her.

The sun was setting on MacDonell castle. Memories of her father were strengthening Deb's body and mind. She was beginning to regain it all. Her body was toned once again from riding with Finnean and every day, she would awaken to the morning mist and practice all that her father had taught her. She would, at times, request David's assistance and they fought each other with various weapons. Deb would out show David at archery and her knife throwing skills were the best that they had ever been. David's sword skills were better than Deb's and it made the two a good match for each other.

They learned from one another's skills and both were better for it. She had the pain of her husband's death pushing her and the difference was that she was trying to honor him, not avenge him. This was making her stronger. Her anger was leaving her mind and she could embrace the life she had ahead of her. She would weep only in silence now and then, for she knew that her tears and pain could never bring Liam back to her. She must keep faith that life would carry on.

The days were passing with few interruptions in daily life. Anne was teaching Deb to read and write even more. Now that Anne was teaching her to write, Deb made herself notes and would study them religiously. She was so interested in learning. It was the very trait that her father saw in her as a young girl. Now as a woman, Anne could see why Deb's father invested so much time and care in rearing her the way he did. It was the greatest gift a young woman could receive during these times. Many were told to be quiet and left to do chores alone with no voice of their own. William saw great value in young Deb Barne. She was a

Douglas at heart and William knew that her father must have been a great man. His daughter proved it and William could tell that David was more and more admiring her beauty and strength.

Anne sat in her window one evening while a young boy played the flute at dusk. A few people were sitting by a fire in the courtyard and David had joined them. In the quiet of the night air, Anne could hear some of the conversation. As she hummed to the notes of the flute, the music stopped and the boy took a drink from the well. David was speaking in a low voice to one of his friends, but Anne suddenly opened her eyes wide as she heard something she only suspected for so long.

"I too have noticed it David, you must tell her. It has been almost a year that she has come to be with us. Her heart must be longing for a man again. She is too young not to."

It was silent a moment and the man added, "I believe that if you do not say something to her, you will lose your chance. A lass like that will not be alone for long. I see the way some look at her."

David said very little, but Anne heard him clearly and it made her heart race.

"I know it, my friend, but I feel a pain in my heart for Liam's soul. How could I not? She loved him. What if she rejects me and I lose her completely?"

Both men then slowly left the courtyard. Anne began to ponder the things that had happened to them all. She heard the words David said and yet, she was not so surprised when she thought on it. The candles in the towers were dimming and the castle was beginning to drift into sleep. This was the time that Anne used to adore the most before Thomas' death. Now it was the quiet that caused her to think about things that she was trying to forget. She knew she had to face her own thoughts and tonight was no different. She knew that Deb was feeling the same things she did; every night, the image of their men came to them. Emotions of pain, loneliness and anger filled their minds.

Anne stood up from her window ledge and smiled gently. She clutched her heart. She had heard something she had felt for so long. David was in love with Deb and Anne needed to find out if Deb felt the same way. How she would do so escaped her, but now that she knew David's feelings for certain, she could not help herself. Deb was truly a daughter to her now, and nothing would make Anne happier than to see Deb joyful again with a loyal man by her side.

Anne once again gazed out the window. There was a mist drifting over the hills in the distance as the candles from the gate cast shadows against the stone walls. The wind was quiet and soft white moths were fluttering around the ledge where she sat. One landed on her hand and she suddenly began to weep gently. She knew more about Deb than she wanted to hold in. She not only wanted to tell her about David, but Anne was holding in information that, at times, she did not want to know. She had been keeping it to herself this entire time. She had to continue until the moment was right to reveal her knowledge.

Deborah Barne was raised by a man who loved her more than a father could love a child. Jacob Douglas was a man of great honor who came from a poor background and turned his daughter into a beautiful, strong woman. He gave her a chance in life where so many others had died from disease, war and famine.

These times saw the life and death of family members time and time again. The wars had subsided with England, but there was still turmoil and quarrels between clans. Some of the nobility was not finished with their taste of English coin. The lands were more peaceful, but they had not seen the last of war and quarreling. The wounds and scars created by the English were never going to disappear completely. The Scots had opened wounds themselves, on the English side. Some were greater than others. Deb bore a scar that she knew not of. Anne looked at Deb and knew her true identity and who she was, but her beginnings were not as she believed.

Anne could not contain what she knew. In her mind, she went over it again and tried to come to terms with it. She couldn't believe it herself until told by an unlikely friend. She pondered what she knew and began to go over it in her head again.

It was a painful thought, but Deb's father was not her true blood after all and her mother's death as tragic as it was, would end up being her salvation from the pain she held in her heart. Her daughter had another man's blood in her veins.

It was not the blood of Jacob Douglas, but he kept his promise to his young wife to never turn his back on his daughter. In his heart however, Jacob knew that he could not see his own eyes behind those of his daughter's. It haunted him, but he created a life for her regardless because behind Deb's eyes there were those of Mary as well. Jacob would do anything to honor her sweet soul. He never said a word to anyone.

Henry knew first-hand of it all. He had been peddling since the age of ten. He lived through the wars of his country by the will of God at times. His crippled physical presence ensured his anonymity from conscription as Henry was a young man of the same age as Jacob Douglas. He made his living in the same town and in the same country side as Jacob Douglas at the time of his wedding to Mary. Henry knew that Mary was Deb's mother and he knew that a high ranking English soldier had raped her. He also knew that Mary had been raped at least two months before she was with Jacob. There was no possible way that the child was his. Henry heard Mary speaking about it to her sister one evening as the sun was falling. They sat under an oak tree by the river and Henry had been sleeping behind the stable that backed the river's edge. He awoke to the voices as one of them was crying.

"Sister, my heart aches to where I cannot stand it! Jacob will leave me. I know it!" Mary was trying to whisper but her emotions were overtaking her.

"Mary calm yourself girl. You have done no wrong! You've been raped. It is not your fault! Are you certain that it cannot be Jacob's?"

"I cannot know for certain, but I do not know! I am so confused! I was with Jacob, but it was so much time before that they came for me! I do not know...I just do not know!"

"I'm afraid it must be then that Jacob is not the father Mary. If it was so much time in between, then I am so sorry. It must and it cannot be his."

Mary fell into her sister's arms weeping. Henry felt almost criminal for listening, but he could never help himself. His face was saddened for the poor girl. Henry knew how much Jacob loved her and would never tell another soul. This was not for him to intrude upon; not however until he met

Anne and Jacob's sweet and beautiful daughter who stole his heart away.

He heard Mary's sister swear that she would never tell a soul; especially not Jacob. When Mary told Jacob through her tears that faithful night that she did not know if Deb was his, she was lying to protect him. She loved Jacob Douglas and wanted her child to have a proper father. It seemed selfish to her at times, but she felt that if Jacob knew the ultimate truth, it would have been worse.

Before he left to take on the Douglas farm, Henry told Anne in confidence thinking that if it was ever revealed to Deb, she would need someone she trusted to be there for her. Henry thought of no one better than Anne.

How he found this out was not a surprise to her. Henry had traveled his entire life through every Scottish village and past every croft on the Scottish landscape. It's how he knew who Deb was before he ever met her; knowing her as the woman who killed Thomas and Anne's son, Gully. He knew Gully as an infant and watched him grow into the tyrant that Deb had faced. Henry had visited the MacDonell castle for years and they had allowed him to travel with them on many occasions on route to various villages and seaport towns. He had met them when they would return from trips to France and Anne would smile every time she saw Henry's crooked little grin. He had friends in the world after all, but when he met Deb, she captured his soul. He knew who she was and made it his last life goal to protect her and help her in any way he could. Henry had a big mouth for certain, but his heart was bigger.

He was a timid little man who had more survival skills than anyone. It was this knowledge and ability to hide and go unnoticed that kept him alive all the years of his life. He spent his days helping others. In fact, it was Henry who tried to help Anne and Thomas with Gully. His potions never did work on the lad, but Henry remained a silent, secret friend of the MacDonell's for years. When he heard of Deb's capture by Gully and his men, he tried to find her, but could not. Once he made his rounds with the villagers, Deb had escaped already and was on her way to find Liam. Henry had been two days away from Dominion castle when he met up with Gully's men who had been searching for Deb. He followed the story from there. It was no accident that he met Deb and Alexander on the road that day and it was no accident that he knew to get Patrick and James to help them. He was playing a part in the story all along, but he just couldn't keep up with some of it. Henry was now aging, but he had been an important part in Deb's journey and now as he faced his own health fading, he needed someone else to understand everything he knew. Anne was the one person he trusted more than anyone with Deb's heart. He was now faithfully watching her father's land while Deb gained her life back. Henry was a guardian angel to Deb but she hadn't realized to what extent.

Chapter Eighteen
Love Again

Cheryl Alleway

Anne walked to her bedside and sat on the edge beside her candle. She wiped her tears and took a deep breath. Who was she to keep these things from Deb? What would their relationship be if their bond of loyalty and honesty was broken? Yet, who was she to create more angst in Deb's life by telling her? Anne did not know what to do. She blew out her candle. Tonight, she would sleep. Tomorrow was a new day.

Deb rose the next day to a chilly air. Her small window was open and she walked over to it to close it. The damp Scottish mist carried the smell of the night's fires. The smoldering scent wafted into the castle and everyone was beginning to wake. Anne was still dozing across the courtyard in her room as her thoughts the night before had kept her awake longer than she would have wanted.

As Deb looked out the window towards the horse stables, she could see Finnean's muzzle anxiously sticking out from his stall. He never liked staying in it, but Deb wanted him safely tucked away at night with his coat wiped down and the burrs plucked from his tail and mane. He seemed to agree to the compromise, but his neighing was distinct and Deb put on her boots and began to tousle her long black hair into a more presentable arrangement.

Before she took one last glance outside, she noticed David walking toward the stables. He was holding his hunting bow and headed for his horse. Before he opened the gate, he stopped to pet Finnean. Deb noticed this and paused to watch. David placed his hand on Finnean's snout and gently caressed him. Finnean instantly stopped neighing and fussing. He blinked his eyes slowly and seemed to fall into the attention from David as he did when Deb greeted him.

Deb smiled curiously as Finnean was not usually as accepting of just anyone getting that close to him. Deb decided to try and get David's attention as she thought it may be enjoyable if she joined him on his hunting outing. She called out to him from her window and her voice echoed down to Finnean's ears as well.

Finnean began bobbing his head again as David turned and looked high up to Deb's window.

"I think he's getting anxious, lass! Why don't you join us?" David shouted back. His heart began to beat a bit more at the thought of being alone with Deb and as he waited for her to make her way down to the courtyard, he turned back to Finnean and said, "Well laddie, I wonder if I will have the courage today? What do you think?"

Finnean brushed his front hooves on the stable floor. David wanted to wait for Deb and added, "Alright now, she's on her way. You'll soon be with her. Trust me lad, I know how you feel."

Deb had grabbed her bow. She was a sight to behold to David as she passed through the entrance to the courtyard from within the castle. She had on her riding leggings, her knee high laced boots, her warm woolen tunic and she had tied most of her hair back with a leather lace. A few long pieces of her dark curly hair were trailing behind her as she walked in her strong gait toward him. He couldn't resist staring, and realized that he was overdoing it so he turned to open the stall that his own horse was in.

Deb made her way to Finnean as well and he pranced out into the courtyard as she set him free. She said good morning to David and said, "If you don't mind, I would like to contribute to the meal tonight! I am anxious to get Finnean his exercise! I think he is too!"

"Of course, I think we would have double the chance to bring a deer home with the two of you by my side." David's face was beaming.

As the two set up the horses, Deb made sure to mount her bow and arrows in the precise location that she would need them should a deer show itself as they rode. Her accuracy while in mid-stride was unmatched at times and David had benefited from riding with her over the past few months. Deb's flexibility as a woman gave her sturdy balance when Finnean was fast paced. It steadied her upper body and allowed for her strong accuracy.

David had been more of a ground fighter. He was strong, stout and his sword technique was envied by many. He had survived many battles alongside the MacDonell clan. When his young wife had died, he was as young as Deb. He understood her pain when Liam was killed and now, almost fourteen years older than Deb, David thought he had found the woman that he was meant to be with. His guilt for Liam's friendship and his love for Deb were now battling inside of him even more. It was a pain that he could no longer hold in.

He wondered if the time were coming for him to reveal his feelings to Deborah Barne. First, he would attempt to find out how she was feeling. They mounted their horses and made a slow pace out through the castle walls. For now, the air was fresh, there was peace on the Inverness fields and Deb was looking more beautiful than ever.

What David didn't notice was Deb's glance upon him as he mounted his horse. She felt something in her gut, but it wasn't something she had allowed herself to feel. It was a feeling of contentment that turned into a mild, but adoring pang within her chest. She hadn't realized that she looked upon him in such a way, but she stayed on course and breathed deeply as the morning air filled her lungs with delight.

Finnean was snorting as he warmed up his muscles with a light jaunt past the castle walls. Deb laughed and patted him on the neck. She leaned forward and put an arm around him. One could see the love she had for him. Finnean in turn held her atop of him as if she were a princess. She had saved him once and had never left his side. When she rode him, he was free. This is what she represented to him and why when they rode together, they were a sight to behold. David sat back on his horse and watched them ride ahead. Deb's sleek form flowed with Finnean's gait as if they were attached. They were one.

Deb pulled her bow out to practice. Without arrows, she released the reigns and laid them loosely on Finnean's neck. As soon as he felt it, he knew what to do. While he rode, she guided his path with light touches to his sides with her feet and knees. It was all he needed. She was then free to use her arms and hands.

She raised the bow and pulled back several times, stretching her arms and warming the bow. David caught up to them and stated, "We're close to the north forest. I think it's a good spot to start with. The does have been seen with fawns and that means there may be a buck nearby as well. Let's ride to the west edge and take a look!"

Deb nodded and the two turned on the trail across the open terrain. Deb's hair was flowing behind her now like dark water and David felt as though he was in heaven as he began to see that Deb was herself again. She was smiling and healthy and the fire was back in her eyes. She was a force to reckon with when she was like this.

Deb Barne was a powerful, vibrant young woman. She would not be found under a man's thumb, or silenced by the back of his hand. Deb was any man's equal in a world where women were so often considered the fairer sex. No, this one was different and she excited him like no one else ever had.

As they pulled up to the edge of the trees, he slowed down and Deb followed in behind. They went quietly in single file and gently brought the two horses to a stop. They dismounted to listen and look for signs of deer.

There were actually plenty of droppings within the underbrush and even a few wolf prints that seemed to be tracking the hoof marks. Deb went up to the horses and touched each of them on the snout.

``Shhhh, boys…quiet now. We need you to be still for a few moments," she said as she stroked their snouts to soothe them.

David had walked around the corner that flanked the field they were in and squatted down.

"These ones seem to be fresh. I think if we sit a bit right in here, we may just have a sighting. They will have heard the horses though, so it will take some time before they feel safe enough to circle around again. Why don't we have bit of bread and let the boys rest?"

Deb agreed and the two took their bows and arrows down from the horses should they need them quickly. They sat down and David pulled out some unleavened bread and a piece of lamb that was left from last night's dinner. They shared a bit of water from a sheep skin flask and David said to Deb, "I'm glad you came, lass. It's much more enjoyable hunting when you have a partner."

She smiled and answered back, "Well, it's something I love to do as well. Besides, maybe we'll get lucky and come home with a few hares on top of it. Imagine the feast we could have tonight!"

David sighed nervously and asked, "So are you feeling more of yourself lately, Deb? You look like it to me. In fact, everyone sees the glow in your face." He added, "I think you look beautiful today especially." He realized what he just said.

Deb felt a slight flush creep into her cheeks. There was that feeling again in her chest. David had never spoken to her like that before. She did not look right at him, but answered back with a smile, "That is a kind thing to say, especially since I did not make myself up very well this morning." She was blushing from her roots to her neck and David saw it.

He now was a bit taken back by her sweet reaction and quickly added, "Deb, I hope it is not too forward to say that you never need to make yourself up. You're perfect the way you are, lass."

Deb looked over at David now realizing what was happening between them. She suddenly felt naive with her thoughts and wondered why she did not expect it. She just kept thinking of Liam so much that she was blinded. She never truly realized that David had been looking at her in this way. *'Was this really happening?'* she thought to herself.

She wasn't ready for it; or so she thought. David was so gentle with his words that she knew he would not presume anything. He wasn't even looking at her as he spoke and it made her smile to think that he was probably very nervous right then. It was uncomfortable, but at the same time so youthful in its emotion that Deb could not help but feel special. She thought it may be best to keep with the task at hand because she could feel David's tension. She decided to change the subject for the time being, but she felt in her gut that something great was happening between them.

"David, I have been thinking of going back to the farm soon. I believe Henry may want to stay on though. It would be most valuable to have him there and I do miss his sweet, crooked smile. I wouldn't be able to afford to pay anyone else to work for me. Henry will have things well maintained and there would be less work to do because of his diligence. What do you think?"

David gazed out into the misty field and sighed quietly. He looked over at Deb and answered honestly, "Well lass, for you, it is a journey that only you can continue at your own pace. But you grew up there. It is your family's home. When I was there, I could see why you and Liam fought for it. I could see why you swore you would go back. In a land that is owned by Lords and Kings, your family is fortunate to answer to no one. The MacDonell's have seen to that. And so I believe that Henry would be more than happy to see you return. I only…". David paused.

"What is it, David?"

David smiled and took a breath. Deb knew that he was going to say something that she was trying to avoid, but then she saw the look in his eyes. It was honest and humble and she felt his heart.

"I just think that maybe it would be beneficial to have someone else with you. Henry is a good man, but Scotland has only just become its own country. There is still unrest with the clans and…your farm is so isolated." He was stuttering as he pretended to be adjusting his bow.

Deb let him speak.

"What I am trying to say is that if there is a need for farm help, I would be happy to help you. I have been well taken care of by the MacDonell's. I have saved much of my coin and if you see it as a necessity, I could join you and help you get your father's land back to where it was before. I am sure that Henry is doing his best, but…well, I just think that you may like to have someone else around."

David looked away when he said his last words and Deb felt an urge to give in to his request. How could she turn him away after all that they had been through? David never allowed himself to be forward with Deb and she knew that she may be keeping walls up that should come down. This man was much older than she was, but something calming came over her when she was with David. The image of a strong loving man caring for her again did not come without guilt. It felt right, but wrong. Why had she not considered it before now? David was bearing his soul and making himself vulnerable. He was alone now as well. He too had lost his love. They should not feel shame for feeling this way after all this time. She was suddenly hit with an epiphany and it was as if a veil had been lifted from her eyes.

Inside, she heard her own voice, *"He is a wonderful man. Why have you been so sightless? I cannot believe what I am feeling. Talk to him! Don't push him away!"*

Deb looked over at David and placed her hand on his. David pulled his head around slowly looking down and then rolled his head up to look into Deb's eyes. She was smiling gently and the misty morning sunlight was framing her beautiful face.

She blinked slowly and when she opened her eyes she said to David's delight, "David you are a gentleman and you have been nothing but good to me. I keep forgetting that you too have battled the same demons inside that I have. We have both lost someone that we loved very much. I know that you may feel something growing between us. I just never looked for it before, but I see it too and I am sorry that I have been so difficult to speak to." She sighed and placed her other hand on David's. "I would be grateful for your help. Maybe it is time that we talk about our friendship as something more?"

David was not blushing anymore. Swallowing a lump in his throat, he looked Deb straight in the eyes this time feeling energy from her words and answered her, "Deborah Barne, I would want nothing more. We shall talk then and make plans. I am sorry if I have been so vague, but it is only out of respect. I must say that these past few months have been glorious ones for me, but torture as well. There is so much I longed to tell you."

He smiled finally, feeling relief from his awkwardness and added, "You are a beautiful woman, Deb. I have wanted to say that for so long."

She thought back and saw it all now. All the small moments, the looks, the willingness and loyalty were all slipping into view. She felt overwhelmed with giddiness as if she was seeing his eyes for the first time in a way she hadn't before. Now there was emotion behind them; a longing that she felt coming from him. It made her feel it too and it was like a wave of love was powering its way through her heart. To know that someone desired her this much was so powerful after all she had been through. She could no longer deny any of it.

Deb reached up and touched David's face, then leaned in and gently caressed his lips with hers. It was innocent and angelic, but David felt as though someone had finally breathed life into his body. He could not believe that this moment was happening, but he knew to be calm for as not to frighten her. Deb was not a woman who was easily manipulated or made to swoon like a girl. She was beyond her years and this is what David noticed in her. He had come this far. He wanted to treat her with the same reverence that he had been feeling for so long. He knew she would appreciate his respect for her and her feelings for Liam. It would not be a man who came on strong that would win this young woman's heart but it would obviously be someone who proved his respect for her through time and patience. David had presented both of these to her and she knew it in her soul.

The two gathered their hunting gear and watered the horses one more time before turning back to the castle. They had nothing to show for the day, but inside, they both knew better. They had found each other's hearts.

As they rode slowly back side by side, they spoke with a comfort that they had both missed for so long. The comfort of having someone by their side that made them feel alive was like basking in the sun. They chatted without awkwardness at last and it was like a weight had been lifted from David's shoulders. Deb thought about it and realized that he had been there every moment, watching, waiting and loving her. How could she have been so blind? She could tell that her face was showing an emotion that she had not allowed herself to feel for so long. She was glowing.

Anne had risen from her slumber and was sitting outside on her balcony watching the children play in the courtyard. She caught the visual of Deb and David riding up to the gate. With patience, she watched intently as they came through, riding slowly amongst the children as they playfully ran beside the horses. Deb and David were both beaming as they laughed with the children and entered the stalls. Anne jumped up from her window stoop as she noticed that look. The look she had been watching for in Deb's face. It was there! She just knew it! She felt it! She could hardly wait until Deb and David separated upon entering the castle interior. Anne rushed down the stone staircase to the hallway where Deb's room was. She found her walking up to her doorway slightly dusty and carrying her bow and arrows at her side.

Deb saw Anne's face filled with glee and held her arms open to greet her as if she had come back from days of being away. Anne held Deb closely saying good morning quickly to her and then burst through Deb's door with her, closing it behind them.

Deb was surprised and wondered what the fuss was about. Anne then took her by the shoulders and pushed her down on the edge of the bed. Deb's eyes were open wide at Anne's enthusiasm, and she was just about to ask her what her excitement was for, when Anne burst out with a point blank question.

"Please tell me that you look this happy for a reason better than bringing home a deer?"

Deb smiled with shock as she answered, "My lady, whatever are you suggesting?"

Anne looked sideways at Deb and answered, "My dear, I have not seen you this happy for a very long time. You are beaming and there is only one thing that makes a woman shine in this way."

Deb chuckled and stood up to take off some of her top layers. She spun around to see Anne's twinkling eyes and knew without a doubt that Anne was seeing right through her. She wondered how long the woman had suspected something. She had never asked her these things before. Why was today so different? There was no denying it though, and if Anne could see it that clearly, there was no use in trying to hide it from her.

"I think you may be referring to the glow one gets when someone else professes feelings for them? I cannot believe how you seem to know these things, my lady! How did you know? *I* didn't know! How could *you*?"

Anne sighed happily and said, "Deb, I have known that this man has had feelings for you for quite some time. In fact, I almost told you, but I thought it best to allow you to discover it for yourself. David is a quiet man and he would never want to jeopardize your happiness...nor would I."

Deb was putting her bow and arrow in the corner and grabbing for a more comfortable tunic and light tan skirt. It fell to the ground and was heavily gathered around her small waist. She tied her hair back and Anne stood up to help her. As Deb gazed into the mirror, Anne looked at her as she tidied up the messy ball Deb had thrown up on her head. She wrapped Deb's long black hair and placed a lovely bone comb in it that had a floral motive cut into its edges. It was Anne's way of slowing Deb down and letting her know that a beautiful young woman should take a moment to make herself presentable. Deb was still such a rugged girl in so many ways and Anne simply wanted to share her knowledge of refinement with her. It was a sweet moment; one that Deb imagined would have happened many times if her own mother had been alive. She was grateful for Anne's loving gesture and stood still like a child being dressed.

As they looked into the mirror together, Anne said, "There are times in our lives when being a woman is the greatest gift of all. We have our challenges and our lives depend on how well we cope with our ever changing world. This is a sentiment that only people with something to live for will understand and you have so much to live for, my dear. Your life is not one story. It is and will be many stories before you are my age."

Deb reached up and placed her hand on Anne's as she held Deb by the shoulders sweetly.

"If I become a woman with your insight and beauty, then my life will be a story that never ends."

Deb smiled as she embraced the moment. She turned around and took Anne's hands.

"My Lady, we have much to talk about. I think you know that I may be leaving the castle soon, and there are things that I want to say to you."

Anne stopped Deb. She took her face in both hands and said, "Not to worry about that right this moment. There will time for all to be discussed. For now, let us enjoy this beautiful day and embrace the joy that you are feeling. I will protect your privacy for the moment, but when everyone sees the two of you together, it will not be kept quiet for long. Take your time. I hope you will stay for as long as you need to prepare. Just allow me a little more time with you both. I want to know that you are leaving with everything you will require."

Deb stood up and hugged Anne. "You have already given that to me. You have been like a mother, Anne. I am forever in your debt."

The two walked through the hallway and down to the kitchen. They passed a small preparation room off the end of the kitchen itself and saw the cooks cutting meat and preparing vegetables for lunch. There was an aroma of blackberry pie wafting from the far end of the kitchen where the fireplaces sat.

Anne and Thomas MacDonell had two huge cooking areas built into the main kitchen so that large groups could be accommodated. A smaller summer kitchen on the other side of the castle yards was used for smaller meals and extra space. Anne often used it herself when the men had been away for long periods of time. The ladies would cook together for the people remaining behind. It was more than the MacDonell castle. It was a home to so many who were loyal to the family.

Anne decided that a small feast would be a wonderful way to announce Deb and David's departure. She knew this day would come. She was even happier that David was a part of it. She could watch Deb leave and feel as though she had all that she needed to repair her life. Anne would send Deb off as though she were her own flesh and blood.

The next few weeks saw the rebirth of Deb and David in the form of a budding young couple. Everyone was pleased with the joining of the two and although they still kept it quiet, Deb and David began to realize that they were not alone any longer. Now they had each other to face the world.

Cheryl Alleway

Chapter Nineteen
Wingless Angels

Cheryl Alleway

There was word sent to the castle that Henry was ailing and that his days were numbered. The Barne family had sent their two boys back down south to check on him. When they returned to the highlands, Henry had lost his hearing all together. He was forgetting to do things and he got lost one night because he could not remember where the main path back to the croft was. He spent the night in the fields before the boys found him the next day. He tried to tell them that he had an injury that caused his hearing loss, but the boys knew that Henry may have been trying to avoid the inevitable.

Deb was very saddened by the news and David knew that their union was meant to be for Deb would need him now more than ever. Anne sent tinctures, medicines and warm clothes with the two in case Henry had lost his will to make his own anymore. She feared that Deb and David would end up burying Henry.

Anne offered to have three of the men travel down with them so that if Henry was in need of care, they could try to bring him back to the castle. They did not know how he was or if he would even make the trip north. They went anyway, just in case. It was not a bad idea in the interim as clan upset had been heard of in the south west. This area was directly in the path that Deb, David and the others would have to take. They did not want to take a longer route in case Henry was in need of immediate care. Deb just wanted to get to him.

On the morning of Deb's twentieth birthday, the skies were gray and the wind was cold. They packed three carts to take home to the farm. One had supplies, seeds, clothing and raw wool. The other carried young lambs; half of them rams and half ewes. They would only stop for short periods to allow them to stretch their legs and drink. Anne also sent three cages of chickens and a pair of geese.

There were weapons as well. Deb knew the value in having a substantial supply of arrows, swords and knives on the farm. She had requested a new bow be crafted before she left. She knew just how it should be built and worked alongside David's friend who was a master craftsman. He used the yew wood she had collected and fit the bow to Deb's frame. It was custom and a thing of beauty.

There was one more thing that Anne wanted to send with them. She knew the trouble with wolves that Deb and her father had had in the past. Henry had a run in with a few himself. Many were killed during the wars by passing armies, but they grew large and mean in Scotland and with a brand new farm of animal scents wafting through the air, Anne new there would be predators coming at some point. The journey south would take days and so she gave Deb two of her prized wolf hounds.

Their names were Brutis and Balgart. The two had even made friends with Finnean. It took a couple of squabbles and one quick snap of the hoof, but once the dogs respected Finnean's strength, they learned to have a valuable respect for the large stallion. Finnean had even allowed them to sleep in his stall one cold night. It was unheard of, but the three became a formidable site. Deb had gotten to know the dogs while hunting and they learned to ride alongside the horses while listening to commands. Brutis outweighed Balgart by at least thirty pounds, and he was easily one hundred and fifty pounds. Their sire remained with Anne at the castle and she knew that there would be enough time in his lifespan to be a father to more faithful pets. Both dogs had run-ins with wolves and both showed their fighting skills well. They were submissive only to those they protected. In a battle, Brutis was a master fighter and still had a scar above his eye that showed his worth. He had instinct and a will to live. Balgart was slightly younger and learning from his older brother. He was fast and hard to catch. They would be very valuable to Deb and David.

They had plenty to take on their journey. Deb was in tears as she left the comfort of Anne's arms in the courtyard. Anne blew her a kiss and everyone waved as the new couple and their friends made their way south once more. It was fall and there would be no time to lose getting back home.

As they passed by the area known to have recently been the site of clan disorder, David and Deb armed themselves. David looked back at the others and they too made themselves ready. If caught in a conflict, they would certainly announce their alliance to the MacDonells, hoping that the clan's reputation would see them through.

William had been diligent to keep the peace in the north, securing his place amongst nobility under the watchful eye of the Lord of the Isles, but there were few that were still feeling the anger that was born during the severe fighting. Nobles and knights became entwined in a game of lies, trickery and survival. The allure of currency and land was used by the English and the Scottish Nobles to turn men against each other, but there were still a larger number of Scots who would give in to nothing. Clans themselves battled for land. The threat of English attacks brought the reality that small clans could not protect themselves alone. There was a need for numbers and a need for leaders who would not back down.

William had taken over for Thomas before the treaty of Northampton gave Scotland the right to have its own government. He had been to every meeting with Thomas; by his side silently watching and listening. Thomas' allegiance to the Lord of the Isles meant his place in Inverness was very secure. Being that the Lord was not known as a warrior but more of a politician, he kept the fighting Thomas MacDonell close by. They met men from every level of Nobility; Scottish, French and English. Some say that Thomas had made a deal with an English Commander. If they broke through Hadrien's wall in sufficient numbers, Perth and Inverness would not be a target. The Lord of the Isles was said to have agreed and added his political thoughts. In return, the MacDonell clan and the northern clans loyal to Islay would not kill any English nobility. The wars were over before the rumor could be disproven. Thomas had heard of it and laughed it off. He would never agree to such a thing. Anyone who attacked his people was fair game, even his own son. Thomas MacDonell could not be bought by any amount of money. He had his own.

No one would ever know for certain how Thomas had such connections, but having a wife that dined with French Nobles' wives on many occasions must have had something to do with it. Thomas was said to have relations with merchants and mercenaries that fought for him. His travels were not secretive, but only his most trusted men would always accompany him. William was one of them. He too stayed quiet about what they really did on their travels.

Anne MacDonell was an underestimated power. Being a woman, she had to use other means of strength to assist her husband. She would relate to the wives and families of the richest people in France and England taking down bridges one conversation at a time behind the battle fields. She was a close confidant of Queen Joan of France and the two women were said to have similar personalities, although Joan was a woman to reckon with when her husband was away and her title of consort was put into place.

Anne was brilliant and knew more about politics than some men of her time. She would discuss how she had another vision of the future for the quarreling countries. The French Pope was seeing the light and Philip VI of France began telling England that they would not be given leeway as they continued to wage wars. Thomas' alliance with the northern clans had given the English cause for concern, but the MacDonells still had their homeland enemies as well.

The Lord of the Isles himself gave Thomas more power than most knew about. Thomas' connections were kept almost secret for decades until the wars began to rage and Robert the Bruce had to make a change before Scotland was lost forever. Thomas had no choice but to come to Robert's side in full force. For years, he fought to bring the north into the forefront of redemption for Scotland.

In the fall of 1329, Robert the Bruce's young son David II had been married to Joan of The Tower; daughter to Edward the II of England and Isabella of France. The treaty of Northampton demanded it and so it was that Robert the Bruce had finally found his life's ambition come to fruition, but his body was deteriorating and disease was taking him fast. Bringing together Scotland, England and France by way of royal marriage was sure to create an alliance with France. Or so he thought.

Anne had a secret relationship with Isabella and the two only met when it was under the utmost secure situations. To be speaking to the wife of the King of England was not a concept many would understand. Anne's intention was to simply calm the waters between the women of power, not to commit treason. They only spoke of what could be compromised upon and Anne was never an enemy of the Queen Isabella, she was a liaison between her people and a woman who had great influence within her own walls. Anne's hope was to create a peaceful joining between the two countries, but from behind closed doors; not on the battlefield. With her ties to France as well, Anne's life was lived in quiet, private conversation on many occasions. Scotland was changing and Deb saw past the drama of the nobles. She saw a calmer and more civilized Scotland and Anne had helped instill this image.

Anne MacDonell had the grace and stature of a queen, but her life was fulfilled in her heart by living with her people and continuing the way of life that made her love her country so much. This unselfish, ability to live side by side with a peasant one day and a Lord's wife the next was Anne's legacy. She felt no one was above another as a human being and she believed that her good fortune was meant as a gift for her to share with those around her. Many had wondered why Thomas and Anne had not been given more status amongst the nobility of their time, but it was said that they had been given opportunity. They agreed early on that theirs was a life meant to be lived where all men lived. Their servants were not treated as such. They lived in the same castle as an extended family alongside the MacDonell's. They ate the same food, drank the same wine and before he was known to be a tyrant, Gully grew up with the other children as if they were siblings. Anne was considered an aunt to most of the children and the women would sit and talk with her about life and what it meant to be living it.

Education was non-existent among the poor, but Anne tried her best to teach as many as she could the basic skills of etiquette, writing and reading. There were conversations that held great attention when Anne spoke of the universities on the main land in France and even in cities like Glasgow. She spoke of people referred to as 'scholars'. They were people of vision. They saw the potential in life and in humans as a race.

Anne would say to the children, "Even though our fathers and brothers are fighting terrible wars, there will be a healing of society here in Scotland. We shall see education become more prevalent. You are the future of this country and for now, we must do what God asks of us in these tormenting times, but do not ever give up faith that there are people in the world that will make change. That change will involve all of you. You must keep your faith and you must believe that Scotland is a country of strength and humanity."

Anne's words echoed in Deb's mind as she and David and the others found themselves close to the Douglas farm. They had been blessed with safe passage and no unrest occurred as they made their way south. It was as if someone was watching over them. They had traveled mostly at night and this too may have given them an advantage.

Now as the sun was setting, Deb took off from the group. She knew exactly where she was now and David and the others watched as she raced ahead.

He said to one of the other men, "I should ride with her. You should still take heed. There is a difficult gully over this hill. Keep to the right side of if to avoid the bogs. Stay straight and do not waiver up and down the hill. Once you feel solid ground. Keep on it. It will not change and you will see the old pathway. It will be small, but trust it and you will not get held up. If you do find trouble, use your horn. The dogs will hear it if we cannot."

With that, David called Brutis and Balgart to follow him. They sprung to his side and soon caught up with Deb and Finnean. They could finally see the croft and were galloping quickly. It was all the dogs could do to keep up. The ground was damp from a recent rain and the familiar smells came wafting into Deb's nose. It was medicating to her heart.

Deb sat high in the saddle as she glanced over the landscape. It was becoming disheveled again and had grown over slightly, but Henry had been keeping a small field intact. There was obviously grain and other vegetables growing. It gave her faith that Henry's time on earth was not over.

David and Deb stopped their horses just outside the gate surrounding the left side of the croft. The dogs sat on David's command and stayed watch with the horses. The old mare that so faithfully had been protecting the farm for so long was no longer there. Deb was not surprised, but it saddened her to think about the loss of such a wonderful animal.

She made her way to the door of the croft and was hoping that Henry would greet them, but the door remained closed. She looked back at David with concern and then opened the door slowly so as not to startle the deaf Henry. She was cautious as he may defend himself if surprised, but as the light came into the room, there sat Henry in the rocker in the corner. The boys had told him that they would send for Deb and he had laid out a simple meal of bread and lamb stew over the fire anticipating their arrival on this day. He guessed correctly after traveling the same paths for so long. He did not act surprised, as they thought he would, when he finally turned to see the beautiful Deb standing in the doorway. It was as if nothing frightened him anymore. He was so peaceful looking; not at all the bouncing little man that Deb knew before.

He got up slowly and his crooked little walk was still evident. He leaned to one side and his head followed a similar path. His face was happy, but more wrinkled and gnarled than ever. He had obviously put on a clean tunic for Deb and she smiled widely upon looking at his sweet eyes. She scurried to him and knelt on one knee holding him in her arms.

Henry closed his eyes and held her tightly. His tiny little body was now smaller and his gentle fingers were bent with enlarged knuckles.

Deb pulled back and kissed Henry's face. "Henry, you handsome devil you! What's this about you getting ill? You are supposed to take care of the rest of us."

Henry could see what Deb was saying and did still have a slight ability to hear muffled sounds, but he said quite loudly, "Well, yu see lassy, I figure that it's time I put mee potions away. I have loved livin' ere' and if I had mee way, I wude be livin' ere' forever. But, time es' tellin' me to slow down and stop actin' like I'eem a yung man. I'eeve missed yu my dear!"

Deb's eyes began to moisten and she hugged Henry again. David came over and shook his hand. "It's good to see you again, Henry."

"Ah David sir, yu are a fine gentleman as alweese. Good to see ya, lad. Good to see ya! Please, I have made enuf food for an armee. I hope ya dinna come alone."

"Oh yes! We have friends that have accompanied us. They should be here in a moment's time. There is so much to talk about, Henry." Deb said.

She was elated to see him standing and talking. She had feared the worst, but for now, he was still Henry. It was all she could hope for. David went to meet the others as they reached the croft. One of the wheels had gotten stuck in the mud, but they were able to release it without calling for help. The animals were unloaded and set free. The lambs were greeted by the older ones that Henry had already on the farm. It was good timing as he had to kill three of his best ewes for food. He kept the ram for breeding and was left with only two ewes. They were getting past the age of healthy pregnancy and the wolves had taken six of the lambs in the summer. Because the old mare had died, there was only Henry to fend them off. He had to deal with three at once and if it were not for his ingenuity with rum soaked burlap sacks set a flame, there would be nothing stopping the wolves from taking them all.

"That is true. 'Tis true! I actually lit one a fire on the tip of hees tail! Oh, Ho Ho! Yu shood 'ave seen them, lassie! I pitched one at 'em the first time and they dinna know what to do with it! Stupid things kept on a goin' for one of me ewes and then I got hees rump right good! It burned hees arse for a few minutes bafor the rat realized that sittin' in the mud was the only thin' that stopped the flames! Oh, Ho Ho, yu shood 'ave seen it!"

"That's a site I would have liked to have seen for sure!" David spouted as he took a sip of wine. Deb was smiling from ear to ear. The other three men had joined them and the group of six talked until Deb felt that Henry needed some sleep. He was starting to get confused by all of the voices and everything just sounded like noise to him.

"Me dear, I do need to lay me head down." Henry was helped up from his chair by David. Deb got up and took his arm. She walked him into the corner nook by the fire and into his bed. The others continued to talk quietly with David as he explained that time was of the essence to return Henry to the castle. They had nothing to slow them down and they should be there far quicker than expected. Then in the midst of their conversation, Deb stepped into their circle and looked back at the now sleeping Henry. She knelt down and her eyes were looking at the floor. When she looked up at David, she spoke with certainty and sadness.

"I don't think you will be taking Henry back with you," she said bluntly.

David put his hand on her shoulder and replied, "If this is what you want, Deb, so be it."

One of the others spoke up and added, "Yes lass, there will be no rush for us to return and we will stay on to help you get settled. Lady Anne told us that if needed, we would not be expected back until two weeks from now."

Deb sighed and put on a brave face. "I do thank you all. It will make the transition much easier and it will allow me to have my hands a bit freer to care for him. It will be a tight fit in here to sleep at night, but it will make the croft warmer at least. He told me not take him away from this place. He knows he's dying and he *wants* to die now that I'm back."

Her head turned quickly and her last words were muffled. She got up and walked outside standing under the moon by the fence gate. David went out to talk to her. The others checked on Henry and stoked the fire. They remained quiet even though they knew Henry could not hear them as he slept.

David caught up slowly with Deb and put his arm around her shoulder. She looked back up at him sweetly and returned her gaze to the misty field. The moon was out and the clouds from the day had passed. Steam from the horse's snouts rose and the dogs were huddled in a hay pile by the sheep enclosure. They perked up when they saw Deb and David. Brutis looked up at her as she was crying softly and Balgart sat beside David pressing up against him. He almost pushed him over.

"It looks like we have everyone's support, Deb," he said with a smiled.

She looked down and patted the top of Brutis's head. He was an ugly animal, almost frightening to some. His dark gray fur was tousled from the wet trip and he was exhausted. Deb had given him and Balgart a rest in the cart a few times. The dogs were fit, but only a horse could make a trip like that and still stand at the end of the day. Brutis's eyes were gentle and he knew his place. Finnean sauntered over as he snorted into the night air. He nuzzled Deb as he always did; this time with some jealously for Brutis and Deb suddenly felt loved more then she had for a long time. She felt as though she had a family again. It was just so strange watching Henry die in her father's bed almost the same way that he had left her a few years before. She was twenty years old now and seventeen seemed like a lifetime ago. She turned to David and he held her in his arms. Pulling back, they said nothing but just gazed into each other's eyes. David placed his hands on her cheeks and kissed her gently on the forehead. He was kind and gentle and Deb felt in her heart for the first time, that this man had been waiting all this time for her without pressure or assumptions. It was time to let life start over.

The next day, Henry rose from his slumber to the scent of warm oats steaming over the fire. He hadn't had oats for some time and it was the most pleasant odor. Deb went to him and helped him up. She placed a shawl around his small shoulders and walked him over to his chair. He sat quietly and ate his meal without speaking. He just looked out the window and at times, Deb wondered if he knew where he really was.

After a while, Deb checked on the men working with David outside. They were doing a wonderful job unloading the rest of the supplies and fixing the roofs on the croft and root cellar. The weasels would no longer get in as David was patching holes at ground level that had been worked at for some time. He gathered stones and built a small base around the shelters to make it harder to dig into the ground. A few thorn bushes threaded through the cracks would help as well.

Deb was content to return to Henry, when suddenly, he was standing up and rummaging through the chest at his bedside. She wondered what he was doing and how he had gotten up, so she walked over and placed her hand on his shoulder. He looked up at her and stated, "I found somethin' under the oak tree, lassie. Dinna know if I shool 'ave been diggin' there, but when it showed itself, I thought maybe I should keep it for ya in case. Just in case. I dinna look at it, I just thought it seemed a wee bit special to put back into the dirty cold ground."

She gently took an old book from him. She sat him down in his chair again and pulled another one over beside him. He watched with a gentle smile as she took a large leather book and gazed at it.

"It was wrapped in a burlap sack, lass. Kind of covered with small stoones. Looked like it was put there; not lost."

Deb was intrigued and felt the front cover of the book. It had nothing on it. It was just a dark leather book about two fingers thickness. She turned it over and there at the bottom were two letters. 'J D'

Anne's lessons had paid off and Deb knew what they were. Her eyes widened. 'Jacob Douglas'

"Henry, did you look inside the book?"

He nodded no, "Dinna think it mee place. I kept it just fer yu lass."

Deb shook her head at Henry. She couldn't believe that he had not even looked inside. In his day, Henry was the nosiest little man around. He had to be. It's how he survived. But this was different. This was not for him to see in his mind.

She turned it back over and slid a large wooden bead out of its eyelet that held the book closed. It was the size of her lap in width and height. It was well worn and she could tell that the book had been put to good use. She couldn't stand it anymore and opened it. As she gazed in silence, it occurred to her that this was something her father had kept. She ran her hand over it softly in amazement. It seemed like a journal, but had little more than pictures in it and numbers at the bottom corners.

At first, she did not equate them to anything and then, it hit her. The images she began to see were unmistakably familiar. The positions the figures were in, the weapons being portrayed, but who were the strange men with dark hair? She had not seen such clothing before except in a picture that Anne had on her wall. It depicted a lady in a beautiful red satin gown wrapped around her with a large band around her waist. The woman had hair, black like Deb's, and bound in a soft bun on her head. She had sticks in her hair and the delicate gold and yellow designs on the skirt that reached the ground gave way to the woman's tiny feet which were fitted with coverings of white material and sandals fitted through her first two toes. Behind the woman, were people depicted in a field working. The people in Anne's painting looked like these men that her father had drawn. Anne had told

Deb that the painting was a gift from the orient, given to her by a Lady from France. It is the only time Deb had ever seen people from that nation; until now.

"What is it, lassie? I've bin dyin' ta know," Henry confessed.

Deb took a breath and answered, "Henry, I think this is my father's journal. I know that he could not write very well; in fact only broken letters at best, but these pictures are so real. Henry, you have seen me fight? You have seen me shoot bow and arrow and you have seen me throw my knife?"

Henry nodded, "Of course, lass. Why eets the very thin' that makes ya soo special."

"Henry, the drawings of these two men...they are the same things that my father taught me. This is the journal he must have kept when he was teaching me."

"Eet's a treasure for sure, lass. Are ya upset with me for diggin' it up?"

"Not one bit! Henry, do you know what this means? Look! There are dates on these pages. My father could at least scribe numbers well. It's how he kept track of his crops. He would draw pictures of the seasons and what seeds he planted. Alongside, he would scribe a date. Henry, according to this book, my father began these drawings before I was even born! I can't believe you found this!"

For that moment in time, Henry felt alive. He felt as though he had given Deb the most special gift possible before he died. He couldn't remember everything he used to know about her, but he knew enough to that she was like family to him.

"Tis almost as eef I was meant ta find it then, because I couldn't have dug eet up now if I tried."

Deb chuckled at Henry's attempt at humor and making fun of himself. "You are a special little man, Henry. You truly are a gift to me. I love you, my sweet friend." She had tears in her eyes as she embraced Henry the Hen, reveling in the feel of him.

The time had come for their friends to go back home so Deb and David saw them off one fateful morning. They turned to look at each other and went inside. Henry was dying, but Deb told the others that she wanted them to make it home before the cold weather became difficult. They sadly said goodbye to Henry and rode into the distance.

David and Deb stayed by Henry's side for two more days and then on the thirty first day of October, Henry the Hen left the world. Deb and David said prayers and dressed him well; wrapping his body in purple thistle and wild violets. Deb placed a poultice and some mint scented tinctures on his chest with his hands holding them. It was how she wanted to remember him.

They buried him deeply so that the wolves would not find his body and covered him with the same stones that were now crumbling on her parent's graves. They took a moment to tidy them up and planted new flowers at their heads. David made new crosses and carved their names into them. It was not far from the graves of Deb's grandparents; Jacob's faithful parents who waited for him for so long. Now they were all together for eternity. There was nothing left to say, and as the sun set that night, Deb and David resigned themselves to the fact that they had much to live for if only for the memories of those that had died before them. There was a new hope in their hearts, even though so much had come to an end. What they lost was heartbreaking, but life was not lived without pain and sorrow. Young Deb was realizing it more and more.

Chapter Twenty
Farewell Home

Cheryl Alleway

Morning came with a strange calmness. Deb and David had fallen asleep in each other's arms. David knew that intimacy would happen when it should and allowing Deb time to decide when that happened was something he did not take for granted. She had been with only one other man in her life and that man was still haunting David as well. He knew spending time together would change that, but being a true gentleman, would touch her heart. David was not a man to grab a woman and take her in the mud. His was a subtle approach that seemed to bode well with Deb. She had always found David to be this way, even though his dreams saw a different scenario. He was deeply in love and time was running out for his chivalry to protect him. No man could resist this woman for too long. There were men in the world who were good and kind and strong at the same time. They didn't have to be animals to be men. David was, at this point, painfully one of them.

    Deb had not really noticed how handsome he was. He stood just slightly taller than she was and his hair was dark brown and tied tightly at the back giving him a sleek look. His eyes were dark blue and he had a smoldering dark complexion.

David's build was that of a man who had worked all his life. He had wide shoulders and thick forearms from splitting wood and using weapons. On his right forearm he had a large scar from battle and his right eye had a smaller scar beneath it. One hardly noticed it though as they looked past at his long dark eyelashes. Deb was now seeing his strong chin and muscular neck. David did not look the age he was in years. He was fit and healthy and blessed with a youthful body.

She noticed his walk, knew his voice and his gentle touch. He had cupped her face in his hands the night they had buried Henry and his eyes were so trusting. She melted into his embrace and knew that she was with someone that made her feel like she did the night her father asked Liam to marry her. The moments that Deb had with Liam were different than those she was experiencing with David and it had been hard for her to let herself feel such things again. Being alone for the rest of her life was not something that she had looked forward to, and to have someone like David right there; right in front of her just when she needed him seemed unbelievable at times, but she knew that David needed her as well. He had been a tortured man in his heart for years. He too had lost love and found it again.

David had gone cold after his wife died. He didn't know how to deal with the loss at first. He threw himself into fighting for Thomas and became as a stone within his heart. When Deb Barne entered his world, his walls came down without effort.

The next day, they went straight to work. There was no time to lose and a surprise visit from two familiar faces made small work of a few chores on their list. As the sun rose above the mist, Sarah and James rode down the trail to the croft. It was a teary eyed moment of happiness when Sarah dismounted and ran to Deb's arms. Not so long ago, Deb saved the life of this young girl who would have been living a life of mental anguish and physical exploitation.

"Oh God, you are a beautiful site, Sarah! You are turning into a woman!" Deb shouted.

"Ah, but right she is!" David added.

"Deb, we heard about you returning and father sent us straight away. If you want us to stay and help for a few days, we have his permission," James stated.

Deb and David were tired and it was an offer they couldn't refuse. David was elated to have James there to help him with the plow. There were a few sheep and three chickens that would need to be slaughtered for the winter. They would dry the meat and add salt to cure it. Eggs were not being produced any longer and so it meant chickens were needed more in the pot than sitting on a nest. Now that Sarah and James were here, two of the birds would be sent back with them for James' family.

Deb and Sarah occupied their time in the potato field. Beside them, Henry had a small, but healthy field of wheat growing. There were small pockets of onion and cabbage that were ready to come in as well. Turnip was a surprise to Deb. It was a wonderful vegetable to keep over the winter months and if covered in bees wax and kept in dry dirt, it lasted longer than most of the other perishables. James had made a beautiful hand carved salt flask for Deb. It was shaped like a small horn and had a rendering of Deb riding Finnean. The flask sat in Deb's hand and extended only slightly from her fingertips. It was so beautifully made. Intricate patterns framed the wide end while the small end had a darker tip with a gentle curve in it. On the end, where the flask was sealed, James had carved the Douglas name as well. It was a precious gift from a young man who had made it through teenage life and was now being given a chance at becoming a man. He had a good start unlike most. James had been courting Sarah now for some time and Deb thought his father had to be almost ready to allow them to marry.

"You look well, Sarah," Deb stated.

Sarah smiled as she dug in the dirt unearthing the jeweled roots beneath.

"As do you, sister. You have been through so much. I wish I could have been with you during your time of need." Sarah didn't want to bring up Liam's death, but she also didn't want to be disrespectful by not asking. Deb knew she was wondering and so she obliged Sarah's obvious curiosity.

"I know, but it did happen fast. I had much love to comfort me. He is with his family now and I have moved on. I had to. For a while though, I did not know what I would do. I had never felt that way before. It was a feeling of complete despair, and I had been there before in Gully's capture, but the difference was that I had hope then. When I realized that Liam was gone for certain, it was an emptiness that I cannot describe."

Sarah nodded and listened intently. "Deb, I am so sorry."

Deb stopped digging for just a moment and looked into Sarah's eyes. She had found her strength again and she let Sarah know it.

She touched the young girl's hand and said, "Love is the greatest gift in life Sarah, but after it is lost, we must try to allow ourselves to find it again. I had many months to thank Liam for being in my life and I know he would not have wanted me to be alone. I know you are curious about David and yes, we are together. I have learned that I have much life still to live. David wants to live it with me. How can I turn that away?"

"I am very glad. He seems to be a good man."

The two looked down the hill to where David and James were working. Deb stated with calmness in her eyes, "Yes…he is."

The day was coming to an end and as the sun began to fall, the clouds rolled in. Rain came and the air became cold. Winter had almost arrived and after Sarah and James left two days later, Deb had time to pull out her father's journal. She sat in his old chair that was in front of the fireplace. He had made it himself and its oversized width made Deb look so small sitting in it. He built it as such so that he could have Deb sit beside him when the night air chilled them. She remembered him, with his arm around her and her mother's blanket wrapped around her shoulders. Her father would tell her stories and he never stopped telling Deb that she was special. She missed him terribly and a tear came to her eye. She wondered if he ever got to hold Mary again.

David came in from gathering the lambs and noticed her quiet demeanor. He took off his coat and hung it by the door. Slowly, he walked over to her and asked, "May I join you?"

She answered, "Of course," and wiped her eyes. David put his arm around her and she felt his cold hands. She pulled the blanket across him as well. He gave her a moment and then asked, "Deb, are you happy?"

Deb was surprised by the question, but answered kindly, "I am now. I cry for the memories I have, not because I am sad. I grieve the images I have in my mind, but I know that there is more right here, right now. I do not take it for granted. This journal is something that I never knew about. The pictures are drawn in my father's hand and I understand all of the effort that he put into raising me. He loved me so much, like no one else."

David looked down at the pages on Deb's lap and said gently, "He loved you more than any father I know. He wanted you to flourish, Deb. It is obvious that he intended great things for you." David looked at the fire and then back at Deb's face. She turned to look at him as well.

"I know that I cannot replace the men in your life that you have lost, but in time, I hope that you see into my heart and know that I will love you with everything I have. I have lost love as well, but with you, I feel as if the heavens have given me a second chance. Fighting is all that I have known for so long. These past few months with you, have shown me that a man does not always have to find power on the battlefield. I know that a man can feel that power from the love of a good woman. You make me feel alive again. I will stand by you for as long as you will have me."

Deb felt overwhelmed by David's words. He touched her face and she closed the journal. She looked into his eyes and took his other hand. Suddenly, they felt passionate warmth between them. It was more powerful than other feelings they had experienced together and now, David could not hold back his feelings any longer. Deb saw it in his face and she felt a wave pass over her. He was strong and masculine as he pulled her in closer to him by her shoulders. Deb moved over standing up slightly as she sat on his lap. David pulled her to his lips and they kissed a kiss so deep that their hearts began to beat fast. David ran his hands over her back and on to her buttocks. Deb felt his heaving chest and opened his tunic revealing his dark, muscular upper body. She put both hands on his face and David stood up carrying her over to the bed while her legs were wrapped around his waist. They were engulfed in the physical intoxication that was taking over and as David lay Deb down softly, she said to him in a whisper, "You no longer have to wait."

David pulled Deb's clothes off slowly and gently revealed her beautiful form. He could not believe he was here with her. She was an angel. Her scars and muscular shape made his pulse race. She was a woman that could not be matched in his eyes. He lost his inhibitions and removed his own garments. She watched him in the fire light. She became engulfed with passion after so many months of trying to forget what it felt like. As they both lay together, bearing their souls to one another, David and Deb fell into a deep trance of passion. The room spun as the fire crackled and their mental anguish was dissolving into a moment of pure desire. Deb knew what David had held in for so long and as they came together in a wave of passionate heat, she too was allowing herself to let go and allow her body the pleasures of the flesh.

David looked down at her as he pushed their bodies together. He was warm and powerful. His arm muscles tensed up as Deb ran her hands over them. She braced herself and pulled up to kiss him.

He pushed her hair back off her face carefully and said quietly, "You are the most beautiful thing I have ever seen." He ran his hand over her breasts feeling her softness. As he touched her waist, his hand moved down to cup her hip and then her thigh. She had to close her eyes as David's strength was taking her to a place of ecstasy.

Deb panted desperately and moaned, "I am yours."

They wound around each other over and over again as passion dissolved their fears and pain. Sweat glistened on their skin and was lit up by the flames of the fire. Deb's hair was draping their bodies and David would gently sweep it from her face, kissing her deeply and bracing himself upon her hips. The room was spinning with pleasure. It was a moment of pure satisfaction and release for them both that had finally come to fruition.

When the climax was over, they breathed heavily in unison and folded back to lie beside one another upon their soft woolen throw. An owl sang a haunting song outside and the moon began to peek through the dark night sky. As David and Deb sighed deeply while lying beside each other, their hands were intertwined. David got up and pulled Deb's night garments over to her. He helped her put on a long linen gown and made sure her hair was pulled back neatly behind her still draping gently over her shoulders. He poured her a cup of water and as he pulled on his trousers, she sat him down and gave him a drink from it. He drank slowly and gazed into the flickering flames. He looked at her again and this time they said nothing. They just sat and looked into each other's eyes for the longest time.

Deb became lost in thought. All that time with Alexander and the others. Was David feeling these things back then? She felt naïve to have not noticed. How could he have held it in so long? She thought of how much integrity he must have in being able to do so. She thanked the heavens for finally giving her sight to see what was right before her. She could see that Liam's memories must have haunted him as well.

Deb sighed with contentment and David laid her down under the sheepskin blanket. He tucked her in with loving hands and sweetly kissed her on the lips. He was tired as well and as he pulled the blanket over himself, she lay on his chest and closed her eyes. She never thought she would feel like this again, but she promised herself she would not feel guilt; only happiness.

David went to sleep that night knowing that he had a woman in his life that would challenge his heart and his body. He would die for her. He stood by her when she wanted to rescue Sarah and the girls. He brought her to Inverness safely when Anne had asked him to. He stood by Deb while she healed from the loss of her husband; always keeping his distance and hiding his true feelings. And as her life seemed to be coming together again, David was once again by her side.

Cheryl Alleway

Chapter Twenty-One
Inverness Skies

Cheryl Alleway

The warmth from the sun came gently upon the west side of the croft. David had stoked the night fire early in the morning and had gone back to sleep. They awoke to a warm room. The smell of smoke drifted lightly through the air and the baying sheep outside told them it was morning. It was deceiving because outside, the first sign of snow was drifting gently down through the cold morning dew. The light skim of iridescent white powder that covered the fields also sat on top of the backs of the animals that formed a tight huddle against the croft. They too were feeling the warmth created from within and took full advantage of it. The back of the croft dug into the hillside making the small building very efficient for its simplicity. There was something to be said for having less at times.

When she rose, Deb hung a warm pot of tea over the amber flames. The large iron hook that held the precious cooking pot creaked as though it had a voice as she pushed it over the fire. She motioned to David to stay in bed he had been up so early. He did not argue as it had taken him a long time to drift back to sleep.

Deb wanted to take this time to look through her father's journal in more depth. She sat in the rocker and bundled up in her lamb skin. The book felt as though it had a current running within. She had noticed it before because she was so ecstatic to receive it, but this second time, she felt it again. It was as if the journal had a small vibration when she held it. She didn't understand what it was, but it was as if she could feel her father's presence. It may have been the sheer overwhelming emotion that it stirred inside of her, but it didn't matter. It was a source of power. The drawings were so well done. Now facing a new page, Deb sat examining it as if it were a treasure.

She gazed at every stroke imagining him putting it on the page with his own hand. With her fingers, she felt the way the ink nib had dug into the paper in places because he had tried to emphasis something. She tried to imagine the two men drawn within the pages. Who were they? Why were all the pages of only their images and her father? As she read the few words and watched the pictures change, a story of sorts came out of the pages.

Jacob had traveled many times to the coast to the merchant docks to seek out materials to use for his swords and archery bows, along with selling his goods.

He would spent many nights at a pub near the town of Aberdeen on the east coast of Scotland. He would sit and listen and watch. He would be gone for a week or more at a time. The people at the seashore were a mix of wealthy travelers, seasoned merchants, vagrant thieves and poor farmers who came to trade and buy supplies.

Jacob found it a challenge to learn as much as he could about the dark world of mercantile. There were many well-known and almost famous merchants who had many men on their crew and sold to everyone who had money including kings and queens.

Before he married Deb's mother, Jacob was fascinated by his trips to the seashore. His father did not like them however, as each trip was dangerous, but Jacob posed as a crippled peddler often blending in unnoticed amongst the poorer class and his nights sitting in pub corners provided him many lessons indeed. He loved to listen to the drunken tales of men who often forgot their tongues to the drink of the night. He gathered this information in a small book. He would record how one man had become well known for slitting a man's throat with his knife throwing techniques. He listened to the tales of sword fighting techniques that were embellished through the night. Jacob had vowed that he would never feel as helpless as he did the day the English dragged him away from his family. Before he had children, he tried to learn as much as he could about defensive fighting techniques. Whether he had a son or daughter did not matter to him. Jacob would not see them take on his same fate.

One man that brought particular interest to Jacob was a man from the country of Korea. He was not a slave, but worked for one of the merchants. This man came into port often from the shores of France aboard one of the ships. How he had come to be so far from his own country was a mystery to Jacob. This merchant he knew had traveled to the orient in search of fine silks and spices where he found the man and his son on a road being assaulted by soldiers that wore the uniform of the Chinese and spoke not a word. It was said that their faces were dark with death and had no feeling or expression. Their horses were large and snorted steaming breath into the cold evening air. They tried to attack the merchant and his men, but they were powerful over the assailants and drove them off. With an angry cry of defeat, the murderous band took flight from the scene.

The Korean man was so grateful for them saving his son's life that he vowed to repay the merchant who did save them and had seen how the man and his son were attempting to defend themselves. They were fighting for their lives with thick branches and stones, rolling out of the path of the blades that attempted to take the horses down at the knees. They fought with mysterious methods Jacob had never seen before. If it were not for being outnumbered, the man and his son were excellent fighters who had nothing but their flexible bodies and rudimentary weapons to defend themselves. The merchant was impressed and promised the man sanctuary upon his ship.

Although a language barrier made it difficult at first to understand each other, the man promised to be the guide while this merchant traveled the orient and for a few years, he and his son sailed upon the ship with gratitude, learning to speak broken Anglo-Norman. There were two French speaking men on board as well and so it was doubly difficult for them to communicate at times. They did well enough to become very invaluable, however. When the ship docked they would seek out the best merchant trails acting as an interpreter and helping them find their way while they did business.

This man fascinated Jacob so much, that he drew pictures of him in his journal. Jacob even drew the man's almond shaped eyes and darker skin. He had never seen an Asian man before. He drew his black hair and soft layered clothing. The colors were simple browns and creams, but they wrapped around him unlike the clothing of the western world. He was short in stature as was his son. They had broad shoulders and a serious expression. These men were so different to Jacob and that was what impressed upon him the most. They were handsome with their dark skin and hair. There was an honest loyalty in their faces that Jacob respected and trusted. Yet, behind the eyes were pain and a longing for home. Jacob understood this feeling in particular.

One night, Jacob approached the man in private on the dock. The man shook his hand after Jacob said hello in his own language. He bowed and Jacob returned in kind.

The man asked Jacob clumsily, "Why you walk with such limp my friend?"

Jacob answered politely by pulling his trousers up and showing the man his wooden leg.

The man was surprised and apologized for his comment. Jacob was not insulted at all. In fact, he had come to the man for a reason and it was he who wanted to be as respectful as possible.

"I was wondering sir, if you would speak to me about the fighting ways from your home."

The man looked down and said, "I sorry friend, but our families hold these things to be sacred and passed down to only who have right to learn. I very sorry, but cannot."

Jacob said quickly, "I understand...but I have listened to the stories you have told about the wars in your country and I believe that we have more in common than you think. The merchant's men told me of your struggle the day they met you and your son, it is no secret that you possess certain skills. I was in a similar situation when they took me from my parents to fight in the wars of our country. I respect the differences between us, but your stories and customs fascinate me. I have never heard of such things before. The merchant's men told me of your fighting techniques and they are most curious to me. I only wish to understand some of your methods."

    This made the man curious, but cautious. He told Jacob that he would ask about him and that if enough people seemed to trust him, he would think about speaking with Jacob again and sharing some of his knowledge. After Jacob explained that he too wished to protect his children one day, the man felt more at ease. The man learned that Jacob had lost his leg in battle and that he went home once again to live with his mother and father. This was very honorable to him as protecting family was the sole reason that his people learned to fight the way that they did.

    Quietly, the two men began talking about the skills that each had learned. Archers in the orient had much different bows and technique, but this was something that the eastern and western countries had in common. Revealing secrets was not something that the Korean man felt comfortable with at first and his son was not pleased that his father was talking to a stranger about something that they had been brought up to protect at all odds. Jacob was highly trustworthy however, and the man saw an aura of innocence and strength around him.

He later told Jacob that this aura represented his child; the child that Jacob had not fathered yet.

They became friends over time and each visit to the docks gave Jacob such happiness when he saw the man with his son. Jacob had gained his trust and finally one night, he presented Jacob with some of the techniques that were taught amongst his family in Korea. These techniques were from what he called SahDoh MuSool. It was their ancient tribal, clan or family martial art. It was highly guarded by generations of families who defended their villages with few weapons and only knowledge and power of the mind and body.

The man that Jacob had come to know was Min. He and his son spoke of the many invasions on their homeland in the North of the Korean territories. The Orient was a land that Jacob had only heard about from merchants. They had thousands of people, vast amounts of silk and spices. Their armies were massive, but the peasants were beginning to see the loss of too many. SahDoh MuSool was created in almost secrecy to help the people defend themselves. Families considered the art to be sacred amongst them. These stories reminded Jacob of the plight of the Scottish people. From a land thousands of miles and oceans away, he met a man who, in Jacob's mind, was a brother and kindred soul. They were both fighting to survive in a world that was war-torn.

"I cannot possibly show you all I have been taught and in respect for son, he wishes you not tell another man about what I about to show you. You must swear on life of your child. Yes, the merchant tells of day they came upon us, but I never discussed my fighting techniques with anyone. Even when he

asked me about what he saw that day, I said nothing and he understands."

Jacob bowed his head as the moon fell upon the three men. They stood on the opposite side of a small bridge that led out of the town from the merchant docks. It was hours into the night that Min asked Jacob to meet them. He did not want anyone to see.

"Of course Min, but how should I explain these unusual methods to others if they see my child using them? I did not know that it was sacred to you. I wish to incorporate them with our traditional methods, but surely they will stand out to those here."

Min knew Jacob would ask and said, "Your child not be told of origin of these skills number one, and your child learn them as if they learn anything else. They are not to teach to anyone else. You tell people if asked, it not for them to know. On this you must not waver. It as simple as that."

Jacob smiled at the simple answer he received and said, "I will honor your request."

He realized that Min was not a man of complication. His answer was direct. Jacob obliged by bowing again. He took out his inkwell, waited and watched, but inside he knew that someday his child may teach their own and so on. He did his best to respect Min who stood before him an innately honorable man.

Min began to speak while he and his son proceeded to perform a series of stances and movements. Jacob had his book out on his lap and was steadily dipping his feather into the ink. He could not write many words and so was the reason for so many pictures drawn within the pages. It would be a visual reference.

Min stated, "Balance between anger and self-control is difficult to maintain unless you understand power within. The day my son and I were attacked, we had to center ourselves or we not have thought clearly. Confusion is enemy. To concentrate is to survive."

Jacob paid attention and said not a word. As Min continued, he felt a deep pain for Min and his son.

"Our minds control bodies. When we frightened, sad, lonely; this when we are vulnerable and cannot fight to best abilities. We must learn to bury our emotions in heat of battle. It is only chance for survival. Emotions make our judgment unclear in moments of quick decision. On day the soldiers took us on road, they had killed my wife and daughter before. Raped my daughter in front of us. Her cries made heart bleed from within. They beat son's back with the handle of their swords as he tried to defend her. My wife beheaded while pressed to her knees in mud. I was held back with rope around my neck. The last thing I saw was fear and pain in her eyes. It was more than I could stand. I felt myself losing control, but I had to gain back or would lose my son as well. Suddenly, I burst free and began to fight in ways of my ancestors. My swift, aggressive release caused the soldiers to lose grip on son just enough that he applied pressure to one of them on neck. The soldier went down and as I struck throat of another, we broke free for only moment to run down road into a clearing. Soldiers were right there instantly, swords drawn. Their blades glistened in sun and one that had killed my wife still had her blood dripping from its tip. There were five of them left and my son and I stood alone facing them."

Min became weary as the memories of his past flowed back into his mind. Min's son touched his shoulder and took over the story. Jacob had hardly ever heard him speak before. The moment had him mesmerized, listening to Min speak.

"My father and I had only sticks and rocks from side of road to defend ourselves with and these sticks kept us alive until merchants arrived, but not before I lost my right ear."

Jacob then noticed the missing ear. There was nothing but a hole now covered by the son's hair.

The young man continued, "Fighting technique using the staff is an accurate and powerful method. If the staff is large enough in width and length, one can protect body from injury from sword. Sword however, will slice staff in half if struck properly. This is key. Along with physical movements of body that are extreme and unpredictable, man can fight for some time against blade if he knows how to counter his opponent mentally as well. Sometimes, on ground and coming from underneath is efficient as well. Large opponent cannot bend well at waist to counter such move, but must be done swiftly and unexpectedly."

Jacob was fascinated by the words being spoken and he drew in his mind what he thought he would have seen that day.

Min continued, "I was filled with anger and revenge and if not for merchants, I would have been killed as well. My son kept us alive and though I lost my wife and daughter, it was clear to me he had learned our ways well."

Min's son bowed his head respectfully at his father's kind and proud words. He would die for his father. Jacob had no doubt in his mind.

"There is difference between justice and vengeance, my friend. One cannot truly be free when taking vengeance alone. There must be purpose and finality when justice is brought. Otherwise, you always feel vengeance calling you. With justice served however, mind will be at peace. Body will be calm once again and you will be able to move on. I have had to release my anger and be thankful my son is still with me. For this I live rest of my life in thanks. I must. Is the only way I can go on. Through meditation, one can release a multitude of negative emotions. This step one!"

Jacob hung his head and raised it slowly to look at Min. He still did not understand the difference between vengeance and justice, but Min's face showed a man who deserved justice for his pain. The soldiers did not steal his livestock or burn his house. They killed his wife and daughter for no reason. This is why Min deserved justice. It would never come however, and now Min had to live knowing this. Jacob began to understand as he thought more and more about Min's words.

"I am so very sorry for what you have been through. Please believe me that I mean no disrespect when I tell you that I have seen much of this evil on the battlefield. The day they took me from my parents, I thought for certain that they would kill them. I have seen many of my age slaughtered before their fifteenth year. I realize now, how lucky I am to be here with you and your son. I may have but one leg, but a life is what we truly long for; a life with peace and the love of family."

"Yes, my friend. Becomes reasoning behind things we will show you. A man should fight to defend only. When men attack other men with vanity and hatred, our countries become black with death and true reason for battle is lost in lust for power. This, I believe, is what you have seen as well. For this reason, I will allow you to learn from us."

Jacob sat back quietly and opened a new page in his journal. Min and his son showed techniques with the arms, wrists and legs. Much of it was like a dance to Jacob, but when Min struck the dummies that were set up as straw sacks, Jacob saw the power in the small man. One would not know it until it was shown in full force. The striking strength and flexibility was unlike any hand-to-hand fighting that Jacob had seen. The moves were calm but distinct. They showed how animal-like reflexes could allow one to strike from below a man's waist level delivering a painful blow to the chest. They showed Jacob techniques to use on the neck region. Sudden pulses with the fingers to the back of the neck nerves could deaden a man's grip on his sword and take all power away from his limb. After that split second while they writhed in pain, Min showed how to bring the man down by twisting the wrist and snapping the more tender bones in the forearm.

It was swift and clean. Cat like movements of the body were key to gaining power over a large assailant with a full-length sword. Getting close to the body from behind and below was crucial. While swinging, the opponent would be caught off guard by the quick kicks that penetrated the center of the body, the sides and head area. Speed, agility, surprise and body manipulation were the main elements to Min's teachings. Jacob put everything into his journal. He knew that he was being given a gift that truly would last a lifetime. That life was that of his unborn child's.

When Jacob met Deb's mother, he kept the journal a secret just as he had promised Min. He would not falter on his promise and for years even after Deb's mother died, he kept it hidden from his little girl. It was sacred to him as well, just as its contents were to his friend Min and his son.

Deb sat back, resting her head on the back of the chair. She tried to allow the story of Min to sink in. The lessons that it taught her were finding places within her heart. Her father had taught her to make everything count, from finding justice in wrongdoings to knowing revenge would merely blacken her soul.

She finally returned to the pages and found it odd that the face of one lone man sat sketched with abrupt strokes on the second to last page. He looked like someone that was of a different social class than Deb's family. His face was clean shaven and his clothing was that of nobility. There was no other detail; just the bust of a man that was a mystery to Deb. There was a page of single letters tucked into the book. It looked like her father had been trying to write individual letters as if he were practicing. She suddenly felt very badly. He must have been so frustrated not being able to read and write properly. She felt so fortunate now that Anne had given her these skills. It was a gift for certain to such a young woman of little means.

Deb pulled out the paper and on the back of it was the same portrait of the clean shaven man. It was a poorer version, but it was him and beside the face was her father's attempt to write what looked like a name. She whispered it out loud to herself and it looked like the name Windserlor.

"Windserlor?" What name was it? She had never heard it before. It was more plainly written, but his lettering was very shaky and she could tell that he had kept going over it with the nib. It was dug into the paper as if in anger. It was very strange, but she also knew her father had met many people in his time. Maybe he was someone with whom her father had bad dealings at the docks?

She also thought that when he wrote in this book, it must have been before he was married because there was not one drawing of her mother or of Deb. He had smaller landscapes of the family farm however, and pictures of what looked like the merchant trails that he had traveled. There were many of the two men who were drawn in the same fighting positions as Deb would use. There were even two pages dedicated to the knife throwing techniques that her father made sure she practiced each day. The tumbling drawings were very accurate as well. In fact, there was even one of a man rolling backwards off his horse with sword in hand. The trick was to stay strong and centered allowing your head to roll off slightly to the side of the horse's haunch. This way, you would not wrench your neck and roll off of your shoulders hopefully landing on both feet. Even if you fell, after you landed, you would at least miss the strike of a hammer axe swinging your way. A sword was no match for it. Keeping your weapon in tact was one rule Jacob never let Deb forget. "When you lose your weapon, you lose your life," he would say.

Deb closed the journal as David rose from his sleep. She smiled at him and got up to stoke the fire. As she gazed into the flames, she could not escape her curiosity and wanted to know who Windserlor was. She wondered if Henry had known the man, but there was no way of knowing. She would ask Anne if she knew the name. She may at least know the family name. It was one Deb had never heard of. She did know that it was English. No mistaking it.

When the morning turned to late evening, David saw a rider coming from the north hill. He made his way carefully through the rough gully that bordered the farm. David attached his sword sheath to his side and Deb took out her bow and arrows and sat them behind a tree. She also took a look around the other side of the croft and made her way up the back hill to take a look through the trees. She and David both knew all too well what a rider could mean. They were often decoys for what was to come and at times pretended to be roving travelers asking questions only to move on and disappear when all the while a more dangerous enemy was hiding out of sight, waiting to attack with the rider's information.

This time, David knew this rider and when Deb made her way back to his location, they could both see that their concern was unnecessary. The rider's name was Horace and he had been sent by Anne to check on Deb and David. Horace was known for his knowledge of the landscape and could travel like a ghost through even saturated enemy territories. David was happy to see him as the two men had grown up together.

"My God lad, how are you?" David shouted.

Horace smiled and came to a stop, getting off his horse right away. "I could be better. I rode all night just thinking about Deb's stew!"

Deb smiled and hugged Horace. "You're just saying that! I'm a terrible cook!" she answered.

"Well, if I had said that, I would go hungry!" They laughed together and made their way into the croft. Horace had good timing as Deb and

David were spent from the day's chores. She had put on a pot of lamb earlier and just added some extra potatoes to satisfy the extra mouth to feed. There was a treat of ale from the castle in Horace's bags and the three friends sat and enjoyed each other's company. Deb tried to tidy herself up a bit and when she turned around and had her hair tied back and a bit of fresh clothing on, the two men turned almost simultaneously out of habit. She didn't notice them looking at her, but David and Horace looked at each other thinking the same thing. She was so beautiful.

Horace respectfully said out loud, "You are a lucky woman Deb, but when you tire of this old man, remember me would you?"

Horace's sense of humor was well known and David they laughed heartily at his merriment. Horace was a gentleman at heart though and Deb knew how to take his words. She walked over and slapped him with the spoon she was holding.

"You best watch your tongue, my friend. Remember who you are teasing! She's better with a weapon than you are!" David was so glad to see his friend.

Deb sat the bowls of steaming stew onto the table and finally asked, "How is Lady Anne and everyone north?"

"Ah, my lady is fine and the castle walls have been somewhat quiet since Northampton was signed by the Bruce, but there is news that has saddened us all. Our King has died, my friends. Sir James Douglas is sailing to Spain to fight against the Moors and it is rumored that he has the Bruce's heart in a case about his neck."

"His heart?" Deb queried in surprise.

"At the request of the dying Bruce himself, it is said. He went horribly we are told. It is not the death that a King of his kind should have been dealt, but you should be proud, Deb. Your clan name is that of one of our guardians. Your braveness must come from it. James has been touted as a great man, but I fear of his return. Time will tell. War is all around us again my friends. It is not over by any means and has drifted upon the shores of the mainland. We are battling enemies on all sides of these lands."

"Who is to lead the Scots in his place?" David asked.

"Scotland will officially be led by the Bruce's young son David II, but he is only a child and guardians will be controlling our interests for now until he is fit to lead us. I fear for them as they attempt to keep Scotland for Edward III is taking the place of his father as well who, as you know, is now also passed for some time. He is much more defiant than his father has been in his final months. Even with the treaty, I fear young David will not be able to live up to his father's expectations if he even had any. The lowlands will become more and more vulnerable, my friends. England will strike again, but we have also made forward marches against them and there still does not seem to be an end. Edward III will not give up hope that he can take Scotland now with Bruce gone. But we hope the guardians will watch our borders and make good decisions."

David paced while he listened to Horace. He was going somewhere with all of this. He hadn't just ridden for days to have Deb's terrible stew and give them an update on the wars.

"Horace, coming to tell us of all of this must mean you have more to say."

"Aiee 'tis true my friend. I will be honest. Anne is worried about the two of you. She feels that there may be border raids occurring more and more. She has asked for me to persuade you to leave the farm and come back to the castle for good."

Deb's eyes widened and she looked at David with angst. Leave the farm for good? How could she? Her family was buried here.

"I understand her concern Horace, but this is my home. I can't just leave. I can't," Deb stated painfully.

David realized that Horace would not have come if he didn't agree whole-heartedly with Anne. What kind of life would it be for them in constant defense of the farm? They could not hold it forever. Deb and Liam couldn't keep it safe from Gully and his men. They were but two people. It may be time to consider Anne's offer.

"Deb, you know that I am the first one to support you as you maintain this home. I was born of the same life. You know I am by your side in whatever you choose, but if this is true, you have to see that there would be no way that you and I could maintain the safety of this place should the English get this far."

He gently added, "Anne has much knowledge of the political gesturing that has been going on, Deb. You know she would not take you from this place unless she knew in her heart that we were in grave danger at some point. You are like a daughter to her. She couldn't stand to lose you too. I think we should consider this as much as I know it pains you."

Horace gave David a look of sadness as he too knew the difficult decision Deb would have to make. This was her home. She was tied to it for life, but he saw danger in their future. They had to leave the farm. There was no other way. There would be safety to the north.

Deb walked outside and placed her hands on the gate. She looked out over the field and Brutis came to her side. He sat beside her and looked up. She looked down and smiled at the furry hound. Finnean sauntered over and bent his neck over the railing. She patted him on the snout and said, "Lad, I think we have one last trip to make to the highlands. This time it is for good, I fear."

She walked up the hill to the grave site where her family and Henry had been laid to rest. The dogs followed her and stayed by her side. When David looked out the door, she was kneeling down on the top of the hill.

"Let her think, lad. This is not an easy choice to make for anyone." Horace placed his hand on David's shoulder and the two gave Deb her space. When she came back down the hill, she was calmer than David expected.

"You know, for years I ran these trails and climbed these trees and watched as animals came and went. My father and I lived and breathed every blade of grass on these hills. I have so much of this dirt under my finger nails. There is so much love here." She poured some hot water from the kettle and sat down with the men. She sipped and then looked at Horace.

Deb said nothing for a moment and then with resolution in her voice she sighed and stated, "We'll leave as Anne is requesting. I don't believe that staying is the right thing to do. I just had to speak to mother and father and feel inside that they would approve. If Anne is correct, life here will be no life at all in the months to come. I think father would want me to make the smart choice. It is my home, but I have family to the north now and it is with all of you that I believe we should be."

"We'll need time," David stated.

"I can stay on and help you prepare to leave, my friends. You'll need to bring many things with you, I am sure. With our three horses, we can pull the cart and ride steadfast. One can ride solo and switch off pulling with the others. I believe most of the fields are prepared already and you may want to leave some things that will weigh us down."

"We'll begin tomorrow. My father's chair is the most important item in this home to me. We'll leave the croft as it is and warn our neighbors as we make the trip north. But David, what of Sarah and James…and their family to the east?"

"Not to worry about them, lass. I have been speaking to others as I rode and many southern families are making their way to the mountains as well. They will be alright." Horace had thought of everything. It was easy to see why he and David were friends. These men were strong of mind and body. Deb felt empowered being with them and blessed that they had entered her life.

"Very good then, let us sleep tonight and tomorrow we'll ready ourselves. We'll leave two days from now." They built a fire for the night and drifted off to sleep knowing that the next day, the farm near Carrick would be behind them.

In the morning, they decided that taking the remaining animals was futile. Anne had more than they would need and so they told families along the way that they were theirs for the taking should they want them. The cart was laden with the most precious items from the croft. Everything was tied down and the winter winds were making the trip difficult. David had placed runners on the cart for easier travel and slopped lard on them to make them move better in the snow. The trail they had taken was just used by merchants the day before and it was packed quite well for miles. As night came, the three would bury themselves, and the dogs, between the trees and the cart to stop the wind and with the horses well covered in sheepskins and their legs wrapped, the group made as warm a huddle as possible when the weather turned treacherous. The castle walls were a most welcoming site indeed when the long trip had finally ended.

They wasted no time getting the horses bedded down out of the wind and into fresh straw for the night. Many small fires had been lit in the courtyard of the castle and for those whose duties required them outside, huddling around the warm flames was a must. Horace made his way to find a bed. David and Deb were headed to the great hall where Anne was said to be having a meal with Margaret and William. They had been given word that William was gifted the official title of earl. They were also discussing the political unrest that was said to be coming and when Deb and David entered the doors, they were elated to see their friends.

"You've arrived!" Anne was gleeful and rushed to Deb to embrace her. She touched David's cold face and smiled graciously. William and Margaret were so pleased and William got up to shake David's hand.

Bowing down before their new earl and lady, Deb and David went to one knee before William.

"Come now! Enough formality! You are family!"

He took Deb's hand and brought her up to his eye level. She was bent down slightly for Deb stood taller than William. He was a robust stout man and when he smiled, he had a warm comforting effect on the room. Without seeing it, one would never know the fighting skills this man had. He was truly a great successor for Thomas.

With Gully gone, there was no true heir to the castle. Angus Og MacDonald, Lord of Islay had sent notification the day before that William would be given the charge of protecting Thomas' branch of the clan. He wanted to meet with him at a future date, but knew that he was not long for the world. It was fate that he had the foresight to give William his position under the circumstances. It was unconventional, but Angus had many under his Lordship and many had stated William's abilities. With much of the clan being carried on through blood lines, William would have more pressure on him to succeed in his role. Angus' son, John, would succeed him and William would need to create a bond with the new Lord as time went by. With neighboring clans such as MacLeod, Cameron and Grant, William would have many to continue good relations with. MacDonell of Kepoch was just south west of Thomas and Anne's castle and it was this area that Gully had avoided the most as he made his way to his father's land on the coast. William would do well, but he would need Anne's support. There was time to build bridges and to take comfort in the fact that many from the south were coming north as

Deb and David did to avoid the southern upset that was to come.

Inverness was a place of strength and strong clans. There would be distaste between them at times, but the following years would see other discontented Scots who lost lands and power during the wars join forces with the English to try and take back what they had lost. Just as Jacob had taught his daughter, the lines between loyalty to Scotland and the need to succeed those who were not giving them what they wanted pushed men to support the English King and make the move to take southern Scotland at places like Halidon Hill and Berwick.

Many times over, the leadership of Scotland was tossed between those who were loyal to its true Scottish roots and those who saw more power in combining forces with Edward of England. King Robert's young son David now had to flee to France and take protection under Phillip IV. The French and the English now looked at each other for battle rights in France and the lowlands of Scotland were under the English thumb. Edward had gained more power over Scotland with Robert the Bruce gone and now many other nobles and Scottish guardians, who tried to protect Scotland, were dead. The northern clans had to find a way to hold on.

Anne was right to have had Deb and David leave the farm. They had been involved in three separate skirmishes and each time Deb and David had been there to protect the highlands. Many had died. Deb and David had both been injured in the attempts and, by the grace of God, they had survived. Anne was in a living hell each time they left and returned. It aged her and she prayed every night for the fighting to end. They had a fortress of clans around them however, and as fate would have it, the castle managed to stay the safe haven it was.

Five years into the changes to their country, twenty-five year old Deb was looking back at what could have been, but now she had a great purpose being a part of Anne's life and the life of those in the north. She was becoming a figure that many revered. Deb Barne was no longer a young farmer's daughter.

Deb spent many of her days thriving in a place that had been kept relatively safe from the onslaughts of the English and their Scottish associations. For the years she spent by David and Anne's side, she became well versed in reading and writing. Anne taught her about social etiquette and the skills that a woman in politics needed in order to be heard and respected. She heard stories of other women who shared her courage and physical fortitude. Anne told her of those before her and of those who were being touted as the next generation of women in Scotland leading the charge against marauders; women who defended their husband's castles while they were at war and succeeded.

Anne was not a fighter, but she continued to meet with those of influence. Whoever she had been speaking with behind closed doors, had kept the high north safe. Only William and Margaret were privy to it. It was how it had to be. It was the way that she and Thomas had made their way through the chaos of it all. Whether with wealth or influence, Anne was certainly a warrior of another kind. She had come from money and married into even more. How deep into the political sea she was in, no one would ever know except those she dealt with.

The new English King was letting it be known each and every battle that he was enforcing his lordship on Scotland. Anne knew that William and Margaret would have a new life and purpose in the north. They were dedicated to the clan and had been forging forward, keeping on the side of the house of Bruce and maintaining their status by upholding Thomas' resolutions. Anne foresaw a second round of wars against Scotland and the French were the only allies of her country who had a clear and determined opinion of Edward's plan to take both lands. With the castle in good hands, she felt it was time to use her connections and try to help her people in the only way she knew how. Her husband and son were gone and Anne's loyalties were with the children and the families of the highlands. It was her purpose all along, but now she was holding Thomas' legacy of dreams. She could not let them die. Without letting on however, Anne had another purpose for a trip to France.

On the morning of June 5, 1334, Anne MacDonell requested her things to be packed and her horses readied for travel. She was headed for the eastern Scottish shores near Aberdeen. There, a private ship would take her and her entourage to the seaside of France and a port near Normandy. Deb and David were asked to accompany her. Anne's relationship with the wealthy and the royals of France needed to be revisited. Her country was becoming a place of such turmoil that she was reaching out to find what could be done and who could help her. Anne was a wonderful person in the eyes of many, but she had many deep secrets she kept as well; secrets that Deb couldn't even begin to know as close as they had become. Anne's place in the world did not come from showing all of the cards she had to deal. She had information that she carried to the French, but no one would know other than the king and queen.

Chapter Twenty-Two
Sea Legs

Cheryl Alleway

Once the journey was underway, Deb sat beside Anne in her carriage and gently asked the question Anne was waiting for.

    The breeze was coming through the sides and Anne sat with a sheer head dress over her graying golden hair, which was placed in a tidy braided bun at the base of her neck. She was pensive but quiet and just tried to enjoy the feeling that maybe, just maybe for a moment she could watch the scenery go by without seeing soldiers, or burned villages, or smell the death in the air. She watched calmly as a king fisher flew past and dove into the river they had come by. It then flew back up to the tree it had been perched in. It obviously missed the fish it had spotted, but it went back to the search; ever diligent and never giving up. It is how Anne lived her life and it was why Deb could not wait any longer.

"Lady Anne, I only wonder what we will be searching for during our trip. Will we be in harm's way? I am ready to protect you at all cost. David is as well. We will not leave your side. You must tell me if our route is near the fighting for we must be wary."

Deb was impatient and nervous of being on a big ship. She had never seen one, let alone sailed on one for any length of time. She was more concerned with what they would find on the shores of France. She had never been anywhere but Scotland. As much as she trusted Anne, she was leery of taking her into an area that was even more dangerous than their homeland.

Anne gently brushed the sheer material from her face and looked at Deb. She smiled confidently knowing that Deb had no idea what was about to happen. It wasn't her intention to worry her, but Anne tried not to divulge too much to Deb in order to keep her level-headed. It was doing the opposite of her intentions and so she spoke briefly, but matter-of-fact, to ease Deb's wandering mind.

"My dear, we are going to be traveling on a ship that belongs to the King of France. His personal soldiers have been tasked with bringing us to his home and with our protection. The path we will travel is a secret one made to protect those of great importance. We will be seeing a tunnel near the beginning of the journey. It was built to mask the arrivals of certain individuals to the shores of France and to bring them to a safe location to continue the journey. The war is bombarding certain areas yes, this is true, but fear not for my safety or the safety of any of you. The next people you see when we arrive will be the guards at the gates of King Phillip's castle. Once there, you will understand more. I seek information and I seek assistance. You must be a part of that." She paused and took a breath, looking out the side again. She placed the thin head piece back over her face and added, "You are an important part of my life and the future of Scotland, my dear Deborah. This trip is also for you. You need to see other parts of the world and other parts of the story that Scotland has been handed. It is your destiny to be with me here on this trip."

    Deb said nothing in return because Anne's words were making her think so deeply that she had to pause to find the words to respond. Her black hair was also tied neatly behind her neck in several braids that had been interwoven into a beautiful ball of texture between her shoulder blades. She was dressed like a lady and Anne had given her perfume and a plush overcoat in the deepest purple to wear over her clothes. She was wearing leather boots that were laced to her knees and upon her wrist she wore a bracelet that David had given to her. It was made with silver and punched into a most wonderful braid with every second hole holding a different coloured stone that had been pressed into place. It fit loosely on Deb's wrist and suited her strength well. It was not dainty or feminine, but rather wide and masculine in nature. It was a beautiful compliment to her outfit and Deb looked as if she were born of nobility. Anne was quite proud of her and when they finally made port, the two women walked beside each other with grace and dignity. Deb felt so special. She felt fortunate to be here on this journey with someone like Anne guiding her and including her in this life. It was a moment she would never forget.

David now saw the two together in full sunlight as Anne was led to the area where the ship was waiting. Deb kept looking in every direction. She had no weapons on her person, except that underneath her skirt laid her father's dagger. She knew how to reach it at a moment's notice should anything happen. Anne kept smiling demurely as the ship came into view. Deb's eyes widened and her heart raced. She had never been on water and Anne had brought with her a tincture that would help settle her stomach should the movement of the water cause Deb to become ill. Riding a horse was one thing, but on a ship, one would need sea legs.

David had wed Deb in a very small ceremony on top of the hill of the castle two years prior. Deb did not take his name however, at David's request. He also suggested she keep her father's clan name of Douglas. Barne was her first husband's name, but David thought it appropriate for her to keep no man's name and follow her father's line instead. It was something he felt strongly about for some reason and Deb agreed. She would live her life as a Douglas. On paper, it was written *Deborah of Douglas*. They did not wish to have a large group watching nor did they feel it mattered. Everyone understood their desire for privacy and so it was that the two confessed their love with only Anne, William and Margaret present. It was a sweet moment that would bond them together and make their lives feel complete. Children had not come and Anne prayed every day that Deb was not barren from her years of extreme physical experiences. She had been thrown from Finnean, kicked and beaten all during the years that her body was just forming into that of a woman. Her female cycle was very weak and her body was extremely muscular for a woman. It may have been how it was meant to be, but Anne knew in her heart that if God saw it fit, Deb would want to be a mother someday soon. Being twenty-five, Deb also was beginning to wonder if it would happen. David never troubled her about it. He loved her and that was all he needed. But he would enjoy it if she were to bear a child of his blood one day.

Right now they had a job to do. They were entering a world they knew very little about. They would be hearing a different language and would have to rely on Anne's abilities to speak it in order to understand. What Anne was hoping to come home with was still unclear, but they knew that she was fulfilling Thomas' dreams of never giving up on their home. What other purpose Anne was taking them there for escaped them.

As the sails billowed in the sea air, Anne's party made their way to the ship's ramp. Anne insisted that Finnean and the other horses come on the trip across the channel. Deb was very concerned about Finnean. He had been through battle and injuries, but he had never been cooped up in the hull of a ship. Anne reassured her that it was done often and he would be fine. They were watched carefully and given large amounts of hay to comfort them. Deb ended up spending most of her time with him and so her fear of being on the ship was consumed by her love for Finnean. Once again, they supported each other. It was a love affair that would never die.

The hours that passed saw a short rain shower and many birds of the sea visited the edges of the ship. Anne stayed inside the captain's cabin most of the time, but she did come out to get fresh air once the ship had made it only two miles from shore. Deb and David gazed in amazement at the view coming from the horizon. It was night-time when they came into view of the shoreline and the ship slowed down, becoming quiet. Anne knew the next step, but she also knew Deb would not be happy about it.

The men were bringing the ship to a full stop, but they were not at shore yet. Deb approached Anne as they all stood upon the ship's deck looking into the distance. The lanterns were all blown out and everyone was made to be silent. "Lady Anne, is there something wrong?" Deb had Anne's shawl with her and placed it upon her shoulders.

Anne touched Deb's hand. "We are entering an area that is the safest place to depart the ship, but we will have to take the smaller boats to get to shore."

"What about Finnean and the other horses?"

"Don't worry, they will sail the ship to port and unload the rest of the cargo. The horses will be brought to us at a secret location. Do not fear. It is only our group that must reach the shore undetected. Once we are clear, the ship is free to pose as it always does…a cargo ship with items for sale and a few horses with which to cart them."

Deb did not like this plan. She hadn't left Finnean for years. They had never been separated. He would be frantic for her. "Please Anne, please, let me stay with Finnean. I cannot leave him."

"You must have faith, dear. I will not take the chance. You must come with us. This country is at war with the very people who have made us come here. You must have faith that Finnean will be alright. He will see you in the morning, I promise."

David put his hands on Deb's shoulders. "It is alright, Deb. Finnean knows two of the men that will stay behind. He trusts them. They will not leave his side. I have told them personally not to."

Deb could face her most mortal enemy with weapon by her side, but Finnean brought out the softer side in her. He saved her over and over again. He had her heart and she was his angel. "If anything happens to him, I don't know what I would do, David."

"I know, but trust Anne's decision. We must."

She was feeling a pain in her heart, but she did as Anne requested. They carefully and quietly unloaded the group onto the two smaller boats that had been taken on the trip. The rest of the team would unload the ship as a merchant crew in port and ride to where Anne, Deb, David and the rest would be waiting. There was simple lodging waiting for them for the night. Even Anne would not complain. She was not above sleeping in a humble place for the night. It was yet another part of the undying devotion to being more than a pampered wife of an earl. She was a person, just like anyone else and she was looking forward to feeling that way. It made her feel closer to the very people she was fighting for. She had the feeling that the days to come would require her to dig down deep and find the woman that many revered and respected as a woman of nobility and wealth.

The air smelled different to Deb. There was sweetness and a subtle scent of oak. They took what gear they could carry and made their way in the darkness to a path that led from the shoreline to a small area in the forest that was surrounded by thick forest. The men with them set up a makeshift canopy for Anne and she found her heavier overcoat to keep her warm. It was summer however the night air by the sea was always cold. The extra dampness was felt by all and they made a fire to sit by. They were safe with a few of the king's men that had been with them for the entire trip. They stayed awake and guarded Anne as if she were a queen.

Deb paced back and forth looking up at the stars and worrying about Finnean. David went to her. He smiled widely as she caught his grin. She looked at him strangely and asked him why he was smiling so.

"You are very charming when you worry about Finnean. I am not mocking you, my love. I am admiring the sweetness that you hold for him. It is endearing to say the least and I do understand. It is how I worry about you. It is how I felt about you for so long. It is an ache in your heart that is unwavering. Soon you will see his handsome face. Please, you must get some rest."

Deb relaxed a bit. It was something that David could always do to her. He had a way about him that was calming and comforting. She turned and kissed him. "Thank you, my love. I will try." She made a place under another canopy that they had erected and David made sure that she had closed her eyes before making his way over to the men who were standing guard.

"My friends, it is a chilly night. Is there anything you need?"

The men graciously declined, and asked no questions, but David could not help notice their gaze in Deb's direction from time to time. David smiled and said, "I know. She is hard not to look at, isn't she?"

The men blinked quickly and turned away. Slightly embarrassed, one apologized, "I meant no harm, sir. She is just unlike many of the women I have ever seen. She is your wife?"

"Yes, by the grace of God. This one is special, gentlemen. She is a force to be reckoned with and Lady Anne thinks of her as a daughter." Suddenly, David realized that these men spoke surprisingly good English. Their accents were extremely strong, but he had no trouble understanding them. Nor did they have trouble understanding him.

"You speak English well."

"We must know English as we are often called upon to spy on them."

"This is logical indeed. It would be dangerous work for certain."

"Many times it has been, but we have learned to blend in. We have English uniforms and traveler's clothing to make us look as though we come from the far East. It is for our king that we challenge our enemies in this way. It is at times the only way." The men gathered around a small fire that one of them had built and David was quite content to know all he could about his knew acquaintances. They were from another country, but David saw such similarities to his fellow soldiers back home. As the moon began to rise, he thought about the value in traveling with Anne. He and Deb seemed to have a different purpose than they thought they ever would. Deb was experiencing so much more than she would have staying on the farm and even though that life would have satisfied them both, he felt destiny had brought them here.

After a warm fire had lulled him to sleep, David said good night to the men and settled in for the night. He did not want to disturb Deb's sleep and lay beside her on a sheepskin blanket. The ground was soft where he settled in and as he faded into sleep, he wondered what dawn would bring. It was long before he smelled the familiar morning dew and the heard the birds wakening their party at a very early hour.

Deb was anxiously waiting with Anne as the two met outside their tents. It was damp and the men had already started a morning fire to boil water and cook a few rabbits they had caught along the way. They would only stay until the others arrived and Anne instructed everyone to be ready to leave as soon as possible. She did not want to waste time getting to the castle. King Robert's young son and his juvenile queen had taken refuge with Phillip of France and Anne wanted to know how they were. She feared for the young boy's life, but his safe passage to the shores of Normandy gave her hope that not all was lost with Scotland. With the Guardians fighting on the homeland to keep Scotland from becoming completely ruled by Edward, her hope was to see the young king return and take his rightful place on Scottish soil, but his fate upon that return was unknown. For now, she was bringing her group to the Sienne River in Paris. They would be heading for the Conciergerie; royal residence of the King and Queen of France.

The sun had fully risen in an attempt to show its power over the morning mist and after it burned through the grey, damp air, a beautiful morning lay before them. Deb had put on more appropriate traveling attire and the men had the tents down and everything packed. Anne waited for a rider to return with news that the others from the ship had made their way to the location and with a smile of relief, she got her wish. Just outside the left bank came word that Finnean and the other horses were spotted, they were making safe passage and would arrive within a short time. Anne took the opportunity to remind everyone of the dangers that they may encounter. She also had changed into more reasonable clothing for the area so as not to appear as her normal self. Deb had never seen her dressed as such and proceeded to compliment her.

"This suits you well, my lady."

"I shall say that I rather enjoy the freedom. As much as I adore a lovely dress, I am quite comfortable indeed. We will have plenty of time for that when we reach Paris." The two smiled at each other as the sound of horses came near. Deb's heart raced as she saw Finnean come into view...once he saw her, the rider got off and let him run to his true owner, but everyone knew he was having quite a time staying atop of the valiant steed. Finnean tolerated him, but when he saw Deb, there was no holding him back. She whistled to him and he came in so fast that many of the others ran backward fearing that he may run them over. Deb and David laughed as Finnean came to a sudden halt right at Deb's feet. He gave a hearty whinny and rose onto his back legs briefly to say hello to his beloved owner. She was relieved as well and David saw that familiar calm come over her when she was with Finnean, but as happy a moment as it was, time was wasting and Anne had everyone organized to leave. The journey into Paris would be safe if everyone did as she asked. They were no longer in Scotland and even though France was their ally, there were English on its land as well.

The first leg of the trip took them from the shores at the edge of Normandy. They would take a similar path as did young King David. To Anne, it was a familiar one. She had traveled many times to the shores of France when she and Thomas were first married. Thomas was a worldly man who had seen the faces of many foreigners even before he had met Anne. They were quiet nobles who educated themselves and felt that to understand one's own country you needed to travel to other parts of the world. Thomas and Anne sat in on many lectures by men who were touted as the greatest minds alive. They had visited universities such as Cohors and had read many books on subjects of science, medicine and much more. They had never wanted to be more than leaders of the people. Thomas had been mentioned in many circles as someone who should strive for a higher position in Scotland, but his role living with his people and educating the young and their families was his way of giving strength to the highlands. Thomas and Anne had a different purpose in life, but always kept the ties with those who were in the roles of leadership. It gave them a distinct attachment to the very people whose lives they were trying to improve and protect. They chose to live with their countrymen and give them the skills they would need to carry on a very proud way of life. By traveling and educating themselves with the wealth they had, they could bring that knowledge back to the people of the highlands and give them the gift of information and insight. This was Thomas' vision all along and so it was that Anne desired to pass this on to Deb and David. She felt it was the greatest gift one could have in life. Defending their land and assisting the king in his wars with the English was an act of loyalty to Thomas. He had made no moves to change his position in the hierarchy and the Bruce respected that. It would take many different men with different skills to protect Scotland and Thomas had found his calling.

For now, Anne remained quiet as she was deep in thought. Something else other than Thomas was on her mind. Deb noticed and rode up beside her mentor. Giving Anne a smile, she did not want to be intrusive, but gently asked if Anne was alright.

"I am just fine, my dear...although the air is becoming cooler."

Deb felt as though this comment was meant to change the subject and she did not wish to be disrespectful. Instead she added, "It is at that. If you require it my lady, I have another blanket behind me."

"Not to worry, I will be just fine. I believe we are getting to the halfway point. Ahead is a small village that we will find shelter in. It is a long used stop for merchant groups. There will be ample room for our horses and shelter for us. Would you please ride back and tell the men that it is there that we will stop for the night?"

"Certainly, my lady." Deb nodded as she slowed up and turned to meet the men near the back. David was riding lead and slowed his own horse to ride beside Anne. She told him that there was something she wanted to talk to him about when they stopped, but she wanted to talk to him alone. David was curious, but why wouldn't she want Deb there as well? He never questioned Anne and so he stayed quiet and continued on as though nothing had changed. As much as he loved Deb, they were in a strange place with many unanswered questions. As to why Anne needed to speak to him, he had no doubt that it was very important and that it involved Deb in some way. He was anxious inside for the entire last leg, but when they finally arrived, he was too busy assisting the men with the horses and gear to think on it much. When they had finally settled into a small set of stalls and a wooden building for them to sleep, Anne motioned for David to follow her and he asked Deb to check on the horses for him while he assisted Anne with planning the next leg of the journey. She had no suspicion. He found himself trying to decide what Anne could possibly want to speak to him about. It was making him nervous, to say the least.

The moon was out and there was a strong odor of ale coming from the small tavern at the end of the path. Surely some of the men had found their way there. Anne had told them to do as they wish but to use decorum with the locals remembering that they were just traveling, though on the hunt for supplies. Anne sat down upon a stone that lay flat by the water. David approached her and found a clear spot on the ground beside her. She pulled a shawl over her shoulders and she seemed very pensive to David as he addressed her. "Lady Anne, are you warm enough?"

His chivalry was enamouring, but she reassured him that she was fine and had something most important to share with him

"My lady, I have tried very hard not to over step my bounds, but you have me puzzled indeed. What it is that you need to discuss?"

"David, your young wife is like a daughter to me and you have proven to be the man that she needed in her life. I believe that she has been pining over her father's journal for years and the thought of this man named Windserlor has disturbed her all this time." She pulled a small flower from its stem in the ground and looked out onto the river and then back at David directly.

"David, Windserlor is here in France."

His face opened up with shock and he shifted his position, "What? The man in her father's journal is here?"

"Yes, he is here and I know where." Anne turned to sit facing David. "This man, David, is an animal at heart. You have to know that he is connected to Deb and her father more than you realize. Windserlor fathered a child against a woman's will. But it was the man she loved that raised the baby girl to be the woman she is today, David."

His face turned dark and he suddenly knew what this was all about. He could say nothing.

"Yes, Windserlor is Deb's birth father, David. He is the villain that appears in her father's journal. Jacob wasn't certain at first, but he found out who he was and kept it a secret. He was the one who loved Deb. He was the one who cared for her and he would never tarnish Mary's memory by hurting the little girl, but now that she has seen the picture, she has never let up trying to understand who he was. She has become obsessive speaking of him to me. I had made it my plight in life to keep the secret that Henry told me before he died. He was privy to it all. I knew of Mary and I felt many years ago that I knew who Deb was. Henry brought it all together. Windserlor is a criminal and I have hired some of the best spies to find him. They have been with us the whole trip."

"Lady Anne, you have held this inside of you all this time? I am so sorry. You do not deserve this burden. Your resilience astonishes me. What do you desire me to do?"

"Deb knows nothing yet, but when we reach the Conciergerie, I will tell her. You can tell her you only just heard of it from me and that I made you swear to wait until I told her myself. I only wanted you to know to help her through it. I have this man's location and if I know your wife, she will need time to take this horrible information into her heart. I fear for the worst, but I believe that if she is never told, it would break the trust we have built. I must tell her. She must have the knowledge of how much Jacob loved her. She will see that it was more than she ever imagined. Her mother's memory meant so much to him. He was a man of great passion for his family and Deb needs to hold onto this. You must help me make her understand, David!" Anne was speaking in a loud whisper at this point and was feeling the pressure of telling that deep, dark secret.

David looked in Anne's eyes and took her hand. He closed his eyes once and when he opened them he stated, "Lady Anne, she will not forsake your love or her father's for this. It will bite her heart knowing what her mother had to endure, but she will not deny you the love you have shown for her. You have given her a life. For this, she will be forever loyal to you. My lady, where is Windserlor?"

"He has been sighted in Bouvray and Patay just south of Paris. The very men you have befriended on this trip will be leaving us once we reach the Conciergerie. They have been chosen by the king, at my request, to capture him and bring him to the castle. I intend to give Deb the opportunity to see his face and let him see the woman that he created. He cannot run nor hide from her questions. She should know that he is to be hung for rape. We have proof that Deb is not the only child he has fathered under the cruelty of this crime. One woman is from this country and anyone who understands the tension between England and France will know how the king took the news. Men rape women every day in this world, but this particular girl was known to the royal court. She is the cousin of the Queen herself. Phillip was easily persuaded to bring Windserlor to justice once I told him of Deb's story as well. So you see lad, this man needed to be stopped for more than Deb's sake. Her mother was not his only victim."

David wanted to kill the man with this knowledge trapped in his mind, but for now, they had to concentrate on the journey to meet the King of France. Anne was anxious to see her friend and confidant, the Queen consort of France, Joan. She was a woman to be admired and respected and it was her additional influence that helped to pay the men who were searching for Windserlor. There was something to be said for the women in Anne's circle of acquaintances. They were mysterious at times, wealthy and dangerous to those who crossed them. Anne certainly did have the connections that Deb and David believed her to have.

Nightfall came and went and the group was quickly on their way and nearing the French river Sienne. Paris could be smelled for two miles away and they knew they were close. The air was changing. Anne knew this area well and they swiftly made their way to the castle entrance where nobles and royalty entered. It came into view like nothing Deb had ever seen. She gazed at the towers and the formal cladding. This castle was very different than Anne's. It was immense and foreboding as it looked down upon the river. The stone was a silvery grey and smooth, unlike the rough Scottish stone that graced Castle MacDonell.

Once they had dismounted from the horses, Deb kissed Finnean and watched him being led to a beautiful stable with the others. She and David looked upon the palace in wonder with large eyes soaking it all within their minds to be forever remembered. As Anne gracefully walked the corridor that she had walked many times before, she looked back at Deb and smiled. She was amazed and had a child-like expression upon her face.

Deb could not believe Anne had lived this life for so long. She was so unassuming on many levels and to think that she could be close to the King and Queen of France was overwhelming. The servants walked past them and nodded their heads politely to Anne and her guests.

There was a short woman who was walking toward them dressed so beautifully that Deb could not take her eyes off her. Her skin was pale and creamy and she had a sweet smile on her face. She greeted Anne and bowed politely taking her hand gently. Anne responded in kind. "Hello, Grace. How are you, my dear?"

The woman seemed very happy to see Anne and answered in French accent, "Very well Madame, now that you are visiting us again. Please, come with me. You must all be tired and in need of a change of clothing."

She looked in Deb's direction and smiled once more. She was so demure and her small body walked gracefully down the hallway to a few rooms that were adjacent to each other. They were spacious and cool, but they were decorated very elaborately with colors so brilliant. Golds, purples, yellows and silk materials adorned the beds and chairs that sat within the rooms. Each fireplace was ample in size and was lit for them as they entered.

David and Deb had their own room as did Anne. The other men had left just as Anne told David they would and she felt that it was time to tell Deb what was happening, but it could wait until after she and David met the king and queen.

David helped Deb with the outfit she had chosen to wear for the evening. She was ravishing. Her dress fell to the floor, cascading from her hips. She had chosen blue velvet and it rose to her waist giving her height even more elegance. Her hair was up with a matching blue pin that Anne had given to her as a gift when they wed. As with any occasion, Deb wore her father's dirk dagger upon her left thigh. No one would know that this beautiful girl was ready to fight at a moment's notice no matter where she was.

David teased her lovingly, "You are your father's daughter, my love. I just hope no one makes the mistake of crossing you tonight."

She smiled and rebutted, "That's what makes it exciting."

David had changed into a clean cream tunic with high collar and an overcoat in dark brown. He was as handsome as ever and Deb could not have been more proud or felt so fortunate. If Jacob was alive, he would be beaming at the sight of his beautiful daughter. Daughter. His daughter. His beautiful daughter. David's smile turned to concern in his mind and it was as if a dark shadow descended over his features as he waited patiently for Anne to tell Deb about Windserlor, but he forced himself to push it all to the back of his mind knowing that this moment was too wonderful to take from her.

They walked out into the hallway and waited for Anne to exit her room. Deb's face lit up when she saw Anne, in all her divine splendour, step out of her room with Grace at her side. She had assisted Anne with her attire and one would believe a queen was walking down the hallway toward them. Deb went to Anne and took both of her hands. The two women just stared at each other. Anne had a tear in her eye, but Deb said quickly, "My lady, you'll ruin your beautiful face."

Anne grinned at the young woman that she had come to love so dearly as her own. She felt in that moment that her life was complete. William and Margaret were taking care of the castle and Deb had David in her life. Anne had one more secret she had to tell the two lovers; one that even David did not now, but it would wait until the evening was over. In that one wonderful moment, they were free, they were together and they were experiencing the joy of what life had given them by staying together and caring for one another. Whether sleeping in a cold shelter under the stars or dining at a banquet table, they were still together. Deb had been given back some of the family she lost so many years ago.

There was music coming from the great hall and Deb was a bit nervous as they came to the entrance. Grace opened the doors and two men stood holding them for the trio. A hearth larger than Deb had ever seen stood in the room to the right. Anne whispered to her that it could roast an entire ox. Deb's eyes widened yet again.

There were many people gathered at tables that were adorned with pheasants, flowers, fruit, bread and more. At the head table above the others, sat the King and Queen of France.

The king noticed Anne and lifted his bejewelled hand to hush the music as their guests walked forward. Everyone was allowed to chat quietly as Grace led them to the front of the room. Phillip and Joan rose and the queen smiled deeply at the sight of her friend, Lady Anne MacDonell. The two met and embraced. They pulled back to look at each other's faces. Anne was fourteen years older than Joan, but the two had much in common including their love for education. Anne spoke to Joan in French and Deb and David stood politely until called upon for introduction. Anne could not have been more proud to have the king and queen meet her friends. Deb bowed respectfully as Anne took her hand and led her and David forward. The king came down from two steps up and addressed Deb and David in a strong French accent, "It is a pleasure to have you both at the Conciergerie." He looked at Deb as were many others and commented to David, "You are a blessed man indeed, my friend."

David smiled and nodded his head up and down, "Thank you, your majesty, your graciousness and hospitality is greatly appreciated."

Joan walked over to David and put out her hand. David bowed on one knee as he held it with an open palm saying, "Thank you for welcoming us, your majesty."

He rose and it was Deb's turn to experience the moment. When Joan came to her, she looked deeply into her eyes and then at Anne. "You have lived a long life already, my dear. I can see it in your eyes. You have the grace of a lady, but in you I see something more. You are fearless in your heart. I see a strength that is rare within such a pretty frame. I am very interested in talking with you more. For now, enjoy your meal and the warmth of the fire. If you need anything throughout your stay, Grace will assist you." Joan knew about Deb's history through her letters back and forth to Anne and she felt a pang of pity for the girl.

Deb bowed lightly and answered gratefully, "Your majesty, your home is so beautiful. We are very grateful for your generosity." Deb's face was as humble and honest as Joan had ever seen. She knew what Anne was doing for her and understood when she looked into Deb's face why Anne had become so attached to her. She would not hesitate to do anything for Anne. Joan knew Deb would understand just how powerful the relationship she had with Anne really was. For now, they would live and they would laugh, enjoy freedom and the comforts of the castle.

The music began again and Deb sat on her chair with her back straight as she watched the entertainers juggle, dance and parade around the room. There was so much food before them that David did not know where to start. Anne ate very little and drank no wine. Deb found it strange as she always enjoyed the red wine made at castle MacDonell, but it was getting late and they were all tired.

As the evening wound down, Deb just sat and looked at the amazing hall they sat within. It was glorious with a vaulted ceiling, rows of pillars and so many candles lit it would take twenty people to snuff them out at the evening's end. White cloths adorned the table under the bountiful food and grapevines were draped around the edges emphasized by intermittent flowers dotting its path. She could not believe the peacock that glorified the center of the king and queen's table. It was unlike anything she had ever seen. The meat had been cooked in the massive hearth she had seen and the aroma permeated the castle halls. Grace diligently marched back and forth filling goblets and adjusting the queen's attire. Anne motioned to Joan that she was ready to retire and she rose up, inviting Deb and David to take their leave as well. After saying good evening respectfully, the three made their way back to their rooms. Anne stopped at hers and asked for David and Deb to join her for a conversation prior to sleep.

She sat quietly and stated, "I believe I spent the majority of my energy on the trip. I am quite tired. How are you both? Did you enjoy your meal?"

Deb blurted out like a young girl, "Oh, Lady Anne! It is so beautiful. The food, the decorations, the people, the clothing and the music...it was so interesting and wonderful. I can't thank you enough!"

David smiled at her as he admired her zest for adventure and new experiences. He too was in awe of the evening.

Anne took a deep breath and suddenly, Deb saw something strange in her face. It was a look of labour and somewhat daunting, but she listened as Anne spoke the words David had been waiting for.

"Deb, my dear, I have shared something with David only in an effort to comfort you when I tell you as well. It was not meant to be deceptive in anyway."

"What is it my lady. Is something wrong?" She glanced at David who sat respectfully quiet.

He swallowed and sat close to her. Deb's brow was furrowed deeply as Anne began to speak.

"You know the man, Winderselor, the one that you so longingly wish to know about?"

"Yes, certainly."

"Deb, this man is alive and he is real. Most importantly, he is here in France."

Deb was shocked and stood up, beginning to pace the floor, "I don't know what to say. I don't even know who he was to my father."

"You don't have to say anything, but you need to know the truth about this man. He is someone your father knew of, yes, but he is also someone your father hated for what he did to your mother. This man is a criminal, my dear, and he has damaged the hearts of more women than you know…more than we all know, I am sure. The guards who traveled with us are en route to capture him and bring him back to the Conciergerie for punishment."

Deb's face flushed; *'for what he did to your mother'*. She heard it over and over again in her head.

"What did this man do to my mother and others?" She was turning dark within her eyes and David tried to settle her just as Liam had always done. "Deb lass, it's going to be alright."

"Alright! Alright? What is this about?"

Anne stood as well and took Deb by the shoulders looking her straight in the eye. She touched her face with her hand and sat Deb down to calm her.

"My dear, your mother was a victim of this man. You are your mother's daughter Deb, but...you...you are also Winderslor's. Jacob raised you knowing this and vowed to love you more than any father could love a daughter."

Deb sat blank faced. She could not speak. This was all too much to take in, but she knew others had suffered as well. This humbled her in the moment and she finally verbalized again what she had heard quite bluntly, "My father Jacob; he was not my real father? My mother was raped by this man and he *is* my real father? He has fathered other children as well this way? He is here in France and you are bringing him here to meet his fate?" She was filled with a hot pain in her chest and her eyes were filling with tears.

She suddenly realized what Anne had done. She realized Joan's involvement. She realized why Jacob would have never shown her the journal and why he buried it. She realized the love Jacob must have had for her to have done what he did and how much he must have loved Mary. Then her heart began to beat with fervor. She could see what kind of man Jacob Douglas truly was and how lucky she was that this monster hadn't been in her life all this time. She felt that Anne had known more about her than she knew about herself and that she had been protecting her all along. She wondered why she wasn't crumbling to the floor. She felt anger instead; anger at this man for harming her mother in such a way; angry that he, like Gully, was allowed to hurt innocent people by hiding behind his men and using his position to get what he wanted. Her father's torment ripped at her heart and she could not believe that he lived all those years without telling her; for her sake. She was not broken as David feared, but sensed how blessed she had been even though she had lost so much.

Deb stood up, surprising them both, and said with a matter of fact tone and presence, "I want to see him when he arrives. He is *not* my father. Jacob Douglas is my father and God be with me when I look into Windserlor's face. He will die with fear in his heart for what he has done. The day I forsake Jacob Douglas is the day I die. I trust you, that what happened to my mother truly happened, but Lady Anne, I loved my father more than anything. I will never deny the life he gave me. Windserlor is just lucky I was not around when he committed this crime against my mother. If I was, he would not be alive today." Deb stood with conviction and David was never more impressed by his young wife.

Anne was in pain for the task she had to perform in telling Deb, but she was so proud of her. She was facing this with the dignity she had been taught and she was standing tall against this man, not allowing him to take her power away. He had already done that to her mother, but Anne had more to say to both Deb and David and she asked them to sit back down for a moment.

"My dear you are my pride and it is with great pain that I have brought this to you. In my heart, I knew that you should be privy to it even though it is a harsh reality to hold. I think of you both as my family, but there is more that I must tell you. I have no blood to carry my life on when I pass and so, it has been written and signed that you will have my fortune when I die. This capture of Windserlor was my last gift to you, Deb. I love you, dear. I love you more than you could ever know. You were brought to me by the angels and for that I am grateful. You will always know that you have worth beyond your past and beyond your experiences. You were sent to us all for a reason, love. You and David must forge a path to greatness together. It is meant to be."

Deb got down on her knees in front of Anne and took her hands. As she looked up at her she asked softly, "Your last gift to me?" David too came in close and sat beside Anne placing his hand upon her shoulder.

"Lady Anne, what are you saying?"

Anne sat steadfast but for one small tear that fell ever so slowly down her cheek. Deb watched as it fell like a feather upon the top of her hand and when she looked back at Anne's face the words she feared came from her lips.

"I am dying. I have tried desperately to relay information back and forth between France and Scotland to quash some of the turmoil on our homelands. I brought you both here to show you what your lives could be and to show you, Deb that you have no demons in your life to hold you back. Windserlor will die a deserving death and you will carry on with the life I have tried to give you. I only hope that you want it. It is the only thing I can give you for I have no children and I must die knowing that you will both have the life you deserve. It is my final wish."

Cheryl Alleway

Chapter Twenty-Three

Enter the Wind

Cheryl Alleway

N ow Deb felt sadness so deep that her stomach was turning. She began to cry and placed her head in Anne's lap. She kissed her hands and gazed up at her like a little girl. This woman had given her everything a mother could and more. They had a bond so strong that Deb could not bear to lose her too. Not Anne too!

"No Anne…please do not say it. There are medical men at the universities here! We can find someone to help you. The queen will help you!"

Anne took a breath and pulled Deb into her arms to embrace her. She said in a quivering voice, "You have already helped me, my dear. You have given me a purpose in my life. I am finished with my journey soon and it is time that I hold Thomas in my arms again."

David sat stunned. He had no words, but chivalry pressed him to place a blanket over Anne's shoulders and say, "You have given *us* a purpose, Lady Anne. For this gift, we are forever loyal."

Deb got up and they both helped Anne lie down in her bed. Deb kissed her cheek once more and they snuffed out her candles. Grace came in after them and Deb asked her kindly to watch Anne closely. She wanted Grace to get her if anything happened through the night.

Grace already knew of Anne's fate as Joan had apprised her. She would tend to Anne's every need while she stayed at the castle. Anne did not wish to die in Scotland. She wanted her people to remember her the way she was. They had already buried too many of their own. She hadn't even told Margaret or William of her impending demise. Anne wanted the castle to carry on with William's leadership. He would guide them well, but Anne did not wish to leave her life until she knew Windserlor was captured. She was willing herself to stay alive, just to know that Deb's life had some closure.

The night saw little sleep for Deb. David had nodded off and she got up and went down to Anne's room to check with Grace. Anne had been sleeping quietly and so Deb returned to her room to sit in the window. The moon was out and there were many lights to challenge the stars. This place was very different than Scotland and as much as Deb had revelled in its majesty, she longed to see her home again. Deb thought Finnean may like a visit and so she put on her overcoat and boots, making her way down the spiralling staircase to the exterior doors. There were three men standing guard and they nodded politely as she asked them to allow her out to see the horses. They wondered why at such an hour, but they also knew that Deb was a special guest and questioning her was inappropriate.

As she wound her way through the courtyard, there she saw her faithful friend. Finnean knew it was her right away when she quietly whistled to him. As she came into view, his eyes opened from their light slumber. He made a muffled sound with his lips and she raised her hands to touch his soft face.

"Finnean, my boy, there have been many things happen in this strange place. I fear we will not have Lady Anne with us much longer. I had no idea that she was…"

A tear was trailing down her cheek. Finnean could smell her anguish as he always had and with a gentle nudge, he pushed her shoulder to move her. She smiled at him and added, "But there's more, lad. Poor mother and father had a sadder start in life than I knew of. I don't care what anyone says. Jacob is my father. This garbage, Windserlor, was definitely not. My heart is too loyal to my upbringing. It means something to me, Finnean. It is who I am inside. Just like my father, I may be cursed with the English by association, but inside, I am a Scot and so are you, lad. You have the heart as well. I am sorry for all of this traveling and strangers. We will be home sooner than you think.

Just enjoy the sweet hay and the pampering. Right now, there is a man being hunted for what he has done. I wish I was part of it, but for Anne's sake, I will be patient and let the men do their job. He is just lucky he did not meet me on the path here and that I knew of his evil doings. It would have saved everyone a lot of trouble."

She brushed Finnean's snout with her hands and he closed his eyes enjoying the attention from his loving partner. With one last kiss, she turned to make her way back into the castle.

Just talking to Finnean released a bit of pressure in her mind. It was time for her to rest.

"Now that is something to see." David was standing above Deb as she opened her eyes finally the next morning. She had slept in later than usual and to no surprise. Grace had already come down to tell David that Anne was fine this morning and that she felt strong enough to come to breakfast. Deb couldn't wait to spend the time with her and her stomach told her that it was time to eat.

The stairway was very chilly that morning. Autumn was on its way and there were rain clouds drifting in on the wind. One could smell them. Grace had assisted Anne with her walk to the great hall where only the king and queen sat ready for morning food and drink. This was a very different arrangement to Anne's castle meals, but she was unique and though Anne was a lady of Scotland, she was not the Queen consort of France.

Warm honey and fresh bread sat upon the long dark table. Alongside it were pieces of pork and venison with a large vessel of fruit. There were cool water jugs waiting and as a special treat, the queen had fruit and meat pies made for the occasion. She knew Anne's favorite was mincemeat. It was decorated with leaves and berries and as they all sat together, Deb wanted to know more about this Windserlor, but first she made sure that Anne was comfortable. She sat beside her as if she were her mother with her hand gently holding one of Anne's and the other cupping her forearm. David sat last out of respect and they all waited for Phillip and Joan to begin. Joan wanted them to feel at ease and simply stated, "Please, mes amis. Begin."

Anne was first to spy the mincemeat and thankfully, she had the appetite today to enjoy it. Grace cut a dainty piece and placed it on a lovely floral dish for her. David and Deb followed suit and as Grace made her way out after the food had been served, Anne asked courteously, "May I have Grace join us? She has been such a kind friend."

Grace looked a bit awkward, but Joan replied, "Of course," and signalled for her to sit beside Anne on the other side. David had been quiet as well. He was feeling a bit overwhelmed at the thought of having to make conversation with royalty such as this. The night before, there was much more sound and activity. It had been more formal, but this was intimate. They would have to try hard so as not to embarrass Anne. She spoke first however, and asked if the soldiers charged with finding Windserlor had been heard from.

"Yes, they have been successful in obtaining the man you call Windserlor, but not without losing one of our own."

Deb's face went white. "You have him? You have Windserlor?"

"It appears so, my dear. He will be brought to the castle within a day and here he will be hung for his dealings. The men had to take him in the night. He was with a small entourage and so it was a small skirmish. It ended quickly. We have sent word to Edward that he is to be hung here in France and that we shall not sway from this decision since he committed crimes of rape against some of our women. There can be no argument from the English. This Windserlor is as much a rat of society and a disgrace to his title to us as to you, my dear." She was looking directly at Deb.

Deb bowed her head politely and said, "Your majesty, I am ever so grateful for your part in bringing him to justice." Her hand was quivering ever so slightly. David noticed and placed his upon it to settle her.

"You need not thank us, but it is our belief that you deserve to see this man hang as much as we do. Now let us enjoy our meal. He will not take that away from us as well today. Please, begin."

To David's surprise, the conversation was easy to follow and the king and queen were quite cordial. He relaxed and felt a peacefulness coming over Deb and radiating to him.

Deb was anxious to see Windserlor's face, but she realized what effort Anne had gone through to make this happen and that was enough to make her feel very privileged. It would not be long before she laid her eyes upon the man that not only raped her mother, but destroyed a part of her father forever. She prepared herself and as the dawn broke the next day, the men were sighted coming up from the southern trail towards the center of Paris.

A bell rang from one of the towers indicating approaching soldiers and when the gates opened, Deb and David were there. With a double glance, Windserlor stared at them for a moment in silence. They stood motionless and sullen as Deb glared back at him, hoping that he knew he was staring at his own offspring. He was injured on the right side of his face, but Deb could still tell from her father's drawing, that this was the man behind the mystery and the years of hatred Jacob had to endure. She could not believe her father's restraint in hunting him down, but alas, he was a humble farmer with a missing leg and a daughter that meant more to him than the sweet taste of revenge. Jacob's purpose was clear when he looked upon his daughter's face. Getting himself killed while taking revenge would do nothing but leave Deb alone in the world. Min's teachings taught Joseph that there were times that one had to release their need for revenge and focus on what they were blessed with in front of them.

  Midday and Windserlor had seen the cold walls of his dungeon room. The king and queen summoned for him to be brought to the great hall. Guards led him down the hallway and past the pillars. He had been given no food as of yet. By design, this weakened him. His hair was tattered and dark. He was still filthy from the fight to bring him in and he still had said nothing. He had been stripped of his English attire and wore nothing but a brown tunic and bottoms that matched. When he walked into the hall, he had a smug look on his face, but Deb had seen this look many times before. What looked like confidence, was fear. Like a trapped animal, he knew he was doomed but he would not give up his persona. David wanted to attack him as he entered the room, but there was no place for that here. The king and queen were sitting quietly when he entered and he was made to go down onto his knees before them. As the queen was given the king's nod to take the lead, she stood and gazed down at the man who had preyed on two of the women he should not have. Anne entered the room off the side with Grace. Deb joined them. They sat down and waited to hear the queen speak.

"You have been brought here for reasons that you must know of. The charges against you are many. For the rape of our own and those of other lands, you are sentenced to death. Do you have anything to say?"

Windserlor just stood there staring at the wall. One could not tell if he was being pompous or brave, but Deb couldn't take it any longer. She stepped forward and requested to speak. Getting the nod from the queen she stood steadfast and looked Windserlor straight in the eye from twenty feet away.

"Do you know me?" she asked Windserlor. He glared at her. Her beauty was all he saw. He didn't listen to her until she lifted her skirt, gripped her father's knife and with pin point precision sent it through the air hitting the target of a large log lying close to the fire area. Windserlor's eyes widened. The knife had grazed his shirt on the way by. He looked down at the tear in his clothing and then up at Deb.

"I don't care who you are. Try that again and I'll show you the floor woman!" The guard grabbed him and pulled him back as he leaned toward Deb. She did not react to him. He noticed this and said, "Well then, who are you? Not that it matters to me. I've never seen you before in my life!"

"Oh but you have! You saw me in the eyes of a young girl named Mary of Scotland and not only did you see me in her eyes, you created me in them!"

"What? I know no Mary of Scotland!"

"Perhaps not by her name, but you did know her. I am her daughter and you, you disgusting devil from hell are the other half of me! Only by blood, thank God above. A man like you could never be a father for it takes a special man to be that for a child. I had a father that loved me despite my creator. May you suffer for what you have done!"

Windserlor didn't want to hear it. The rape of Mary occurred more than twenty five years prior and he did not remember her or any of the others of that time.

He did manage to spit out something that would cost him dearly. "If I fathered you then lucky for you that you do not have only dirty Scot's blood coursing through your veins! You've got English blood in you! Your worth lies only in this fact! You should be thanking me!"

The queen wanted to surge forward, but before she could think about it, Deb raced ahead lifting her skirt while spinning around and striking Windserlor in the face with her boot. The kick was so powerful that he flew out of the guards' arms and landed hard on the floor cutting his lip. As he raised his evil face to look at her, blood streaming down his chin. She saw fear in his eyes for the first time. The king sprang forward and shouted to the guard to grab him and stand him up. He had seen enough.

"My dear, do not waste one more moment on this vile creature. His time is done. You will not change him. He is destined to live with his demons in hell. Guards! Take him to his room. Prepare him for the courtyard!"

David had not made a move throughout the incident. Deb could handle herself and he wanted her to feel independence and release on her own.

This was her moment to vent her anger upon Windserlor.

It wasn't enough for Deb and the king knew this. He felt for her and did not scold her for her actions, but praised her. "You are skilled but I am sorry that I cannot allow you to kill him. He must die under our laws. Do not worry. He will be dead before this day is over."

Deb and David spent time in the garden to calm her nerves. She knew what she wanted to do but was forbidden. Queen Joan entered the courtyard with Grace and sat beside Deb. She stood up to bow to the queen.

Joan motioned for her to sit. "Please, formalities can be forgiven at this moment. I wish to speak to you both." Grace left Joan's side and David moved closer to the two women. Joan was someone of a serious nature, but they could see a gentler side of her as she spoke the words that Deb could not bring herself to accept.

"My friends, our Lady Anne is going to expire by the day's end. She does not want you to see it occur and has asked me to keep you from her room."

Deb's eyes welled up and Joan took her hand. "Please your majesty, I must be with her."

"I know this is what you desire, but Anne wants you to remember her in a different way. This is why she came here to die. She does not want her people to see her demise. So much suffering, so much sadness I see in your faces. You have lived a life of strife. Your country is in chaos and we see the threat of ours becoming war torn as well. We must keep in our minds the reason that we are given our strengths. In this life, we see many people come and go. They influence us and those around us to move forward whether with happiness or pain. We learn that life is much more than simply living. It is our destiny to reach for our futures and plan for a better world to come to us. It takes diligence, courage, strength and resilience."

She looked directly at Deb and she sat up straight as the queen said with resolution, "Anne has told me of your journey, Deborah of Douglas. She has told me of Thomas' impression of you and the future he saw for you. You are special, my dear. You must know in your heart that you are a rarity in this world. Anne gave you a part of her life that she would have given her own child. It is you, Deb. It is you that she wants to see succeed in life. She loves you more than you know and she will die knowing that you have come to us. The king and I wish for you to be our guests until you feel it appropriate to go home, but you have been given Anne's wealth and her life's lessons. She wishes for you to have a good life. If you return to Scotland, you will return to war. If this is what you choose, I honour you and will send supplies...as much as you require, but should you ever wish to leave Scotland, you have a place here."

Deb and David sat dumbfounded. They never would have believed that their humble lives would mean so much to the Queen of France or that she would accept them without noble status. Anne had obviously painted a picture for Joan that convinced her of their worth. For now, David and Deb needed to attend to two things before returning home. Windserlor was to be hanged at noon and Anne was about to pass from this world and into the next at any moment.

As they waited in the great hall, Grace ran to Deb and took her hand. "My lady! Anne has changed her mind. She wants you by her side! She is leaving us!"

Deb raced down the hall past Grace who was running at full tilt. When she burst open Anne's door, Anne lifted one hand with a fragile shake and called out in a soft tone, "Deb child, please hold my hand!"

Deb fell to the floor on her knees as she kissed Anne's face gently and taking her trembling hand.

"I did not want you to see me like this, but I cannot leave this world without seeing your face one more time."

Deb was wiping tears from her face as she listened to Anne's last words.

"I want you to live. I want you to be the person you are inside. Don't ever forget my love for you. I have seen many people die without love or family. Today I die with my daughter holding my hand."

Deb fell onto Anne's chest and wept. She had no words. David now rushed in and put his arm around them both. Lady Anne looked up one last time and stated, "David, love her, care for her. Stay with each other."

Deb stopped breathing for a moment and as she finally took in a slow breath, she felt the life leave Anne's body. Anne MacDonell was gone.

Grace peered around the door frame and had tears in her own eyes. She had known Anne for years and was deeply saddened by the loss of her. She slipped quietly down the hall to tell the king and queen the news, but not without placing her hand on her mouth so that her cries would be silenced.

Joan sat stoic in her chair. She had cried many tears for her friend but now, she and Phillip had to contain themselves. Windserlor was readied in the south courtyard. She took a cross from the table in her room and placed its chain around her neck. She kissed it and the two made their way down the hallway instructing Grace to return to Anne's side with a few other women to prepare her and her chamber.

As people from the castle gathered, Phillip and Joan took their seats. Deb and David had spent their last moments with Anne and were making their way to the courtyard as well. Joan could not believe they had the fortitude after what just happened and it was proven once again that Anne had described them correctly. David and Deb stood out as they courageously made their way to their seats. Deb bowed in front of the king and bowed again to kiss Joan's hand. She had tears in her eyes. Joan placed the other on Deb's cheek as the two women looked at each other with sympathy and friendship. It settled Deb somewhat. They gathered themselves and turned as Windserlor was brought into the courtyard and stood upon the place where he would be hanged for his crimes.

A man stood and spoke for the king, who wished not to say another word about the animal that stood before him.

"You have been found guilty of the rape of numerous women including that of the royal family. For this charge you are sentenced to be hanged by the neck until dead."

Windserlor said nothing and it was fitting because if he had spoken one word, Deb would have pounced on him from her seat. David took her hand and she sat strong.

The hangman placed the noose around Windserlor's neck and tightened it. A burlap sack was placed on his head and as Deb closed her eyes for a moment to envision her mother's and Anne's faces, she heard the drop. When she opened her eyes, Windserlor hung dangling from his now broken neck and a quiet fell upon the courtyard. The king motioned to the men to wait until they were sure and then, the body was taken away.

He stood, finally, and stated, "Today we have lost an evil entity, but we are also mourning the loss of Lady Anne MacDonell."

The people were saddened indeed as many had met Anne on her visits to see Joan.

"We shall join in the great hall to honour her memory and to feast together in celebration of her life."

One by one, people left the courtyard in a sullen saunter. Deb and David waited and joined the king and queen.

As the afternoon ended, they retired to their room to sleep and comfort each other. They were not disturbed and Deb fell asleep that evening by the fire in David's arms. He gazed into the flames wondering what they would do now. Scotland was on his mind and he knew that Deb would miss her home as well.

After a few days, they had buried Anne in a quiet ceremony and packed their things. Finnean was anxious for Deb to ride again and with a small group accompanying them, David and Deb said goodbye to The King and Queen of France. Grace came to say goodbye as well and as she met Deb's eyes, the two instantly knew that they would be friends forever. Grace was a sweet, gentle soul. Deb felt in some way that other than her beauty, she was not unlike Henry. She was loyal and unassuming. It was not hard to see why Anne loved her so dearly. Grace was just a small part of Anne's life away from the fields of Scotland and most would never know just how much she lived and learned while traveling.

She and Thomas would always remain a bit mysterious. Deb knew the woman who gave her life back and now, for whatever reason, her future was also a gift that could never be repaid. She did however, ponder deeply on how, or why, she was given this destiny, but as David had put it, when dying; peace often only comes when one's love and earthly possessions are passed onto someone they trust will use them both wisely.

"Your father felt this as he raised you, Deb. He knew he would leave one day and he instilled the very qualities within you that Anne recognized. His legacy is being honoured even more than he probably ever imagined. You have made him proud from the heavens. I know he and your mother look upon you with contentment."

"It is like a dream, David. I feel pain and sorrow, but there is also hope surging in my chest even more than before. Then I sense danger and I hold onto my father's words. Like a tug of war in my heart, I see our future in a field of mist. At times I see the glory of redemption, but I will not forget those who have guided us to this place in life. I hear them clearly." She looked down at herself.

A small, almost unnoticeable curve was appearing on Deb's body. She was with child. She and David were unsure at first and kept it quiet while on their journey for fear of Anne worrying about her safety even more, but there was no doubt now as her body was changing.

After making their way back to the shore the ship was loaded. Deb and David met on the deck as the wind blew through their hair and the sea cleansed their minds. The journey home would be bitter sweet at best, but Anne had given them a life they never dreamed of having and as the sun was setting, David looked down at Deb and placed his hand upon her belly. "You are glowing. Soon, Finnean will have to learn to ride with two passengers."

Deb smiled softly and placed her hand upon David's. "Yes, my only wish would be that he or she does not see all that we have in this world. We must try to protect our child, David. We must try."

David nodded his head, gently placing a hand around her shoulders. They both fell silent as they watched sea birds fly above them. The ship turned for its final leg of the journey and sailed toward the Scottish coastline with its precious cargo.

Watch for more from author Cheryl Alleway by visiting her at http://allewaybooks.com.